Praise for Fiona Palmer

'Palmer is at the top of her game here'

iBOOKS EDITOR

'Fiona Palmer just keeps getting better'

RACHAEL JOHNS

'Her scenes are vivid and genuine, just as her characters are'

BOOK'D OUT

'A heartfelt tale of how long-held secrets can catch up with even the closest of mates'

YOURS MAGAZINE

Fiona PALMER

Secrets Between Friends

hachette
AUSTRALIA

hachette
AUSTRALIA

First published in Australia and New Zealand in 2017
by Hachette Australia
(an imprint of Hachette Australia Pty Limited)
Level 17, 207 Kent Street, Sydney NSW 2000
www.hachette.com.au

10 9 8 7 6 5 4 3 2 1

This edition published in 2018

 A catalogue record for this
book is available from the
NATIONAL
LIBRARY National Library of Australia
OF AUSTRALIA

ISBN 978 0 7336 4041 4 (paperback)

Cover design by Christabella Designs
Cover photographs courtesy of Shutterstock and Arcangel
Author photo courtesy of Craig Peihopa
Text design by Bookhouse, Sydney
Typeset in Sabon LT Pro by Bookhouse, Sydney
Printed and bound in Great Britain by Clays Ltd, Elcograf S.p.A

To Rachael Johns – thank you for asking me to go on a cruise with you!

Prologue

THE TV BLARED LOUDLY WITH MALE VOICES WHILE ON THE screen tiny men in white clothes stood on a green field. Jessica's dad sat in his tattered brown chair directly opposite with a can of beer in his hand. She'd learned quickly that this position meant he didn't like to be disturbed. Don't ask him questions, don't tell him you're hungry and don't ask if he'll come to watch you ride your bike. But Jess badly wanted to show her dad how well she could ride her bike now, even if it was only up and down their driveway. She was nearly six and wanted to ride on the road like the boy down the street, but her mum wouldn't let her.

'Chris, keep it down, buddy!' shouted her dad as Chris started to throw his toys out of the box again.

The booming voice made Chris pause mid-throw and then sit down to play quietly in the corner. Dad liked Chris, because he was a boy, but still Chris knew when he had to be good. Dad's voice was always a second away from a growl.

Jess went into the kitchen, where her mum was cutting up a carrot on the green bench top.

'Mum, can I go ride my bike?'

'Sure, honey, just stay on the driveway,' she replied without looking up from her task.

Jess badly wanted to tell her dad she was off to ride her bike but she didn't want to bring out the bad dad. The one that moved like an angry bear, throwing around its strong arms dangerously and spitting from the mouth, teeth glistening. Jess was scared of that dad and so she left him be and kept her lips pressed tightly as she walked past to the front door.

Outside, it was warm but not too hot; just right for riding her bike. It sat where she had left it, propped up against the fence near the yellow Holden. The bike had only two wheels; her mum had taken off the trainer wheels a while ago. The bike hadn't been new when she got it, she could tell, but it had been repainted and on the handlebars sat pink tassels that fluttered as she went faster and faster. Jess climbed on, the torn black seat no longer prickling her bottom now that her mum had covered it with tape. Mum had watched her ride that day. If only Dad would. Maybe if he saw how well she could ride he'd be nicer?

Down the driveway she swerved around the grass that grew through the cracked cement, pretending it was her own special race track. Only once did she miss a tight turn and end up on the scraggly, weedy lawn. Mum was always asking her dad to mow it.

She quickly righted her bike. The driveway was so small and boring; she wanted to be a big kid and ride their street.

It was quiet, their house was at the end of the road, so cars didn't come along very often.

Jess glanced back at the house and then rode down the driveway onto the road before turning back to the driveway. Nothing bad happened, so she did it again, this time going further, and this time seeing the boy who lived further along the street. He was on his bike too, riding on the road, but she could see his dad sitting by their square mailbox watching.

She gritted her teeth and pushed hard on the pedals. Down the street she flew as if she owned it, all the while smiling, almost giggling with the feeling the speed brought.

It took a moment to realise she'd fallen off, that she was lying on the road, her bike was on top of her and parts of her body hurt. She began to cry.

'Are you okay?'

She opened her eyes to see the boy leaning over her. He went to pick up her bike but then his dad took over and lifted it off like it was a feather.

'Are you okay, sweetie?' said the man. His voice was soft and gentle.

It made Jess stop crying but her tears still ran down her face.

'Oh, you've hurt your knee,' said the boy as she sat up.

'Come and sit on the kerb and I'll get you a Band-Aid, maybe a few,' said the boy's father.

Her skin was scraped from her knee, burning as if it were on fire. Jess sniffled as her bottom lip quivered.

The nice man had helped her walk to the edge of the bitumen and laid her bike down. The boy sat beside her.

'So, you're a girl?' he said as he looked at her. 'I only have a brother.'

'Me too,' said Jess. 'He touches all my toys.'

'So does mine. I'm Peter,' he said holding out his hand.

Jess just continued to hug her legs until he dropped it.

'You're supposed to tell me your name. I've seen you at your house, riding your bike. You're getting really good.'

Jess sat up straighter. At least someone had noticed. 'I'm Jess. Why are you so nice?' Jess was only used to her dad and Chris; so far boys weren't much fun.

'Nice? I'm just trying to be helpful. Dad always says I should be kind and helpful to girls 'cause my mum is a girl. Do you go to school? I do, I'm going to be in year one next year.'

Before Jess could reply, his dad came back and carefully put the Band-Aids over her sores. 'There you go, now that's better, isn't it,' he said in a soothing voice.

'Dad, this is Jess. Can we ride together?'

Jess looked down at her feet, her face heating up.

'Hi Jess. I'm Mr Wellstead. You can ride together, if it's okay with Jess's parents.'

Jess swallowed and quickly muttered the words, 'I'm not allowed to ride on the road. I'm supposed to stay on the driveway.' Jess squeezed her eyes shut and pulled her shoulders towards her head, bracing for a clip over the ears or some form of punishment. But none came.

'Hmm, I see,' said Mr Wellstead. 'Shall we go and speak to them?'

Jess's heart raced at the thought that Mr Wellstead would dob her in and then surely she would get a walloping.

She stayed silent as Mr Wellstead walked her back to her house, Peter pushing her bike. The closer they got to home the slower her movements became.

'It's okay,' said a soft voice suddenly. 'You won't get into trouble.'

She looked up slowly. Mr Wellstead's face wasn't like her dad's. It wasn't red and blotchy, and he smiled a lot.

'Come on,' he said softly.

Mr Wellstead knocked on their door as if there wasn't a care in the world.

Her dad came to the door.

'Yeah?' was all he said, can of beer still in his hand.

'Hi. I'm Edward Wellstead from down the road. I was just wondering if Jess was allowed to ride on the street with my son Peter. I'll keep an eye on them both.'

Jess saw her mum walk up behind her dad as he looked from Mr Wellstead, to Peter and then to her. 'Please, Dad,' she said. 'I'll be good.'

He shrugged and disappeared back to the TV.

Her mum, still standing behind the flywire door, added, 'Just for half an hour then come back for dinner.' Her eyes flicked back to Mr Wellstead. 'Thank you,' she added, then watched them leave.

Jess turned as fast as she could, not quite believing that they hadn't noticed the Band-Aids on her knee.

'Off you go,' Mr Wellstead said with a smile. 'Just always check for cars down the end of the street and come straight to the footpath when you see one.'

Peter gave her the bike and ran along the pathway back to his own. 'Yay, this will be so much fun. My brother can't ride a bike yet. We're going to be friends, Jess. I know it.'

Her sore knee was forgotten as she climbed onto her bike,

and she laughed when Peter lifted his feet off the pedals. 'Look at me!'

'I can do that too,' said Jess, following suit.

Jess rode her bike and not once did she think of her dad. Of what might come later.

Today was the best. Being with Peter was the most fun she'd ever had. And he said they were going to be friends. Her first real friend.

1

Abbie

ABIGAIL SHELDON STEPPED OUT OF HER CAR AND MANAGED to lock it, tie her hair up and keep her handbag on her shoulder all in one movement. She was in deep trouble. No thanks to the thick traffic due to the Sculpture by the Sea exhibit on the beach. She'd actually gone to see the seventy-six sculptures over the weekend, more so to distract herself but had been pleasantly surprised and had loved walking the white beaches with the Indian Ocean crashing at her feet as the sun set. It had been the best afternoon she'd had in ages. If only she could go back to that moment now. Half an hour late for work already and she still had to get from the parking area up a flight of stairs to the office. Those stairs seemed like Mount Everest lately. As fast as her tired legs could go she headed to the main door, thankful she'd worn flats. They didn't look as nice as her black heels did with her pencil grey skirt and sleeveless white shirt, but in the Perth heat and her current mood, she was too tired to care. Although she shouldn't complain, if she lived further

1

north, the dry heat would be a constant, or at the tip of Western Australia where it was a sweaty hot in the tropics. Luckily the cruise she was about to take was going south of the state to lush green areas and sky-blue seas.

'Hi Abbie, just getting in?' said Nita. Her chestnut hair was pulled back tightly into a bun and her heels click-clacked against the cement floor as she made her way past carrying a folder. 'I'm off to the open house in Cottesloe. Park Street,' she said, the corner of her mouth curling up ever so slightly.

Abbie forced a smile to her face. Nita knew that house was in Abbie's portfolio, and the fact she was politely rubbing it in made Abbie hate her fake smile even more. 'Good luck,' Abbie replied in her best sing-song voice as she pushed open the glass doors and headed for the stairs. Nita was hardly out of earshot before Abbie was swearing under her breath as she took each step.

'Abbie, nice of you to join us,' said Derek, her boss.

He stood at the top of the stairs with a smug look on his Botox-filled face. Abbie bet he'd seen her car come in and had been waiting for this moment.

'Sorry, Derek, I got held up with traffic again. I wanted to check the Park Street property was all set for the open house before I came to work,' she said breathlessly, which was odd for someone of her slender, athletic build. It seemed like only days ago Jim had told her she was looking all willowy like a runway model; only now did she realise maybe it wasn't a compliment. 'Also, I have a doctor's appointment at one. Hopefully it won't take too long. I really need to sort out this flu, I can't seem to shake it.'

Derek's face reddened slightly – he knew she'd had a few doctor's appointments lately – as he stepped back so she could pass. Her last boss had been a flexible guy who rewarded hard work. Derek, on the other hand, wanted all work with no bend. Strike one was her forced absences due to this ongoing flu; strike two was her lateness, even though she'd checked the house this morning, which was work related. He'd been so close to firing her the second he saw her today, she could tell. His right eye twitched and his face was still red. She'd stretched her welcome these past few weeks but had put in plenty of overtime so her work hadn't suffered. Her clients came first. With her breath back, Abbie stepped around him and headed to her office.

'Nita is doing the Park Street house. It's too important,' he said before clearing his throat.

Abbie heard his reprimand loud and clear. She wanted to tell him where he could shove that Park Street house, but instead she just nodded.

The day her boss had retired and Derek had taken his place had been the beginning of the end. At least it had helped make up her mind about starting her own business, something she'd dreamed of since entering the real-estate market and quickly climbing the ranks. She had the knowledge and the determination. Her last boss had been so supportive, helping and guiding her in the right direction. Derek didn't want to hear about it. He wanted her under his thumb.

Abbie just needed the energy to walk away, she thought, sitting down in her chair and letting her handbag slide from her shoulder as if it weighed a tonne. Bending down, she pulled out her make-up mirror from her bag. She could hardly see her eyes for the dark circles around them. *Derek probably thinks I'm on drugs*, she thought. Being late meant she'd skipped the full face of make-up, which was a mistake. Concealer had been her best friend lately. Putting her mirror away, she glanced at her neat desk.

A yellow sticky note grabbed her attention like a flashing neon light. Scribbled in neat writing was the date and time she was due to meet Peter and Jess.

For the first time that day, she smiled. It would be so good to catch up with her friends again and talk about their trip. Abbie was so excited about their upcoming boat cruise reunion. Ten years since they'd graduated high school together. With everything that had been going on, the cruise was her beacon of light. Three days of nothing but fun, friendship and relaxation. Depart Fremantle, sail the seas in comfort plus a day stopover in gorgeous Albany where the white beaches are so crisp, before floating back to Fremantle. *The place to leave your troubles behind*, the glossy brochure had boasted.

She could still remember the time she first met Jess. It was the fourth week of year eight and she'd noticed the girl, who was in most of her classes, hanging out with a year-nine boy. Normally it would give a girl some school credit, but this boy was gangly and geeky and the other girls started to tease her. 'Is that your *boy*friend, Jessica?' they would taunt, and Jess would deny it, saying he was just her friend, which only made them tease her more. It annoyed Abbie but she didn't do anything about it – not until one day when Jess caught her up in the corridor.

'Abbie, Abbie, sorry but you dropped this,' she'd said, holding out a bit of paper that Abbie had scribbled notes on during

class. Not really notes, they were love hearts with *Abbie &
John* in them. The year-eleven head boy. Her secret crush. Yet
Jess handed it over, even after seeing what was written on it,
and with a smile walked off. Not a word was uttered about it,
no gossip spread. From that moment on Abbie knew that Jess
was a girl she could trust. So, when the other girls teased her
about the boy a few days later, Abbie stepped in and told them
to grow up. 'Come on, Jess, they're just jealous because they
don't even know how to talk to boys, let alone have one as a
friend.' Abbie had taken her hand and led her away from them.

Hell, where had the time gone? Abbie was twenty-seven
with not much to show for it. Yet another thing to add to her
list of failures. It was growing day by day. If it kept up like
this she might need more note paper.

She twisted the end of her long black hair as her eyes moved
across to another bright sticky note. *One o'clock, Doctor Rikes.*

God, how she hated that sticky note. It had tortured her
from the moment she stuck it up on her wall. Not even the
bright pink could sway the feeling of dread it brought. But
today was the day. With some luck she'd get some answers.

Abbie let her head fall to the desk and rest against the cold
melamine. She just had to get through the next few hours
without screaming, swearing at Derek or curling up in a ball
under her desk.

2

Ricki

'HI, RICKI. READY TO HEAD HOME?'

'You bet,' said Ricki Van Leeuwin as she passed her colleague Jolene in the hospital corridor.

Ricki stifled a yawn as she headed back to the nurses' desk to prepare for handover. Pulling out her phone, she read the message from Peter.

Hi honey, I have dinner sorted, dishes are done, and so is the washing. See you soon.

Ricki smiled. How would she cope without Peter taking care of her? The best thing she'd done was move in with him after a year together; he was the yin to her yang. Ricki was slack when it came to housecleaning and was quite happy to live off frozen dinners and two-minute noodles, but Peter cooked and cleaned as well as ran his own business. This last year living together had made her life so much easier and happier, yet her teeth automatically grated together as she felt something deep down that wanted to dispute it.

'Rickster!'

A hand curled around her arm and stopped her next step. Ricki turned to see Teresa, an enrolled nurse she spent many shifts with, who was smiling much too brightly for someone who was also at the end of her shift. Teresa's blue uniform had light blue strips around the V-neck and Ricki's was white to distinguish their roles.

A nurse was the only thing Ricki had ever wanted to be. Since that day in year eight, when she'd witnessed Jess accidentally catch her sleeve on fire with the Bunsen burner, nursing had been her calling. Ricki had felt compelled to rush to Jess's aid back then, working on instinct she'd helped put out the flames and then dragged her to the sink to put her arm under the tap. 'Are you okay, Jess? Does it sting?'

Ricki had looked into Jess's eyes and seen how hard she was fighting to keep tears at bay.

'You know my name?' she'd said softly and then smiled. 'Thanks, Ricki, I think I'm okay. It hurts but I'll live.'

'Hey, you know my name too. Cool.' The teacher asked Ricki to take her to the nurse's office. 'I think it's not that deep a burn, it's when you can't feel it that it's a deep burn.'

'Thank you for helping me, and for keeping me company. You'd make a great nurse, Ricki,' Jess had said, grinning. 'You seem to know so much.'

For the first time in weeks, at the new school, Ricki had felt like she had a real friend. Her primary school was a long way from here and none of her friends were at this high school, which had made her feel lost, like a ping-pong ball bouncing from place to place. Yet helping Jess had felt right, and she was so nice; it became the beginning of a close friendship and the direction of her career.

Ricki smiled as she adjusted her uniform and looked at Teresa, who was now by her side. 'What's up?' The hospital seemed quiet for the moment; usually that meant the calm before the storm.

'You've got Miguel for handover. Lucky girl. Can I tag along?'

'You wish.' Ricki dug into her pocket until she found her last piece of chewie and popped it in her mouth.

'Did you just come from Mr Chan?' added Teresa.

'Yeah, nasty infection and the skin is going necrotic. Smells foul.' Luckily the chewie was removing the smell that had seemed to lodge itself in her nasal passages and throat. 'I've got to go, I want to pick up some paperwork before handover.'

Ricki waved goodbye as she continued on her way down the corridor. She didn't want Teresa tagging along – she was younger and prone to flirtations when attractive nurses or doctors were nearby. Not that Ricki wanted Miguel all to herself; he was gorgeous with olive skin, thanks to his Brazilian heritage but it was more about hearing his stories. He was new, filling in for one of their regulars who had taken maternity leave, and Ricki had learned he'd been volunteering overseas in places like Cambodia. That had been her dream.

'Hello Ricki, how was your day?' His voice was warm, deep with only the faintest accent. Miguel's parents moved to Australia before he was born so even though he looked exotic he was still Aussie.

He was leaning against the high desk. Only he could make the nurse's uniform look sexy. Or maybe it was his smile. Or the neatly clipped dark hair.

Ricki reached up to her high ponytail, now a droopy mess. Her long blonde locks were normally her best feature – just not at the end of a shift. Why couldn't Miguel be the one taking her through a handover instead of the other way around; then she'd be looking fresh and her lip gloss would still be on her lips.

'Long, as usual. So, how are you settling in? Different hospital same job?' Ricki leaned against the desk beside him as she reached for her paperwork.

Miguel's lopsided smile revealed his perfect white teeth. 'It's okay. I'm very adaptable.'

'I bet. So, you worked in Cambodia and Peru? Do you mind me asking you a bit about your work over there?' He shook his head, so she fired off a question as she finished her paperwork, her eyes on the notes but her ears taking in his words. 'What made you go?'

He shrugged. 'I just knew I wanted to go overseas. I grew up with trips to Brazil as well as seeing family in Peru and it was mainly in Peru where I saw the sick children. It struck a chord with me and my mum said if it worried me that much I should do something about it. So I studied to become a nurse and a uni friend told me about GGC Volunteers. I've been volunteering for them ever since.' His hands came together, as if he were praying. 'It's amazing, Ricki. Truly.'

They started down the corridor to visit the patients she was handing over to Miguel for his shift.

'Will you go back to Cambodia?'

'For sure,' he said. 'I'm planning my next trip now.'

His dark, almost black eyes hit her with such intensity it was like looking up at the night sky with all its infinite possibilities and uncharted territory.

'Seeing the slums was a shock. I don't think anyone could really be prepared for the sights and smells. The main entrance is generally covered by fetid sewerage water, which the kids use as a pool.' Miguel screwed up his face. 'We provided medical care to all members of the community, not just the kids. I stayed in Phnom Penh and the clinic is sixteen kilometres away. It's a modern house just a couple of hundred metres from the slums.'

They paused the conversation as they came to their first patient. 'Mr Gow has come in so we can help him manage his Type One diabetes. How are you feeling, Mr Gow?' she asked.

'Food's not great,' he said with a frown.

Miguel looked at his charts as Ricki added, 'I've just done Mr Gow's blood levels and they're within parameters as authorised by his GP. BGLs are due again pre-dinner and his insulin is due at dinner time.' Ricki introduced Miguel. 'Mr Gow sadly lost his wife recently,' she said while gently holding his frail hand. Ricki knew that Mr Gow's wife had looked after him well, and without her he was struggling to control his diabetes.

'I bet she was a marvellous woman, right, Mr Gow?' Miguel said, giving him a wink. 'Kept you on the straight and narrow, no doubt?'

'That she was and yes she did,' said Mr Gow. 'She was a hard woman at times, but I know it was for my own good. She had a heart of gold, my Meryl. She ran a tight ship.'

'And I bet you feel like your ship's lost its anchor and you're floating out to sea?'

Mr Gow turned his sad grey eyes up to Miguel and nodded.

'She's still with you, in here,' said Miguel touching his chest. 'So, you've got to look after yourself. Imagine what she'd be saying about this.'

Mr Gow's eyes widened. 'She'd be none too pleased. My ears would be ringing.' He chuckled, smiling for the first time that day.

Miguel pressed the old man's shoulder gently and smiled. 'I bet you know exactly what she'd say. You should still listen to her, she's right,' he said. 'I'll be back to check on you later.'

Seeing Mr Gow smile was the best thing Ricki had seen all day, and she couldn't help her own grin as she saw the way Miguel had with people. It wasn't just his open face and good looks. He had a big genuine heart.

They continued on their rounds, and in the moments between the patients Ricki probed Miguel for more information. 'So, what kind of cases did you see over there?'

'Diarrhoea, chest infections, broken arms, eye infections, fevers, skin conditions, infected wounds.' Miguel stopped walking and almost squinted at Ricki. 'You know, you should go. They're always looking for volunteers, and it will change your life,' he said, smiling. 'Google GGC Volunteers tonight.'

'What a challenge! You make it sound so amazing,' she said, almost gushing.

He smiled and it made her pulse flip. Teresa was right, he was gorgeous.

'That's because it *is* amazing. Really, do yourself a favour and check it out. I'm going back soon. You could come with me?'

Ricki laughed. 'I'll check it out,' she said.

As for the rest – well, that was just a pipe dream.

⚓

'Hey Ricki, how was your day?' asked Peter as he opened the front door.

Ricki kicked off her shoes outside – they never went inside the house if she could help it – and Peter pulled her into a hug, but she quickly drew back. 'Ew, germs on my clothes. Wait till I've had a shower, babe. My day was okay. How was yours?'

'Didn't get electrocuted or sued,' he said with a smile. His standard reply for his work as an electrician.

He was changed out of his work clothes, showered and in black shorts and a surf singlet. Peter was handsome. He was tall, with blond, almost shaggy hair and a lean, tanned body that came from all the surfing on the weekends. A stark contrast to the lanky boy she'd met through Jess at high school. It sometimes seemed like yesterday when Peter had come up to Jess at lunchtime asking if she was okay, wondering why she hadn't met him for lunch.

'Oh, it's okay, Peter,' she'd said. 'I've found some friends. This is Abbie and Ricki.'

His face had been very pimply but he was thoughtful in the way he looked out for Jess. But they didn't become good friends with Peter until they started hanging out together. It was Peter who told them that Jess's home life wasn't ideal.

'So, a good day then.' Ricki smiled too. She couldn't help it. He always knew how to brighten her mood. 'I'm dying for a shower. How long till dinner?'

'Ready in forty, I just want to crackle up the roast.'

'Oh yum.' Ricki groaned as she headed towards the bedroom while Peter went into the kitchen.

She emptied out her pockets with the usual – scissors, Micropore tape, two black pens, IV cap, alcohol wipes, notepad and chewing-gum wrappers – before dumping her uniform in its special basket and heading to the shower.

After a good long soak, she dressed in shorts and a T-shirt and went into her office.

Within seconds she'd found the page. As she read the stories from the volunteers in Vietnam and Cambodia, she felt the stirring of old dreams and desires deep in her chest. She went to the bookcase and withdrew a file, a collection of letters in separate labelled partitions, each holding information on her World Vision sponsor children. The first: Sainatu from Malawi; then Gertrude from Zambia. As a child she'd written to them regularly and kept their letters even though in the beginning they were few and far between. As she got older she sponsored more: Siyabonga from Zimbabwe was six; Ezekiel from Tanzania was seven. This was why she became a nurse, to help disadvantaged children. In high school, second year, they'd had a nursing student talk to their class about her overseas work. She'd shown photos of a small village with sick kids, and from that moment Ricki's path had been written for her. Maybe it was the exotic location or the adorable kids or maybe the way the nurse spoke so passionately about her role – it didn't matter, Ricki was smitten with the whole idea. She'd done the first part: become the nurse, working hard towards her goal, but somehow she'd got stuck, the rest of her dream incomplete.

'This is what I love about you,' said Peter suddenly from the doorway, his face aglow.

'What?' she asked curiously.

'Ricki, you're a messy kind of girl – clothes usually lie where you take them off, towel left on the bed after a shower, your stuff scattered everywhere – and yet those folders of your kids' letters are so immaculately organised. I love how much they mean to you.'

Peter held steady eye contact, pupils large and shining with adoration. Ricki knew how much he loved kids too, it was one thing they shared. Only, she didn't really want her own, not yet.

'I know, I'm a strange one,' she said, closing her folder and running her hand over it, over the photos of the kids on each cover.

'Come on, strange one, dinner's ready.'

Ricki exited the website, glad that Peter hadn't noticed what was on the screen. Maybe she'd bring up the subject, just test the waters and see how Peter would feel about her going overseas for a little while. Yet just the thought caused the hair on the back of her neck to prickle. Peter loved their life just as it was; she couldn't imagine how he would cope with her going overseas for a year or even six months. With a sigh she got up. She knew what had happened to her dream, to a degree. Peter had happened. Not that she blamed him, how could she when he was such an amazing man. Peter had compassion and loyalty in spades. He was the guy mothers wanted their daughters to marry, her mum included. But deep down she felt the regret and wondered if she could live with it.

The upcoming cruise was a bright spot, though; it was exciting just thinking about it. She missed her friends, saddened by how easily the routine of life got in the way of the time they used to spend together. This trip would be great, help them renew and strengthen their friendship. Just what she needed.

3

Jess

'BYE, MISS RANDALL. SEE YOU NEXT TERM.'

'Goodbye, Matilda. Have a great break.' Jessica Randall smiled at the enthusiastic seven-year-old who was still waving.

As Jess packed up her desk she mused that Matilda wasn't the only one happy for a break from school. Teaching was what she loved, but that didn't mean it was easy, especially because she was also raising a sixteen-month-old on her own. But Jess refused to let her life derail because of her son; instead she'd been determined to get back to work and had found a great shared job in Wandering, a tiny country town an hour and a half from the city. She shared teaching the year ones with another working mum, Janice, and so far they had made a success of it.

Jess brushed a hand through her straight shoulder-length blonde hair; it had once been quite long but she'd opted for an easier style after Ollie was born. Quickly she moved around the small classroom, pulling down the last of the decorations for this term's theme of Australian Animals. Next term would be a new one, which she and Janice were planning together.

When everything was packed up, Jess put her hands on her hips and surveyed the quiet, empty room. It had been a relaxed day with lots of sport, so she'd worn shorts, a light-blue polo shirt and her running shoes. She did love Fridays the most.

'Rather sad like this, isn't it?'

Jess smiled at the school cleaner who stood in the doorway watching her pack up. 'It is a bit. I'm all done if you wanted to make a start in here, Thea?'

'Righto, thanks. So, all set for your cruise?'

Thea wheeled in a big vacuum cleaner and put it in the corner by the power point.

'Not really. It'll be the first time I'm away from Ollie,' said Jess truthfully. In just two terms she had come to love the people of Wandering; the small, close-knit community had been so embracing and concerned for her and Ollie's welfare. It had been the right decision to move here from Perth. It felt like she had a family, and lots of people were happy to help watch Ollie if she needed. She never had time to feel alone or isolated when there was so much to do. Like the book club, the crochet club, playgroup for Ollie, reading time at the CRC Library, plus throw in her school work and Jess just didn't have much time left to dwell on her situation. No wonder people always talked about the benefits of living in a small community. In a way this town had saved her.

'Ollie will be fine with your mum. She'll spoil him rotten and he'll hardly miss you.'

'It's not Ollie I'm worried about,' said Jess with a laugh. 'I know he'll be fine. Not sure I'll cope.'

'You deserve a break, so make sure you make the most of this trip.'

Jess put her handbag in the box of classroom items and picked it up. 'Thanks, Thea, you have a good break too. I'll see you next term.'

It was only a few minutes' drive back to her house. It was an old three-bedroom building but it was perfect for just the two of them. Her neighbour Marian helped her keep the garden nice and babysat Ollie when she had to work. Jess was just offloading the box onto the kitchen bench when Marian came through the front door.

'Yoo hoo, it's only us.'

Marian entered the kitchen, with Ollie on her hip. Jess smiled the moment she saw her boy with his curly blond mop and vibrant blue eyes. His little chubby cheeks melted her heart and his arms immediately reached out for her.

'Hello, my Ollie,' she said, pulling him into her arms and covering him in kisses until he wiggled in annoyance. 'Thanks, Marian. Would you like a cuppa?'

Marian was in her sixties, her husband had passed away a year earlier and she'd been rather melancholy. But Ollie had been her saving grace, if Jess believed what the locals told her. Looking after him had given her something to brighten her day, especially with her family in the city.

'No thanks, love, I'll let you unpack your school things and get ready for your holiday.' Marian smiled. She brushed back her short grey hair and turned her eyes to Ollie. They shone bright with love for him. 'He was a wonderful boy for me today, even had a sleep. I'll miss you both.'

Jess hugged Marian. 'We'll miss you too. Thanks, Marian. I couldn't do any of this without you.'

'My pleasure. And don't worry about a thing while you're gone. I'll keep an eye on the garden for you.'

Jess didn't know what she'd done to deserve Marian or the life she'd made for herself in Wandering. *If only Mum was more like you*, Jess thought and then felt shame burn her cheeks. Her mum had done the best she could, and if having a child had taught Jess anything it was that people shouldn't judge. Motherhood was hard and it didn't come with an instruction manual. Having a difficult husband hadn't helped her mum either.

After Marian went home Jess left the box of unpacking and lay on the floor next to Ollie while he played with his toys. He was the most important man in her life. Ollie held out a red block for her and she took it, watching him stack the rest. Then he stood up and tottered off to his pop-up tent in the corner of the lounge room. She still marvelled at his new skill of walking. How quickly he was growing up.

Her phone rang and as she reached for her mobile she watched Ollie pick up a block and hold it to his ear, mimicking her.

Jess smiled when she saw the caller name. 'Hello Peter Pan.'

'Hi Jess.' His voice was smooth and warm like melted chocolate.

'Are you packed yet?' he asked.

'No. I just finished school. Gee, give me time. I'm not coming to Perth till tomorrow.'

'Are you still up for helping me on Monday? I can't do it without you. You and Abbie know Ricki probably better than I do.'

'Peter, you're the one who wants to marry her. I really think it should be something that comes from your heart, not what we think.' Just saying the word *marry* made Jess uncomfortable. It was strange; she'd got used to her best friends dating, even moving in together, but marriage? Something about it made her heart race. If she hadn't borne witness to Peter's parents' happy marriage, she wasn't sure she would believe in it at all.

'I know, but I want it to be perfect.'

'She'll marry you regardless, Pete. You could get her a ring of copper and she'd say yes.' *She'd be bloody mad if she didn't*, thought Jess. Pete was the catch of the century.

Ollie came up to her, still talking on his pretend phone. He dropped the block and held out his hand. 'Ta. Ta,' he said.

'Is that Ollie?' said Peter. 'Can I talk to him?'

'Sure,' said Jess holding her mobile up to Ollie's ear. 'Say hello to Pete.'

Ollie tried to hold the phone. She could see his eyes light up as Peter spoke to him but he didn't answer. Jess laughed and brought the phone back to her ear. 'He's like a deer in the headlights, the moment he gets a chance to talk on a phone he goes all quiet.'

'I miss the little guy. Can't wait to catch up with you both. It's been ages. This cruise is going to be awesome,' said Peter.

Jess wished she could share his enthusiasm. Something niggled in the back of her mind and she couldn't shake it. Fear? Anxiety? She'd been excited about the trip since its conception, so why the sudden worry? She didn't want to dig further and find out why. Not yet.

In year eight they'd gone on a school camp to Albany, around five hours' drive from Perth through wide open countryside, to see Whale World and the Princess Royal Fortress, which was now home to the award-winning National ANZAC Centre. It had been the few days there that had cemented their newfound friendship into best friends; from that moment forth Abbie, Ricki and Jess were inseparable. Over wine and cheese about six months ago the topic of school had come up, and the fact that it was ten years since they had graduated, and Jess suggested they re-do their trip to Albany. Abbie, who for all her frank and forward personality was quite sentimental, had whole-heartedly agreed. It was a pretty place with beautiful beaches and green hills that remained a special place for all of them.

'We should go by boat. It would be perfect for us. No long drive in the car – instead we can drink and eat our way to Albany!'

'I've always wanted to try a cruise,' Ricki had said. 'There's something magical about the idea of sailing out on an endless ocean.'

So, it was set. Abbie took the lead and booked their tickets. A three-day trip. No turning back.

But now with Peter coming along it didn't seem as exciting. He'd convinced them all to let him come, promising to give them space. But he wanted to use the cruise as a romantic way to propose to Ricki. Who were Jess and Abbie to refuse him?

'Yeah, the trip will be great,' said Jess, remembering Peter was still on the line.

'Too right. Well, I've got to go, I'm still on a job. I'll see you next week. Love you, Jess,' he said, his usual sign-off.

'Love you too, Pete.'

And it was the truth.

4

Abbie

ABBIE SAT IN THE HOSPITAL WAITING ROOM, HER HAND automatically finding its way to her neck to feel the lump she knew was there. Her doctor had been monitoring it and she'd had an ultrasound followed by a blood test but neither had been conclusive. The lump, which Jim had found when massaging her one night, didn't seem to be shrinking, so her doctor had referred her to a general surgeon for a fine-needle aspiration.

And so, here she was.

Only, now she was doing it alone. Jim had disappeared about the time he'd found the lump. Not that the lump had been the issue. No, it was the tall, leggy blonde receptionist from his law office that had drawn him away. Abbie still hadn't come to terms with arriving home from work one afternoon to find his bags packed and him loading his car.

'Sorry Abbie, I'm moving out. I left a note on the table that explains everything.'

Of course when she'd picked her jaw up off the floor she'd managed to ask him why.

'I'm in love with Julie. I've tried to fight it, honestly I have, but she's my soul mate.'

Jim had put it in such a way that she would almost have felt bad if she attempted to make him stay. How could she come between him and his soul mate? Hadn't she been that to him over the past three-and-a-half years?

'I'm so sorry,' he'd said. 'I didn't want to hurt you. But there's no easy way to do this.'

Didn't want to hurt me? she'd wanted to scream. It was a punch to the gut as she'd struggled for air. As he'd finished packing the car, Abbie's mind had ticked over. Office calls to Julie for work, Julie rocking up to collect papers, Julie this and Julie that. 'How long has it been going on?' she'd managed to ask.

Jim had stood by his BMW, a leather bag hanging from his shoulder, looking ever so handsome in his perfectly tailored suit. It was his dark-blue one, her favourite.

'You owe me the truth,' she'd added. Of all the things she could have said and asked, this was what she wanted to know the most before the man she loved walked out of their home.

Jim had lifted a shoulder, winced a bit and then said, 'About a year.'

At this point the tears had finally fallen. Abbie would never forget the look on Jim's face in that moment. As if he wanted to hug her but knew they were well past that.

'I'm sorry, Abbie. I can't keep living a lie. I'll sort out the rest later. I think a clean break is best.'

She'd had a bad day at work, and she simply didn't have the energy to fight for Jim. She was in shock. Had that been his plan? Stun her and exit quickly before the fireworks? But Abbie couldn't muster any fireworks. No anger. No frustration. Just a sense of defeat and a feeling she'd lost control of her life.

Then he'd got in his car and driven away. Just like that. No wonder she'd been feeling like shit for the past few months. Her life felt as if it had derailed and she was travelling along unknown tracks, rough and bumpy as the world flashed past in a blur. She hadn't told a soul. Too scared it would make it real. Too worried she would cry. Too fearful she would fall apart. But for those first few weeks she had fallen apart, every night in her bed alone, in the dark. Crying herself to sleep, wondering what she'd done wrong and then feeling bad for thinking it had been her fault. This was on Jim, and slowly she'd started to heal. She'd drawn on her inner strength to overcome this hurdle, like all the hurdles in the past. Whether it be attaining the job she'd been told she wasn't qualified for by a male peer, or shooting until her shoulder was black and blue until she'd hit two clay targets. Abbie didn't want to live by regret or fear, or stay stuck in the past. She was all for going forward. Even if forward meant this waiting room.

An old lady sitting across from her with grey curls and a blue tracksuit coughed badly, her handbag slipping off her lap and spilling all sorts of pills, pens and lipsticks across the floor. Abbie jumped up and hurried over. She'd watched the old lady walk in earlier and take an age to sit on one of the uninviting white chairs.

'It's all right, don't move, I'll get it for you,' said Abbie with a smile as she swiftly gathered the woman's things. 'There you go.' She popped the large purse back on her lap.

'Oh, thank you so much, dear. It would have taken me all day to get down there and pick everything up. My Roger used to call my bag the Tardis,' she said with a chuckle. 'You seem too young and healthy to be in a place like this,' she added, prying a little.

'Just a check-up. You?' she asked as she sat beside the lady. Her grandmother had loved to chat; she had grown lonely after Gramps died, and so Abbie had made a point of visiting her regularly. Just for a cuppa and a few hours of chitchat, even if it was mainly about the cat or her latest ailments. Until Abbie had lost her too.

'I'm in for my dodgy hip. They think there might be cancer in it.'

'Oh no. Are you here alone?'

'Yes, they're all busy. It's okay. My son Paul is coming as soon as he can, he had a meeting he couldn't get out of.'

Abbie's heart melted. She had been by her granddad's side every moment she could when he was sick. It was still a raw wound, with Gramps and Grams passing on within the past few years, eight months apart.

'I'm sure he'll be here soon, then.'

'Miss Sheldon, the doctor will see you now,' the receptionist called out.

Abbie nodded, and touched the lady's arm beside her. 'Take care, and I hope it all works out.'

'Thank you, I won't forget your kindness.'

Abbie knew the woman didn't just mean picking up her spilled bag. 'My pleasure,' she said.

The doctor's room felt small and sterile, with minimal furniture. Abbie clenched her hands. It wasn't the doctor she feared, more like his giant needle.

The surgeon walked in with a file, her file. He didn't look at her until he was seated at his desk.

'Abbie?' She nodded. 'I'll just have a quick feel, if you don't mind.'

Nodding again, she sat still as the middle-aged man moved towards her and prodded her neck with his cold hands, making a series of noises she couldn't interpret as good or bad.

Eventually he sat back down. His green eyes assessed her further as he asked a few questions, the same ones her previous doctor had asked. How did she feel? Was she tired? Any night sweats? Any itching?

She answered them, even though they both knew the answers were in her file.

'I don't want to do the needle aspiration today, Abbie,' he said, matter-of-fact.

Abbie sat straighter, noting the serious expression on his face. 'You don't?'

Shaking his head slowly, he said, 'I'd rather remove the lymph gland entirely in hospital and biopsy it.'

'Oh, okay.'

'Just to be on the safe side. It will give us a better indication of what's going on. I can fit you in at the start of next week. Do you have any questions?'

Abbie found this to be a stupid question. How could she ask something she didn't know to ask? She didn't know where to start, so instead replied with a polite, 'No.'

Leaving the hospital, with her biopsy booked in for Tuesday, Abbie told herself that it couldn't be anything really bad. Could it? Not when the ultrasound and blood tests hadn't revealed much. With everything going on in her life with work, and Jim trying to get her to pay out his half of the house, Abbie didn't have time to dwell on her unhappy body. She had been putting most of it down to stress, but might it be more?

When Abbie got back to the office she took her time climbing the steps. One at a time like an old lady with a bad hip. She smiled as the Tardis bag lady came to mind, but it made her miss Gramps and Grams, and as she looked up and saw Derek she was on the verge of tears.

'Good, you're back. Nita needs a hand with the Park Street house,' he said, pausing on his way to his office.

Abbie saw red. 'Sorry,' she replied dismissively, 'I don't have the time. I have a few new clients interested in selling, plus one keen on the Melba Street home.' Abbie continued to her desk and almost smirked at the look on his face. Tansy, the receptionist, gave her a surreptitious thumbs-up as she went past.

Abbie plonked her bag down on her desk as Derek arrived in a whoosh.

'I beg your pardon? I asked you to go and help Nita.'

'Yes, and I explained why I couldn't. Besides, you told me you had given the Park Street home to her this morning. I'm sure she'll figure it out.'

Tansy was standing up so she could see over the open-plan office dividers. Eric and Maree, both property managers, stood up to watch the show too. Nita was nowhere to be seen.

His shoulders tightened and his chest expanded. 'I've had

enough of your tardiness and your attitude, Abbie. This is the last straw or you'll be looking for another job.'

'Quite frankly, I've had enough of your bullying, *Derek*,' Abbie retorted without a second thought. 'You treat Eric like he's never managed a property before, yet he's one of the best I've worked with. You make Tansy get you coffee like she's your personal slave not the over-qualified receptionist she is. This was a great place to work until you turned up.'

Derek was past tomato red, his eyes bulged and his neck skin jiggled like a turkey's.

'That's it,' he said, raising his hand and pointing at her like a naughty child. 'You're fired.'

Abbie blinked twice as his words sank in. *Like hell*, she thought. She would not go down so easily. 'No, I quit,' she stated firmly. She took delight in the way his fat lips wobbled as he gasped for air like an oxygen-starved fish. His eyes were ready for war, his mind already thinking up a retort, but she wasn't going to let him get a word in. 'Besides,' she pounced quickly, 'we all know you're sleeping with Nita. One day your wife will find out and I hope she rips you a new one.' Abbie slung her bag back on her shoulder and walked out of the office. Eric gave her a silent clap, his grin reward enough. For a brief moment her head fog cleared and she had a glimpse of freedom.

She'd made it to the bottom of those blasted stairs when Tansy caught her up.

'Abbie. I'll get all your stuff together and drop it around later.' Tansy held her by the shoulders, her tattooed wrist just poking out as her blouse sleeves rose up her arms. 'Let me know when you get your business going and you need a receptionist.

I'll be there with bells on. You were amazing. Derek's gone and shut himself in his office.'

'I hope he's not too hard on you all because of me.' Abbie frowned. Tansy's nose-stud diamond sparkled in the light. She was young and a little hip but she did her job brilliantly.

'I doubt it. He's realised we all know about Nita now.'

'Good. And yes, I'd love for you to come and work for me. One day. When I get my shit together.'

'I believe in you. We all do. You've done so much for me and believed in us all. If you ever need anything, call.' Tansy pulled her into a hug. 'You should see the smile on Eric's face. He can't wait for Nita to appear.' Tansy eyeballed Abbie for a moment, her face growing serious. 'What are you going to do now?'

'Go home. Take an extended holiday. I was due to start my two weeks' break on Monday anyway. Now that can be my two weeks' notice,' she said with a wink. Having no work to keep her mind busy was going to drive her insane, but she wouldn't let Tansy see defeat. Squaring her shoulders, Abbie shot her a smile. 'I'll talk to you soon. Let me know the fallout goss.'

'I will, for sure.'

'Thank you. You're the best, Tansy. And tell Derek to fetch his own damn coffee.'

⚓

When Abbie arrived home, she unlocked the door with her new key. She'd had the locks changed after coming home to find that Jim had let himself in to take more of his things – only he'd helped himself to her favourite books and DVDs, plus some of her plants. It had pissed her off. He didn't deserve anything. As it was she wasn't going to pay him half of the house. No, Jim's decision was going to leave him with less than he'd bargained for.

Abbie shut the front door and walked down the passage to the kitchen. She dropped her bag, opened the fridge for her favourite bottle of wine and grabbed a glass. She carried it back to the couch and put on the TV. No more Derek. No more Jim. She could focus on what *she* wanted in life. Tears blurred her vision as she battled to stay in control. What did she want? How could she not feel cheated, hard done by, scared and alone? So many emotions; she didn't know what to fight first. Her belly rumbled; she had a craving for ice cream. It wouldn't go with her wine, but maybe she'd try it anyway. She had to have something she could control. Suddenly she burst out laughing at the craziness of what was now her life. The tears rolled down her face as she laughed and laughed until they were big shaky sobs that had her screaming into the nearest cushion.

5

Jess

JESS SAT OUTSIDE HER OLD HOME, LEANING AGAINST THE red-brick wall while watching Ollie pull leaves off the shrub beside her as they both waited for her mum to return. It was quiet here in the cul de sac street with older neighbours. One had waved as she'd driven past while they were watering their front garden while other homes remained silent, still, gardens overgrown with their owners away with work. Two streets back was a main road, busy with the afternoon commute and one street to the left was a park where Jess used to go with her friends. Even now she could hear some kids enjoying the small park which offered a place to run and play. She took it all in, familiar and strange, while she waited. She'd told April the exact time that they planned to arrive, give or take five minutes, and still her mum managed to forget.

'Jess, is that you?'

Peter's mum, who still lived a few houses down, was walking up the road waving. The same road she and Peter had ridden their bikes on. The memory made her grin as Lucy came closer. Her shoulders square, her walk elegant and her graceful long limbs. A lovely woman, tall with short brown hair and wearing ironed cargo shorts and a pretty white blouse. Not like Jess's mother, who loved floral pants and bright tops with colourful bags and big necklaces. Nothing she wore ever matched, but that's how April liked it. Jess couldn't convince her otherwise when she was embarrassed by her mum's attire as a teenager, but now she wouldn't change it for the world. It was who she was.

Jess picked up Ollie and met Lucy on the edge of the road. Lucy wrapped them both in a hug the moment she was near.

'Peter said you'd be up today, so I've been keeping a lookout. Gosh, love, it's so great to see you. How's little Ollie? My, how he's grown!' Lucy reached for Ollie and tried to hug the squirming boy. 'He looks so much like you. But I guess we all say that, especially not knowing what his dad looks like.'

Jess cringed inside, trying not to take Lucy's words to heart.

'He's walking now.'

'Really? Wow. What a clever boy,' she said kissing his cheek.

Jess smiled. Lucy was like her second mum. When the heat had got too hot at home she'd always found a sanctuary at their place. Peter often said his mum would have loved to have had a girl, and in the end Jess had become that substitute. It was Lucy who taught her how to cook and sew, who braided her hair and let her wear her high heels, who doted on her.

'Lost your key, love?' asked Lucy.

'No, Mum had to change the locks because she lost her set, and I haven't got a copy yet. I got her one of those locked boxes to put the spare in on the side of the house, but she's forgotten that code too.'

Lucy gave her a knowing smile. 'Ah, here she is.'

They all waved at the little red Suzuki Swift as it came towards them.

'I'll let you catch up. Pop over for a cuppa. Eddie would love to see you and Ollie.'

'Will do. Thanks, Lucy. Bye.'

Jess got to her mum's car as she was getting out, but before she could speak, April took one look at them and burst into tears, then gestured for them to hug her quickly.

'Oh Mum, it hasn't been that long,' she said. The hug lasted a while but Jess enjoyed the warmth of her mum's arms, the scent of her favourite perfume and the frangipani washing powder she always used.

'It's been too long. Oh, Ollie come to Nanny. Look how much you've grown,' said April, pouting. She smothered the boy in more kisses and blew raspberries down his arms until he giggled. 'Doesn't he have the cutest laugh? I could just eat you up, Ollie. Come on, let's get you inside.' April kept Ollie on her hip and headed to the front door after locking her car. 'Sorry I wasn't here to greet you, love. I hadn't forgotten. I was with a friend – she's having troubles like I am with Christopher, and I lost track of time. It's such an awful thing. I'm starting to think you did the right thing by moving to the country.'

'My little brother in trouble again?' Jess sighed heavily as she was hit with a vision of walking in on him smoking marijuana in the small back shed when he was eighteen, followed by a few years later when he'd progressed to cocaine and now ice. Jess shuddered and pushed those memories from her mind. Things she'd seen and never told a soul.

Inside the house they walked across old patterned carpets and past faded material couches now covered with crochet rugs. They were the ones she'd grown up sitting on, except for the new recliner in the corner, which she'd pitched in with Chris and bought their mum one year for Christmas. The whole house was loaded with childhood memories, not many of them happy, but she tried to only remember the good times, like when she and Chris would build cubbies out of sheets in the dining room. Mum would always find time to play with them, if Dad wasn't home. She'd crawl under the table, bringing them chocolate biscuits she'd hidden away for them.

Jess put Ollie down and he went immediately to the glass door where her mum's tiny Cavalier King Charles Spaniel watched, wagging its tail. Ollie put his hands against the glass and squealed at the dog. Jess had been given a kitten for her ninth birthday, but it died not long after when her dad kicked it in a fit of rage. Jess had never wanted another pet. Her mum had got the dog after her father had left but by then it was too late for Jess. The whole episode had scarred her for life and she couldn't bring herself to get a pet. Maybe when Ollie was older, maybe.

April flicked on the kettle while Jess pulled out a stool next to the small green breakfast bar. 'Is Chris not any better, Mum?' she said seriously, her excitement to be home now replaced by worry.

'I don't think so, darling. He told me he'd got clean but my friend's daughter saw him at a party the other day and he was using, she was positive. She's heard on the grapevine that Chris might be dealing too. They do that to pay for their habit.' April sagged against the breakfast bar and looked as if she'd aged thirty years. 'I don't know what else to do, Jessica. What did I do wrong? How did he end up this way? How do I help him when he refuses to talk to me?'

April's hands trembled as she clutched them together, her eyes a mix of worry, agony and pain. Jess felt the same churn in her belly.

'Mum, it's not your fault, but it might be Dad's. If he'd been a better role model and father, then maybe Chris wouldn't be searching for something more all the time. I'm not sure what we can do for him except offer to be there for him.'

Her brother was managing his drug habit, like so many others, but at what point would it all explode? Did he have to hit rock bottom before he'd get help? Did they have to force him into rehab for a habit he swore was just an occasional bit of fun? When did they try to intervene? And when would it end? When he was caught by police or dead in a gutter? He'd been fired from so many jobs. The last she'd heard he was working for a construction company and living with one of his mates. The previous job he'd been fired for theft of some power tools.

Jess glanced at Ollie and felt the weight of the future crash down on her. Would Ollie end up like Chris because he didn't have a father to guide him?

'Ollie will be fine, love,' said April, watching Jess closely. 'You're a better mother than I was. I should have got rid of your father years before he left, but I was scared and weak and now look at Chris. You're stronger than I am.'

'Aw, Mum.' Jess reached out and held her hands.

'Enough of depressing talk.' April got out some cups and made them tea. 'How have you been? How's the teaching going? Tell me all about your little kids and this trip. Have you seen Peter yet?'

'I love my classroom, Mum. I'm so happy there and I wish you'd come and visit me soon. You'd love it. I haven't seen Peter yet, but I'll message him now. I think he's going to drop around and say hi. I'll probably meet him over at his folks' place.'

'Well, I have to help out at the centre at three and I'll be gone for a few hours,' said April.

'That's okay. I'll put dinner on and tidy up for you.' Jess knew her mum loved it when she cooked for her. April would rather spend her time helping at the centre, where they sorted donations and made sure the right people got them, mostly domestic-abuse victims starting over, and held meetings for women like her. April had become passionate about this cause. After Jess's father had left, it was the centre April had turned to, which had taken strength and courage. To see her mum admit what she'd been through, to embrace it and move forward, had been a long, steady journey. The ladies at the centre had given her confidence a boost, helped her see she was strong and could be independent. Some days Jess wondered if she couldn't have done more to help her mum get through the tough times, but she was just a kid trying to find her own way to survive and was busy getting through school and university. Either way, April had slowly transformed and Jess was so proud. Hopefully Ollie would be proud of her one day too.

⚓

When her mum left for the centre, Ollie was just waking up from his nap in the cot in her old room. She dressed him in

his best clothes and freshened up to head over to see Lucy
and Eddie.

'Are you ready to go see Gran Lucy and Pop Eddie?' she
said to Ollie as she locked up and started down the street.

She'd messaged Peter and he said he'd be on his way shortly
after he finished wiring up an air conditioner. Jess felt the
butterflies in her belly take flight as she got closer to her second
home – closer to Peter. It had been months since they'd caught
up, briefly, at Ollie's first birthday party. She'd been so busy
organising it that they hadn't really had a proper chat. Life
had kept them both busy, but they still texted and spoke on
the phone all the time. Peter was a stickler for keeping their
regular Friday chats. *Love you, Jess.*

Jess put Ollie down and let him walk up the garden path
to the front door. This entrance had always seemed so magical to
Jess, but it was just a large wooden door. Yet even now she felt
its power; behind it was a sanctuary.

She knocked and called out. 'Hello, anyone home?'

Lucy appeared. 'Come in, come in. Oh, look at you go, Ollie.'

Lucy stood back and watched Ollie walk inside as Jess held
his hand for extra balance.

'He is just divine. I wish Peter would hurry up and give me
a grandie.'

Jess had to bite her tongue. If only Lucy knew how close
he was to proposing. Kids would no doubt be just around
the corner. After he'd convinced Ricki, that is. Jess had spent
many years with Ricki, and having kids just didn't seem to
fit into her life plan. But people's dreams changed – and why
wouldn't Ricki want to have babies with Peter? They'd be the
most gorgeous darlings.

'Eddie, they're here. Look at Ollie,' called Lucy, staying close by Ollie's side.

Jess looked up to see a tall, solid man step into the room. He wore jeans and a polo shirt. He was handsome for his age, his short hair just greying near his sideburns. To Jess he hadn't changed much over the years, just a few more lines and grey flecks. She saw Peter in his eyes and the strong shape of his jaw.

Ollie's eyes grew wide upon seeing Eddie, who got down on his knees and produced a little toy truck. 'Hello, Ollie. By crikey have you grown into a strapping young man.'

Ollie didn't even glance at Jess to see if the coast was clear, instead he reached out for the toy, balancing on his own two feet as he stepped towards Eddie.

'Ta, ta,' said Ollie.

Eddie marvelled at the little boy walking towards him and offered up his reward before gathering Ollie up into his arms. Ollie, who wasn't keen on strangers, seemed happy with Eddie.

'I think he likes you,' said Jess.

'Then he'll love me after we show him the toy box.'

They followed Eddie and Ollie into the kitchen, Eddie put Ollie by the toy box by the far wall and helped him pull out a toy phone, blocks and assorted other toys. 'Lucy had a friend wanting to get rid of these, so she snapped them up so Ollie would have something to play with when you visit,' said Eddie.

'Oh, that is so sweet,' Jess replied, touched by their thoughtfulness. There was also an edge of sadness that niggled her. She pushed it away.

'They'll always be handy,' said Lucy, with a smile.

After some time playing on the floor with the toys Eddie left Ollie to it and jumped up to hug Jess.

'It's so good to see you too, Jess. We miss having you pop by. The boys aren't so good at it.'

Jess returned the hug and revelled in Eddie's warm embrace and manly scent. She used to dream that Eddie was her father. Who knew what she would have turned out like if she didn't have the love from a wonderful man like Eddie?

'It's a bit hard for Scott to visit when he's in Spain, dear,' said Lucy as she began to fill the kettle.

'Peter said he'd made it to Spain. Scott is really living the life,' Jess said as she moved to the fridge and looked at all the post-cards Lucy gestured to.

'He sends one every week, or from every new place he visits. We've promised to meet up with him when he makes it to Rome. Eddie has booked in his holidays from work already.'

They sat around the kitchen table, in the middle of which stood a lovely vase full of flowers from Lucy's garden, and talked about Scott's travels while Eddie and Lucy took turns playing with Ollie and spoiling him with little treats to eat.

'Hello, can I come in? I'm dying for a coffee!'

Peter's voice rang out through the house and Lucy jumped up to let him in as Jess felt that strange flutter in her lower belly and her foot began to tap against the floor. Should she get up or wait for him to walk in? She wrung her hands together and sucked her bottom lip between her teeth.

'Where's my girl?' Peter called out.

Jess looked up as Peter came into the room. He was as tall as his dad, but his hair was much blonder and looking messed up from work, which somehow looked as sexy as hell. Or was it that cute, perfect-teeth smile? As a kid he'd been scrawny, worn braces and had glasses, but he'd morphed into a tanned, ripped surfing god. It took all her effort not to gawk. But beneath all that was her best friend, and it was his heart that she loved the most. Peter opened his arms and smiled at her.

'Get in here *now*,' he demanded cheekily.

Jess smiled as she got up and stepped into his embrace.

'I can't believe how long it's been,' said Peter, not letting her go. His hand reached up and felt her hair. 'You've cut it off? It looks cute.'

'I doubt it's cute, but it's my mum look,' she said with a chuckle.

Finally he let her go but kept her within arm's reach, his hands holding her shoulders as he checked her over. 'Man, are you a sight for sore eyes.'

Peter had a way of making Jess feel like she was the most important girl in his life. She could literally feel herself glowing just being near him.

'Where's Ollie?'

At the mention of his name Ollie paused what he was doing. He saw Jess with Peter and walked over, grabbing her leg and looking up at him.

'Can I pick him up?' asked Peter.

'Sure. I can't guarantee he'll stay there.'

Peter bent down and smiled. 'Hello there, buddy. Gonna come to Uncle Pete?' he said holding out his large hands.

Ollie tilted his head a fraction then reached out for Peter's hands. Not needing any more encouragement, Peter lifted him up, almost throwing him into the air. Ollie looked shocked at first, but then he smiled and threw his body back. 'More!'

Peter lifted him up high again and again and the house was filled with Ollie's infectious laughter.

Jess couldn't help but watch them with adoration. The two men she loved most in this world. Ollie would be okay if they could keep Peter in their life. Who knew what the future would hold after he married Ricki and they had their own kids, but with a bit of luck Pete could still offer the support and positive male influence that Ollie would need, just as Eddie had been for her.

Peter had been at Ollie's birth, along with Ricki and Abbie, and for that she would always be grateful. Her friends were there when she'd cried after finding out she was pregnant, and they had supported her decision to keep her baby even though she didn't want the dad involved. One drunken night, in a fit of depression, jealousy and rare bravado, she had created Ollie. What at first had seemed like a massive mistake had since turned into the centre of her life, and she wouldn't change it for the world. Because of Ollie, Jess knew she would survive. She had to, for him. And because of Ollie she knew she could endure loving her best friend from afar and be happy even though he would never be hers. At least he was still in their lives, a great fatherly influence for her son. And Pete loved her, even if it was as a sister. Thoughts of them being a family began to manifest, but with practised ease she forced them back.

And maybe one day her heart and soul would stop wanting him. It had to. Until then she would have to fight the desires and stay in control.

6

Ricki

RICKI CHECKED HER PONYTAIL WASN'T TOO DROOPY AND dug her lip gloss from her pocket, recoating her lips again even though it was towards the end of her shift. It was hard to look any good in her nursing uniform. On the upside, everyone else was in one too.

With a sigh she headed out of the bathroom; if she took much longer Heather might put out a missing-persons report. Ricki had enjoyed her shift today, working with Miguel, whose stories and plans for his next trip were an escape from her mundane life, and also spending time with her patients, who seemed genuinely thankful and appreciative of her efforts, especially the parents of little Molly, who would go home after nearly dying from a spider bite. But then there was Heather. Major bitch boss from hell. Satan must have rejected her and sent her back to wreak havoc on the poor innocent nursing staff at the Southern Health Campus.

'Ricki, there you are. Where have you been? This isn't good enough. Molly's family is waiting to take her home. It should have been done already,' said Heather as she clicked the end of her pen in quick succession.

Speak of the devil, she thought. With her red hair, dyed to an artificial brightness, Heather just needed some horns and red contacts and she'd be set for a Halloween costume.

There was no point trying to tell Heather that if she hadn't just gone to the bathroom right then her bladder would have exploded since she'd been hanging onto it for most of the shift. No, that was still no excuse. Nurses didn't have time for luxuries like peeing and eating. Ricki swallowed the retort burning on her tongue, nodded and headed towards Molly's room.

'She's got a major red hot chilli stuck up her behind today,' came a whisper.

Ricki laughed, then clapped her hand over her mouth so Heather wouldn't reprimand her for having fun. Miguel smiled, and she forgot about her painful boss. 'I'm glad the smile's back on your face,' he said as his eyes watched her intently.

Butterflies took flight in her belly. Was Miguel flirting with her? She watched as he reached for a chart by his patient's bed, his forearm tanned and strong. She loved watching him work, those hands so gentle and nurturing, his way of putting people instantly at ease.

And yet he could put Ricki on edge, filling her with a sudden hit of adrenaline. Feeling lightheaded, she tried to focus on what she was supposed to be doing. What was it again?

A little girl sat up on her bed, dark curls falling around her face and her arm still bandaged. 'Ah, Miss Molly. You get to go home today. Are you excited?'

She nodded her head and Ricki glanced at her mum, who was sitting beside the bed collecting the comfort toys she'd brought in for her daughter.

'We all are,' her mum said with relief.

It had been a long, hard slog for Molly after the redback spider bite, but things had turned out as well as they had dared to hope.

'I'm going to miss your smile, Miss Molly,' said Ricki as she did a last round of obs. 'You're good to go. Just go to the desk to sign the papers on your way out,' she said to the mother.

'Thank you.'

'Bye,' said Molly, waving to Ricki and Miguel.

'You'd be amazing in Cambodia,' said Miguel as he joined her by the empty bed. 'You're so good with kids.'

Ricki laughed. 'You really want me to go, don't you, Miguel?'

'Of course. I can see it burning in your eyes. You're a born healer, Ricki, and you would thrive in that environment.' He shot a glance in Heather's direction. Nothing more needed to be said. 'Will you come and have a coffee with me after the shift? At the cafe?'

Her heart pounded strangely. Was it nerves? Fear? Anticipation? He was a good friend but Ricki picked up an undertone that he would like much more. Sometimes she thought she was being silly, dreaming of something exciting and new, wanting to be liked by the hot guy everyone fancied. And yet his shifts were lining up with hers and he always made an effort to say hello or eat his lunch with her. At first she thought it was because she was so interested in his overseas work, maybe he just liked having someone to talk to about it.

Yet, the looks were starting to linger. His smiles seemed only for her.

'Sure, I'm just about to do sign-off with Teresa. I'll meet you there in five.'

Miguel waved and walked out of the room.

Ricki felt a giddying sensation that seemed to come with a warning. But it was just coffee, between friends. That was all. He was so different to Peter. Peter had never been out of Australia, nor did any sort of travel interest him. Yet Ricki had been putting money into a travel account since she could remember – the only problem was, she hadn't left the state either. One day she should really try and rectify that, with or without Peter.

⚓

Miguel was waiting for her in the far corner, the quietest spot in the room.

'Hey, you. I got you a coffee,' he said, pushing the cup forward. 'And something to eat.'

'Oh, you're a life saver,' she said, taking a big sip of the coffee and then reaching for the slice of chocolate cake. 'This is today's lunch. Thank you. My shout next time.'

Miguel's laugh was soft and sexy. She couldn't help but smile.

'I'll hold you to that,' he said, his eyes fixed on hers. She could tell he had something on his mind. He shuffled his chair in closer and leaned towards her. Ricki quickly swallowed her mouthful and chased it down with more coffee. Suddenly her throat was very dry.

'I need to talk to you,' Miguel said quietly, his fingers tapping the tabletop nervously.

Ricki felt her legs tingle in anticipation. 'Yeah, sure,' she almost squeaked. 'You can tell me anything.' Over the past few weeks as she and Miguel had grown closer she had mentioned Peter a few times, but it hadn't stopped the flirting. Maybe Miguel didn't care? She could only guess at what he was about to say, but she couldn't help but wonder – hope? – if it was about her. Her fingers tightened around her cup so hard she was close to spilling coffee everywhere.

'Good, I'm glad. I feel the same way about you; that's why I have to tell you I'm worried about Marni.'

Ricki pulled a face. Marni? That new young nurse? What did she have to do with anything? Did he like her?

'I'm worried she's been stealing meds from the patients. I've been watching her, and I think they're for her. Well, that's just my guess. Have you noticed anything? What should I do? I'm really worried – patients are still in pain when they shouldn't be. Mr Dennis in room nine is as tough as they come, so when he complains of pain I'm worried.'

Ricki nodded, still too shocked to come up with a response.

'And Hilda in room three has been managing after her op with the pain, but now all of a sudden it hurts. She should be improving and I've checked her over, she's healing beautifully. I know my patients, Ricki. I really feel they aren't getting their meds, and it's always when Marni's been on the rounds.' Miguel reached out and gripped Ricki's hand. 'I don't know what I should do.'

Ricki shook her head, trying to process this information. Glancing down at the table, she scratched at a mark, trying not to be disappointed that Miguel wasn't expressing feeling things for her. With a deep breath she mentally shook herself and tried to get a grip. 'Marni. I haven't worked with her much.' She couldn't look up at Miguel yet. 'Let me think.' Closing her eyes, she tried to focus on the shifts with Marni.

'Have you ever issued out drugs with her?' he probed. She lifted her head. 'For fours or eights? Did she offer to deliver the meds?'

Ricki held up her hand to slow him down. He still held her other hand and she wasn't ready to break that connection. 'Yeah, for both fours and eights.' Schedule 4 and Schedule 8 drugs were kept in the medicine room. They needed a key to get into the 4 cupboard, which held mainly antibiotics and strong pain killers; they needed another key to unlock the 8s cupboard, which was the strong stuff, including morphine and methadone. Two people had to sign the drugs out and then administer them to the patient. 'She said once that she'd deliver them but I went with her anyway because I like to stick to the rules in that regard.'

Miguel glanced around and pulled his hand away as a few nurses walked past, but his voice remained at a whisper. 'On my first shift with her she told me she'd deliver the drugs and I let her – as one of my patients took a bad turn. Now I'm wondering if I didn't just play into her hands? I can see them suffering, Ricki. It makes me furious.'

Ricki frowned, her heart going out to Miguel. 'Don't beat yourself up. All we can do for now is to cover our arses and make sure we deliver the drugs properly. I've heard of some nurses swapping the pills with similar-looking ones before they give them to the patient. But we can't accuse her of anything without proof. Let's keep our eyes open and just play it day by day, yeah?'

He smiled. 'Thanks, Ricki. I feel better not having to carry this on my own. And I'm sorry to dump you with it—'

She shook her head and cut him off. 'No, don't be. We've got to stick together and look out for each other. It's a tough job. I'm glad you came to me. I'll be more aware now too.'

They sat watching each other for a moment. Ricki could have sworn there was electricity in the air.

'Do you have to rush off home? Can you stay for a bit longer? I haven't told you about the trip to Vietnam that started my whole career off yet,' he teased. 'I'm sure I can put you to sleep.'

She laughed. 'You know I want to hear everything. I'd love to stay. I don't need to rush home.' And she didn't. Peter had a job north of the river and wouldn't be back until late. There was nothing waiting for her except housework and catching up on the shows she always recorded on Foxtel.

They talked for over an hour before Miguel said he had to go. 'Sorry, I have a class to get to.'

'Oh?' she replied as they stood and made their way to the car park.

'I'm learning Khmer. It'll make things easier when I go back to Cambodia. I was terrible at languages at school, but now I've been to these places it's different. I just love it.'

'Wow, that's cool. Say something,' she urged.

'*Tau neak sok sapbaiy teh?*' he said softly.

The words sounded so exotic and made Miguel twice as sexy. He rubbed the back of his neck as they walked and Ricki had to try hard not to stare. How could someone make something so simple look so hot?

'What did you say?'

Miguel smiled as he stopped by her car. Only now did she realise he'd walked her here instead of going off to his own. It felt like a date.

'Thanks for the talk,' he said, ignoring her question.

Ricki soon forgot it as well when he reached out and pulled her into a hug. Not a quick I-don't-really-like-contact hug but a slow, long I-really-feel-you kind of hug. The kind that connects two people on a personal, intimate level. Or was that just because he smelled good, even after a hospital shift?

'See you tomorrow,' he said eventually, pulling away and walking towards his car.

Ricki watched him leave and realised she never hugged Peter like that, at least not while she was still in her uniform. It took all her concentration to fish out her car keys, but eventually she was on her way home while the words he'd spoken echoed through her mind.

7

Jess

JESS SAW PETER FIRST. SHE WOULD RECOGNISE HIM IN ANY crowd with his height and surfie good looks. Beside him sat Abbie, long black hair cascading down her back. They were chatting on one of the island seats in the shopping centre waiting for her to join them. Jess was always a clock watcher and arrived early if not on time. That was until she'd had Ollie; now she was simply grateful to actually turn up to things. She glanced at Ollie on her hip as she strode along trying not to think of how long her friends had been waiting. Ollie held up his hand – slightly sticky from leftover breakfast she must have missed – and placed it on her face.

'Thanks darling,' she sighed. Yet she smiled because he made her heart burst with love and she found it hard to look away from his gorgeous, innocent blue eyes. She hadn't bothered with his stroller, because that would have taken even longer to organise.

As Peter saw her and waved, Jess's belly dropped. She really didn't want to be here today, helping him buy a ring for someone else, even if it was her best friend.

With two steps to go until she reached them, she sucked in a deep breath and plastered on a smile. 'Hey, guys. Sorry I'm late.'

Peter jumped up to hug her and took Ollie from her arms.

After hugging Abbie, which was like hugging a thin tree, she held her shoulders and squinted at her. 'Big night out, Abs?'

'Urgh, you could say that. What gave it away – the black circles or my general disdain for life right now?'

Jess smirked. She'd loved that about Abbie from the moment Abbie had stood up for her at high school. Her bravery in the face of bullies and her quick wit made her something to behold. Jess could never get the words out right and so remained silent most of the time, but when Abbie spoke people listened. Once when they were fourteen and sunbaking at the beach, a man approached them. He was old and creepy, yet when he'd asked if he could buy them an ice cream and join them, Jess had wanted to shrink to nothing. But Abbie had sat up and said, 'Sure. While you're at it, go ask my dad over there if he'd like one. See the big guy by the rocks. He works at a prison. He could use an ice cream, he's pretty grumpy.'

Needless to say, the guy took one look at the big bloke Abbie had pointed out and took off.

'How do you do that?' Jess had asked, glancing at the big bloke Abbie had claimed as her father.

Abbie had shrugged. 'He's lucky I didn't call him a paedophile. And that big bloke we passed on our way to the beach seemed like the right kind of guy to protect us,' she said with a smirk.

Just so calm and cool under pressure was Abbie. Jess felt safe with her.

'It's so nice to be here with you and not at work,' Abbie said to her now.

'Oh, that's right, your new boss. Is he still being a dick?' Jess said.

'Yep. Doubt that will change.' Abbie flicked her large brown eyes away. They settled on Ollie. 'Hey, little man. Look at you.'

Abbie held his hand and smiled. She liked kids; she just didn't want any until her career was sorted. And then there was Ricki, who was brilliant with kids but didn't want any either. Out of her friends, Peter was the one who gushed over Ollie. Which was fine by her, as long as someone was keen to help carry him around the shops today.

'Can we get a coffee first?' asked Abbie. 'I'm slowly dying here,' she said.

'Yeah, great idea. Mum only has instant coffee, and I swear it's the same tin from when we were at high school.'

'There's a good coffee shop down the end, and it does nice pastries,' said Peter, leading the way. 'What do you think, Ollie? Are you allowed some treats?'

Jess slipped her arm through Abbie's as they walked behind Peter, Ollie happy in his arms. It was a rare moment she could relax.

'It's so good to catch up again. I miss you guys so much,' said Jess.

Abbie nodded and squeezed her arm tighter but it was a forced smile that came to her lips. *Man, you must really be hungover*, thought Jess. When they got on the boat Jess was going to let loose and have a few drinks with her friends. It felt like years since they'd all had a good time together.

They sat against the wall of the coffee shop so Ollie could stand on the booth seat and walk between Jess and Peter. Abbie sat opposite them and inhaled her coffee when it arrived. Jess sipped hers while helping Ollie eat his giant cookie.

'So, what's happening these days?' she asked Abbie. 'How's Jim? How are your folks – are they still loving the grey-nomad thing? I can remember them talking about taking that trip decades ago; it must be nice for them to finally be off doing it.' Jess was half-expecting a call any day now saying Jim had proposed. It couldn't be far off. Her coffee momentarily soured in her mouth as she realised both her closest girlfriends were happily in relationships, living with their partners, building lives. Jess didn't have a partner, but Ollie was more than enough. Except on the nights Ollie was sick; she'd get so scared, doubt what she was doing, get no sleep and wish there was someone to help her. Those days were tough. But she'd made it this far on her own.

'Jim is Jim. Work is work. And I haven't heard from the folks in nearly three weeks, so I'm guessing they're either having a ball or dead. I'm sure they're just busy exploring the delights of South Australia before they head towards Tasmania. But I'm happy for them. They saved hard to get that caravan and four-wheel drive and then to set off on their dream after all these years of hard work. I'm really proud. They still have a year and a half on their journey but I bet anything they keep finding new places to explore.'

'It sounds amazing. I bet you miss them.'

'I do, but this is their time now.'

Abbie's eyes sparkled with pride. Her house could have burned to the ground, yet she'd keep that from her parents so it wouldn't interrupt their trip. She was very selfless like that, putting other people's needs before her own.

'What about you, Peter, what's with this bloody idea to propose to Ricki? Living together is working for you, then?' said Abbie, turning the focus on him.

Jess could swear she saw uncertainty flicker through his eyes, or maybe it was the bright lights of the coffee shop. 'You shouldn't need us for this too, Pete. A ring should come from the heart,' Jess added.

He watched as Ollie walked along the seat to him and climbed onto his lap. 'It's the next step. We're cruising along, and marriage and kids is what comes next. Why wait? Ollie needs a friend to play with, right? And as for the ring – I'm still trying to figure her out and I don't want to screw this up. I want something she'll love.'

'What do you mean you haven't figured her out yet?' said Jess.

Peter tilted his head back so it was out of reach from Ollie's hands as he flapped them about dancing to the music filtered through the shop. 'You know, I'll try to do something nice and bring her a rug when she's cold and it will be the wrong one, or I'll make her a coffee when she feels like a hot chocolate. I never seem to read her right. It will come eventually, but for now I need your help. Please,' he begged. 'Jewellery is girls' stuff, so you two should be pros at this.'

Dimples appeared with his smile and Jess knew she'd never say 'no' to him.

'Thanks, Jess,' he said.

'I'll ignore your sexist remark. *I* don't like jewellery. I've worn the same diamond earrings for the past three years,' Abbie smiled cheekily. 'But I don't have much else to do, so I'll gladly help you spend your money, Pete baby.' Abbie picked up her spoon and ran it around her cup as she yawned.

'So, there are two jewellery shops in here. Which one first, and what style and price range are we talking?' said Jess, forcing all other thoughts away. This was how life was now, for her, for Peter.

Ollie had finished using Peter as a jungle gym and now held out a fork. 'Ta, ta,' he said pointedly to Jess. She put a bit of his biscuit on the end of it for him but made him sit to eat it.

'Well, let's start at the closest one, and I guess something simple for Ricki,' said Peter. His left eyebrow rose as if he wasn't sure.

'Yes, you're right. Ricki likes simple, easy and minimal.' Jess watched him relax knowing he'd got something right. She reached over and gripped his hand. 'It's supposed to be fun, Peter, not a chore. She'll love it regardless. Don't stress.'

'Jess is right. Ricki doesn't like too much bling, so you need something classical and uncluttered.'

Peter got up. 'Right, let's get this show on the road.' He reached for Ollie, putting his empty fork on the table. If that had been Jess, Ollie would have made a performance for taking the fork off him, yet with Peter he went happily back to his arms. Little rascal.

Normally, shopping with Abbie was like having four seasons in one day. She'd be off like a mini rocket, and even in heels she'd clip-clop through the shops as if time were a pressing issue. But today she took her time, and Jess liked seeing her going slowly for a change.

'So, what are you going to do with your time until we leave next week?' Jess asked.

'As little as possible.' Abbie shrugged and buried her hands into her knee-length black knit cardigan. She wore it over a white singlet and skinny jeans. So simple, yet on Abbie it looked amazing. Jess felt frumpish beside her. Her jeans were a snug fit around her wide hips, and her boobs threatened to overflow her bra. Luckily she wore a large, baggy shirt to keep them under wraps. She'd been meaning to get the next-size-up bra but hadn't had time. Maybe after they selected the ring and if Ollie was still in good spirits she could do a little shopping for herself. But that was a big *if*. If she could be bothered, too.

At the first jewellery shop, Peter stood in the middle and looked around. His eyes found hers and he looked like a drowning rat begging to be saved. Jess rolled her eyes and with Abbie's help they found the engagement-ring section and asked the sales lady to bring a few out from behind the glass.

'Come and look, Pete,' said Abbie waving him over. 'We're not picking this thing for you.'

Jess took Ollie from him and put him down so he could walk around while Abbie showed Peter through the rings she thought Ricki would like. It was hard work stopping Ollie from smearing his little handprints all over the glass display cabinets but she managed, just, all the time wishing she had brought the stroller.

'Jess, what do you think?' Pete turned to her, his brow creased. He looked panicked, like the day all those years ago that he'd hit the cricket ball through the shed window, knowing his dad was going to go ballistic, especially because it had only been replaced the week before from their last backyard cricket game.

'Here, I'll take him,' said Abbie, reaching for Ollie and leading him to a plush chair, where they snuggled in together and Abbie pulled out her phone to distract him.

Jess turned her attention to the three rings Peter had selected with Abbie's help. Two were yellow gold and the other was white gold. Jess loved the white gold with its cluster of tiny diamonds, but Ricki had always liked yellow gold with her complexion. 'Stick with yellow gold. And my guess would be more like this one,' she said pointing to the solitaire ring with the large diamond as the centrepiece.

Peter let out a deep breath. Then he looked up at the sales lady. 'Thank you. I'll think on it a bit. Cheers.'

'Take your time,' she said. 'It's an important thing not to be rushed into.' And she gave him a reassuring wink.

As they headed to the next jewellery store Ollie spotted a kids' car ride and Peter fished out some coins from his pocket.

'You'll never get him off it now, you do realise,' said Jess, already anticipating the tantrum.

Abbie ducked off to the bathroom while they waited by Ollie. Next to the car that rolled up and down causing Ollie to squeal in delight was a stand with balls containing tiny gifts – all you needed was fifty cents. Peter popped in a coin and retrieved his plastic ball – inside he found a little metal ring with a red love heart on it.

'Aw, see now that's the kind of ring I'd love.' Jess tried it on her finger and admired it. 'It's not about the cut of the diamond or its size or the cost, for me it's the love that comes with it. The special moment where a guy would give me this because he was so overcome with love and couldn't wait to go ring shopping.' Jess stared at the ring, almost picturing the moment as if it were real. Peter laughed and she looked up as she gave it back. 'What?'

'Nothing.' His smile was sincere. 'You're beautiful when you go off in your own world.'

The light danced in his blue eyes and filled her heart, easing away the loneliness. Peter was her home growing up, he made the world colourful and safe, and looking at him now Jess realised he always would bring that inner peace and protection.

They smiled at each other until Ollie started to shake the car to make it rock again.

Abbie was walking back towards them, so Jess held out her hands. 'Time to go, Ollie,' she said, bracing herself for the sixteen-month-old attitude and pout.

Beside her Peter tucked the little heart ring into his pocket and used the plastic ball to distract Ollie as he pulled him from the car. In no time they were all moving towards the next jewellery shop. Jess couldn't help the sigh of relief. Her friends didn't realise just how much it meant to have someone take care of a situation, to have one less tantrum to deal with, the scene, the glances, the judgement. It all rattled around her head like stress balls, but for today, in that moment, she'd been given a little slice of heaven.

An hour later, Peter had finally settled on a large solitaire diamond ring. He should have been excited, yet his face looked tinged with green.

'I hope she doesn't lose it. I hope *I* don't,' he said worriedly as he handed over his credit card.

'Deed's done now, Pete.' Abbie smiled and rested her hand on his arm. 'Today has been fun. I've missed you crazy kids.'

In that moment Abbie's eyes actually smiled too. It had been more than a hangover, Jess realised now. It wasn't just Abbie's empty smiles, it was the lethargy in the way she moved, it was the moments of sadness, despair even. Whatever it was, Jess couldn't put a finger on it but she made a mental note to spend some alone time with Abbie and find out what was troubling her. Maybe there were problems at home with Jim. Or at work. 'Hey, do you want to have lunch again tomorrow or later in the week?' Jess asked.

Abbie looked a bit shocked. 'Oh, um, that sounds lovely, Jess, but . . .' She cleared her throat. 'I've got a few things to get done before the cruise. I'm sorry.'

Jess detected more to the story. Maybe it was the way Abbie kept scratching at her skin – was it nerves? – and the fact that earlier she'd said she had nothing on for the week.

'We'll have time on the boat. Yeah?' said Abbie quickly, a bit too quickly.

'I feel like I should celebrate with a beer,' Pete jumped in before Jess could reply. 'Who's keen to have one at our old stomping ground with lunch?'

He looked like a lost teenager at a party, unsure and nervous, needing his friends around him for support. This had been a big step for him and for a moment Jess wondered if his whole heart was in it. Or perhaps he was only worried Ricki would say no.

'Sure, sounds good,' said Abbie, flicking her hair over her shoulder, seemingly happy for the distraction.

Jess sighed and smiled; shopping for herself would have to wait, as usual. 'Okay, I'm in too.'

⚓

The Duke was a two-storey refitted 1850s building with unpolished timber floors, exposed brick walls and hearty meals. The black metal and solid wood furniture gave it a warm, industrial feel. Peter collected a high chair for Ollie and the foursome automatically went to their favourite table, a slab from a tree positioned near a large window framed with bricks. The rest of the wall was covered with plaster and painted in a soft mocha tone.

With Ollie tucked in tight, they relaxed and gave their orders to Pete, who went to relay them to the barman.

'A bourbon?' said Jess at Abbie's order.

'I'm on holidays. Fu— . . . dge it, I say,' she said raising her glass before covering her mouth with her hand. 'Sorry, Ollie.'

'He can't say much, so I'm not worried he'll repeat it, but it's a day that's not far off.'

By the time Ollie's meal arrived, Jess was feeling a little on edge as Ollie had got impatient, and tired. She had resorted to using her phone to keep him occupied and that bought them some time, well enough that Peter and Abbie could talk. Jess was flat out making sure Ollie didn't press something he shouldn't and almost cried out 'Thank God' when his lunch arrived.

Jess was feeding Ollie his pasta when a voice she hadn't heard in a while made her body tense. So much so, she dropped Ollie's fork onto his high chair.

'Fancy seeing you mob here. Hey, sis.'

Jess was almost too afraid to meet his eyes, of what she'd see, but slowly they rose, finding familiar features but a different face. Her jaw ached from clasping her teeth together. 'Hi, Chris,' Jess said flatly.

'G'day, Chris, it's been a long time.' Peter got up to shake his hand and towered over Chris, who, like his mum, was a good inch shorter than Jess. His dark, wayward hair was their father's, and he and Jess shared similar blue eyes – though his looked tired. *He's probably half-drunk*, thought Jess. *Or maybe high.* She pinched her lips together. It was hard not to feel the abyss that had grown between them, more so since he'd got mixed up with drugs. Chris had taken life badly, felt as if he'd been dealt poor cards and liked to blame others for it. He accused their mum of driving their dad away. There were days Jess had seen their mum bear the brunt of his harsh words, and not once did she set him right. Jess loved her brother, but he was making it really hard, and right now she didn't like him much at all.

'Yeah, sure has. How's Scott doing these days?' asked Chris, although he didn't wait for an answer. Chris and Scott had played together as kids, but when he was eleven and Jess's dad left, Chris and Scott drifted apart and joined different crowds. 'I didn't know you were back,' said Chris, glancing at Ollie. 'Heck, he's grown.'

'Not for long.' Her brow furrowed. Was it awful that she didn't want him to know she was around? That she didn't want him to drop by their mum's house? Her temple pounded with an oncoming migraine. She didn't want Chris anywhere near Ollie, even though he was Ollie's only uncle. The mistrust burned inside her, but when it came to her son she wouldn't risk anything.

'Hey, Ollie. It's Uncle Chris.'

Chris frowned when Ollie didn't pay him any notice, too intent on getting the pasta from his bowl to his mouth. Jess wasn't going fast enough, so he pushed his fingers into his dinner, grabbing a handful.

'Don't take it personally, he just doesn't remember you.' Jess noted her brother's slight sideways shuffle as he wiped his nose on his shirt. He'd had a few beers, for sure.

'Yeah, whatever. Hey, have you got any money, sis?'

Chris only called her *sis* when he was sucking up.

'No, sorry.'

'How 'bout you guys? I just ran out, wouldn't mind another few beers though,' he almost begged.

Abbie glanced at Jess and then turned around to face Chris. 'Sorry, mate, I only have my card.' To prove her point she lifted up her phone.

'I've only got shrapnel,' said Pete, pulling out the last of the coins from his pocket.

Chris's eye twitched and he shook his head. 'No worries, I guess I'll leave you to it.' Before he went he glanced longingly at Ollie, the corner of his lips tugging up. 'He looks like you, Jess, when you were little. Remember that photo Mum had on the fridge of us?' Then his head twitched as if shaking the memory away. 'See you, guys. Bye, sis.'

The soft expression changed when he glanced to her. Without so much as a smile he turned and went back to the bar.

'Wow,' said Peter. 'He doesn't look so good.'

Jess could see that Peter was shocked to see the state of Chris. Her once strong-looking brother, once handsome too, now barely had any meat on his bones to stop his skin from wrinkling, which aged him dramatically. His face was blotchy, his eyes drawn and tired. Everyone talked about the ice epidemic and how it was getting out of control. But no one seemed to have any brilliant ideas on how to stop it or save people from its ravages, nothing that gave them the tools to help Chris now. Not when he didn't want help. Just money.

'I know. I know.' It was all she could manage to say as a sudden wave of emotion threatened to come crashing down. She focused on Ollie's mouth as he ate, anything but the faces of her friends. That would make Chris's state more real.

'How long has he been using?' said Abbie. 'I mean, beyond the usual parties.'

Jess shrugged. 'I don't know.' How could she tell them she'd known that Chris had been doing drugs for years? That maybe if she'd said something in the beginning, he might not be like this? 'Mum's been trying to handle it, but with how he feels about her I think it's pushed him the other way. I don't know what to do either. I have Ollie to worry about, and Chris is an adult.' Jess sighed. 'If I say anything to him, he gets upset. And so far he's managing to work and get by. Maybe it's something he has to do on his own. I don't know.' Jess kissed Ollie's hand to hide her trembling lips. She wouldn't fall to pieces in the pub. She had to be strong.

Neither of her friends had an answer, and everyone seemed relieved when the waiter brought over their meals. As they dug in, the conversation moved back to safe territory.

'Do you remember the time all three of us girls were dancing on this table while we sang "Eagle Rock"?' said Abbie as her hand brushed across the top.

Peter laughed. 'That was until Gerry the barman came and busted you all.'

Abbie's eyes grew wide. 'That's right, 'cause we all dropped our pants while the song was on! It's what you have to do.'

'But Gerry loved us, he wasn't really mad,' said Jess. 'He was the best barman.'

Abbie got up. 'No, he loved *you*. I'm getting another drink. Same again?' she asked them.

Peter asked for a Coke this time, so did Jess. He smiled after Abbie as she made her way to the bar.

'What did she mean? Gerry didn't like me.' He'd been managing the pub at that time, had been here for years. 'I wonder where he is?'

'Gerry went back to Ireland about six months ago. You wouldn't look his way, and it gutted him.'

She stared at Peter, her mouth open.

He chuckled, and she relaxed. 'You're so easy. No, his mum got sick, so he left. And yes, seriously he did have a thing for you. Couldn't you tell?'

'No. Really? There were a few times I thought he might be keen, but I don't know, I guess he wasn't my type.'

Jess glanced over at Abbie chatting to Chris at the bar, and tried to push away the sudden uneasiness this sight brought.

'Who *is* your type? Ollie's father?'

'Pardon?' Jess looked back to Peter. When he repeated his question, she wished he hadn't. 'I guess he had to be, in a way.

I slept with him.' Her heart jumped at the possible directions this conversation might take.

'Haven't looked him up?'

Jess screwed up her brow. 'No. I told you it was an accident. A good one, I guess,' she added, glancing at her son. 'But I didn't know his last name and I figure there's a good reason for that. One-night stands happen, Pete. Two ships passing in the night. Except I was left with a lasting reminder.'

Peter reached across and touched her hand, and instantly her body relaxed a little. 'I'm sorry. I didn't mean to upset you. It's just sad that Ollie won't get to know his dad. I love my dad.'

'Yeah, I love your father too. But mine's a dipshit I never want back in my life. I'd hate for Ollie's dad to be like that. So, at least this way he's safe. He has you and your dad. It was all *I* ever needed.' She could tell by the way his eyes glittered with tenderness that he knew. He'd been there through it all: the times she'd told him her darkest fears and the scariest moments when her dad lashed out. He'd want to call the police and she'd beg him not to; it would only make it worse. So, he said nothing.

Peter had always kept her secrets.

8

Abbie

ABBIE OPENED HER HEAVY EYES AND BLINKED AT THE brightness. 'Am I still alive?' she croaked.

But there was no one in her room, so she closed them again as a dull ache pulsed around her neck and her head felt groggy. She wanted – needed – a coffee. Suddenly she had a vision of the first time she'd met Jim: heading to her favourite coffee shop for her morning fix and this man opening the door for her. He did it while talking with a mate, as if it was as natural as scratching his head. That was what she'd noticed first. Then the next day they'd arrived at the line together and he'd let her go in front. That's when she'd noticed his eyes, like the new leaves on her gardenia bush, the purest green without blemish, and the thickness of his hair brushed into place but without fancy product to keep it there. The next day she'd been disappointed to not meet 'green eyes' again and had walked out with her coffee only to nearly collide with him heading to the door at a rate of knots.

'Oh, sorry, I was in a rush.' Then he'd smiled. 'To catch you actually,' he'd admitted, his face colouring slightly.

Abbie had been smitten. They had been amazing moments, and she found herself smiling now at the memory. Just that feeling, the first pangs of desire. No matter what she thought of Jim now, she wouldn't want to give back those moments. They were happy then.

Besides, who really knew how life was going to work out? It could all change at the flick of a wrist.

With a sigh she tried to open her eyes again but gave up.

It had been a long day. It started with fasting, which wasn't hard because she'd been too nervous to eat, so her last main meal had been at the pub with Peter and Jess.

A taxi had dropped her off at the hospital – early, as instructed – with her small bag of clothes hugged to her side. At least this hospital was far away from Ricki's and there was no way they'd cross paths. Abbie didn't know what the surgery would result in, but she guessed that once this was done everything could go back to normal. Well, as close to normal as her life lately could be. It was as if she were a ship in a glass bottle, her life carefully built with steady hands and tweezers, only for someone to come along and shake the hell out of it. Nothing was where it once belonged. Things were broken. Shattered.

A nurse had settled her in, and she had met the surgeon just before going into the operating theatre, where he'd marked the site on her neck, talking her through it briefly. Enough to satisfy her curiosity without being an information overload and possibly freaking her out.

'So, will I feel any of it?' she'd replied when he asked if she had any questions.

'No, it's performed under a general anaesthetic, so you won't be awake during the procedure. Once you're asleep, local anaesthetic will be injected into the area of surgery to provide additional comfort after the operation.' His voice was deep and confident, as if he'd done this a million times.

Abbie took comfort in that. Even if he did look a little on the young side. But it was better than some old guy with shaky hands, like the doctor from her last visit to hospital, when she was twelve and getting her tonsils out. But at least she'd had her whole family for support and reassurance; today she'd faced this alone. Why worry anyone when it could be nothing?

'How are you feeling?' came a soft voice.

Abbie cracked open an eye to see a nurse standing nearby. 'Crappy.'

The nurse smiled. 'Well, I have some pain relief for you and I can organise some anti-nausea medication if you need it?'

Abbie shook her head.

'Do you have family with you?' she asked as she did Abbie's observations.

'No.'

The nurse's lips thinned as she pressed them together.

Abbie lifted her hand to her neck and felt the dressing. It hurt when she swallowed.

'You can eat and drink as soon as you're able, but it might be slightly uncomfortable.'

It was already uncomfortable. She closed her eyes and tried to imagine a place far away from the white walls and sterile smell.

⚓

Abbie slowly chowed down on some rubbery hospital food. It wasn't so bad; at least there were people about, unlike at her house. Maybe she should get a cat? The only downside to this hospital stay was that she missed her relaxing glass of wine. Today's nurse was a lovely bloke who liked to whistle all sorts of tunes from 'You are my sunshine' to 'Thunderstruck'. The bright side of Jim leaving was that she was now free to see other men. Only, she'd loved Jim these past three years – she thought he would be with her for life, so how did she move on from that? It still confused her. What had she missed? Were there signs that he wasn't happy? Sure their sex life had basically disappeared but they were both extremely busy with work. She swallowed another bite, not so painful this time, and pondered her situation. Did she become too focused on her job? Did she not ask Jim enough about his? Abbie couldn't see where it had all gone wrong, and she'd said as much to Jim. He'd given her the usual *It's not you, it's me* line. It had made her want to barf on the spot or throw her phone at him. Apparently he just fell in love with another woman. As simple as that.

Abbie sighed heavily and let her fork crash noisily to her plate.

'That bad, is it?' said the nurse, whose name was Shane. He gave her an understanding look. 'At least you get to eat. My lunch consisted of a muesli bar.'

'You're free to eat mine.'

He smiled and looked at her sideways as he checked her neck. 'No, it's hospital food. Pass,' he said, deadpan. Abbie grinned. 'That's better. First time I've seen you smile. It's not so bad, either. It's no Julia Roberts, but it'll do.'

Abbie was still grinning. She liked his flippant bedside manner. He was probably someone she'd enjoy the company of; they could bitch about the world together. Except for the metal band on his finger. Typical.

'So, will I live?'

'Probably not,' he said shaking his head. He flipped the sheet back and checked out her legs. 'Looking good.' He winked. 'Been for a few walks?'

'Only to the toilet. It's numb around the wound, is that normal?' She didn't want to sound like a worry wart but it had to be asked.

'It's normal, Abbie. You should be right to go home tomorrow. Have you taken time off work?'

She almost threw her head back and laughed, but the soreness stopped her and laughing wasn't so easy either. Instead she settled for a gurgled chuckle. 'If you must know, I quit my job. Told my boss to shove it in not-so-polite terms.'

Shane paused what he was doing. 'Oh, do tell. Was he or she an arse?'

'Yes, *he* was. Treated everyone like crap, and I'd had enough. So, now I have all the time in the world off from work. Oh, but I'm off on a boat cruise next week with my friends. Will I be okay with this?' she said gesturing to her neck with her long elegant fingers.

'I don't see why not, just take it easy. You might be able to get the stitches out before you go. Check with the doctor when he stops by. I'm sure your friends will take good care of you.'

Abbie pushed her tray table away and played with the hem on the sheet. 'My friends don't know. My family doesn't even know,' she said suddenly, unsure why she'd told Shane more than she'd told anyone else. Maybe because he was a stranger and a nurse, so there would be no pity, no judgement or sadness – or any other emotions Abbie didn't want to deal with.

'You've done this alone? No one, no boyfriend?' Shane's mouth dropped open.

It wasn't pity she saw in his eyes but amazement, and for a moment Abbie felt strong and capable of handling this on her own.

'No boyfriend. He left me for another woman.'

'No way, you're gorgeous. Do you have a weird foot fetish or something he couldn't handle?'

'Ha, I wish. Then I'd make better sense of it all. Nup, he just fell in love with someone else.'

'Shit, Abbie, it sounds like you've been put through the wringer lately. This cruise sounds like the perfect pick-me-up. You deserve some fun.' Shane frowned. 'Just not too much fun, you don't want to go pushing too hard after surgery.'

'Yes, Nurse Shane,' she said giving him a salute.

'I'm going to miss you around here. I like patients with spunk.' He put her chart back, squeezed her hand and then left her room.

⚓

Arriving home with her bag and different clothes, she felt strange. A little lonely. Almost as if nothing at all had happened, yet inside she felt different. Deep down in the darkest place bubbling away like molten tar was fear, but she wouldn't let it out. Not yet.

After digging through her bag for her key, she unlocked the door to find a note that had been slid under it. Her hand surprisingly didn't shake as she recognised the handwriting. It was from Jim.

Why won't you answer my phone calls? Why have you changed the locks? Call me! Abbie, I want to be civil about this. Please can we stay friends?

She dropped the bit of paper and walked over it as she stepped inside, locking the door behind her. Her house smelled a bit funny, like the mice had run amok while she'd been gone, tinged with stale air and the rubbish bin in the kitchen she'd forgotten to empty. 'Great. Welcome home, Abbie.' She dumped her bags and sat on the couch, putting her feet up on the coffee table. *Let's live on the wild side,* she thought.

After the bustle of the hospital, the house was eerily silent. Maybe she did need a cat. Or a boisterous dog who would demand her attention. Her phone had a few messages from her friends about the cruise, mainly asking what she was packing; she'd barred Jim's number, so she wasn't getting his usual onslaught of calls and texts. She sat in the darkened room for a while, unsure of what to do next. Getting home had worn her out – so much so that she couldn't be bothered to get back up to crawl into her bed. Instead she reached for the TV remote. Beside it was the slip of paper Chris had given to her at the pub that day, telling her to call him if she ever needed a pick-me-up. Abbie had decided against telling Jess, and even now she wondered why she'd kept his mobile number. How could she help him when her life was upside down? Abbie left the number alone; she didn't need any party drugs, and, besides, the hospital ones were doing just fine for now. Instead she dragged the tiger-print mink rug that was draped over the couch to her. As she flicked through the channels she wondered if this was how her future would be, and then she realised she was too tired to care.

That tiredness lasted the rest of the week, and it was only by the weekend that she started to tidy the house and pack for the trip. She also shopped for scarves and outfits that would cover her neck. And in case they didn't work, she came up with a story about having a mole cut out. It would be something they'd believe.

Packing up her bags, double checking she had everything, she locked up and headed off to her doctor's appointment. From there she'd go straight to the Fremantle Terminal where their cruise ship would be waiting.

Abbie sat on the hard examination table in a cold room. The temperature wasn't especially low, but random shivers kept coming over her, and her hands were white where they clenched the table.

'Relax, Abbie, they won't hurt to take out. Just look away,' said the doctor as he came closer and removed her bandage. 'We also have your results back. The biopsy showed that you have Hodgkin's Lymphoma.'

'What?' said Abbie, pulling away from him suddenly as if he'd cut her. She blinked rapidly, trying to follow what he'd said. One minute he was talking stitches, the next Hodgkin's Lymphoma. *What the hell?!* was what she really wanted to say, but instead she managed: 'Is that cancer?'

All this time she had never really thought it would be cancer – well, worst-case scenario maybe – but none of her early results had shown much, and she wasn't feeling sick, so she'd pushed it from her mind. She'd been more focused on her surgery and stitches than anything else.

'Sorry, Abbie.'

Weren't doctors supposed to soften the blow, or at least ease into it, not *BAM!* you have cancer? She gazed at him as if he had three heads but he ignored her and continued removing her stitches. 'This is a shitty way of distracting your patients,' she said with a strangled laugh. The look he gave her, probably the same one he gave every patient he had to break bad news to, only made her feel worse. Tears swam in her eyes, threatening to spill, but she blinked them back. She would not fall to pieces. She would *not*. Forcing down the black thoughts, she breathed deeply and asked her first question. 'What does all this mean? It's a form of cancer, right?'

He nodded and then, as his hands moved swiftly, practiced, to remove the last of the stitches, he gave her the medical version of the disease. But Abbie had trouble following, her mind was wandering and her pulse was pounding so hard it almost drowned out his words.

'What happens from here?' she asked finally.

'I will refer you to an oncologist to have more tests done so the disease can be staged.'

'Okay. And what's staged?' This bloody boat cruise was going to cause problems. Abbie didn't want to cancel it though, because it could be the last bit of fun she might have in a long, long time. Plus they would want to know why she'd pulled out.

'It means we can tell what stage the disease is at. A CT scan and a PET scan and some bloods will be taken. For example, if you're a stage two, that means it's restricted to your neck, and in the other side gland also. But,' he said touching her shoulder gently, 'there's no point worrying until we have all the data.'

'Could it mean chemotherapy?'

He nodded. 'Yes, and radiation. That's why it's important to get your stage sorted, and then the course of action can be set.'

Abbie's hand went to her long hair, letting it slide through her fingers like silk. Chemo meant no hair usually. *God. Oh, God.*

Suddenly Abbie was standing back at her car, with no recollection of how she got there. She locked herself in, then put her hands on the steering wheel and burst into tears. The whole time the doctor had avoided the word cancer; it was always Hodgkin's Lymphoma or Hodgkin's Disease, to the point Abbie was struggling to actually associate it with the big C.

The night sweats, the itching, the tiredness – apparently they were all a part of it.

'Shit!' she screamed out through her tears and hit the steering wheel, making the horn go off and scaring an old couple walking past. 'Why me?' she sobbed. 'What the hell did I do to have my life turn to crap?'

Abbie cried messily for what felt like an age, until finally, with zero visibility, she felt through her handbag for tissues and tried to wipe her face and blow her nose. She had to gather herself before she met up with Jess, Ricki and Peter. If she looked a right mess her friends would worry and ask questions, and Abbie couldn't tell them, she couldn't repeat the doctor's words. Maybe if she didn't, then it wouldn't be real – she would come back from the cruise and find that this had all been a strange nightmare.

Checking her watch she realised she had a bit of time left – enough for a stiff drink to calm her nerves. With a last wipe at her eyes she threw the tissues on the passenger seat and started the car. Then with her phone she googled the nearest pub to the port.

Hell, if she was going to die she might as well enjoy the bit of life she had left. And nothing said 'fun' like a great scotch or a nice glass of red. Actually maybe both were needed to put the fire back in her veins and the courage back in her heart to face her friends without falling apart. She would not ruin this trip for them. Or for herself.

9

Ricki

'OH, COME ON, RICKI,' PETER HAD SAID TO HER. 'YOU shouldn't work the day we leave. The ship leaves port this afternoon!'

'But they're short staffed and Heather's on my case,' she'd told him, without quite meeting his eye.

Truthfully, it wasn't Heather or the staffing shortages. Something else was pulling her to the hospital and making work a joy that not even She-Devil Heather could kill. And Ricki knew exactly what it was the moment she spotted him at the end of the corridor. Heather was talking to him and another nurse but he turned towards her and smiled. Ricki's heart flipped, and a warm tingle spread to her fingers and toes.

But Heather saw her and immediately began to put the boot in. 'You're la—' But she didn't finish as she looked at the clock and realised Ricki was early.

That shut you up, Ricki thought, and for good measure she shot Heather a sweet, sugary smile.

Earlier in the week, while Ricki created a diversion, Miguel had slipped a mild laxative into Heather's coffee, and they'd watched all day as Heather's painful rants were cut short as she ducked off to the loo. Ricki had taken great delight in waiting for her to exit the bathroom on one occasion. 'Oh, *there* you are, Heather, you're needed back at the desk.' The knowing smile was all she could give Heather now.

Ricki paused beside Miguel.

'What's up?' she asked.

For once Heather's eyes were soft and her expression solemn. 'I was just mentioning that the little boy who came in yesterday from the bike fall passed away this morning.'

'Oh no.' Ricki put her hand to her mouth. 'Dan was so tough.'

Heather nodded and with a weighted sigh moped back to her office.

Miguel touched Ricki's hand. 'Poor kid,' he said softly. 'He wasn't even ten. Such a waste.'

Dan had been riding his bike without a helmet when he fell off. He had told his mum about his sore knee and elbows, but it wasn't until the next morning that he woke up with a headache, didn't want to eat and was lethargic. His mum saw a bump on his head and brought him into the hospital.

When Ricki had asked Dan how he was feeling, he'd looked up at her with big eyes half-hidden behind his floppy fringe and said, 'I'm okay. My head hurts a bit.'

And then he started to vomit. The poor kid apologised, still trying to be tough, but Miguel had to scoop him up when he started to collapse. He had paid no care to the vomit covering the boy, and focused on getting Dan to wake as they took him to a bed while trying to calm his hysterical mother.

'Let us do our job and help him. We'll take good care of him,' Miguel had promised. 'Just give us some room,' he'd pleaded softly, his voice calming Dan's mother.

After a CT scan, the diagnosis was a right temporal fracture of the skull and a right temporal epidural haematoma. Dan went straight into emergency surgery, and the whole time he'd been so brave. Ricki could see it in his eyes, not wanting to worry his mum. Even Ricki gave him greater odds than the 50/50 chance the doctor had estimated. He was a tough kid, he'd pull through. Or so she'd thought.

'I can't believe it.' Ricki hated these days. It was always sad to lose patients, but kids were especially brutal for her; they were often the strongest patients, ones who faced the scariest challenges, and they always managed a smile.

'I feel for his mum too,' said Miguel. 'A helmet would have saved his life. That's going to haunt her.' He wasn't trying to assign blame, Ricki knew. His eyes were full of sorrow. He simply understood people's pain.

They walked down the corridor together, Miguel's broad shoulders and his hand brushing against her with each stride. When Ricki glanced across to him, he gave her a sad smile.

'It reminds you how short life is, doesn't it? And that living in the moment is sometimes taken for granted,' he whispered, leaning close to her ear.

It wasn't his gently caressing words that made her heart skip a beat but the simmering heat that radiated from his dark chocolate eyes. That gaze made her knees go weak, and when his fingers brushed hers she felt sparks like static.

'Thank God, I never thought this shift would end,' said

Teresa, suddenly appearing, looking exhausted but relieved to see them. 'Seeing you means it must be nearly over.'

'Tough night?'

Teresa nodded as her shoulders hunched over. 'You ready to get this handover done?'

'Lead the way,' said Ricki. As she stepped in behind Teresa she turned back to Miguel and saw his gaze roaming up her body. Had he been looking at her backside? She felt a blush creep up through her skin. 'I'll see you around.'

'Yes, you will,' he said and then winked.

If it wasn't for Teresa grabbing her arm, Ricki might have tripped over her feet and fallen flat on the floor.

'Gosh, I feel like I never get to talk to you anymore,' said Teresa, pulling her in close as they headed off to get the paperwork for handover.

Ricki let herself be guided, not listening to a word her friend said, focusing all her attention instead on that wink.

The rest of her morning flew by, and yet the moments she crossed paths with Miguel seemed to slow as they moved around each other, her senses aware, her skin on edge, her breath catching in her throat. At one point he asked if she could help him get a patient into a wheelchair.

'Thanks, Ricki. Now, Mrs Carmichael, we'll just get you in this chair and then I can whiz you across for your scan.'

Ricki did as he asked, helping the patient to the edge of the bed, and then on his count they manoeuvred her up and then back down into the chair. The whole time it felt as if the air had been sucked out of the room, and all Ricki could hear was the smooth sound of Miguel's voice as he gave directions and reassured his patient. Her heart raced like she'd been injected with adrenaline. She was aware of his every move, the rustle of his uniform, the flex of his forearms and his sexy scent, so much better than the hospital smells. He was her escape from confinement, from a stuffy closed box; he was the doorway that led to a green park full of jasmine and earthy wood.

And right now, he was all she could think about.

It was as if she lived in two worlds: one at home with Peter, and a completely different one here at work with Miguel.

'Thank you,' he said, drinking her in before he pushed Mrs Carmichael down the corridor.

Temptation.

She tried to focus on thoughts of Peter, but her whole body reacted to Miguel like no other man before. The things he made her feel. The way she could just listen to him talk. Ricki didn't have any answers. Only feelings.

The thought of leaving Miguel and going away on this cruise was terrifying and yet she needed space, to think rationally, which was impossible to do at work, when every time she saw Miguel they shared lingering looks. It had been building, burning to a point where she ached to see him. Light would burst inside her from just his smile alone; her own drug, her own little addiction.

An hour later she was walking towards the small room where they'd sometimes take a moment to eat or have a quick cuppa, when she saw Miguel stick his head out and gesture to her. There was something naughty simmering in his smile.

'What's—' she began to say before he dragged her inside the room. He shut it, pushing Ricki against the door and locking it in one swift motion. 'Miguel?' she whispered.

He was so close, his hands resting against the door, one either side of her head. He inched closer, until she could feel the heat of his body.

'Life is short, no?' His focus was on her lips.

She'd never seen his eyes look so dark, brimming with passion. She moistened her lips with a quick flick of her tongue.

He groaned ever so quietly and as he leaned in further she could feel him, the length of him, and her insides turned molten.

'Life is short, Ricki.' Her name was hardly audible as his lips brushed against hers.

They were so soft. Better than she'd imagined. And she had imagined on more than a few occasions.

His lips teased hers, little nibbles, and then as she opened them a fraction his tongue brushed across. Whatever thoughts she had of this being wrong were dashed in a heartbeat as her body took over. Ricki kissed him back, her hands going around his backside, pulling him against her. He was so hard, her body trembled. The kiss deepened, grew feverish as they tasted each other.

Miguel's hands left the door and cupped her face. Ricki breathed him in, tasting coffee and mint. And when his hand pressed against her bare skin, her nerves quivered. She pressed back, rocking her hips against him, building into a roaring fire that demanded more.

Someone laughed outside the door and they broke apart, breathing heavily, watching each other, lips wet with moisture.

Miguel stepped back a fraction, slightly out of breath.

'I better get back or Heather will be on our case. I'm sorry, I just had to do that,' he said before unlocking the door.

Ricki stepped away so he could open it but before he did he kissed her one last time.

'You're an amazing woman, Ricki.'

With that parting statement he left, and Ricki stumbled to a chair and sat down before her legs gave out. *Oh. My. God.*

She stared at the table, at her trembling hands that rested on it. She was so turned on. If they'd had time, Ricki realised with a mix of excitement and shame, she wouldn't have stopped it. She was powerless against her feelings for him. Even now she felt the loss of him, the unfairness of not being able to finish what they'd started. She would feel the ache between her thighs for the rest of the shift. Every time she thought about the kiss, his touch . . . even now she felt the ache build again.

'Oh, hey, here you are. Did you want to do the meds with me?' asked Jolene, suddenly crashing into Ricki's thoughts.

'Ah, yeah sure.' Ricki got up quickly, trying to focus.

'Are you okay?' Jolene frowned. 'You look a bit flushed. It would be awful if you came down with something before your cruise. You know they might not let you on if you're sick?'

'Really? Bugger. I'm sure it's nothing. Just need more water,' said Ricki, forcing her hands to steady as she poured a glass. The cool liquid gave her time to gather herself. She could have probably done with a super-cold shower too. Or maybe liquid nitrogen to put out her fire.

It wasn't until Jolene asked what time Ricki was meeting Peter for the cruise that Ricki snapped back into reality.

Peter.

What had she done? She had thought she was happily in love with Peter, but if she was, then how could she do this? She didn't want to hurt him; Peter didn't deserve that. Was there something wrong with her? Did she just want to be liked, lusted after, looked at the way Miguel looked at her?

'Ricki, have you got that?' said Jolene as she shook the pills in front of her.

'Yeah, yeah,' said Ricki, forcing her thoughts from her mind so she could check the pills and sign the form.

On the last run of rounds to distribute the medication, she saw Miguel. He didn't give her his usual smile; no, this time he almost looked pained as his stare went straight to her lips as if remembering . . . everything.

No one had looked at her like she was worth devouring in such a long time.

'How's it going?' he croaked out as they left the room at the same time.

'Okay, I guess. You?'

He glanced around before adjusting himself. 'Wish I could get this to disappear. I almost had until I saw you again.'

Tingles ran down her spine as the pressure of his hard shape flooded her memory. 'What *was* all that, Miguel?' she whispered, desperate to know but afraid of the answer.

'I thought it was pretty obvious,' he said as they walked to the hand-wash bay together. 'I couldn't let you disappear on your boat without a proper goodbye.' He shrugged. 'I'm sorry. I like to jump at life when I can, and I've been pushing these feelings away for so long . . . I got sick of fighting. Do you regret it?'

The deep sorrow skirting the black centres of his eyes expressed as much, and she felt his genuine panic that he'd overstepped, perhaps even ruined their friendship.

Ricki thought hard for a moment and then said what she felt. 'I don't regret it.' Even now her body was screaming for release, to finish what they'd started.

Then he hit her with a sledgehammer.

'I . . . um . . . I'm leaving soon,' he stammered.

'What?' No. He couldn't leave. He would take all the light.

'My trip to Cambodia, it's time to join the program over there for six months. You could come with me?' His words hung in the air, hopeful.

'This place will be unbearable without you here,' she said. And it was the truth. He'd become her comrade, a true friend, and she had lived her dreams through his stories. 'I wish you weren't going.' Her lips dropped at the corners and she knew she was being selfish.

'What's stopping you from coming? I know it's been your dream. Maybe you need to think about what you really want from life and what will make you happy. Because I want you to be happy, Ricki. I care about you.' He reached up to brush away a loose strand of her hair, but he pulled back at the last minute.

'When you get off shift, meet me here,' she said suddenly as she glanced at the nearby door.

He frowned but nodded. 'Okay.' He washed his hands and dried them as Ricki washed hers. 'I'll see you in just over an hour.'

Checking his watch, he turned and went, leaving Ricki with her thoughts. She felt a hole in her chest, as if he'd gone already. She couldn't let him leave without a proper goodbye. Ricki knew what she wanted, knew it wasn't right. But it was something she needed. Desperately.

⚓

An hour later as he walked back to that spot, Ricki was leaning against the door not far from the wash basin, her hand on the door knob, her eyes checking the corridor.

Before he could even open his mouth she pulled him into the room and closed the door.

It was dark, windowless, but she could see the shelves for storage, a mop and bucket in one corner and a big metal cupboard. She locked the heavy door.

'Ricki?' His voice was hopeful.

'I wanted to say goodbye too,' she said reaching for him.

Miguel needed no further prompting, pressing her back against the solid door.

Ricki found his lips and then his tongue. A groan escaped – it was hers – as he nestled between her. Together the heat was unbearable. *Too many clothes*, she thought.

His hands slid under her uniform, along her skin up to her breasts. He cupped them both, then went under her bra to seek out her nipples. His fingers were gentle and yet each brush of her delicate skin sent ripples right to her lower belly. Needing more, wanting to feel him, Ricki let her hand roam down his chest.

He kissed along her neck as she dipped her hand into his pants. Skin to skin she held him. His hips almost bucked from her touch and she felt his teeth graze her skin. Ricki couldn't think about anything other than this moment. She was being swept along the stream, unable to stop the strength of the force.

One hand shifted from her breast, down the front of her uniform, under the band and down deep into warmth.

'Jesus,' she panted. Nothing was in her mind except the pure pleasure of his touch and how much she wanted more.

If she wasn't in a hospital storeroom, she would have Miguel, and that thought scared her. She released him and moved her hands to outside his clothes, wrapping her arms around him and clinging tightly. 'I don't want you to leave,' she whispered, the pain suddenly sharp and real.

His heavy breathing began to ease as he too disentangled his hands from her lower body, all the while nuzzling into her neck. 'I'm going to miss you.' He pulled back, staring into her eyes with determination. 'I know you're with . . . someone, but look me up if that ever changes. Okay?' Then he kissed her. 'Goodbye, Ricki. Make sure you find your happiness.'

Then he was gone.

10

Jess

'AND IF HE WAKES AT NIGHT, TRY HIS DUMMY OR HIS SPECIAL blue blanket. But don't pick him up, he'll go back to sleep if you leave quickly. Also in the bag is his medication, stuff for his gums or if he runs a fever . . . do you want me to run you through the dosage?' said Jess as she reached for the colourful bag sitting on the table.

'Darling,' said April, intercepting Jess's hand. 'I managed to raise you and your brother from birth, I'm pretty sure I can handle it.'

Jess blinked at her mum. 'Sorry. It's just . . .'

'He's your baby boy, and you're going to miss him like crazy, I know. I'll take good care of him. And Lucy has already offered to babysit if I need a break.'

Jess nodded and let out her breath. Yes, her mum had raised them just fine, but that was years ago, and April had moments of forgetfulness. Last night Jess had dreamed her mum had gone off to help at the centre and left Ollie behind. It was easily done when you weren't used to having a baby around. Even Jess had done it herself once: not long after she'd brought Ollie home from hospital she'd gone to the shops and had made it halfway out of the car park before remembering that Ollie was still asleep in the back of the car. She'd felt so bloody awful. She'd run back like a mad woman, crying as she'd opened the car, woke him up to hold him close and kept apologising while people walked past thinking she was some crazed lady. She'd put Ollie in the car and driven back home, she couldn't face shopping after that.

'I've got the ship number in case you can't get through to me,' said Jess, pushing the memory and the worry away, and handing her mum the piece of paper from her pocket. 'I don't think we get service out at sea.'

April smiled. 'Have you got everything you need?'

Jess looked around her mum's house, at her travel bag sitting by the front door along with her handbag. Her phone was in her pocket. 'I think I'm ready.'

They loaded up April's car with her bags and Ollie and then headed to Fremantle. The whole ride Jess's hands rested in her lap, her fingers nervously tapping and her eyes darting back to Ollie, who was happily watching the cars go past his window.

'You okay, love?' asked April as she glanced across while they sat at a red light. 'Excited about the trip with the girls?'

'Oh, yes, I am,' she said, looking back to Ollie.

'Nothing bad is going to happen to Ollie while you're away. It's just the first time you've been apart from him. Try to have some fun and make the most of it while you can – these moments are rare when you have cherubs.'

Jess studied her mum as she drove through the traffic. A calmness radiated from her, allowing Jess to feel more at ease. 'Thanks, Mum.' At times her mum was amazing – she had survived a bad marriage, became a single mum and gave great advice. Then there were times when Jess wondered how April survived on her own when she was a serial key misplacer and so forgetful that getting her checked for Alzheimer's was on Jess's to-do list. Some days Jess actually wondered if it was an after-effect of her dad's fists or perhaps the time he threw her out of his path and she'd fallen, hitting her head on a chair. Jess had only been nine at the time. She'd sat with her mum, silently crying while squeezing her hand and hoping she'd wake up. Jess often thought of that moment: her fear, too scared to move from her mum's side, too scared to ring an ambulance in case her dad saw her using the phone. Counting to a hundred had kept her going. April had woken up at eighty-nine. If Jess had reached a hundred, she would have run to Peter's place for help. That was always her fall-back plan, but fortunately that moment had been the worst she'd witnessed. But sometimes she had to wonder if he was the cause of her mum's forgetfulness.

'Oh, look, there's the ship. Wow, it's so big,' said April as she pulled into the large parking area by the dock.

The ship was docked behind the Fremantle Passenger Terminal, but it was like trying to hide an elephant behind a shrub.

'Oh my gosh!' Jess had tried to imagine the size of the ship but nothing came close as it now sat before her, making everything seem so small beside it. How was it possible that something so big could stay afloat? The *Pacific Eden*, with its decks upon decks, was like a skyscraper on water. It was hard not to be excited to see something so magical that screamed: *Let me take you to some place exotic!*

⚓

'Don't worry, we'll distract you,' said a familiar voice as Jess watched her mum's car disappear from view. She turned and was lifted into a Pete-style bear hug. Even though the hot afternoon sun beat down, intensified by all the black bitumen, she still welcomed his hug.

'Hey Ricki,' she said, laughing as Pete let her go so she could hug her friend. 'You look beat. Late night?' Jess wiggled her eyebrows.

'No, nothing like that. Early shift at the hospital. How are you? Did you pack your dress for the Gatsby party? I heard two women talking about it over there; they say it's the best thing about the trip.'

Jess nodded, and suddenly Ricki pointed. 'Oh, here's Abbie. I was wondering what was taking her so long.'

Pete rushed down the steps to help Abbie from the taxi. As he pulled her luggage from the boot Abbie paid the driver and then got out, nearly fell over and then laughed.

Jess and Ricki glanced at each other then back at Abbie.

'Are you drunk?' said Ricki when Abbie made it to their side. 'And what happened to your neck?'

Abbie smiled. 'I had a few while I was waiting.' She gave them a wink. 'You two will need to catch up quick when we get on the boat. Oh, and this,' she added airily, her eyes flicking away for a moment. 'I had a funny spot cut out just in case. The doctor said it looked suspicious.'

Ricki frowned for a second. 'Better to be on the safe side.'

'Where's Jim?' asked Jess. 'I would have thought he'd drop you off.'

Abbie gripped her bag as if to steady herself, and shrugged. 'He's at work. We said our goodbyes,' she said, fiddling with the carry handle.

'All right, let's go get checked in,' said Peter, leading the charge towards the security terminal.

Half an hour later they wound back out into the salty air on the other side of the terminal.

'Right, don't lose these,' Jess said, handing out their plastic cards that would serve as ID, room key and credit card while on board. No one was taking any notice of her and she realised why when she glanced up at the *Pacific Eden*. 'Oh wow. It's massive,' said Jess. Her mouth fell open as her eyes climbed up the many rows of tiny cabin windows and deck railings.

'Let's get on. This is getting exciting now,' said Ricki as they headed for the walkway, *Welcome* written along it, their access to the ship. Six orange lifeboats, which she hoped wouldn't have to be used, stood out against the vibrant white of the ship. They walked onto the narrow wooden deck, which ran the whole length of the ship and its polish shimmered in the Fremantle heat. They were the only ones walking along it to the sign pointing their entry into the inside of the ship, besides two uniformed staff further up painting the outside railings. It must be a constant job, trying to paint the whole ship and it would be a must in the salty sea air.

'Did you know it holds twelve hundred guests?' said Peter as he looked it over with a male eye. 'Just imagine how many tonnes this ship must weigh!' They followed the small red arrow through two opened doors, stepping onto carpet where they were met by two staff standing at a lectern scanning in people's passes as they entered.

'This is so cool,' said Abbie as she gazed across at what resembled a fancy hotel lobby, with plush patterned carpets and elegant lighting.

'Shall we go straight to our cabins, drop off our bags and then explore?' said Jess. 'We're room 5126,' she added, looking at her plastic card. Jess gazed around the section of the ship they had entered. It was an atrium open to a few levels, with lifts to one side and a wide carpeted circular staircase on the other that took you up the open levels. A gleaming gold handrail set off the luxurious feel, topped off with the royal patterned floor covering and a huge sparkly chandelier that draped in the centre like a cascading diamond necklace. It even had its own scent, as if the area had been freshly aired with jasmine and the rails polished for hours before their arrival.

'What level are we on now?' said Peter as he wandered off to another set of stairs leading down, these clearly marked level eight. 'Hey, we've got to go down three flights to get to our cabin floor.'

Peter was almost as excited as the little kid who rushed past him in bright red shoes, to race down the stairs, only to come back up moments later and yell out to his sister to follow him. Meanwhile their parents were trying to take in the sights and keep track of where their kids were heading off to.

Jess smiled as they followed Peter down the stairs while the two excited kids were called back. Beside her Abbie used the handrail to guide her down. Maybe the pre-launch drinks were getting the better of her friend. Luckily they weren't out to sea yet.

Disembarking the stairs on level five they wandered down a long corridor filled with endless doors among exhilarated couples, families and friends who were also trying to find their cabins. Hyped-up voices filled the air as new places were explored.

'Shit, how will we find our rooms when we're staggering around drunk?' said Ricki.

Jess smiled again; the excitement was infectious. Ricki had finally perked up a bit and Abbie was already in a happy place.

'Here we are, right next to each other,' said Jess.

'God, I hope the walls are soundproof,' said Abbie with a snort.

⚓

'Right,' said Abbie. 'Three hours till we set sail. Shall we get a drink?'

'Yes, let's.' Jess needed one for her nerves, for leaving Ollie but also for being so close to Peter again. It was so much easier speaking to him over the phone; in person she saw his gorgeous smile and those vivid blue eyes, and she couldn't run away from his essence, a mixture of soapy vanilla and salt. Nor could she avoid his hugs, which had always felt like home or the beach. He surfed that much it was as if he was the salty crisp ocean waves. Before this cruise was over Peter would be an engaged man. Off the market for good. Yes, a drink was exactly what she needed.

Outside their rooms two stewards were nearby in their cream shorts and turquoise tops sorting out their supply trolleys ready to start turning down beds for night time. Both smiled and bent their heads in greeting as they set off. Ricki gave them a wave before looping her arm through Abbie's and heading off in front, leaving Peter by Jess's side.

His fingers brushed against her arm. 'Relax. Smile.'

Jess was too tightly wound to relax, like a knotted ball of string, but she tried a smile.

'Hmm, we'll work on that.'

They passed a young couple, hands clasped together and oozing love, who had just boarded, looking for their cabin, before climbing the stairs towards the restaurants. 'Shall we make a booking for tomorrow night?' Jess asked. 'While we're here?'

As they turned the corner they found a small line of people doing just that.

'Yeah, good idea,' said Abbie, who seemed to be travelling a bit better after some water and time.

Ricki was staring at a wall poster of the ship's layout while her fingers traced her lips.

'Where are we, Ricki?' asked Jess, only to have her question go unanswered. Jess waved her hand in front of her face. 'Ricki?'

'Huh? What?' Ricki's eyebrows shot up. 'What did I miss?'

'Dinner? Tonight?' said Abbie.

'Come on, Abs, we'll sort it out,' said Peter, who led Abbie away.

'Sounds good,' said Jess before she turned back to Ricki. 'Hey, are you okay?' she said softly.

Ricki nodded, her hair cascading down her back in golden waves. 'Yeah, I'm fine. Just head stuck back at work still.'

Jess frowned. 'Something happen?' Agony flashed across

Ricki's face and Jess leaned over to hug her. 'We're here for you if you need to talk about it.'

'Thanks.' Ricki sighed, casting a quick look in the direction Peter and Abbie had gone. 'I sooooo need a drink.'

Suddenly Jess got another vibe. Maybe it was nothing, but she couldn't help feeling that Ricki wasn't happy that Peter had come on this trip. She could be reading it wrong; maybe they'd had a fight before coming aboard, there could be a million reasons. But there wasn't time to dwell now – Abbie was back, with Peter a step behind, and she was on a mission.

'All done, let's drink!'

Jess smiled at the return of her friend's energy.

Abbie led them through two drinking areas, each with its own colour scheme and furnishings, before stopping at the third because she loved the blue, black and silver hues of the bar decor.

Each with a drink, they found a spot on the velvet blue lounge by the large window framed by black curtains. The plush sapphire and black carpet and black tables gave the room a sexy, sleek feel. It was even better because they had the place to themselves.

Jess sat back and looked out the window. Beyond the terminal the streets of Fremantle were busy with people going about their day, finishing work, cars back and forth. Some looking towards the *Pacific Eden*, no doubt with envy. A flutter of excitement rippled under her skin. She and her friends were the lucky ones, and the *Eden* was taking them on an adventure.

In three hours she would put an ocean between her and Ollie for the first time. Held captive by the ship, unable to leave.

A warm hand gently squeezed hers. She turned away from the window to see Peter giving her an understanding smile. He didn't say anything, his touch and smile said it all.

In three hours she would also be stuck in close quarters with Peter, with no escape. *Hell.*

11

Ricki

RICKI LISTENED TO ABBIE TALK ABOUT THE GUY WHO HAD tried to crack onto her at the pub before she'd arrived at the terminal – but her eyes were on Peter as he held Jess's hand. Their friendship had always been close, they were tactile friends who always hugged when they saw each other. It had never bothered Ricki, because they were like that before she started dating Peter; she knew the deal, and Jess was, after all, her best friend. But now, as she watched the understanding float between her partner and her best friend, she wondered: Did she have that with Peter? Did they really understand each other? Should she be jealous? Straightaway she flicked that thought from her mind. After what she'd just done with Miguel, she would never have a right to be jealous. But the fact that she *wasn't* jealous worried her. Did she not love Peter as much as she should? Surely if she loved him, then she never would have noticed Miguel. If she loved Peter, then she never would have dreamed of hurting him. And yet she'd lost her way, lost her common sense, lost respect for their relationship. Just thinking about it made her gut churn and her cheeks flush with shame – but worse was that if she had the time over again with Miguel, she probably wouldn't change a thing.

She took a big sip of her margarita, chomped through some ice and nodded at Abbie as if she had heard every word. But her mind was miles away.

A cheater.

That's what she was. Did that make her a horrible person? *Of course it does!* she screamed in her mind. Peter didn't deserve that. He was the perfect guy. He took such good care of her and he loved her. And this was how she repaid him.

Yet even as she reprimanded herself, she couldn't help but think about Miguel, growing warm at the thought of being with him, remembering the electric interaction. Was she in love with Miguel too, or was it just lust? *How does anyone make sense of this stuff?* she thought desperately, avoiding looking anywhere near Peter. Downing the last of her drink, she got up. 'Anyone for another?'

'Me please,' said Abbie.

Peter and Jess were so immersed in their conversation they had made it only halfway through theirs.

At the bar she ordered drinks for herself and Abbie, using her room card, but her mind still spun. What did she do now? Break up with Peter? She couldn't be with Miguel; he was leaving. Did she want to be with him more than with Peter? Did she up and leave her life to be with Miguel?

Her heart ached sharply at the thought, but as she glanced over at Peter she felt a deeper love for him, one built on shared experience and time together. Should she put this thing with

Miguel behind her, try to live on with the secret, or should she tell Peter and risk hurting him, losing him? *And how the hell do I figure it out sleeping next to him in that tiny cabin?* she asked herself.

Ricki cursed under her breath and carried the drinks back to their spot. 'When we finish these shall we go explore some more?' Any form of distraction would do.

'Thanks. Yep, sounds like a plan. I wonder what the theatre area looks like. We must get to all the comedy shows. I could use a good laugh,' said Abbie.

'I agree.'

⚓

'I'm glad none of us gets seasick,' said Jess as she finished the last of her Mexican wrap.

They had sat on stools by the window to eat their meals, looking out over Fremantle as the light faded from the day. Behind them more and more people came to eat at the relaxed cafe area called The Pantry. With a huge selection of food to choose from some people had done quite a few circular laps around the centre island. Ricki had gone around twice and settled on the fish and chips in the cute little basket with paper that was made to look like newspapers.

'A shame we can't fish,' said Peter glancing at Ricki.

She smiled as she thought of the time they had spent a week fishing up north at Kalbarri. They chartered a boat and went out deep-sea fishing, and she ended up out-fishing Peter. He caught a snapper, while she caught a large tuna and some trevally. But it evened up when they went down the estuary and he caught the most mulloway.

That had been a great week. They'd fished, laughed, drank the local beverages and tasted great food. That was over a year ago now, before they moved in together. Had their relationship just grown stale? Should they have taken more trips and adventures together? Is that what she was missing? He worked hard, she worked hard; somewhere in there had they lost themselves?

Ricki dusted the salt from her chips off her hands. 'You realise this cruise is the first real holiday we've had since Kalbarri,' she said to Peter.

He cocked his head to the side, he'd been about to eat a chip. 'Really? Hmm, well, we'll have to fix that.' Then he winked and smiled as if he knew something she didn't.

'This is the first holiday I've had ever,' said Jess. 'At least you guys have been *somewhere*. And Abbie and Jim went to Bali. I've never even been on a plane.'

'Maybe Abbie and Jim can get married in Bali and then you'll have to go on a plane,' said Ricki.

Abbie coughed as she choked on her rice.

Ricki resisted the urge to whack her on the back, and handed her some water instead. From the corner of her eye she saw Jess and Peter share a smile, and she had a strange sensation, as if she were being left out of a secret.

'Hey, we're moving,' said Abbie as she recovered from her coughing fit. 'Let's go up top and watch.'

Out in the fresh salty air, they watched the captain navigate the narrow water canal towards the wide ocean. On one side were two big ships next to cranes by the loading docks in the industrial area where hundreds of sea containers sat lined up like coloured bricks. The setting sun filled the sky with a golden glow that was mirrored against the dark water and again onshore with the streetlights, illuminating the cars and chunky buildings in Fremantle. As they reached open water they could see back to the fishing boat harbour and beach. Boats and yachts moored together, and large pine trees that stood proud in the Esplanade Park where the Ferris wheel's lights twinkled brightly. Into the big blue ocean they went, while the boat churned up a whitewash path behind them. Soon the air turned cold as the sun dropped below the sea, and they remained silent for those moments as it disappeared, the slosh of water against the boat and the burble of the motor the only accompaniment. Ricki felt the bustle of the city drain from her body and she started to relax.

'We are officially on our cruise,' she said with a grin.

'So, gang, what's next?' said Jess.

'Which bar are we going to tonight? Should we check out that band?' said Abbie as her hair whipped around her face.

'I want to have a shower and get dressed up a bit first,' said Jess.

'I wouldn't mind changing too,' agreed Ricki. She had showered after her shift, but if they were going to the bar, she could do better than jeans and Vans. As much as she loved her collection of T-shirts and jeans, she also enjoyed dressing up for occasions.

'I vote shower.' Abbie held up her hand and then took off towards their rooms.

'I guess that's that,' said Peter. 'I'll go to the bar and find us a spot, then. Maybe do a spot of taste-testing the beers.'

Ricki looked him up and down; so familiar, and yet suddenly she felt shy. He already looked so handsome in his denim

shorts and short-sleeved V-neck shirt in a deep dark blue. He
half-raised an eyebrow when he saw her eyes tracing the lines
of his body, and she managed a quick smile for him before
following the girls.

When they reached the long narrow corridor of cabins, Abbie
began to run. 'I bags first shower!' she called with a laugh.

'Damn.' Jess slowed her pace.

'Don't worry, Jess, use our shower,' said Ricki. 'I'm only
going to get changed.' She opened the door and then handed
her key card to Jess.

'Oh, thanks, Ricki. I'll grab my towel and bits.'

As Ricki rummaged through her case for a pair of heels
and a skirt, she was already considering how drunk she might
need to get in order to go straight to sleep tonight while Peter
lay beside her. The bed seemed to pulse, its white sheets bright
like fluorescent lights, drawing her eyes to it. She couldn't let
Peter touch her right now, her head wasn't right.

Changing quickly, she left the cabin as Jess entered.

'I'm going up to the bar. See you when you get there.' Ricki
quickly headed past her friend, ignoring the confused expression on her face. That was possibly the worst thing about
dating her friend's friend: she couldn't talk to Jess about her
problems. Maybe Abbie would listen, but she was in a happy
relationship with Jim, and she loved Peter like a brother too.
Maybe they were all too close. She couldn't really talk to either
of her friends.

Ricki felt more alone than ever.

12

Jess

JESS PUT DOWN HER TOWEL AND TOILETRY BAG AND SURVEYED the small bathroom. On one side the shower hung over a pint-sized bath tub, the toilet squeezed between that and the sink on the other side. Compact – a little cramped – but to Jess it was still perfect because it was all hers. This would be the first shower she could remember in a long time in which she didn't have to worry about getting out and back to Ollie or any interruptions or crying; she could simply relax.

Feeling a bubble of excitement, she started her favourite playlist on her phone and then undressed to the sound of P!nk's 'Just Like Fire'.

'Oh my God,' she said as the warm water ran over her skin. 'Bliss.'

The boat rocked gently, every now and then reminding her that they were out at sea. She sang along to the song in her head, belting out the words silently, as if she had an audience of thousands as she washed the shampoo from her hair.

Suddenly she saw the shower curtain move, and before she could think how to react, she saw a man step into her shower. She turned just as he spoke. 'It's okay, babe, it's just me.'

Peter was completely naked, and she watched, shocked into silence, as he realised what was going on; that she wasn't Ricki.

With bravado she didn't know she had, she smiled nervously and said, 'Sorry, you've got the wrong woman.' P!nk was still singing in the background, oblivious to the commotion in the small bathroom.

'What the . . . *Jess*?' His eyes bulged.

She may have been trying to look cool, calm and collected, but inside her heart was racing. Her eyes quickly snuck a peek at his nakedness. He was a Michelangelo sculpture. And she was a curvy, busty mum. She suddenly felt exposed, her hands folding across her lower body.

'Shit, I'm so sorry. I thought you were Ricki. She loves P!nk.' His eyes went to her breasts. 'Oh, my God.' He slapped his hands over his eyes. 'I'm so sorry.' His hands dropped to his mouth, his eyes returning to her.

The water was washing the last of the shampoo bubbles over her skin. His eyes tracked the movement as the suds fell over her breasts, then he paused as if recalculating their size. But he didn't stop there, further they dropped. Her belly flipped as she tried to remain calm. 'Have you quite finished your tour?' she said nervously.

Peter cleared his throat and suddenly put his hands over his groin as if he'd only just realised he was also naked. But his large hands didn't, or couldn't, hide his excitement.

'Well, this is awkward,' he said, cocking his head to the side. Peter seemed muddled yet his eyes kept darting along

her body. 'I'm feeling rather confused right now. I'm just . . .
I don't . . . God, I can't think straight!'

Jess almost smiled. 'Sorry, Ricki said I should use your
shower.' The way Peter was looking at her made her feel
suddenly powerful. She leaned back into the water to wash
off some soap, her nipples hard, her body giving away her
inner thoughts and desires. Long-buried dreams popped up
and taunted her. What if she reached out and touched him?
Did he see his best friend right now or did he see a woman?

Peter swallowed. She could tell he was gnashing his teeth
together. Was he thinking about the same thing that she was:
the last time they'd seen each other naked?

'I'll be out in two seconds. Do you want to wait or share
my water?' Jess needed conditioner in her hair, but right now
escaping the confined space seemed a greater priority. Quickly,
before she did something reckless, again. Something that could
threaten their entire relationship, not to mention her friendship
with Ricki.

'Um, ah.' He winced and tried to cover himself but realised
it was impossible and let his hands drop back to his sides. 'I
will need a shower. A very cold shower.' He frowned.

Jess had rarely seen Peter lost for words. His face was
flushed, a mixture of confusion and turmoil. She tipped her
head to the side, a chuckle escaping her lips before pulling the
curtain back and stepping out. 'It's all yours,' she said casually
but inside she was anything but calm. Her nerve endings sizzled
and she wished she'd turned the water cold herself.

'Shit.'

'You okay?' she asked as she wrapped the towel around her.

'Cold water isn't nice,' he said, his voice laced with humour.

Jess dried her hair a bit and then patted down some of her skin. As she looked up into the mirror she caught Peter's gaze through a crack in the shower curtain, watching intently as she towelled her chest, then his eyes rose to meet hers. The breath caught in her throat as they watched each other, no words spoken, no movements made, just those bright blue eyes filled with a fire and confusion she'd never seen before.

The song on her phone ended. Tearing her eyes away from Peter, she turned it off before another one could start.

'Jess?' His voice was a low growl.

She collected her clothes and toiletry bag before glancing back at him through the gap in the curtain. His cold shower wasn't helping. Was this an awakening, a revelation for Peter to finally realise Jess was actually a real woman? He looked as if he wanted to say something, but stopped himself.

She gave him a smile, to let him know all was okay. Then she exited the bathroom, shutting the door and leaning against it. *Oh my God*, she mouthed silently. *Did that just freaking happen?*

She could hear him moving about, leaning against the wall and then a groan. Jess moved away from the door into the sitting area, her thoughts slamming into each other and making no sense. One thing was clear, though: the image of his naked body would be burned into her brain for life.

After drying and dressing in record time, she snuck back to her room to finish her make-up, not game to be there when he got out.

'Is that you, Jess?' asked Abbie when she closed their cabin door.

'Yep.'

'Gosh, you were quick. I'm only just out of the shower now.'

Yeah, but you didn't have a naked man in yours, she thought. Jess shivered and tried to towel her hair off while not thinking of Peter. *Just pretend it never happened*, she tried to convince herself.

'Wow, you look hot,' said Abbie as she stepped out of the bathroom in a fitted coffee-coloured dress.

Jess *was* hot, still flushed from Peter's openly staring gaze. She would never forget it. 'Thanks, Abs, so do you. It's nice to frock up for once, and step out of mum mode.'

'Well, in that skirt and top you might find yourself a night companion. Oh, on that topic: if that happens I'll hang out at the bar till morning or sleep on a couch there.' Abbie winked.

'No, I couldn't do that.'

'Of course you can, sweet pea. This trip is going to be epic. Let's party hard, get drunk and have one-night stands like we're teenagers.'

Jess opened her mouth in disbelief at Abbie's words.

'I was kidding,' Abbie added and smiled. 'We're not teenagers, are we?' With a wink and a chuckle she picked up her room card and slipped it down her top. 'You ready?'

'Ready as I'll ever be.' Jess adjusted her gold strappy top that complemented her black pencil skirt. She couldn't go braless like Ricki sometimes did; her breasts were likely to shoot out the sides of her top if she lifted her arms, and dancing would be totally out of the question.

'Leave your top alone, you look fabulous. I want to dive into your cleavage. You have the best boobs, Jess.'

Jess tried not to think of her cleavage as they made their way to meet Peter and Ricki at the open bar area. Her belly fluttered at the thought of seeing him again. *God, don't go bright red*, she willed herself.

'Oh, there they are.' Abbie grabbed her hand and almost dragged her along, causing her to stumble in her black high heels – or was that the sight of Peter lounging in the black leather couch, his shirt open at the front and his hair still damp from his shower? Their shower.

A shiver shot down her spine.

In front of him on a low black table sat a selection of cocktails in vibrant blues, lime and burnt orange, decorated with fruit and fancy straws in glasses shaped like curvaceous women. Heavy grey curtains hung from the walls covering the windows and the thick grey carpet felt soft even though Jess's heels were starting to hurt her feet. Peter was watching the band set up in the front corner while Ricki sat in a single silver high-backed chair on the other side of the table. Had Peter told Ricki about their encounter? Would she be upset, or would she find it hilarious?

Abbie sat in the spare chair next to Ricki, leaving Jess the leather couch beside Peter. He sat up, but he didn't move away from her.

'Glad you girls could finally make it. Pick a drink, any drink,' said Ricki before sipping her green one.

Peter lifted a packet of Pringles from beside him on the couch and slid some out of the container. He always ate when he was stressed. *Is he stressed?* Jess wondered, trying to remember to keep her shoulders back so her top didn't gape while also trying *not* to visualise Peter naked, all the while not knowing what he thought about the whole ordeal.

'What's this?' said Abbie.

'Sorry, got hungry.' He offered his chips around.

When he got to Jess she smiled. 'Thanks, Peter. My favourite.'
He looked at her for a moment and then returned her smile. His eyes dropped to her top, or maybe lack of, before he quickly dragged his hand over his face, rubbing his eyes. Then he tipped out another handful of chips and started to munch while staring at the floor as if it were a Sudoku puzzle.

'Hey, Jess, I met the drummer. He's cute and single,' said Ricki.

'Oh yeah, you could totally go there,' added Abbie as she leaned forward to get a good look at said drummer.

'No. No. NO.' Jess sat up straight and pointed a finger at her friends. 'I did *not* come on this trip so you could set me up with random guys. I don't need your pity. I'll find someone when I'm ready.'

'How about him, he's cute,' said Abbie as a guy in tight black jeans walked past her chair. He heard her, glanced back at them, smiled and kept walking.

Jess threw up her arms. 'What if I already have a guy?'

They stopped, watching her. Even Peter paused mid-crunch.

'Do you?' he mumbled through his mouthful.

'What, Wandering has single blokes?' said Ricki. 'Aren't they all married farmers?'

'You would have told us, wouldn't you?' said Abbie. Then she frowned as if she'd said something wrong.

'Do you really?' asked Peter again. He moved to touch her hand but then stopped.

'Yes, I have a cute one who likes to dribble on me,' she said, then laughed when the girls rolled their eyes at her. 'No, of course I don't,' she admitted with a sigh. 'But it doesn't mean I want to be set up or sleep with some random stranger because you guys think I need to.'

'You've already done that,' said Ricki. 'Remember Ollie?' She winked.

'Exactly, Ricki. I've learned my lesson.'

'Always wear a condom,' said Abbie with a smirk before she sucked the last of her drink and put the glass back on the table. 'Have you decided what you're going to tell Ollie about his dad when he's older?'

They'd asked her this after she'd given birth, but Jess had brushed them away. She had plenty of time to figure that out, she had told herself. Only, time had flown and soon Ollie would realise that other kids had two parents. 'The truth, I suppose.' But she couldn't tell Ollie the real truth, not yet, he was too young for all that. 'Mainly that I didn't know who his dad was.' Her cling-to line; the one she'd told her friends from the start.

'One-night-stand man. Has a ring to it.' Abbie reached for the cocktail menu.

'Gee, this place is filling up. Hope the band starts soon, I feel like dancing,' said Ricki, and Jess was grateful for the change of topic.

It didn't take them long to get through their cocktails while they listened to the band warm up.

'They should be all right if they can manage to get through a whole song,' said Ricki, who pulled a face every time they started a song only to cut it short. 'Another round?' she asked after putting her empty glass down.

'Yep, my shout.' Abbie stood.

Beside Jess, Peter had been rather quiet.

When Ricki and Abbie headed to the bar she turned to him and asked, 'You okay?'

He rested his head in his hand as he stared at her. 'I don't know, Jess. I can't seem to clear my head.' His brow creased as his gaze dropped to her chest. 'That top is not helping. Geez,' he groaned. Peter leaned further forward, putting his elbows on his knees. 'Since when did you have such nice . . .' He flicked his fingers towards her breasts. 'It's messing with my head, 'cause I know what they look like underneath.'

'It's just a body, Peter. Same one I've had for years.' Jess was smiling, even let out a little chuckle, though truth be told she couldn't look at him without thinking the same. His snug jeans didn't leave much to her imagination.

'You think this is so funny, don't you? You like watching me squirm.'

'Maybe a little. It's not often I get to see you tongue-tied. Gosh, Peter, anyone would think you hadn't seen a pair of breasts before.' It was meant as a gentle tease, but just saying the words made her breath catch at the idea that her breasts were on Peter's mind. A tiny bit of hope sparked in the dark.

'I can't believe you're not freaked out like I am, Jess. I was naked too,' he whispered. 'What am I missing?' he said. 'Why are you so calm?'

He turned, his stare diving deep into her soul.

Oh, she was far from calm. If Peter wasn't so busy with his own thoughts and really looked at her, he would see that clearly for himself. She gripped the hem of her skirt, clinging to it as if it were a security blanket. She knew she'd have to tell him something now. Not the whole truth – that wasn't an option – but enough to show him why she wasn't overly shocked to see him naked.

'We've already seen each other naked, Peter, once before. Don't you remember?' He screwed his face up. 'We were very intoxicated, mind you, so maybe you don't remember it and I've got a lot curvier after having Ollie, but it's not anything you haven't seen before.' Jess watched him for a reaction, some form of recognition, but there was nothing.

'What do you mean? When? I don't remember you naked *at all* and I'm sure as shit I wouldn't forget something like that.' His eyes found her breasts again and he slapped his hand over his eyes with a grunt. 'I would totally remember them.'

Jess felt the heat rise in her cheeks and her chest tighten. If that was a compliment, she'd take it.

'You wiped yourself out that night, Abbie said you were out cold on the back lawn the next morning. Maybe that's why you don't remember it. You know the party we had when you were flatting with Guy? Jim was there with Abbie, and Ricki brought some of her friends from work? Guy set the barbecue on fire and you had to take over so he didn't burn all the sausages?' She searched his eyes when he dropped his hand from his face, waiting, hoping, but they were blank.

'Was that the night he was trying to win over one of the nurses?' He nodded. 'I think that was the night Ricki and I had our first kiss.'

'Bingo,' said Jess, smiling warmly. 'You remember it?'

'Only that bit. The rest of the night is still a blur,' he said. 'Whose idea was it to start making cocktails?' He looked at her again, closely. 'And to get naked?'

'That was Abbie with her new cocktail book. It wasn't ever going to end well.'

That night had probably been Jess's only chance to let Peter know how she felt, but fate had other plans and he'd ended up with Ricki. And she couldn't risk him asking for more details, so she jumped ahead. 'Speaking of Ricki. When are you going to pop the question?' Jess stole a glance to the bar. Both girls were in no rush to get back and had settled on stools, chatting.

'I was going to do it tonight, but I might save it for tomorrow now. Or even when we stop over in Albany. On a beach could be nice. Maybe even wait for the trip home.'

She shot him a confused look and waited.

'I don't know. She was a bit upset after work. Lost a kid. It always affects her and she's been having a tough time. It's had her stressed out and I'm trying to be understanding. I hope this trip will help. She's been a bit distant.'

Jess sipped her drink, not sure what to say.

He sighed heavily. 'Everything seems so out of plumb lately. And I hate the fact that you live so far away.'

Jess put her hand on his knee and gently squeezed. It was hard not to touch him – it came so naturally. 'I'm sure it'll work out. We all have bad days. And we talk on the phone.'

'I know, but it's not the same. I miss hanging out. Now you have another bloke who's more important than me.' His eyes sparkled as he grinned. 'Just remember that I've known you longer than Ollie.'

She put her arm around his shoulder and shook him gently. 'Peter, you don't need me anymore. Soon you'll have a wife and kids and you'll be too busy to talk to me.' Jess could already see how it would turn out. They would grow further and further apart as their busy lives took over. It hurt, so much, but Jess had to be realistic; it was the only way she and Ollie would cope.

'That would never happen. I need you in my life, Jess. You're family.'

'I feel the same,' she said. She knew it was true, but she also knew that she couldn't sit back and watch him play happy families while her heart broke. Being in such close proximity to him again – and especially after the shower debacle – made her realise that she would never stop loving Peter. The only way to avoid dragging her heart through barbed wire would be to cut all ties with him, to stand on her own two feet and pour all her love into Ollie.

She downed the last of her drink as her thoughts grew more determined. If Peter was going to marry Ricki, then Jess had to end their friendship, which would upset her relationships with Ricki and Abbie, because she couldn't see one without the other. It meant living her life without being able to call on Peter for anything, no more hugs, and no more blue eyes. And it would change things with her friends forever. Starting over. It wouldn't be easy, but she had to look forward. She still had her mum and Ollie. She could build a new life for them in Wandering. If she didn't completely rip her heart from her chest. Jess closed her eyes as she realised this cruise might be the last time she spent with her best friends and the man she loved. When they returned to Fremantle, life as she knew it would change.

13

Abbie

'WHAT'S UP WITH YOU? YOU SEEM DISTRACTED,' SAID ABBIE.

'Is it that obvious?' said Ricki as she sat on a stool by the bar, leaning forward, hands around her drink.

'To me it is. Someone die?'

Ricki paused, with a half-smile that quickly turned into a grimace. 'Yes, but it's more than that. Only, I don't want to tell you because you'll hate me and probably disown me as a friend.'

Abbie quickly sat on the stool next to hers and reached for her drink. Leaning closer to Ricki, she spoke quietly. 'Oh, I'm sorry you lost a patient, I know how hard it is for you. As for the other thing, do tell. I'll always be your friend. Well, that is unless you killed someone, then maybe not unless it was an accident at work. Wrong meds?' Abbie tried to make her friend smile, but she couldn't. 'Come on?'

Ricki winced, her shoulders sagged. 'There's a guy at work,' she said then stopped, glancing at Abbie. 'Miguel.'

Abbie waited.

Ricki glanced towards Peter, then turned her back towards him as she spoke. 'I kind of made out with him.'

'What?' Abbie screwed up her face, ignoring the woman beside her who scoffed at her outburst. Ricki had cheated on Peter? How was that possible? She hadn't expected that from her friend, and it was especially hard to swallow after Jim's betrayal. But this was her best friend and she could tell Ricki was in turmoil. She was punishing herself enough already, judging by the stress wrinkles on her face and her glassy eyes. Jim had left Abbie for another woman; Ricki was cheating on Peter; and Peter was about to propose to Ricki. *Jesus*.

'I know, I suck.'

Abbie, her mind in utter confusion, reached over and gripped Ricki's hand anyway. 'What's going on, my friend?' Now she wished Ricki hadn't told her. *Me and my big mouth*, she thought. A secret to keep from Peter.

'I don't know. I'm so confused. We hit it off straightaway.'

As Ricki told her about Miguel and his overseas work, Abbie saw the light in her friend's eyes and heard the excitement in her voice – it was like Ricki was when she started nursing and continually told them her dreams of doing something similar.

'I see the attraction. He's living the life you dreamed of. Is he cute?'

Ricki's eyes sparkled and she nodded. 'Yes, he's gorgeous. And we were good friends and we flirted a little, which makes life more fun. I found myself eager to get to work for a change, and when I'm with him I'm always happy and he makes me laugh.' Ricki paused, chewing her bottom lip. 'I haven't felt like that with Peter for a while now. Am I acting out because I'm bored or is it real with Miguel?'

'Gosh, love, don't ask me. I'm not qualified to answer that. Only you can.' Abbie didn't know the answers to anything anymore. She had no job, no boyfriend, and was possibly dying. Hell, maybe she should party hard before she was six feet under. Sex with an attractive man who wasn't Jim was starting to sound very good. Abbie had cheated on a guy before, in her last year of high school – but it didn't seem to count when you were young and carefree. It all changed when you got older and relationships became serious. You were supposed to find that one you were going to marry and make a life with, have kids, juggle motherhood and a job and clean up after everyone. Whose idea was that? At least Ricki had options.

'I love Peter, but the thought of marrying him and having kids scares me. I know it's not a prison sentence, the old ball and chain, but it feels like it would be. I feel so awful thinking like that.'

Abbie was itching to tell her that Peter had marrying on his mind. As she glanced over she saw that at this moment Peter was leaning in close to Jess as they spoke, and anyone would think *they* were the couple. Whatever they were discussing, it looked serious too. *Hell, this trip's looking more and more like a disaster*, Abbie thought as she looked back to Ricki, who was clearly lost in her own thoughts. Would she turn down Peter's proposal? Or would she say yes out of duty?

'So . . . was he good?' Abbie said eventually.

Ricki studied her for a moment before a smile appeared. 'Yes, scorching hot. Neither of us could fight it. I didn't have sex with him but, Abbie, I really wanted to. It took a huge effort to stop.' Ricki winced. 'It was breathtaking, but now

I feel horrible. I love Peter and I don't want to hurt him but I wouldn't have done this if I was truly happy, right?'

Abbie looked into her drink. She should blink but couldn't bring herself to do it as her mind replayed Ricki's words. *If I was truly happy.* Had Jim not been happy with her? Had it got stale and boring? Is that why he was distracted by someone else, or was his new girl just better suited to him? A better match, the one, his soul mate?

Abbie had not been enough, like Peter wasn't enough for Ricki. It was hard not to feel the pang of pain, of worthlessness. Cast aside like a defective apple on the sorting tray. Were her faults too much for him? Her mouth always got her into trouble. Or was it more about chemistry? Did this new girl turn him on more?

'Abbie?'

'Oh, sorry. Was just thinking.'

'I'm sorry for dumping this on you. You must despise me for what I've done?'

Ricki's face looked like it would crumble into a million pieces.

'No. No, I don't. We all make mistakes and do rash things. Who am I to judge?' She gave Ricki a warm, reassuring smile. 'Are you going to tell him?'

'I don't know. Right now I'm finding it hard to be close to him. It feels wrong. Can you keep it a secret until I figure it out? Please?'

Abbie gritted her teeth. If she spoke now she'd probably spill the beans about the proposal. So, she pushed it aside and nodded. But even with all that, she felt a little bit of sympathy for Ricki. Abbie could see how hard this was for her. Had Jim struggled with it too? Had he tried to ignore his feelings for *the other woman* before he gave in? And the way Ricki had lit up talking about Miguel and his work overseas – Abbie hadn't seen that Ricki in a long time. Clearly it stirred something young and wild inside her. Maybe if Abbie survived this cancer, then she should go off to find herself; set up her own business or travel the world.

She had to survive first.

Her throat constricted with a sudden wave of fear. She couldn't let it win. Wouldn't let it win. Taking a deep breath, she imagined putting her scary thoughts into a jar and sealing the lid tightly before tucking it down at the back of a dark shelf. Thoughts like cancer eating through her body did nothing but turn her into a mess. This trip wasn't about doom and gloom.

'Bartender, another two, please,' she said after drinking the dregs from her glass. She handed over her room card. 'Let's drink to shit moments.'

'Anyone ever said you swear too much?' said Ricki with a grin.

'Yeah, you have many times. It's how I express my feelings.'

'And that, my dear, is why we love you. I wouldn't want you any other way,' said Ricki leaning over and hugging her. 'Thank you for listening and trying to understand, especially about keeping this from Peter. I need time to sort out what I want.'

'I know. Just don't leave it too long.'

⚓

An hour later they were dancing up a storm, shoes discarded by the chairs and a mash of bodies on the small dance floor in front of the band. Abbie felt free in the music, lost in the moment, nothing but the guitar and drum beat pulsing through her mind. No fear. No waiting. No future scenarios.

There was a young blond-haired guy dancing behind her, rubbing up close as they moved to the beat, occasionally holding her hips and kissing her neck. Abbie laughed as Jess bumped into them – it had taken a few drinks but she was finally letting her hair down and dancing like a woman possessed. Or a woman free of kids for the night. Abbie glanced across to see Ricki dancing by herself in the crowd. Peter moved closer to her on the dance floor, but when he reached out to her she suddenly stopped dancing and motioned she needed a drink before disappearing from the floor. He saw Abbie watching and shrugged. Abbie's gut tightened. A wave of tiredness rippled through her.

Mr Blondie drew her back against his chest. He touched her hand and she felt him slip something into it. Abbie squinted down through the flicker of dancing lights and saw a pill. She looked over her shoulder at him. He smiled and nodded, then winked as he popped something into his mouth. When she didn't follow suit he shouted over the music, 'Don't you ever want to escape life?'

She did. Right now she wanted to forget everything. Cancer. Jim. Her job. Peter and Ricki. Abbie swallowed the little coloured pill.

And twenty minutes later she was filled with energy. Like she used to feel before her body had been invaded. Alert, she danced like she was born for it. Arms draped around Mr Blondie. Two hours later, and she was still dancing. Another hour saw two of her friends disappear, but Abbie was lost in the moment. The music pulsed through her body, bringing it alive, and the flashing lights took her away. She no longer knew where she was. Cancer was the furthest thing from her mind.

14

Ricki

RICKI DIDN'T WANT TO GO BACK TO HER CABIN; BACK TO Peter, who might want something more than someone to sleep beside. She couldn't do it. It didn't feel right, or fair.

So, she stayed on the dance floor, to keep an eye on Abbie was her excuse. And she wanted to be with Abbie, who knew her secret and hadn't judged her. Abbie had listened. That was more than Ricki probably deserved. It was nice to know that one mistake didn't kill a friendship. Not that she thought of being with Miguel as a mistake – only the way it had happened. She should have restrained herself, or at least broken up with Peter before she went near Miguel. But she hadn't.

She drank a glass of water, her eyes scanning the room for Abbie.

It was long past midnight. Ricki's feet were hurting. She wanted to lie down but she needed to check on Abbie first. Still scanning the crowd, looking for Abbie's long raven hair, she saw some sort of commotion at the corner of the dance floor. A fight maybe. No, people were gathered around someone on the floor. Ricki headed straight there, her nursing instinct kicking in. She pushed her way between two women and saw the raven hair fanned out on the floor.

'Abbie!'

Ricki kneeled beside her friend and immediately felt her forehead. Abbie was burning up. *Oh, God, Abbie, what happened to you?* she thought frantically. She knew she needed to focus, but concern was making her slow to act.

'Let me through, I'm the ship's doctor.'

A man in dress pants and a buttoned olive shirt pressed his way into the circle, his almost-black eyes instantly taking in the situation. He didn't speak, just checked Abbie until she started to respond to him. He glanced at Ricki. 'Is she your friend? Has she taken anything?'

'Yes. And I don't know. I wouldn't have thought so,' said Ricki, suddenly scared.

'Right, let's get her rehydrated.'

The man and Ricki helped Abbie up. She was trying to focus, blinking rapidly, but she was weak, and holding her head up was proving difficult for her. Her cheeks were flushed, her lips dry. She was in no state to walk, and suddenly strong arms scooped her up as if she were no more than a small child, and the doctor carried her from the crowd on the dance floor.

He headed to a long sofa while Ricki got two glasses of water from the bar, suddenly realising what this could be. The man had placed Abbie directly under an air conditioner and was now taking her pulse.

Abbie groaned and tried to hold her head with her free hand.

'Here, drink this.' Ricki pushed the glass into her hand and then guided it to her lips. She made her drink half the glass before stopping for a break.

'How are you feeling?' the doctor asked Abbie, watching her carefully.

Ricki could see him checking her pupils, his hand still on her wrist monitoring her pulse.

'I'm okay. Feel silly, but I'm okay. I need water.'

'Yes, keep hydrated,' he said sternly.

'Thank you . . .' she said, looking enquiringly to the man.

'Alex.' He glanced at Ricki. His face was handsome and sincere. 'She'll be fine.'

'Thank you, Alex. This is so not like Abbie,' she said as she made her friend drink the last of the water.

Abbie turned to Alex and frowned. 'Wow, you're sexy. Those eyes.' Abbie reached for his face, her fingers gently caressing his cheek.

Alex smiled and looked to Ricki. 'Is that normal?'

Ricki laughed. 'Yes, yes it is. Abbie has no . . .' Ricki was trying to think how to put it, but Abbie beat her to it.

'I have no filter. I see bullshit, I say so. I see something beautiful, I comment. Why beat around the bush?' Abbie's head dropped as if her words were the last of her energy spent.

'That's an admirable quality,' said Alex as he lifted her head to check her pupils.

Her bottom lip started to quiver. 'No, it's not,' she said as her eyes welled with tears. 'It's probably why Jim left me. I'm not good enough.' Tears dropped, trailing down her smooth skin.

Ricki blinked, wondering if she'd heard right. Jim had left her? How could that be? Ricki had thought they were the real deal. But the tears? Ricki knew how much it took to make Abbie cry.

'Oh, shit, Abs, has he really?' Ricki wrung her hands together, her shoulders tightening as if she were trapped in a vice and someone was slowly turning the handle. Her breath became shallow and painful. If Jim and Abbie couldn't make it work, then how would Ricki with Peter?

Abbie nodded and sniffed as Alex handed her a tissue.

'Not too many tears. You're already dehydrated,' he said with a wink.

Abbie smiled and took the other glass of water he held out.

'He must be a jerk to walk away from such a stunning woman.'

Abbie's lips twitched up. 'Thanks for trying.'

'Hey, I'm speaking the truth. Take it from someone who's been where you are. It gets better over time, and in the end you realise you're much better off without them. Why be with someone who wasn't the right one for you?' Alex reached across and squeezed her hand.

Ricki blinked, her heart thumping. Even though his words were for Abbie, they resonated with her. She couldn't string Peter along. It was simple: she wasn't the right woman for him. He deserved someone who wanted the same things as he did, just as Ricki needed to find her own happiness. The sooner she told him the better. It seemed the wrong timing to do it on the cruise, but the moment they got off and were back home, she'd end their relationship. Immediately she felt relief flood through her as the idea grew. Suddenly life seemed a little clearer. Yes, she would break up with Peter and move out. She could leave work and go overseas. There would be nothing stopping her. Her heart began to race with all the possibilities.

'Who would walk away from *you*?' said Abbie to Alex.

His forehead creased as he swallowed slowly. 'My wife. After two years of marriage.'

'Oh, no, sorry,' said Abbie. Her tears had stopped falling but her eyes were still watery.

'It was over a year ago now. At the time it was awful, painful and I thought I'd never get over it – but here I am, enjoying life and happy to see what it brings.'

Abbie sucked her bottom lip in. 'I bet a woman passed out on the floor was not what you were hoping for.'

'Shit no,' he said.

Ricki laughed. *You two would make a good pair*, she thought.

'Anyway. It's morning already and I should get to bed, I have work in a few hours,' he said with a warm smile.

He made a few final checks and then, seemingly satisfied, he stood. The band had played their last set and were now packing up. A small crowd still lingered, but their voices were quiet. Even the light machine had been switched off.

'It's okay, I'm a nurse, I'll keep an eye on her,' said Ricki.

He nodded, went to move but then turned back to Abbie, his face creased in seriousness. 'Be careful what you take on board this ship. If something goes wrong we're a long way from a hospital. I know you don't want to be told how to live your life, but, please, no more. I hate losing good people.'

Then he left, disappearing through a door at the back of the bar room. Ricki turned to face Abbie, hoping his words had sunk in.

'What the hell were you thinking taking . . . stuff?' she said. 'You scared the crap out of me.'

Abbie put her hand up and then moved it to her temple. 'I'm sorry. I just wanted to forget everything, you know? With Jim and my job.'

Ricki was about to continue her rant when she pulled up short. 'What do you mean? What about your job?' Could this night get any crazier? What was going on with Abbie?

'Oh,' said Abbie as if just realising her slip. 'Um, I quit. My boss was a jerk, so I told him where he could shove his job, more or less. So, no job and no Jim. Life's just dandy.'

Abbie spoke with customary sarcasm, but beneath her bravado Ricki saw pain and misery, and her heart ached for her friend.

'Abbie, why didn't you tell me? Oh my God. When did all this happen?'

Abbie leaned back on the seat and groaned. Her head was probably pounding. *Serves you right*, thought Ricki in a moment of anger. Abbie had truly scared her. It was so out of character, but then again she *had* lost Jim and her job. Ricki couldn't stay angry even for two seconds. 'I'm so sorry. I wish I'd known. I wouldn't have dumped my mess on you, especially if I'd known about Jim.'

'It's not your fault,' said Abbie through closed eyes as her head rested on the back of the couch. 'Jim wanted to be with her more. Nothing anyone could have done.'

'Who is she?' Ricki asked softly.

'His receptionist, Julie. And the worst thing is I actually liked her. She's a bubbly, pretty blonde with big boobs, but I didn't ever feel threatened. I thought we were solid.' She paused for a deep breath. 'He left a while ago now. He's had feelings for her for nearly a year. He's moved in with her. His soul mate, apparently.'

Ricki took the glass from Abbie and put it on the table, but continued to hold her hand. A whole year Jim had been seeing this other woman. How did he live with himself? Ricki had been with Miguel one day and already it was killing her. But if she was truthful she'd had feelings for Miguel a lot longer, she just hadn't been game to admit it to herself.

'Why didn't you tell me, or Jess? We could have been there for you.'

'I know. I was embarrassed, ashamed, felt stupid. A whole year and I had no idea. Maybe I really didn't know him as well as I thought.' Abbie lifted her head so she could look her in the eye. 'He said he'd tried to fight it, Ricki, but in the end he couldn't. Don't make the same mistake with Peter. Don't keep him hanging on the end of a burning bit of string. End it straightaway if it's what you want. Or come clean if it was a big mistake. Don't do what Jim did. Please.'

Ricki wiggled her nose as her eyes prickled with tears. 'I won't, I promise, I'm going to sort it out. But what about Jess? Are you going to tell her about all this? What are you going to do about work?'

'Ricki, I have no freakin' clue. At the moment I'm just taking every day as it comes. I don't want to tell Jess, can you do it? And what about you – are you going to tell her about Miguel?'

'You know I can't. Her loyalty to Peter is probably stronger than our friendship. He's like family to her. No. I can't tell her anything until I talk to Peter.' Ricki sighed. 'Life can seem great one minute and then a shit-hole mess the next. What do we do, Abbie?'

'We do the only thing we can do. Live each day as it comes, try to be good people while pursuing happiness.'

It sounded easy. But it wasn't.

15

Jess

THERE WAS A SOFT KNOCK AT THE DOOR, AND JESS OPENED it before Abbie woke.

'Hi, you. Wanna go get some brekkie?' said Peter almost shyly, looking her up and down in her denim cut-offs and singlet. He ran his hand through his hair, messing it up and yet it still looked good. 'I think it's just going to be you and me for a while. Is Abs still out to it?'

Jess chuckled and opened the door further so Peter could see Abbie sprawled over the bed in last night's dress, no shoes and her hair over her face.

'Funny, I have her exact clone in my room. Did you get to speak to her at all last night, I mean this morning?' asked Peter, nodding towards the sleeping figure.

'No, but I did wake when she came in. Ricki helped her to bed and she was asleep pretty quick. Did you with Ricki?'

He shook his head, his hair brushing across his tanned forehead. 'No, I heard her groan as she crawled on top of the bed. And that's how I found her when I woke up. I guess you're stuck with me till probably lunchtime.'

She smiled. 'Shall we grab some coffees and pastries from the bakery and nab some sun lounges?'

Peter smiled, and Jess tried to keep her breathing steady as his eyes shone at her. 'You read my mind.'

⚓

'Hmm, I'm glad I don't get seasick. But still it's an incredible view to get used to,' said Jess as she lay back on her sun lounge. In saying that, her stomach flipped. All she could see was ocean, endless ocean, and the sky light blue with yellow hues from the morning sun.

Here on deck eleven it was noticeably louder, mainly from the music playing and the kids splashing and squealing in the pool. One child had blond hair like Ollie, bringing her boy to mind. The area was spacious, the whole level open with only large windows at either end and the massive sun roof retracted so the morning rays came straight in along with fresh air, if a little salty. The cream sun lounges and day beds that surrounded the centre pool were covered with the *Eden*'s blue-and-white striped towels and scattered with bright yellow cushions. A handful of adults kicked back either reading, chatting or ordering drinks from the staff who wandered past in their black uniforms collecting empty glasses and taking orders.

Peter stretched out on the empty sun lounge beside Jess's, brushing pastry crumbs from his shirt before putting his hands behind his head. 'This is better. Think I could almost have a snooze after that *pain au chocolat*,' he said.

As Jess fished out her book from her bag, Peter flipped onto his side so he could see her. The electric blue of his eyes watched her carefully.

She rested the book on her lap and faced him. 'What?'

'There's one thing that's been bugging me,' he said finally, as if weighing his words.

Jess couldn't read his expression. It was serious, yet there was mischief in his eyes, especially after she had caught him looking over her body. She'd seen this look before, back when they were thirteen and he'd asked her if she'd been kissed yet and would she want to practise on him.

'What were you thinking now?' he asked. 'You got that little dimple that appears when you're remembering something good.'

'No, you don't get to say something's bugging you and then change the subject,' she said. 'Besides . . . I'm not sure if it was good.'

'Tell me yours, then I'll tell you mine?' His eyes swirled with teasing and the corner of his lips curled.

Jess sighed; he wouldn't stop until he knew. 'I was thinking about our first kiss when we were thirteen. Do you remember it?'

His eyebrows shot up. '*That's* what you were thinking about?' His fingers went to his lips, brushing them. 'Quite frankly, I'm offended that you'd think I'd forget that weird, messy kiss,' he said with a chuckle.

'It was at your place behind the old cubby house. It was my first kiss, but I was so sure it wasn't yours.'

'Oh, believe me it was my first. I was such a dork. Why did you think I hit you up for a kiss?'

'Gee, thanks, but you soon made up for it. Probably kissed all the girls in year twelve.' By his last year at school he'd grown lean and muscly from all his surfing. Add the tan and the blond hair, and he was Mr Popular. But Jess had loved him long before then.

'I have some experience now. It would be much better, I'm sure.' He winked.

His gaze remained on her, steadfast. Her breath caught. She watched him swallow and press his lips together as if a kiss was exactly what he was thinking about now.

Jess felt the air crackle. This was new territory, they'd never flirted before, if that's what this was. Whatever it was, Jess liked the sensation of it on her skin.

'It *was* much better,' she agreed with a smirk.

Those eyes narrowed, eyebrows shot skywards. 'See. Something is amiss. This thing that's bugging me, I can't get it out of my head. Yesterday you said we've seen each other naked before, and now you act like you've kissed me, not including the teenage debacle.'

'Gosh, you catch on quick, Peter Wellstead.' She smiled, even though she knew she was dancing in dangerous territory. She'd never dared to tease him like this before. But he was teasing her back, and she liked it. His gaze was so intense she wanted to look away, in case he could read her deepest desires, but those vibrant blue eyes were like electricity, lighting up her body.

He let out a low growl. 'Oh my God, tell me already. Why do I not remember any of this? Are you making it up? Teasing me?'

'Now, Peter Pan, would I lie to you?' Jess almost flinched at her own words. She was a terrible liar, but with age came practice.

'Come on. I'm dying here.'

He dropped his bottom lip like he used to when she'd take his favourite toy. They'd had plenty of fights when they were younger, like siblings. And then when he grew popular Jess got grumpy because she was left out and felt jealous. But Peter didn't give up on her, he still came to see her if he had time on the weekends. He refused to let the gap between them grow, which only made her love him more.

'Okay, okay. Well, back at that party with the cocktails—'

'Did we kiss there?' he cut in.

'You going to let me tell the story?' He zipped his lips and let her continue. 'It was after you and Ricki kissed.'

Peter laughed. 'God, that sounds bad. It was a messy night. At least I remember that much. The night was still young then.'

'Yes. Anyway, it was much later into the night, or morning, I can't remember,' she said with a laugh. Jess pressed her lips together before she continued to keep her nervous excitement at bay. 'So . . . um . . . by any chance do you remember sleeping with someone that night?'

Peter's eyes widened. 'Ah, yeah. How did you know that?'

'So, you remember being with someone?'

He went a little pink. 'Well, not exactly.'

It was Jess's turn to raise her eyebrows.

'Actually, I don't remember much of it.' He screwed his face up. 'Okay, okay, I don't remember any of it. I'd never been that wasted before in my life, I can't understand why or how I came to be sleeping on the lawn.' He hung his head. 'I know, I feel really crappy about it.'

'But you know you slept with someone?'

'Well, yes because when I crawled back into bed the next night, there were telltale signs – like women's red lacy underwear in my bed. I asked Guy if he'd seen me take anyone into my room, but he couldn't remember much either. I really don't know who I ended up with, and I wasn't about to go around waving the undies asking who they belonged to. I thought maybe it was Ricki, but the fact she never brought it up made me think it wasn't. And by then we had something going on and I didn't want to complicate things.'

Jess's heart had stopped, her blood sitting still in her veins while her brain was spinning trying to take it all in. Since that night she wasn't sure if Peter couldn't remember or had forgotten it on purpose, but now she knew for sure. He had no idea!

'So, you think it was Ricki?'

Peter closed his eyes for a moment. 'Mmm, well yeah, 'cause we'd kissed earlier that night out by the barbecue and I'm guessing one thing led to another. Then the next day she rang up and asked me out. The rest is history. What's all this got to do with anything, anyway?'

Jess put her face in her hands and took a couple of deep breaths. Was this something she should share? No one knew the truth, not Ricki, not Abbie – not even Peter, it seemed. Jess was the master secret keeper, after all. She'd never told anyone the full story about her dad, the things she'd seen; Peter, Ricki and Abbie only knew the scraps she'd given them. She'd never told anyone about Chris and what she'd seen. Back in school other girls couldn't wait to pass on secrets, but not Jess. But maybe it was time to change that.

'Jess, you're freaking me out, what aren't you saying? Do you know who it was? Was it Ricki? Did she say something?'

Damn it, she thought. So many questions, just not the right ones. 'Did you ever wonder why Ricki didn't bring it up?' When he shrugged she continued. 'Because it wasn't her, you idiot.'

He sat up, and moved towards her so his legs rested against her sun lounge. 'Really? Who was it? How come you know?'

Jess felt her heart in her throat. *Just say it!* she screamed at herself. 'The red lace undies were mine, Pete.' And there it was. Finally it was out in the open. All this time she thought he wanted to forget it, pretend it hadn't happened, that being friends must have been more important. All that agony – when he simply didn't remember it. Suddenly she smiled from relief. But Peter's face showed no relief, more like shock. He looked a little pale, the whites of his eyes bright and his mouth open.

'Say what?'

'The red undies were mine. That was me in your bed.'

He blinked at her, once, twice, three times. 'No way. What? I slept with *you*?' He looked down into his lap and squinted, as if trying to force a memory that simply wasn't there. Eventually he shook his head and looked up at her. 'You and me?'

'Bingo. Surprise,' she said with a nervous smile.

Peter lay back on his chair, his eyes not leaving her face. 'I don't . . . I can't . . . shit, *really*? Why didn't you ever say anything? How did that happen?'

'Well, we took off our clothes—'

'Ha ha,' he said dryly. 'Jess, how could I not know this? Why didn't you tell me?'

He was staring at her, drinking her in, searching her face for the answers, which only made her body heat more. 'Sorry,' she said nervously. 'But I didn't know you weren't going to remember it. Afterwards . . .' Gosh, how did she put this without bringing up the pain it had caused. 'After we'd, well, you looked at me and said, "Holy shit, that shouldn't have happened." You threw your hands over your face and groaned. I saw in your face the regret and I wasn't going to hang around and listen to whatever you said next. I took off home.' Jess shrugged as if his words and that moment hadn't gutted her. 'And then you and Ricki happened, so the rest is history.'

He remained silent.

'Gee, is it that hard to believe? I'm a woman, you're a man. These things happen. We're not really family, you know.' Jess suddenly felt uncertain about where this conversation might lead. About everything.

'I know that,' he said softly. His brow scrunched as if in silent agony. 'It's just I don't remember saying that to you and I can see you've taken my words not how I would have intended. Jess, you know you've always been my best friend, someone I want to take care of, but yesterday in the shower . . . Whenever I've let myself start to see you in that way, I've managed to rein it in.' He cleared his throat. 'Jess, it's not that it's hard to believe; I'm just struggling with the fact it happened when I've spent so many times keeping myself behind the line. My words wouldn't have been out of not wanting to be with you, it's because I never wanted to cross that line, didn't want to ruin what we have, never wanted to put you in a situation where I put my wants over your needs. I've tried so hard to not go there. So those words were me being disappointed in myself, not you. I can honestly say that's what I would have been thinking.' Peter shook his head, squeezed his eyes shut for a moment before he continued. 'It makes total sense why I wrote myself off now. God I was an idiot.'

Jess let out her breath slowly. Were these things he was saying true? Had he thought of her like that at times? Just the possibility of it made her feel like she was floating off the sun lounge. Her eyes didn't leave his face as she waited for him to continue.

'Our friendship means the world to me. I never wanted to jeopardise that.'

All this time she'd thought it had been her he didn't want, when the truth was he'd had moments where he wanted to overstep. Wow.

The noise of the kids in the pool faded, leaving only the sound of her shallow breaths and his, as they watched each other, thinking, sorting, wondering.

After what felt like minutes he asked, 'Was it good?'

A glimmer of a grin. A cheeky one at that.

Jess laughed, relieved to break the intensity. 'Yeah, I think it was. We were both drunk, though, so it wasn't going to break records,' she teased.

He frowned. 'I do feel ripped off. A little jealous that you can remember it and I can't.' He was playing with the bottom of his shirt, twisting it in his fingers. 'How did we end up like that anyway? Was it something I did?'

Jess swallowed hard. 'No, it was all me. Kind of silly, really. After seeing you kiss Ricki I guess I felt I was missing out or something,' she said, trying to sound a little vague. 'So, I found you alone later, pulled you into your room and kissed you. It was dark, we'd had a lot to drink, and you weren't to know I'd pounce on you. It's not normally what I'd do.'

'True,' he said, watching her, a question forming in his eyes. 'But . . . was it just the alcohol? Or did you . . .' He stopped, and his eyes bored into hers until she couldn't look away no matter how much she wanted to. 'Did you have feelings for me?'

Jess's heart raced. Why couldn't Peter have asked her this years ago, not now when he was in a relationship and about to make it permanent? Bloody hell, regret hit her hard, why couldn't she have kept her mouth shut? How did she word this without ruining everything? The lie was too hard so she answered him by shaking her head. 'But I've always loved you Peter. How could I not?' she said and patted his knee playfully. His eyes studied her for a moment, and she forced herself to meet his gaze, to not look away.

His lips twitched. 'So, the kisses were okay? Better than our first?'

Relief flooded her limbs. He'd brought it so far. 'Much better. So good in fact we didn't stop. You can guess the rest.'

'No, tell me it all in great detail,' he teased, his energy suddenly renewed.

'Ha ha, not now, not ever,' she said. 'Besides, it worked out for the best because now you're with Ricki and you're about to pop the question. It was obviously meant to be.'

'You and fate. You always believe things happen for a reason, don't you?'

In this moment Jess knew she should tell him she needed distance, that fate now meant their friendship had to change, but she couldn't bring herself to do it. How could she sever such an important friendship – the one constant in her life until Ollie had come along? But once Peter was married and had a family, then he'd be okay. He wouldn't need Jess in his life. He wouldn't understand, but maybe one day down the track she'd tell him why she'd had to leave. One day maybe they could be friends again, whenever her heart decided to let him go.

16

Abbie

ABBIE EVENTUALLY SURFACED IN THE AFTERNOON, AFTER A long shower and many glasses of water. She pulled on shorts and a sleeveless shirt and slowly made her way out of her cabin. She ignored the stairs and went straight for the elevator; going down was okay, but up was like climbing a mountain and Abbie had no strength for it. Even last night she'd noticed how quickly she'd been puffed on the dance floor, until she'd swallowed that pill – then she'd felt alive and well. But it hadn't fixed anything, had merely given her a moment of freedom, a moment to forget everything that had come her way in the past few months.

As the lift doors began to close a man scooted in.

'Hi, Abbie, how are you feeling?'

She squinted at him; something seemed familiar. His dark eyes were gorgeous, like shiny black pearls. His hair was thick, black strands framing his handsome face. He was tall and strong, like a real country man, but something about the way he held himself told her that this man didn't have to work for his body, it was just built this way. She could tell by the way his jeans wrapped around his shaped legs and his white shirt tightened on his biceps. He couldn't be more than ten years older than her, she figured.

'How do I know you?' she said, brushing her hair back off her shoulder as she studied him, her mind casting back. Dancing. Falling. The floor. Dark eyes. 'You helped me last night, with Ricki?'

'Yes. Alex,' he said holding out his hand.

Abbie shook it firmly. 'Thank you, Alex. Not my finest hour.'

'I'm glad you're okay. Feeling better?'

She was, and the scent of him, leather notes highlighted with coffee, seemed to snap her awake like smelling salts. 'I am. Thanks for asking.' She saw him look at the dressing on her neck but he didn't ask about it.

The lift stopped at deck nine, where an older lady with lots of flashy jewellery and far too much perfume got on. It was so bad, Abbie pretended to cough just so she could cover her nose. And then the elevator stopped at deck ten and the woman got off.

'Wow, that's strong. Instant headache,' said Alex once the doors closed and the elevator continued on its way.

'I was thinking the same thing. Perfume needs to come with strict guidelines. It's not for bathing in.'

They shared a smile.

'Where's your friend? Ricki?'

'Um, good question. They're all off somewhere.' She shrugged. 'I'm hoping I might find them in The Pantry having lunch. Not sure if I feel like eating, though.' Abbie screwed her nose up as the doors opened and the smells of cooked food filled the air. 'Ah, nup. Can't do it.'

Alex touched her arm gently. 'Would you like to head outside to the terrace and I'll bring you some fruit?'

'Really?' Abbie grinned. 'Don't you have anything better to do? Friends to see?'

He shook his head. 'Maybe we can keep each other company over lunch seeing as we're both friendless.'

The smell was making her stomach roll and in the end his offer was too good to refuse. 'What's the quickest way out?'

'Around the corner there's a door that goes straight out onto the back deck. How do you like your coffee?'

'Black and strong. Thank you. Again.'

He smiled and almost bowed to her. For a moment she was mesmerised, but as the smell of food lingered she held her breath and darted for the outside door, trying to ignore all the people eating.

Outside the breeze whipped around her face, instant relief of cool salty air. The cloudless sky was bright and she had to squint until she adjusted to it. The glare was intensified by the reflected sunlight off the Prussian blue ocean, which seemed to paint the wave crests silver.

She was facing the rear of the boat. The deck ran to the back edge of the ship, and stairs with solid wood rails either side led to the next level down to the pool surrounded by black layabout chairs. Some were filled with ladies reading books with drinks beside them, some had towels thrown across them. Three people relaxed in the pool, arms over the edge as they looked out to sea. It was a picture of wonder, something from a cruise brochure but even better in real life.

She stepped towards an empty chair but paused by the person occupying the nearest one.

'Ricki!'

Her friend was lying back with her sunnies on, sleeping.

Abbie walked over and stretched out on the chair beside her. 'Ricki?' Abbie reached over and touched her arm.

Ricki stirred, turning her head to the side. 'Abbie. How did you find me?'

'By fluke, really. I couldn't stomach the smells inside.'

'Ha, me neither. I came out here for a bit and . . .' She looked around blearily. 'I feel shattered, like if I've worked a double shift.' Ricki adjusted her sunglasses. 'It's all your fault, you know,' she said teasingly.

'Argh, don't remind me. I feel terrible enough as it is. Sorry again, about all that.'

'We aren't young anymore, Abbie. By now we're supposed to be responsible adults and have our lives going to plan,' said Ricki.

'Ha. I thought I had. Now it's all turned to crap and I feel like I'm bobbing about in the sea waiting for a shark to eat me.' Staring at the ocean, she watched the churned white caps from the ship's movements. Maybe it would be easier if she jumped overboard. Eaten by a shark would be an experience, or maybe she'd sink to the bottom of the ocean like an anchor. Abbie had watched her granddad die a long, slow and painful death from cancer. She didn't want that; she'd rather go while she still had her hair and full body function. Gramps was the love of her life for many years. His dry sense of humour and grumpy-old-man ways kept her entertained and in awe, and watching him die had destroyed her. Every time she visited him, his eyes filled with pain and suffering, she knew he wanted to die on his own terms and not be stuck in a hospital being poked and prodded. Every visit he said the same thing to her. 'I just want to die.'

Damn cancer.

'I see you found a friend after all,' said Alex as he stood between them. 'Hello, Ricki.'

'Hi, Alex.'

He held out a bowl of fruit and a coffee for Abbie. He had a basket of hot chips in his other hand which he picked at.

'Oh, you are such a life saver. Thanks.' She drew up her legs to make room for him to sit next to her.

'Would you like something, Ricki?' he asked when he caught her eyeing off Abbie's coffee.

'No, thank you. I had one earlier,' she said with a smile. 'So, where are you from, Alex?'

'Griffith, country New South Wales. But after my divorce I needed a change from small-town life. I went on a cruise and ended up in Western Australia, and then I fell in love with Perth. So, when this job came up, it seemed like the right step. I moved there about six months ago.'

'Wow,' said Ricki. 'I envy your ability to make a big change.'

He squinted against the sun and pulled out his sunnies from his shirt pocket. Abbie would rather he left those dark eyes uncovered; they were like a little atlas she was trying to navigate her way around, figure out what made Alex tick. He seemed honest and thoughtful, and happy to talk about his private mess. Abbie had to try hard to not watch him eat. He had nice lips. She was surprised he even wanted to be near her after last night, or was it early this morning? Her face started to burn but she shook it off. He wouldn't be here if he didn't want to be.

'I often wonder about moving, but I've been scared about taking that leap,' said Ricki.

'Trust me, it's better to do it and have tried than not to and regret it. You can always go home afterwards.' He glanced between them. 'So, are you both from Perth? What do you do?'

'Yep, from Perth,' said Abbie.

'I'm a nurse and Abbie works in real estate. She wants to start her own business,' added Ricki.

Abbie glanced overboard. 'It's not as exciting as working on a cruise ship,' she said, shutting down talk about her future.

Alex finished the last of his chips and brushed the salt off his fingers. 'It's a job that still has its moments and speaking of, I must head off,' he said as he stood, towering over them both.

'Oh, don't feel like you have to leave. Feel free to stay and keep us company,' said Ricki.

'No, no, I'd love to, but I do have to start my shift,' he said glancing at his watch. 'It was nice to chat to you both. I'm sure I'll see you around again.'

'Thank you for lunch,' said Abbie. He gave her a smile, which sparkled in his eyes, and she couldn't stop herself from watching him walk back inside.

'He is delish,' said Ricki. 'Why didn't you convince him to stay? I reckon he would have if *you'd* asked.' She rested her head back on the chair, taking up her previous sleeping position.

'Bullshit. He had somewhere to be.'

'Come *on*. Maybe an ocean-voyage rendezvous with Doctor Alex is just what you need to move on from Jim.'

Abbie spluttered as she sipped her coffee, spilling some down her chin. 'Damn it.' She turned to Ricki. 'I don't think I'm ready to start a new relationship yet.' *Or ever*, she thought.

'I'm not telling you to marry the bloke, but to have some fun. Maybe when we reach Albany you can see if he's free for a beach walk. You're a sexy single adult and so is he. There is nothing wrong in this scenario.'

Abbie looked at her friend. 'Have you seen Peter yet?' she asked.

Ricki's forehead creased and her lips pulled into a thin line. 'Nope. He'll be off with Jess somewhere. I'm actually thinking of going back to the room and watching a movie. Maybe I'll feel like eating later. At least that way we can be found. Want to join me?' Ricki sat up. 'I won't be offended if you fall asleep,' she said with a grin.

'You know what, that sounds about all I can muster at the moment. We'll need to build up our energy for tonight anyway. That comedy show's at seven, and then the Gatsby party is afterwards. We can't miss the show. I need a few laughs.'

'You and me both,' said Ricki with a sigh. 'Gee, they really pack a lot of events into a day aboard the ship don't they?'

But Abbie didn't really hear her as she gazed into the deep endless water and for a moment contemplated its sweet release.

The swell held her hypnotised until she felt the brush of her friend's fingers against her skin.

'Come on. Let's go.'

17

Jess

'WHAT? AM I BORING YOU ALREADY?' ASKED PETER AS HE pushed his lunch plate away. 'You've been staring out that window since we got here. Don't you love me anymore?' He pouted.

Jess tried to smile. 'Sorry, no, I was just thinking.' *God, how do I start? Will he hate me?* Her eyes traced his lean jaw, up to his perfect lips and then the small laughter lines around his eyes. She knew every spot, scar and faint sun-kissed freckle as if it were her own skin. Giving up Peter felt like giving up a part of herself, but she couldn't live like this anymore.

'Seems serious. You've got that eye twitch happening.' He reached over and brushed his thumb down the side of her face as if it would help her relax.

It did anything but.

Jess grabbed his hand and pulled it away. 'Peter, I need to talk to you. Seriously.' She frowned as if to stress her point. She glanced around The Pantry, it was buzzing half-full of people eating merrily, enjoying the ship's ambience, but she and Peter were in the far corner by the window, secluded.

'Okay,' he said sitting up curiously. 'I'm all ears.'

'Well . . . I've decided to stay in Wandering and make it my home. It will give Ollie a stable home.'

He frowned as if he'd been expecting a different reply. Then his face went taut as her words sank in. 'I assumed you'd come back to teach closer to home. Be closer to me so I can be there for you and Ollie.'

Her held breath rushed out between her lips. 'That's just it, Pete. You're about to get married, start your own family and concentrate on your own life. You can't be there for us too. You've always been a knight, coming to my rescue, and I know you'd drop everything to help me. That's who you are, but you can't anymore, not for me. I need to stand on my own two feet and take care of my own family without relying on you.'

He put his elbow on the table and rested his chin on his hand. His brow creased in confusion. 'But you're my best friend. I have to stay in touch with you and care for you. We're practically family.'

'I know that. But I can't do it anymore, Peter. I need to focus on Ollie.'

'Can't do what? What are you saying, Jess?'

His face was so close, his eyes full of questions as they searched for answers. He moved his hand to touch her fingers but she pulled back. She could see the surprise, the hurt, in his eyes at her movement, but she couldn't handle his caress, not now.

'I'm saying that I'm going to let you live your life in peace.

I won't come back to Perth much if I can help it and I won't be calling you anymore and I won't answer yours.'

He sat up as if her words had burned him. 'What! I need our phone calls. This is ludicrous, Jess.'

Jess sighed. *Why can't I simply invent a boyfriend and make it sound real?* she admonished herself. But she couldn't. Not with Peter. 'Peter, it's not right that we have so much contact. I'm too dependent on you and I need to find my own way. I also have to let you go so you can focus on Ricki. She'll need you, especially when you have kids.' How did she leave Peter without actually saying, *I'm totally in love with you, you bastard, and I can't handle seeing you playing happy families without me, so I'm cutting off all ties.* Being truthful could ruin everything – but then again, she was probably going to ruin everything now anyway. But at least this way would give her time and maybe later down the track she'd be able to handle being friends again.

'What is this bullshit, Jess?' he growled. He leaned forward, his jaw pulsing. 'You can't be serious. I don't believe any of it. And what about Ricki – you're never going to see her? What's really wrong?' He shoved his hand through his hair, and Jess started tapping her nails on the tabletop. Her foot jiggled uncontrollably.

Sucking in a deep breath, she tried to calm herself before saying, 'I'm growing up, Peter. I'm taking charge of my life.'

His voice softened. 'Come on, Jess, you don't mean it?'

Standing up quickly, she checked her watch. 'I have to get ready for my massage.'

'Jess, you can't go, not now. Let's talk this through.' He moved to reach for her but hesitated.

'I'm really sorry, Peter. Don't hate me. Please. All I want is for you to be happy.' She gave him a smile before walking away. He got up to follow her but she put up her hand.

'I could never hate you,' he said. 'I don't understand what this is about. Please, Jess.'

Seeing him confused, in pain, was pulling at her heart strings. 'I have to go. I'm sorry.' She walked off quickly and didn't look back, but back in her cabin, with no sign of Abbie, she burst into tears. Crawling onto her bed, she let herself grieve.

⚓

'Hey you,' Ricki said with a smile as she came into the cabin. Jess, after wallowing in self-pity as long as she dared, had showered, changed and was about to head out.

'Hi,' said Jess, putting on her best smile; focusing on someone other than herself would help her move forward. 'How are you feeling? Have you seen Abbie?' Ricki seemed distracted, her eyes heavy.

'I'm fine now. Abbie and I have been watching a movie next door while we recovered. Only, now I'm hungry, and I'm off to find supplies, but I was hoping to find you first.' She glanced towards the cabin door. 'Are you off for your massage?' she asked.

'Yep. Want to walk with me? I'll drop you off at the lolly shop so you can get your sugar fix.'

Ricki nodded as they made their way out to the corridor. 'Sounds good. And, I need to talk to you. About Abbie.'

Was this what had Ricki looking so dishevelled? 'What about her? Did something happen last night?'

'Yes, but that's not what this is about.' She waited until the lift doors had closed before she continued. 'Firstly, Jim left her for Julie, his receptionist.'

Jess swore, then covered her mouth. 'He didn't!'

Ricki nodded. 'He did. And she also quit her job.'

'Oh, no, really? Poor Abbie. That new boss, Derek. Why didn't she tell me?'

'I only found out by accident. I don't think she planned on telling us at all.' Ricki shook her head, her hair cascading loosely down her back.

'It explains her behaviour. I thought she was making the most of being away with us, but she's got so much else going on. I can't believe Jim left her. I thought those two would get married. Did she say much else?'

'No.' Ricki pressed her lips together as she turned away to trace the bamboo wallpaper in the lift. 'I thought they'd marry too. She wanted me to tell you so she didn't have to. She doesn't want a big deal made out of it. You know Abbie.'

'Yep, but still, I can't believe she didn't confide in us.' Jess's face suddenly burned, her words echoing through her mind as she realised she wasn't the only one hiding secrets from her friends. 'Is she okay, do you think?'

'I don't know. She went a bit wild last night, but I'm sure it was just to let off some steam. She'd hate for us to make a circus out of it, so I'm going to let it slide for now. Let's make sure we're there for her,' she said as the doors opened and they stepped out. 'We could take her out for dinner and a movie or have a few girlie nights at her place. I might even spend a few nights with her when we get back,' said Ricki.

'But you'll be . . .' Her words died on her lips as she realised she was about to say *newly engaged*. 'I mean, I'll be back in Wandering. But I'll try.'

Ricki gave her a quick hug and then left as Jess made her way to the day spa and Ricki headed for the lolly shop. As she lay naked on the table minutes later, with soft music playing in the background, Jess willed herself to forget everything and enjoy this moment. Who knew when she'd ever have the chance again?

18

Abbie

'COME ON, RICKI, WHAT DID YOU FORGET?' ABBIE SAID AS she opened the cabin door. Only, it was Peter. 'Oh, it's you.'

'Sorry to disappoint,' he said blankly.

'You didn't,' she said as he came and sat on the bench seat next to the table. 'Ricki and I have been watching a movie. She just stepped out to get some food, and . . .' She stopped. 'You okay, Peter? You seem distracted.'

He sat hunched over, staring at the half-empty water bottle on the table.

'Are you having second thoughts about proposing?' she ventured, sitting next to him. 'Or is it something else?' She touched his arm and he jumped. 'Pete?'

His head turned slowly to her, his eyes the most lifeless she'd ever seen them.

'Is Jess okay, do you know?' he asked eventually, his voice strained.

'As far as I know. Why?'

'She just told me, more or less, that she didn't want us to be friends anymore. That she didn't want me in her life.'

Abbie frowned, wondering if she'd heard right. 'Surely you got the wrong end of the stick.'

'Nope. She made it clear.'

'But you guys are joined at the hip.' Abbie's head was spinning. What the hell was going on with her friends lately? Were they all in some quarter-life crisis?

'I'm totally confused. Is something going on in her life? Does she have a new man?'

'Nup, no bloke that I'm aware of. So, what was her reason?'

Peter sighed deeply and went back to staring at the water. 'Some crap about needing to stand on her own two feet. That she needed to think about Ollie and that I'd be too busy with Ricki and my own family.' He reached up, scrunching yesterday's activities sheet in his hand and then throwing it across the room. 'I don't get why she suddenly decided she doesn't want me in her life anymore. I don't get it at all.'

Abbie didn't get it either. What was worse was that she had a fair idea that Ricki was going to say no, so there would be no engagement and no future kids. Abbie had always known that Jess kept her cards close to her chest — after all, it was Peter who told them about Jess's abusive dad all those years ago, and that was only because they couldn't understand why Jess wouldn't let them stay over — but Abbie hadn't really considered how much complexity lay behind that sweet face. Jess would have made a great actress.

'Stuffed if I know,' said Abbie truthfully. 'But if you like I'll have a talk with her later. It could just be a passing phase,

Peter. I'm sure she didn't really mean it. How could you two not be in each other's lives?'

'Exactly,' he said, slapping his leg. 'I love her to bits. I know she loves me too, so I can't figure out what's wrong. I'm actually worried that something serious has happened and she's trying to shut me out.'

'Good luck with that. Jess won't talk unless she's ready.' Abbie had never seen Peter look so gutted. He was a glass-half-full guy, and together with Jess the two were like a sugar overdose in a sun-filled room with rainbows and fairies. It was sickening but adorable. Yet Jess had a darkness that was hidden deep, secrets and memories that were never shared unless she felt like sharing. They'd been seventeen, nearly two years after her dad had left, when Jess first told Abbie about her fear of him returning. They were sitting on the beach at twilight, talking about a girl they knew from school who'd been in a car crash. Maybe all the sad talk had just been the right time for her to mention it, but the moment made Abbie feel closer to Jess than ever.

'Did he ever hurt you?' Abbie had asked. Usually Jess cleverly evaded these types of questions, but not that night.

'Only a few times, pushing me out of the way, slaps to the head, he even kicked me a few times. Once he ripped my arm so hard he dislocated it. But he did all the really bad stuff to Mum. And Chris escaped it all. Mum and I protected him, shielded him from the worst of it.'

Abbie had been unnerved by the coldness of Jess's voice, the disjointed way she spoke about it. To see the woman she was today, no one would ever know what she'd lived through.

Peter sighed again, almost angrily, frustrated. 'I can't not have Jess in my life, Abs. It's not a future I can imagine. She can't mean it?'

Abbie grabbed his hand. 'Give her time. Try not to worry. I'll talk to her.'

He looked hopeful. 'Thanks. I'd really appreciate it.'

'And what about Ricki? When's the proposal?'

He tilted his head to the side. 'I was going to do it after the comedy show tonight maybe, before we head off to the Gatsby party. She should be in a good mood then,' he said with a weak smile. 'Do you think I shouldn't?'

Uncertainty filled his eyes.

'This is something only you can do, Peter. Best thing I can say is to really search your heart and listen to what it tells you. You don't have to rush into this. There's no expiry date.'

He pulled a face. 'You know, Abbie, that's the most profound thing I've ever heard you say.'

'Yeah, well, I do have a heart somewhere and it works on occasion. But only for those special folks I love.' She grinned, glad he was looking better. 'Now, shall I go and give you and Ricki some alone time? I feel as if I've monopolised her lately.'

'No, stay. We'll have time later. Besides, I'm betting you're starving by now.'

'I *am* a little hungry. But when Ricki gets back I might wander off around the ship for a look-see. Make the most of it.'

Before Peter could reply, they heard the door open, and Ricki came in carrying two huge red cups filled with lollies.

'I couldn't help it, I went for the naughty stuff. We're on holidays, after all, and sugar is needed to keep our energy up,' she said with a grin that faltered slightly as Ricki realised Peter was in the cabin too.

'Hi, Pete,' she said as Abbie jumped up to grab her cup. 'Sorry, I didn't get you one. But you can share mine.' Ricki sat on the end of her bed while Abbie stayed by the door.

'Actually, take mine – but save me some. I'm going to take a stroll and maybe catch up with Jess after her massage. I'll see you both later,' Abbie said. She grabbed a handful of lollies and passed the cup to Peter – then quickly ducked out the door. *And you two sort out your shit!* she wanted to add.

⚓

Abbie wandered along, enjoying the sweets and the alone time as she made her way towards the day spa.

'Ah, just in time,' she said as Jess walked out looking a little sleepy.

'Abs, what are you doing here?' she asked.

'Waiting for you, actually. Good massage?' she asked.

'The best. Make sure you get Elsa.'

Jess smiled, and Abbie couldn't see anything out of the ordinary. 'What are you going to do now?'

Jess shrugged. 'I'm thinking I might go for a swim. I've never been swimming on a ship before.'

'Good idea. You might find some young hunk while you're at it.'

'If I do I'll be sure to ask him if he has a brother.'

Abbie chuckled as they started to walk. 'Yes, you do that,' she said, and then added more quietly. 'So, how are you going, Jess. I mean, really?'

Jess frowned a fraction but then smiled and replied, 'Good. I love being a mother, and I love my little classroom, and the folks in Wandering are fabulous. I feel like for once I've got my life almost sorted.'

Despite her smile, there was a flicker of doubt in her eyes, as she crossed her arms.

Abbie wasn't fooled. 'So, what's the go with you and Peter, then?'

Jess's mouth dropped open. 'What do you mean?' she said as she glanced away, chewing her lip.

'You know what I mean. I just saw Peter and he was rather confused, Jess. What's going on in your pretty little head, my friend?' Abbie reached out and tugged at Jess's arm until she relaxed and let Abbie hold her hand. 'Talk to me, Jess.'

'What, like you did about Jim?' she said softly.

Abbie flinched, but she knew Jess was right. 'Touché.' She sighed. 'I was too embarrassed to tell you both that Jim had left me.'

Jess watched her, clearly weighing up her words. 'You know we only want to be there for you. We could have made a Jim voodoo doll and stabbed pins in it for you,' she said with a smirk. 'Or just been an ear. I'm not embarrassed about my issue, just sad I guess. It's nobody's problem except mine and I'm just trying to deal with it the best way I can.'

'And as you just said, I want to be there for you. What's going on?' Abbie saw the heartache in Jess's expression, her tight lips, her glistening eyes. Suddenly, she knew. 'Oh. Are you still in love with Peter?' she said tenderly. 'Even after all these years?'

Jess frowned, maybe a little miffed that Abbie had guessed so correctly, but she nodded nonetheless. 'How did you know?'

'It was the only thing that made sense. Why else would you turn away from him? Only Ricki and I know how you really felt for Peter in school because we found your diary that time. I guess if we hadn't we never would have known. You did a good job of hiding it so it was easy for us to forget about it later. But you don't have to cut him out of your life, Jess.' Abbie burned to tell Jess about Ricki's affair and how they might not actually get married, but she pressed her lips together and kept the secret.

'Oh, I do. I survived him buying the ring, but spending so much time with him again is too hard. I thought having Ollie and moving away would change things, but when I'm with Pete, when he hugs me, touches me ... Abbie, I can't keep living like this. I need to let him go. It's been bad enough watching him and Ricki hold hands, or kiss. I won't be able to do their wedding.'

'Oh, shit, Jess. I didn't realise it was that bad for you. I'm sorry.'

'You weren't to know. I tried to hide it. I tried to be the good, supportive friend. But not anymore. I need to move on. Sometimes it's too much hard work keeping all this stuff to myself. I don't know why I feel the need to hold onto it.'

Abbie hugged her. 'Have you told him how you feel?'

'No. That would be wrong when he's about to marry Ricki.'

'Why is it? It's giving him all his options before he makes a choice that could affect the rest of his life. Wouldn't you want all your cards on the table before a big decision?'

'I guess. But I don't want to ruin anything. And I couldn't do that to Ricki.'

'You're afraid to tell him, I get that. And afraid to hurt Ricki too. But she wouldn't want to be with Peter if he's meant to be your soul mate. I understand if you're afraid he might not understand or feel the same, but Jess, what you're doing to him now is going to ruin your friendship with him and Ricki anyway so what have you got to lose?'

Jess sighed. 'I guess you're right. When you put it like that, I have at least a small chance, and he will know the truth. Bit clever, aren't you,' she said, squeezing Abbie's hand.

19

Ricki

'DO YOU WANT ANY MORE?' SHE ASKED PETER, PUTTING THE cup of lollies down. He shook his head. He'd been quiet since she returned and Abbie had done a runner. Ricki knew that Abbie didn't want to be her Peter buffer and, really, she couldn't blame her. This was Ricki's mess, not Abbie's.

Ricki had tiptoed around Peter, his solemn mood making her wonder if it was something she'd done, but he still smiled and replied to her questions. If he was cross with her usually she got a heated look and curt answers.

She squeezed his shoulder. 'Are you okay? Not seasick?'

He blinked and shook his head. She'd always thought Peter was attractive; well, at least after he grew out of that gangly stage. It wasn't until he hit seventeen that he hit smoking-hot status and everyone wanted him. Even Jess once had a crush on him. But Ricki had always known him as Jess's friend and a sweet guy. She'd never thought about dating him until they kissed that night when the moment was just right. They'd been chatting alone by the barbecue and she'd leaned over and kissed him. As simple as that. It was funny how one kiss had made her think differently about Peter, and she'd gone home wanting to taste more of him, feel those sun-kissed abs and run her hands through his sand-coloured hair. He'd accepted her offer of a date, which had taken her by surprise, and afterwards she'd gone around to Jess's place.

'We're going out on a date and I wanted to check if that was okay by you?' she'd asked her best friend.

Jess's face had shown shock but she'd quickly masked it. 'Sure, why would it worry me?'

'Um, because you two are so close and, well, you used to be in love with him. I wanted to check, you know. I don't want it to be weird between us all.'

'If he's keen to go out with you, Ricki, then who am I to stand in his way? He's my best friend. Just don't hurt him.'

'Yeah, I know. I have all our friendships to think about if it goes south, but I think it's worth the risk. He's great.'

'That he is,' Jess had said before saying she had to get back to sorting out her lesson plan for her new class.

Ricki remembered feeling like it was the start of something new, and as she studied Peter now she still felt that concern for his wellbeing and a deep-rooted love for him that came from their long association – but was that enough to sustain a relationship when she wasn't really happy?

'No, I'm fine,' he said. 'My mind is miles away though. What time's your massage? I can walk you there and then hang out at the pool till you're done.'

'Sure, let's get out of here.'

⚓

An hour and a half later, as if floating in her own bubble of relaxation, Ricki left the day spa and found the sun lounge on which Pete was sprawled, his body stretched out and his head resting on one of the big yellow cushions. His phone sat on his chest, screen down and his fingers weaved together below it, his eyes masked by dark sunglasses. He didn't stir as she sat beside him.

'Hey you. Are you asleep?'

'No. How was your massage?' he said softly.

'Lovely. I nearly nodded off at one point and I still feel really relaxed and sleepy.'

Pete nodded and returned his gaze to the pool with a slight frown. Ricki followed suit and saw four people swimming, two women and two men. One of the latter was in his early twenties, and the other looked like a hairy seal.

'Urgh,' she said quietly, 'that's enough to put me off swimming.'

'Not Jess, she's in there.'

Ricki looked again and realised the busty girl in the black bikini was Jess. 'Wow, Jess looks good. You'd never think she'd had a kid, except for the stretch marks.'

'I think that just adds character,' he said. 'I don't remember her having such big boobs, though.'

Ricki laughed. 'Oh, Peter, she's always had them, maybe they're a bit bigger since Ollie. She just doesn't get them out usually. I'm glad she's feeling relaxed enough to wear her bikini. I like seeing her that way. You know, having Ollie has changed her, I reckon.'

Peter shifted awkwardly on the sun lounge. 'You think? How?'

'She's more confident, she knows what she wants. She has Ollie and her job. When she has him in her arms it's the happiest I've ever seen her.' Would anything in life ever give her that much enjoyment? It certainly wasn't her work anymore, nor living with Peter. She did imagine children in her arms, but the ones in her mind were skinny, with tight black curls and bellies big from hunger.

'Do you think Jess will ever find a husband? Someone to be there for Ollie?' asked Peter.

'Who knows? At the moment she only has eyes for Ollie. But I hope she keeps herself open for love when it comes her way. Right now I'd say she was happy being a single mum. Jess would never find a man just for the sake of Ollie having a father,' she said.

Peter stared off into the distance and Ricki studied him silently. He was so handsome and sweet, but she found herself almost wishing the cruise was over so she could end it with him and stop feeling like she was lying to him, stringing him along.

Her building thoughts, the smell of chlorine, the loud kids and the music were all getting too much for Ricki. A dull thud had begun in her temple.

'Hey, Pete, I'm going to go back to the cabin for a shower, wash this oil off.'

'Okay, babe,' he said casually.

Her lips curled up as she walked away. She would miss him, there was no doubt about it. Everyone loved Peter.

20

Jess

JESS KNEW SHE WAS BEING WATCHED. PETER'S GAZE WAS unnerving, making her self-conscious and yet her body was alert to his attention. Even when Ricki sat beside him for a moment before leaving he'd not diverted his eyes.

Eventually it was too much and she needed to escape. She climbed out of the pool, dripping water, leaving wet footprints on the deck. She stopped to help pick up a little girl who had fallen over, and as she made her way back to her sun lounge she saw Peter stand and move towards her.

Shit.

She quickly tied one of the blue-and-white striped towels around her waist and grabbed the rest of her things. Slipping on her sandals, she headed across the deck for the stairs.

'Jess.'

She looked straight ahead as she took the stairs two at a time. She had made it down to the next midway level before his hand latched onto her arm.

'Hey, Jess, wait up.'

Expelling her held breath with force, she turned to face him. 'Hey, Peter.'

Water dripped from her hair as she clutched her shirt, sunglasses and book against her.

'We need to talk,' he said, frowning.

Jess squeezed her eyes shut as if that would make him disappear. 'There's nothing much to say,' she said.

'No, that's where you're wrong. There's lots to say. I don't understand how you can throw away years and years of friendship like this, Jess. Please. Help me to understand. Have I done something wrong?'

'I can't, Peter. And no, it's not you. It's me. You have to trust me that this is the right thing for us both.'

Jess turned to step down the next flight of stairs but he held her fast.

'Bullshit.'

He pushed her gently towards the corner of the stairs as a couple moved past.

'Bullshit,' he said again but quieter. 'Jess, this is you and me we're talking about. Us. You don't walk away from what we have.'

His eyes softened and he reached up and brushed her wet hair from her face.

'It's always been you and me against the world. Why would you want to change that?'

Tears welled in her eyes. Damn him for being so tender, so handsome and so irresistible. But that was the issue right there.

'I can't do it anymore, Pete.' It was whispered so quietly

that Jess wondered if she'd even spoken the words. She tried to leave. 'Let me go. Please, Peter.'

'I can't, Jess. Not until you tell me why. Why are you doing this?' he begged.

'I can't handle it,' she gasped as a tear spilled down. He reached for her cheek but she pulled back sharply. 'You can't do that anymore. You can't touch me,' she spat out.

His face showed his shock. 'I'm sorry,' he said, his hand dropping away from her instantly. 'I didn't realise it offended you.'

Her body crumpled, her gut twisted.

'That's the problem,' she said softly. 'It doesn't. It's the opposite. And with you proposing to Ricki I can't let it continue anymore. It's killing me.' There, she'd said it, sort of.

Bloody men. Do I really have to spell it out? she thought as Abbie's words came back to haunt her: *What have you got to lose?*

So, she jumped. 'I love you, Pete.'

The words were out before she lost her nerve. And with them came relief, a weight off her chest.

'And I love you too, Jess. Always will.' His lips curled and his face softened.

Jess wanted to grab him by the shoulders and shake him. 'Oh, Peter. You really don't get it, do you? I'm *in love* with you. As in, I want to kiss you, and not just on the cheek. The fact that it took all my effort not to jump you in the shower kind of love. Passionate. Deep.'

His eyes grew wide. 'You love me?' He leaned closer, his breath caressing her face. 'Since when?'

'Since forever, Peter. Just ask the girls. I've been in love with you since we were kids. I was always too afraid to tell you in case I lost you as a friend. That's why I slept with you at the party. But now that you're going to marry Ricki I can't be around you anymore. It's been hard enough to see you with her, and I need to cut ties and move on. I'm trying to do what's right for both of us.' She let her things drop to the floor as she raised her hands to his face. 'I will always love you, Peter. You've been there for me, protected me, supported me, and now it's time I make my own way in life.' She pushed up on her toes so she could kiss him, just long enough to feel the heat of him and enjoy the softness of his lips before she pulled away, picked up her things and quickly descended the steps without turning back.

⚓

The pounding of her heart was all she could hear on her way back to the cabin. How she managed to find her way back was a miracle, because she didn't remember the journey at all. The cabin was empty, so Jess quickly jumped in the shower, and as the hot water rushed over her body so did her tears. Lots and lots of blistering tears. Some from the release of finally telling Peter how she felt; some for the loss she knew was coming.

Twenty minutes later the door to the bathroom opened.

'Hey, it's only me,' said Abbie as she used the toilet.

'How was your massage?' said Jess as she tried to gather herself from her sob session.

'Great. I'll jump in the shower after you. Nearly time for our early dinner, then the comedy show.'

Jess froze. The show. Peter planned to propose to Ricki after it.

'And following that is the Gatsby party. Here's to shaking some tassels and feathers on the dance floor,' Abbie added as she washed up.

Jess got out, her toes and fingers like soggy prunes.

'You okay?' asked Abbie.

Jess frowned. *Am I that easy to read?* 'How can you tell?'

'I just can,' she said with a smile and sat on the edge of the bed, waiting. 'Tell me. Peter?'

Jess nodded as she held up her black sequinned dress. 'I told him how I felt. Like you said, what do I have to lose?'

Abbie clapped her hands together and smiled. 'Good on you, Jess. I'm proud of you. Now the ball is in Peter's court. If anything, you've given him something to think about and maybe it will help him understand why you need to walk away for a while.'

Jess wondered why Abbie didn't seem more concerned at how this would affect Ricki. Maybe she thought Jess was better suited to Peter? 'Yeah, I guess.'

'It'll be okay,' said Abbie, reaching out to hug Jess. 'It really will.'

As Abbie showered, Jess slipped into her dress. It had a high side split with a matching sequinned headpiece with black feathers; she teamed this with black gloves and lots of pearls – in her ears, around her neck and on her wrist.

Half an hour later and they were nearly ready.

'Hot to trot, Jess. Does this pass?' Abbie adjusted her red tassel dress. She wore a red sequinned headpiece with a white feather boa around her neck, to cover her pink scar, and matching white heels.

'Stunning, darling.'

They grinned like schoolgirls. It reminded Jess of the time they'd dressed up for their year eleven ball, feeling so beautiful and grown up, when life was easier. They laughed so much that night, drunk on their own happiness at just being together. Young and free.

'I haven't dressed up like this in ages. We used to host all the dress-up parties, what happened?'

'Well, I don't know about you, but I had a kid,' said Jess with a laugh. She leaned in towards the mirror to check the make-up Abbie had applied for her. She was going for a sexy, sultry look, more daring than Jess would usually do, but she had to admit it looked good with her costume.

A moment later Ricki banged on their door.

'You two ready?' came her muffled voice.

Suddenly Jess wasn't sure if she'd be able to walk on her heels in this state, especially knowing Peter was outside. Had he told Ricki about her declaration? Would Ricki hate her? Abbie opened the door and they stepped into the corridor.

Ricki wolf whistled and clapped at their outfits; the smile on her face immediately put Jess at ease; there was no anger there, no resentment. Ricki wore a green silk dress that fell to the floor, a green feather boa around her shoulders and red feathers in her hair. Jess didn't want to look at Peter but couldn't help herself. Heat found her cheeks, remembering the parting kiss she'd given him to leave no doubt in his mind. He was wearing black dress pants with a black long-sleeved dress shirt, a skinny white tie and white suspenders. A black fedora sat on his head, its white band blending perfectly with his outfit. The small area where they stood suddenly smelled of warm spices, leather and a signature woody character of the aftershave Peter always wore. Her eyes closed as she breathed him in, her insides turning to jelly, her mind going places it shouldn't. Damn, he smelled so good. Telling Peter hadn't changed anything, this was still really hard. And now it would be awkward.

She glanced at his face, unable to resist. But his eyes were on her dress. Getting through dinner without having to look him in the eye was the next challenge.

'Let's go.' Abbie grabbed her arm and they led the way, passing more people dressed in 1920s attire. Some people didn't dress up but that was life on the ship. You could partake in all the activities, some or none.

The Dragon Lady was their restaurant for the night, and it was busy. Black lattice illuminated by blue lights divided the room into secluded sections, some areas had cushions on the floor with low tables. They took their seats by thick heavy curtains with a small black table and chairs where the lattice around them created mystery. Satay and lemongrass wafted in the air and it mixed with the clang of cutlery and throng of voices. Staff in black uniforms wandered around the tables making sure guests were catered for.

'Check out our menu,' said Peter who sat beside Ricki and opposite Abbie. He picked up the folded origami-like shape on the table.

Jess let out a shaky sigh upon hearing Peter talk. She sat like a block of ice, too afraid to look Peter or Ricki in the eye. Jess opened her menu, glad for the distraction, and saw a mouth-watering selection of Asian flavours.

The conversation was a bit stop–start, Jess and Peter avoiding each other but still talking within the group. Over the barbe-cued chicken satay sticks with crunchy peanut sauce they were all subdued, sticking to the safe topics of sport, movies and memories from school days and the bands they'd loved.

On the few occasions Peter's eyes had lingered, Jess had tried to read them but couldn't. Was he thinking about Jess's declaration, or was he focused on making the night perfect for his proposal? Every time her mind wandered, her stomach would knot up and she would lose track of the conversation. Most of the time she would put food in her mouth and pretend she couldn't talk, with a shrug or nod of her head.

As they were leaving for The Marquee, the theatre area, she found herself studying Peter, looking for a ring box. There was nothing in his back pockets, and she wasn't game to get caught staring at the front.

Peter glanced back with an unknown look in his eye, as he watched her for a moment. Was he wondering how to be around her now? Maybe wondering how he ever missed it? Or was he merely confused? Maybe he would agree that going their separate ways was for the best, which would devastate her, but she couldn't see any other option.

'Let's sit here,' said Ricki, finding a spot on the second tier.

'Actually, I'd like to go down there,' said Jess, suddenly needing to be away from the lovebirds. She pointed to a spot closer to the stage where a few women with pink feather boas sat.

'Yes, we'll go down there and let you two have some time to yourselves,' added Abbie.

Jess tried to hide her cringe. Would he ask Ricki after the show or halfway through?

Once the engagement was announced she would have to play the excited friend. Maybe she should jump ship now? Only the thought of Ollie kept her sane. Just a few more nights and she'd see her baby boy.

'You don't have to,' said Ricki quickly. 'Please stay. This was a girls' trip, after all!'

'We'll see you at the end,' said Abbie as she ushered Jess towards the stairs leading to the lower level.

Jess would never forget the look of unease on Ricki's face, bordering on fear. Before she could wonder what it was all about, the ship rolled and she grabbed the rail to steady herself. When she glanced back, Ricki was sitting down beside Peter, facing the front. Well, it didn't matter now. Soon the most amazing guy would ask Ricki to marry him and she'd be the happiest girl on this ship.

While Jess was the saddest.

21

Ricki

'I WONDER IF WE'LL RECOGNISE ANY OF THE COMEDIANS. Probably not,' said Ricki as she settled in next to Peter. She'd have words with Abbie later for leaving her side. Part of her wondered if Abbie considered this her punishment, to endure alone time with Peter knowing what she'd done. She was probably right. Ricki had started trying to figure out a way to tell Peter that she wanted to break up. She didn't want to mention Miguel – no need to hurt Peter any more than she had to – but she was worried he might not let her go easily, that if she told him she wanted to go overseas he would support her and try to maintain a long-distance relationship.

'We might get a surprise,' said Peter.

His reply was so delayed and she'd been so busy in her own mind that she was momentarily lost.

Peter stood up. 'I'll go get drinks. Wine?' he asked.

'Great idea,' she said with relief. He walked away, past the beautiful mosaic wall beside them that seemed to spread up across the wall like an old oak tree. The room was filling up fast, about half the people in Gatsby costumes, men in suits, ladies in sequins or tassels with lots of feathers and pearl necklaces. Those who didn't dress up were still in good clothes but sat back watching the loose feathers float from costumes.

When he returned, the lights had dimmed and a short dark lady emerged onto the stage with a hand-held microphone. Red plush curtains swayed behind her, the only indication they were at sea. She introduced the show and the comedians to come, then smoothly transitioned into jokes about old ladies, taking the mickey out of herself. The next act had a guitar and sang funny songs he'd made up. Each act was as hilarious as the one before but they covered different ground, one man did Tom Cruise impersonations and overall it was a brilliant show.

The hour passed in rapid time, Ricki getting lost in the laughter and glad for the distraction. Even Peter seemed to relax into his old self.

As they left The Marquee, Peter took her hand and led her up to the top deck, suggesting they check out the night sky. Outside, she shivered in the cool air, a change from the heat of the day, and headed to the rail. The moon was full and bright, throwing light over the ship and the white caps of the ocean. And its image glittered across the water like liquid silver.

Ricki looked up at the stars and for a moment felt like Rose on the *Titanic* – only, without the sinking ship. She turned to tell Peter and found him standing behind her, his arm outstretched with a red box in his hand. He was staring at the open box, his forehead creased. Then he closed the box and folded it into his hand out of sight.

'Peter?'

He glanced up at her, his expression unreadable.

'Was that what I think it was?' Ricki pointed to his hand. 'Are you going to propose?' she said suddenly. Her stomach flipped as realisation sank in.

'I was,' he said softly, tucking the box into his pocket.

Ricki felt as if all the blood had suddenly rushed out her big toe. 'Oh, no, Peter.' How could this be happening? 'No, no, no. I'm so sorry. I can't marry you.' Her hand covered her mouth as she waited for his reaction.

He smiled at her suddenly. Not the reaction she was expecting. Now she was really confused.

'That's okay. I just realised I don't want to marry you either. No offence,' he added.

Ricki tilted her head as she frowned. 'Oh. Really?'

He nodded. 'So, you don't want to marry me?'

All of a sudden the time felt right, and Ricki's hands clasped around his. 'Peter, I've realised I'm not really happy. I don't want to get married, I don't want to be at that stage of my life yet. I want to go overseas and experience life. And . . .' She paused, flinching. 'I'm sorry, but I don't think I can do that with you. I don't want to hurt you, but I don't want to be in a relationship anymore. I want us to break up, go our separate ways and hopefully remain friends.'

She knew she was asking a lot, to remain friends. When did that ever really happen? But she had to say it because it was true. They'd been good friends before, and he was a part of their group. She hoped one day it wouldn't be awkward and their friendship would remain, but she didn't have a crystal ball.

'Okay.' Peter blinked, let go of her hand and gripped the railing.

'Okay? Are you sure?' she said, her heart racing and her skin thankful for the cool night air.

Peter turned to her, his eyes sparkling with stars from the sky. 'How long have you been unhappy?'

His voice was calm, soft, with maybe even a hint of concern.

She shrugged. 'I don't know. I think it happened without me realising it. I guess it was not long after moving in, when things became a routine.' She cringed at her own hurtful words.

His knuckles went white and she felt bad for being so honest.

'I'm sorry I didn't realise you felt that way. I guess I've been a bit blind myself.' He sighed heavily. 'To a lot of things, really.'

'It's not your fault, Peter. Don't blame yourself. This is all me.' *More than you know.* 'I do love you and care for you, but I think we want different things.'

He nodded, his face turned towards the moon. Ricki didn't know what else to say, but kept blathering to fill the awkward silence.

'I think you want marriage and children. I don't, not yet at least. I feel really bad, Peter, for letting it get to this point.' Knocking him back when he was about to propose, it was worse than worse. But it was done now. 'I don't want to hurt you. I'm sorry.'

He glanced at her now, and in his reaction she didn't see anger, hatred or disappointment; instead he was just an eerie quiet, blankness, plain and unreadable. In a way, it was much more frightening. Did he truly understand what was happening? Was he suppressing it?

'I don't want you to be unhappy, Ricki.' Another long pause. 'So, I guess this is it for us?'

'I guess it is.'

They turned and faced each other, and Ricki held out her hand to him. 'I won't ever regret being with you, Peter. I still care deeply for you, always will, but I think I *will* regret not following my heart and my dreams.'

He reached for it and gripped tightly. 'I think we all deserve to be happy.' Then his lips twitched to the side and he let go, turned and walked away.

Ricki watched him leave right up until he disappeared through the door, then she let out a big sigh that turned into a sob. Too many emotions. She should be happy, but she was still in turmoil and it would take a while to figure out the next step. Life as she knew it had changed forever.

She just hoped it was for the better, and that this wasn't the biggest mistake of her life.

22

Jess

'DAMN FUNNY, SHE WAS,' SAID ABBIE AS THEY MADE THEIR way to the Blue Room where sexy, warm velvet textures and music-themed decor emphasised its Gatsby-clad occupants.

'It was fantastic. That guy looked so much like Tom Cruise, that smile and the glasses did it. What a crack-up.' And for that whole hour she forgot about Peter. With the gags coming thick and fast she didn't have time. It was a sweet release.

'This is pretty cool.' Abbie waved her arm out where people in flapper dresses and vintage suits mixed while a live band played jazz nearby.

Jess smiled. 'Look they even have special Gatsby cocktails.'

Grabbing the drinks list, they made their selection and Abbie gave their order to the barman.

Jess looked out the nearby window at the moon shimmering across the water. The trumpet playing in the background reverberated along her spine, sending tingles across her skin. So romantic. The perfect night for a proposal. Were they outside?

In The Marquee still, on their way to the costume party – or were they back at their cabin? Her chest grew tight.

'Stop that.'

The command startled her. Abbie shook her head. 'No thinking about it. And don't try to deny it; I can see that worry line on your forehead working overtime. Forget about it, you're with me now and we're going to have a fab time. Don't let what *might* be happening control your night.'

Her words were strong and Jess knew her friend was right.

Soon their cocktails – 'Between the Sheets' for Abbie, 'Bee's Knees' for Jess – were finished, and Jess was starting to relax.

'Right, let's ditch our shoes back in the room and go dancing,' said Abbie. 'I want to dance all night long and have more Between the Sheets,' she added with a laugh.

They were just about to leave when a tall man with dark eyes only for Abbie approached them. He wore a black buttoned shirt open at the neck revealing tanned skin, and a black fedora with a white band. *Hmm*, thought Jess as she watched Abbie's reaction. *This could be interesting.*

'Hi, Abbie.'

'Hiya, Alex. This is my friend Jess. Jess, this is Alex.'

Jess shook his hand with a smile and a quick sideways glance at Abbie. *Where'd you find this one?* her eyes said, but Abbie did a convincing impression of not seeing.

'Sorry, we were about to head off,' Abbie said to Alex.

'You stay,' said Jess quickly. 'I'll take your shoes down.' Jess held out her hand, only just refraining from giving her a secret wink.

Abbie glanced between Jess and Alex before smiling and nodding. 'Yeah, okay. Thanks, Jess.' She sat back down, slipped

off her shoes and handed them over before gesturing to Alex
to take Jess's place.

'I'll be right back. Then we can hit the dance floor. You'll
have to join us, Alex.'

'Sounds like a good plan.' His smile was rich and warm.

Jess took her time heading down to the cabin, thinking
Abbie wouldn't be worried about how long she spent with a
sexy man beside her. In her happy daze she walked down the
narrow door-lined corridor and didn't recognise the figure
leaning against the door until it was too late to turn around.

There was nowhere to hide, no open door to duck through.
With all the effort she could muster, Jess smiled.

'Hi Peter, how's it all going?' she said, trying to remain
calm. 'Where's Ricki?'

'I don't know,' said Peter.

Jess stopped short of him as she tried to figure out his reply.
But the gap she left was soon closed as Peter launched towards
her and reached for her arms, causing Abbie's shoes to swing
in her hands.

'Oh, Jess, I couldn't do it,' he said.

'What?'

Peter let her go and paced in a tight circle, pulling his fedora
off his head and ruffling up his hair.

What couldn't he do? Propose? Could she even dare to hope?

'Peter?' she squeaked, finding it hard to breathe, let alone talk.

Finally he paused, those eyes resting on her face. 'Ricki said
no. But I hadn't even proposed. I was standing there, box in
my hand when I stopped and thought about it.' Peter held his
hand out, re-enacting the moment.

Ricki said no. It was all Jess had heard, but she tried to focus on whatever else Peter was trying to say.

'I thought . . . in that moment . . . that I could lose you. And I faltered. I thought if I had to choose between you and Ricki—' He paused, searching her face. 'But before I'd even finished my own question my brain was shouting you. It's always you, Jess. I can't see a future without you in it. I don't want anyone else if I can't have you in my life.' He sighed, and then managed a smile. 'It was so simple. All these years I've been fighting my feelings for you to save our friendship. If I'd known you felt the same way . . .'

Jess blinked, staring at the face that had always fascinated her; from the sandy hair that seemed to have a life of its own to those eyes that had always been her safety, her home.

Peter dropped his hat and cupped her face in his hands, his thumbs gentle on her cheeks.

'In that moment I knew I didn't want to marry Ricki, and I closed the box.'

It was hard to focus on his words when she was hypnotised by his moving lips and the soft movements of his thumbs against her skin, but she knew it was important. One of the most important moments of her life.

'So, you're not engaged? Not getting married?' She needed to hear it again. Just to be sure.

'No, Jess. I'm not engaged. I'm not even in a relationship anymore. But there *is* one thing I haven't been able to stop thinking about, one thing I need more of.'

With that final statement he leaned in and kissed her. Not a peck on the cheek, not a quick brush on the forehead. No, this was a heated kiss on the lips.

After what seemed like minutes he paused, his breath caressing her face. 'It seems so unfair that we've kissed and I can't remember it. It bugs me and it's time to fix it.'

Abbie's shoes fell from Jess's fingers and her hands went to his waist as he deepened the kiss. Just like that night they spent together, which he didn't remember, the kiss was hot, sexy and electrifying. But this was much, much better. It was clearer. Her memory had faded over time and this renewal eclipsed everything.

Her hands snaked around his back as he pressed against her, his tongue searching. Jess groaned just as Peter's name was yelled.

Only, she hadn't yelled it, but the voice was familiar. Pulling away, she tried to clear the passion that had fogged her mind.

Peter turned and Jess looked over his shoulder to see Ricki standing there with her mouth open.

'Peter? Jess? What the hell!' She turned on her heel and ran off down the corridor.

Peter pulled away and swore.

Jess leaned back against the wall and put her hand over her eyes. 'I better go after her.'

'Me too. She shouldn't have to see that.' Peter reached out and touched her arm. 'Are you okay?'

Jess pulled her hand down, saw his face and smiled regardless of the situation. 'I'll be okay. We better go and find her. She's going to hate us. I'll get Abbie, too.'

Peter didn't let her go just yet. 'Can we talk about this later? About all of it?'

Jess could only nod. Inside she was trying not to get her hopes up. She didn't want to be a rebound fling or a passing phase. She was still scared of getting hurt, and she had Ollie to think of.

Jess watched Peter leave and then quickly dug out her room key card. She threw Abbie's shoes on the floor and changed into her sandals, then hurried back out.

As Jess rushed towards Abbie she felt bad for interrupting what was clearly an in-depth conversation, but as soon as Abbie spotted her she stood up.

'What's wrong?'

'Long story, but we need to find Ricki,' she said, shooting an apologetic smile to Alex.

Abbie caught on quickly and turned to Alex. 'I'm so sorry. I have to go. It's been nice chatting to you again.'

'Anything I can help with?' he offered.

'No,' said Jess quickly. 'Thank you anyway.'

'Thanks, Alex. Bye,' said Abbie as Jess took her hand and pulled her from the bar.

'What's wrong?' said Abbie quickly.

'Ricki saw Peter kissing me and ran off,' said Jess as heat filled her cheeks. How could Abbie not think Jess was horrible after what she had done?

Abbie stopped suddenly. 'Oh. My. God. How did that happen?'

'Long story short: he didn't propose, said he chose me instead, we kissed, Ricki saw, now Ricki's angry.'

To Jess's astonishment, and relief, Abbie looked almost excited that she'd kissed Peter.

'I thought you'd be angry?'

'Bollocks. You two are meant to be together; who am I to stand in the way of that? But we should definitely see how Ricki is.' Then Abbie turned and strolled towards the front of the ship. 'Where are we looking? The dance floor?' she asked hopefully as Jess caught her up.

'I don't know. She could have gone anywhere.'

'So, was it everything you expected?' asked Abbie, her bare feet moving along the carpet with a childlike care factor.

'Was what?' said Jess. Her mind was in total chaos, emotions mashing together. She was angry with herself, for not being able to think clearly and for hurting Ricki. Yet she could hardly believe what had happened and was beyond excited. Her hopes were raised and yet caution sirens were blaring.

'The kiss, Jess.'

Her lips spread automatically into a big grin despite her mixed emotions. 'Oh yes, it was amazing.' That was her happy moment. 'But I can't enjoy it, I feel bad.'

'You're too self-sacrificing, Jess.'

'Not right now, I'm not.'

⚓

After an hour of searching the length and breadth of the entire ship, they ran into Peter in the atrium.

'Any luck?' asked Jess. Her eyes were eating Peter up, especially when he gave her a heated smile that was for her alone.

'It's bloody impossible. We'll have to wait until she comes back to the cabin,' he said. 'She has to sleep at some point, right?' He sounded hopeful, but his heavy sigh and the drop of his shoulders said otherwise. 'This isn't how I thought anything would turn out,' he said rubbing his face.

Abbie gripped his shoulder. 'She's a big girl, Peter. Don't be too hard on yourself. Who wants to go dancing? The jazz band is fabulous.'

Jess shook her head, turning to stare at Abbie. '*Dancing?*

No, I'm going to bed. I don't feel up to it.' She glanced at Peter. So much needed to be said, but now wasn't the time.

He smiled weakly. 'I'm sorry to put you in this position, Jess. I don't know where my head was.'

But the spark she saw in his eyes said they both knew exactly where his mind had been, and suddenly the heat in the air intensified and her heart raced.

She hugged Abbie goodbye. 'Don't worry about disturbing me when you get in, okay? Make the most of the Gatsby party.' None of this was Abbie's fault and she deserved a little fun. 'Go find Alex,' she said with a wink. 'But remember we dock in Albany tomorrow!' The thought of reaching Albany, the place where the girls' friendship really began, made her pause. Could they sort this out tomorrow? Could they move past it?

'Ha. Maybe I will. Yes, I'll try to behave.'

Jess suddenly felt adrift. Normally she would hug Peter too, but now it suddenly seemed wrong, especially because it meant so much more to both of them. Instead, she gave him a little wave.

'I'll see you tomorrow. Good luck.'

'Thanks, Jess. Yes, we'll talk tomorrow.'

All she wanted was his reassuring arms wrapped around her. His breath on her neck. The feel of his hard body against hers. It felt like it was within her grasp but one step either way and it could be so easily missed. She had waited this long; she could wait another night, another week or even another month.

For now she was going to fall asleep remembering that kiss, and dreaming that it might happen again.

23

Abbie

'OH, WHAT A NIGHT! SO, YOU TOOK MY ADVICE DID YOU, Peter Pan?' said Abbie as Jess left and the two of them stood in the middle of the huge atrium. A staircase circled half the room, edged with gold and thick royal blue drop curtains, up to the next level, and a white and gold pole rose up the centre of the three open floors, making it seem like they were in a luxurious hotel, not on a ship. The only other people here were two young women trying to get signals on their phones. Together they headed up the stairs towards the Blue Room, towards the swing and blue notes of jazz.

Peter cocked his head to the side and studied her.

'As a matter of fact I did think about what you said. I wondered why I was really proposing, and the only reason I had was it was the next step. Marriage, kids.' He shrugged.

'See, you're a duty-bound man, Peter. You do what is expected *but* do you do what your heart wants?'

His lips curled into a grin. 'I believe I just did.' Then the smile faded. 'It all turned to shit, though.' He forced a small laugh. 'It turns out Ricki didn't want to marry me anyway, or even be with me at all. Don't know what I'll do with that ring . . . But at the same time, kissing Jess was like nothing I've ever experienced before. It was deep, layers and layers deeper . . .' His words trailed away.

Abbie grinned and gripped his shoulder. 'I understand. You two are soul mates, I reckon. Some people live a whole life and never find that one person.'

'So, Jim wasn't it?'

'Hell, no. In fact, I'm glad he's gone and I'm not wasting my life with someone who wasn't the one for me, you know what I mean? Screw Jim. From this day forth I will not think of him again, and I'm going to enjoy life to the fullest.' She wrapped her arms around Peter. 'So, what do you say, Peter Pan, will you dance with me and help me celebrate this life? Besides, I think you have more chance of finding Ricki on the dance floor than anywhere else on this ship. And I need someone to party with.' She pouted, and she saw the smile in his eyes before it even reached his lips.

'All right, you twisted my arm. Besides, I owe you one. You saved me.'

'Damn right I did. Let's go, my boy.' Abbie led him through the shimmering bodies that held champagne in long glass flutes to the dance floor by the band where feather boas were twirled and tassels shaken. The room had filled since they'd been searching for Ricki and she glanced around, wondering if Alex was still here. Peter was watching the trumpet player with awe and then he took her hand and started to copy the people beside them doing the Charleston. Abbie was in fits of giggles in no time trying to keep up with him.

Abbie didn't see Alex again. Instead, when they were beat, they staggered back to the cabins. When Peter saw that Ricki was asleep inside their cabin, he asked to sleep on Abbie and Jess's floor for the few remaining hours until the sun came up.

'I don't think she'd be happy to see me right now. Best wait for the morning,' he said as they entered Abbie's room.

'Shh,' said Abbie loudly as she threw Peter a pillow from her bed. 'We'll sort it out tomorrow. Somehow.'

⚓

Abbie woke to movement. Through sleep-heavy eyes she saw that Jess was up and dressed, her pyjamas replaced by a cute knee-length white dress. Her friend stood next to Peter, who was snoring softly, sprawled out on the floor. Jess bent and brushed his hair from his face and smiled.

'Morning,' Abbie croaked.

Jess looked up, not at all fazed by being caught ogling Peter. 'Hey, how are you?'

'Shattered. I can't feel my feet. That'll teach me to dance barefoot for hours.'

'It's early, I'm going for breakfast. Then I might wander off the ship to see Albany while I wait for you lot. Text me and I'll let you know where I am.'

'Okay.' Abbie's eyes had shut before the door.

The next time she woke up something had hit her. Prying her eyes open she saw Peter standing over her, a pillow in his hands. 'Wakey, wakey, Abs. Hungry yet?'

He was still in last night's clothes minus the hat and tie, and his hair was fanned out on one side where he'd been sleeping.

'Why are you so perky?' she groaned. 'You slept on the floor, remember?'

'And I bloody feel like it. Stiff joints, but it could be from the dancing too,' he said with a smirk as he headed for the door. 'But I need a shower and food, and I'm guessing so do you. It's nearly eight-thirty and we're already docked in Albany, let's not waste a minute.'

⚓

Outside the cabin window was a round ocean inlet edged by green hilly ranges, some covered with rocks. Further out from the circular harbour, islands rose out of the dark blue sea, half rock, half green with vegetation and totally wild and natural. Untouched and perfect in the morning light. The whole magical scene stirred an excitement in Abbie to get out and explore.

After a shower that should have been quick but for her aching muscles, she threw on a soft blue maxi dress, no longer worried about covering her new scar, and then slipped on her thongs and left the cabin just as Peter was about to bang on her door.

'Good timing,' he said with a smirk. He was wearing denim shorts and a plain T-shirt, his standard uniform for non-work days.

'Where's Ricki?' she asked, looking towards the cabin next door.

His smirk faded as he replied. 'I don't know, but I want to get this sorted sooner rather than later.'

'Don't worry too much, Peter. She's a big girl, she probably needed some space. When we booked this trip the plan was to be at the ANZAC Centre at eleven. I'm sure she'll be there at our reunion spot. It's what this whole trip's about.'

'I hope you're right.'

They had some light food and juice before heading outside, off the walkway and onto the dock in Albany. Past the port area Mount Clarence rose up before them, a morning mist clinging to its green peak. It was a bright day, but a cool breeze softened the summer heat a little, and there was a buzz around as more people left the ship to explore the small country city. They were all guided to buses that ferried them uphill to York Street, the main strip of Albany. It was a very hilly place, green and rolling, which made it feel cosy and peaceful, so different from the bustle of Perth.

'Albany is known as the city of roundabouts, for those who are visiting for the first time,' said the heavy-set bus driver. 'And we are about to do a Yorkie,' he said loudly, then chuckled to himself. 'Which is cruising up and down York Street.'

The driver's booming voice continued, providing a running commentary on the landmarks and noteworthy spots. The street was wide with heritage green lamps that hung over the road like heavy flower heads and wide footpaths on either side made it perfect for walking tourists and shoppers. Massive pine trees grew next to old churches and you could see the town's age in the older-style buildings that lined the road. Abbie tried to pay polite attention but was preoccupied with her signal-restored phone and quickly messaged Jess, just as her phone vibrated with a new text: a reminder of her medical appointment, date and time. She groaned, turning the screen away so Peter couldn't see it. *Like I need a reminder.*

The bus dropped them off in a large public area by the local library.

'Come on, this way,' Abbie said to Peter. 'Jess said she's having a coffee near the old church.' She followed Jess's directions to find her friend looking up at the church bell tower.

'We found you,' said Abbie.

'Hey, guys. Did you know that the stone construction for the Church of St John the Evangelist started in 1840 and it was the first Western Australian church to be consecrated, in 1848?'

'What does that even mean?' said Peter, who gave Jess a warm smile.

Upon seeing Peter, Jess's face glowed and Abbie felt the sizzle in the air.

'Did you swallow the information pamphlet?' asked Abbie.

'Maybe,' said Jess with a grin. 'I'm glad you two could make it. It's not as much fun without having someone to share these things with. I like this place so much. It has such a lovely feel. I'm glad we came back.'

'It's my first time here. I'm looking forward to the beaches,' said Peter, looking around. 'Have you seen Ricki?' he added, turning back to Jess, his smile fading a little.

'No, but Abbie could text her now, at least see if she's okay?' Jess turned to Abbie, her face pleading.

'Oh, cut the puppy-dog face, I'll send her a text. But first, where can I get good coffee?' she asked eyeing off Jess's cup.

Jess pointed her across the street and Abbie set off, taking with her Peter's order and her own determination to give the two time to talk.

When she got back they were sitting quietly under the shade of a large tree next to the church.

'Here it is,' she said loudly before they saw her.

'Thanks, Abbie.' Peter stood up and took his coffee. 'I'm going to get something more to eat. Jess said there are some great cafes down the road. I'll be back shortly. Just text me if you decide to wander. Jess mentioned visiting the museum and going on the replica brig *Amity*.'

'Sure. I don't mind getting on another ship,' she laughed.

Abbie glanced from Peter's retreating back to Jess as she sat down where he'd been. 'Is everything okay?' she said.

Jess shrugged, a melancholy smile straining as she sighed. 'I don't know.'

'Did you talk?'

'Yeah, he told me about you guys dancing up a storm. We skirted around the big issue for a while. He asked if the kiss was okay.' Jess's smile was genuine this time. 'That's probably the only thing I'm sure of at the moment,' she said.

'What do you mean? I thought I'd be catching you two making out again.' Abbie adjusted her long dress and stretched out her lower legs in the sun. She didn't have to give a flying duck about cancer now, not when it was already invading her body. *Have some more*, she felt like screaming, taunting the sun to kiss her skin with its power. *I dare you*. What's a melanoma to add to the mix?

Jess laughed. 'Oh, if only it was that easy. Everything is too new and strange, I think. And then there's Ricki. I don't want to hurt her. And Peter, I told him I don't want to be a rebound. My heart couldn't handle it if this all went pear-shaped. I told him I wanted to go slow, very slow.'

'How did he take that?'

'I'm not sure, he was quiet and then you came back.'

'Hmm, sorry.'

'Don't be. It'll be good for him to have time to think this through. I'm worried that it might be a passing phase for him. I tell him I'm in love with him and suddenly he has feelings for me. What if they suddenly disappear too?'

'Honey, I think he's always had feelings. It's just that he's *suddenly* realised it. Don't be too hard on him. I'm sure he knows how he's feeling and that he loves you deeply.'

'But what if he's confused over friendship love and family love, and it's not the passionate sort that I feel?'

Abbie turned to Jess. 'What is it, Jess? Why are you fighting this?' Jess was trying to say something, Abbie could feel it. Jess was building so many walls between the things she wanted most.

'You have to understand, I thought this day would never happen.' Jess sighed so heavily that it was almost a grunt. 'I never thought that Peter could ever be mine, that he didn't feel the same as I did. I thought he chose Ricki over me, even after we slept together. And then, he and Ricki seemed so happy, you know – I never thought they would split up.'

Abbie threw up a hand. 'Back the truck up. Did you say you *slept with him*?' Abbie's jaw dropped and she was thankful she hadn't gone for a sip of coffee or else it would be sprayed all over both of them. Had Peter and Jess cheated on Ricki?

'Don't look at me like that! It was before they got together. It was at a party a while back . . . Do you remember when Jim had just got that tattoo under his arm?'

Abbie looked at Jess while her mind caught up. 'The night they had their first kiss? When I caught them snogging by the barbie.' Abbie remembered it. It had been a great night. Jim had been fun, attentive. His new tattoo had been a surprise, something he'd always wanted to do, apparently. Only now did Abbie wonder if that hadn't been the first sign of change. The Julie change.

'Yes, that's the one. Anyway, seeing that made me insanely jealous. I drank a lot that night, which gave me a bit of bravado so I followed him to his room and seduced him.'

'Go on. Details, please,' said Abbie inching closer.

'I remember walking in there and shutting the door. He was standing by his wardrobe without his shirt. He was a little drunk, but all I really remember is just wanting to touch him. Next thing I knew, my hands were all over him. Hot kisses, more clothes coming off.'

Abbie smiled because her friend was smiling at the memory and it was contagious. 'And?'

'And afterwards he kinda freaked out over the whole thing. I grabbed my clothes and went home.'

'Well, that explains why you disappeared and why he hit the drink pretty hard. He seemed so angry later that night. I get it now.'

Jess nodded. 'He said he was angry at himself for letting it happen, that he never wanted to cross that line and ruin our friendship. Little did he know it's exactly what I wanted. Anyway, I was waiting for him to call, for us to talk about it, but it never happened. I assumed he regretted it and didn't want to talk about it ever again. Next thing, he's off on a date with Ricki. He's never mentioned it since, so I figured he erased it from his mind like a big fat mistake. Or so I thought, I only just found out he didn't even remember it.'

'He didn't remember *having sex with you*?'

'Yeah, he wrote himself off that badly he can't remember much of that night, including what we got up to.' Jess shrugged.

Abbie, through years of friendship, knew there was heavy pain in that simple shrug. 'Oh, Jess. That's so sad. Why didn't you tell me this sooner? You should have fought for your man.' Abbie sighed. 'But that's not your MO, is it? You would have seen them happily dating and taken a step back. You would have thought yourself not good enough.'

Jess's cheeks reddened. 'I thought if he wanted me he would have come for me. I gave him that time to decide, and I figured when he didn't say anything it was his way of trying to keep things the way they were.'

'So, what's holding you back now?'

Her eyebrows shot up. 'I'm scared. It's not just me I have to worry about. It's Ollie. What if it doesn't work and he leaves?'

Abbie smiled and said sadly, 'That's relationships.' And didn't Abbie know it.

But Jess was staring into space. Something heavier was weighing on her mind, behind her tightly closed doors. Jess blinked, eyes suddenly glassy as a tear rolled down her cheek.

'Jess, oh honey.' Abbie shuffled closer and put her arm around her friend. 'Tell me, please, I hate seeing you try to keep so much to yourself. You have friends so you don't have to carry it all by yourself.'

'It's Ollie's father,' she sobbed, flicking her tears from her face.

'What about him?'

Jess held her breath for what seemed like ages. And then it gushed out with rushed words. 'It's Peter.' Her green eyes were glistening but solid in the truth.

Abbie felt as if Jess's words had slapped her. 'What? Really?' She was momentarily speechless, as shock and disappointment at being kept in the dark battled in her mind. Eventually she managed to look back at Jess. 'How *the hell* did you keep that a secret? And *why* would you?'

'Well, remember that I didn't find out until I was nearly six months. I was still getting my period, I just thought I was getting fat. It wasn't until you made me go see a doctor about my belly in case I had a tumour or cyst growing that I found out, and remember the shock?'

Abbie nodded. 'Yeah, that was some surprise.' Especially considering they made Jess do a home kit early on and it came back negative.

'So, it was a huge surprise when I eventually found out, and by then he was happily with Ricki.'

'Yes, but he's the father. He wants kids. He would have dropped everything to be with . . .' Abbie's voice faded away as she finally understood. 'You didn't want him like that, did you?'

Jess's hair brushed her shoulders as she shook her head. 'No, I know Peter. He would have sacrificed his relationship with Ricki to support me and Ollie. He would have given up his happiness with her for us. I didn't want his duty of care, Abbie, I wanted his love. It would have killed me having him so involved in my son's life, our life, out of duty.'

'Yes, *and love*. It might have grown into love. Did you ever think of that?'

'And have Ricki hate me in the process? What if Ricki *was* his match, his perfect one? I didn't want to mess with that, I love them both. I know it probably sounds really selfish, but I did what I thought was right for me at the time. I needed all my friends around me then.'

Abbie sighed. 'No, you put your friends first instead of yourself. I don't know anyone more selfless than you, Jess. I'd never tag you as selfish. No one who really knows you would.'

'But I was.'

'You were protecting your heart, and Peter's and Ricki's at the same time. You were trying to let Peter have his happiness. You love him that much you put his life first.'

Jess stared down at her coffee cup as people walked along the sloped street nearby. 'He gave me Ollie. I knew I could be happy with that. This way we all got to be happy.'

'So, you created a one-night stand. And you went through everything by yourself. Ricki and Peter were at Ollie's birth, for God's sake. How did you cope?'

'Ollie,' Jess replied simply. 'Truly, I'm so in love with him. He's my world.'

'Would you have ever told Pete? Will you now?'

Jess gave out a strangled laugh. 'That's the funny bit – he'll probably hate me for keeping this from him. We can't start something with a secret like that hanging over our heads. That's why I'm keeping him at arm's length. I know I have to tell him but I'm scared it may kill whatever respect he had for me.'

'I see your dilemma.' Abbie took a sip of her coolish coffee and swallowed it down like it was a lump of clay.

Affairs, secret babies, cancer. Lots of secrets between friends. Only, Abbie didn't plan to share her secret. Not yet. Not unless she had to.

Some things were better left unsaid.

24

Ricki

RICKI LOOKED OUT OVER ONE OF THE MOST SPECTACULAR harbours she had ever seen, King George Sound, from the top of Mount Clarence; the brilliant blue of the ocean was edged with cliffs, and a scattering of islands rose covered in granite rock and vegetation. The man on the bus announced that whales and dolphins could be seen here all the time in season, but all she saw today was a large industrial ship on its way out past the islands into deeper water.

Ricki sucked in a breath that was earthy, damp, salty and carried the scent of the surrounding bush as she walked to the edge of Convoy Lookout. As she let it out she wondered what the hell she was doing. Not even the crisp sea air could clear her mind or give her some clarity, nor could the ships, boats and birdlife distract her thoughts.

Why was she even feeling so hurt and hard done by? Sure, it was a shock to see Peter and Jess going for it, but Ricki had done much more than that. She had no right to be upset, and yet she was.

She couldn't cut her feelings for Peter off like that. Yes, they had ended it, but it still hurt. Her brain was going around and around in circles, pain and guilt vying for precedence.

She'd been kind of relieved and yet disappointed when Peter didn't come back to the cabin last night. If they'd come looking for her she hadn't seen them as she wandered the ship in a daze. Getting off the ship early this morning had been a godsend, and after walking around Albany she had headed up to the highest hill; there were a few, but Mount Clarence was special, and the old fort at the top still amazed her even being her second visit. It also overlooked the harbour and Vancouver Peninsula where the *Pacific Eden* had come in to dock.

She wanted to wait for the girls to visit the new ANZAC Centre – after all, that's what this whole trip had been planned around – so instead she strolled around the old guns and through the bunkers and took in the views from on top of the mountain. The thought of facing Jess made her feel uneasy. It helped put her thoughts into perspective to imagine the ships in port, ready to fight in World War I. Thousands off to their deaths, and here she was worried about one kiss. There was no comparison.

She spent a lot of time gazing out to sea as if it held the meaning of life. Or at least some answers. Humans were strange beings, full of jumbled-up emotions. Was she really in a position to criticise Peter or Jess?

Jess.

Growing up, she'd always bored them to death with 'Peter this' and 'Peter that'. It made sense when they found her journal containing confessions about Peter. She was a girl in love, but they all thought it had passed long ago. And Jess had given Ricki her blessing to date him. Jess never made a move on him. So, why now?

'Not planning on jumping, are you?'

Ricki didn't have to turn to know Abbie was standing there with her hands on her hips. She could even imagine the raised eyebrows and frank expression on her face.

'About time you showed up,' she said plainly. When she did turn she saw Abbie wasn't alone; Jess stood beside her looking remorseful with her hands clasped in front of her white dress.

'Ricki.' Jess broke the silence. 'Please, I need to explain. What you saw shouldn't have happened,' she gushed.

'Yep, it shouldn't have. Peter was going to propose to me, next thing he's kissing you? How does that happen?' With Abbie standing by, Ricki knew she couldn't let her hurt take hold, not when Abbie knew her secret. But Ricki couldn't stop the questions from coming out.

'It was the first time we've kissed, I promise,' said Jess. 'Well, besides the night we slept together, before you were even dating, and a really awkward bad first kiss when we were kids.'

Jess was rambling, her hands waving about like a magical whomping willow tree, but Ricki's mind was on replay suddenly, retracing Jess's words. 'Did you just say you've slept with Peter?' It was almost too crazy to believe.

Jess nodded, her green eyes wide and almost frightened.

'Oh my God. Why has no one ever mentioned this! I can't believe Peter didn't even tell me. What else has he kept from me?' She felt her agitation build, despite her best efforts to stay rational.

'It was before you two got together, Ricki,' Jess stressed.

Ricki opened her mouth to speak but was cut off by Abbie.

'Oh, for God's sake, give it a rest, Ricki. You cheated on Peter. Don't even think about lecturing Jess. Their kiss might have been a shock, but it was above board.'

Ricki's mouth dropped open as Abbie sat down on a nearby seat as if suddenly she was exhausted from her outburst. Ricki wanted to be angry at Abbie too, but deep down she knew she deserved it. Abbie was being truthful, as usual. Her timing just sucked, as usual.

'You cheated on Peter? When? With who?' Jess covered her mouth. 'How could you?' Her voice was high and indignant. A moment later she asked, 'Is that why you broke up?'

An elderly couple strolled past hand in hand and Ricki waited until there was some space between them before speaking. 'It only just happened. That's why I broke it off. And I didn't sleep with anyone, I just . . .'

'*You* broke it off?' Jess's head dropped, her hair falling forward like a wall hiding half her face.

Ricki could see the pain and knew that her confession would be twice as painful for Peter.

'But Ricki? Peter is—'

'Freaking perfect, I know. I know, okay!' she screamed. 'I know.' The elderly couple glanced back.

Jess straightened her shoulders. 'He didn't deserve that,' she said.

'Oh, for shit's sake.' Abbie stood up and headed towards the ANZAC Centre across the lawn. 'I can't handle this anymore. You two bickering over nothing. It's not like either of you is an angel. First World problems, people. First-freaking-World problems.'

And with that she stomped off and didn't look back.

Ricki turned back to Jess. 'What was all that about?'

'Stuffed if I know.' Jess turned on her heel and followed Abbie.

Jess's words echoed in Ricki's head like relentless waves crashing against the shore in a storm.

How could you?

How could you?

Ricki had asked herself the same thing over and over, and as she watched her two closest friends walk away from her, the question rang in her head again.

How could she?

25

Jess

JESS STORMED OFF TOWARDS ONE OF THE BUSES THAT WAS taking the ship's passengers around Albany. She didn't care where this one was headed, she needed to be anywhere but here. She couldn't visit the ANZAC Centre feeling like she did, it deserved the time and respect to be seen properly. Right now she was too upset and confused. Lashing out at Ricki had made her feel better for a moment, but now the weight of her own actions and secrets was bearing down on her.

The driver took them down the hill and around Mount Clarence along the water's edge to Middleton Beach. As she climbed off the bus she gulped in the air full of salty sea spray and headed out across the soft expanse of lawn past rows of lush green pine trees tall and majestic like Christmas trees waiting to be adorned with ornaments. Giggling kids ran past her holding the long-fallen pine fingers trying to whip each other with them. The white sand beckoned, such a vibrant white that demanded to be experienced. She took off her shoes and sank her toes into it, finally stopping to catch her breath and thoughts.

She closed her eyes, even though the view before her was magnificent, as her mind ran wild.

'Hey, are you okay?' A hand touched her shoulder and Peter's words followed. 'I was lying under one of the pine trees when you powered out of that bus like your arse was on fire,' he said with a smirk.

Jess opened her eyes at him then closed him out again. Right now she simply couldn't handle jokes, even from Peter.

'Come on. Even a little smile?' He turned her towards him and she opened her eyes and focused on his body. The white cotton of his T-shirt sat snugly over his skin and his scent enveloped her, breaking down her walls. All too soon her eyes lifted, meeting his bright blue ones. He was the white of the sand and the blue of the sea. This was where Peter belonged, on a beautiful beach.

'See, was that so hard? What's going on?' His gaze delved into her soul. 'I know you, so don't give me the "I'm fine" line.'

Those eyes seemed to see all, her defences were useless and she crumbled.

'I saw Ricki.'

Everything went blurry as tears threatened. She wanted to go home and hug her son.

His lips drew tight. 'Oh, Jess. Was it that awful? I'm so sorry, you shouldn't have had to do that on your own.' He pulled her into a hug right there on the beach with waves crashing in the background, children laughing and seagulls calling to their friends.

Jess let him hold her in his arms. Her body reacted on instinct – he was her home, her safe place – as she sagged against him. For a moment she breathed him in, felt the strength of his body and the caress and comfort of his arms. It was as close to Ollie as she could get right now. She got her breathing under control, kept the tears at bay and finally managed to speak.

'It's ruined our reunion. And I wasn't alone. Abbie was there.' She stopped herself from saying more; telling Peter about Ricki's unfaithfulness would only hurt him. It wasn't for her to tell. Just like she knew how much it would hurt him when he found out about Ollie. Guilt was eating at her, and what made her so confused about Ricki's betrayal was that she was no better. What she had kept secret was much, much worse.

'Good.' Peter indicated to a building nestled at the bottom of the hill at the end of the beach. 'Feel like a hot chocolate?' he asked.

Did they make a 'clear away the guilt hot chocolate'? 'Yes, sounds perfect. Thanks, Peter.' Arm in arm they strolled along the beach, kicking sand, towards the coffee shop.

Growing up, whenever her dad had gone on a bender, she'd go straight to Peter's place the next morning while her dad slept it off. His mum had always made her a hot chocolate with marshmallows, and accompanied it with a chocolate biscuit. Jess would take care to wear a long-sleeved shirt to hide any of the marks that made her feel so ashamed. Only now did Jess figure out that Peter's mum knew what was going on and that her place had become a sanctuary. The hot chocolates had become her remedy for a bad night, and as they grew older Peter became the one who mastered the hot-chocolate making.

In the dark hours of the night when her dad was yelling abuse at them all and they'd tiptoe around the house to avoid upsetting him, Jess would always think about marshmallows bobbing around in the chocolate, slightly melting. A simple drink had become a lifeline, and so had Peter.

It was Peter who told her she shouldn't give up teaching just because she had Ollie.

'You can still have it all,' he'd told her as he nursed a three-day-old Ollie. 'Take this little guy on the journey with you. You have all our support.'

How could I not love you? she thought as she watched him order their drinks. But it was bittersweet. *Will you love me when I tell you the truth?*

'They'll bring them over shortly,' said Peter as he guided her to a table outside the cafe.

He sat close so their arms and legs touched. It was how they always were in each other's company; like two magnets, they had no personal space, it was always shared.

'Thank you.' She reached for his hand and threaded her fingers through his, noting the look of surprise on his face.

'What were you just thinking?' he asked softly.

She spilled her thoughts. 'That no one else will ever love you as much as I do. No one else knows you like I do.' She smiled and he returned it.

'That I do believe. I feel exactly the same, Jess. I know you want to go slow with this, I understand what's at stake. I don't want to lose our friendship either. Ever.'

'I know, Peter. I've been too scared to risk it.'

'Then why did you tell me now?' His forehead creased under his flop of hair.

'Well, I was moving on already. I'd vowed to let you go, to let you be happy – I just couldn't be there to watch it. So, in the end it didn't matter if I told you and you walked away. I was prepared to try to live my life without you.'

Peter shook his head and waited until the waiter had placed their mugs in front of them. 'I'm so glad you told me,' he said when they were alone again. 'But you know, I would never have let you walk away. I would have kept calling, visiting and hounding you until you changed your mind. A life without you, and Ollie, is not a reality I want.'

They sipped their hot chocolates, Peter watching her over the rim of his mug.

'If you hadn't done that, Jess, then I wouldn't have searched my feelings and understood how deep they ran. I don't know how I could have missed it.'

'Sometimes I think we're pretty good at lying to ourselves. Our head tries to tell us what it wants or thinks we need, but it's our heart that has the final say. Well, that's what I believe.'

He bumped her shoulder. 'When did you get so clever?'

'Maybe having a child puts things into perspective. I don't know.'

They gazed at each other as if they didn't already know every line, every freckle.

'So, what happens now?' Peter asked eventually.

'Ease into it?' said Jess.

'Can I kiss you again?' There was a naughty spark to his smile that she couldn't resist.

'If you can control yourself,' she teased.

Peter reached for her slowly, holding her close, his eyes not wavering from hers as their lips touched. It started soft, slow but built quickly with an instant heat as if the pin had been pulled on a grenade. When they finally unglued themselves they were both breathing heavily. Jess looked around to check they hadn't been too public, but no one seemed to notice; the locals were too busy watching their kids play in the water or on the nearby swing set.

'Oh, I like doing that, very much,' murmured Peter.

Jess smiled, but in the back recess of her mind still lurked fear and worry. She had protected her heart for so long, this still seemed fraught with danger. And what about Ollie? Could Peter forgive her the greatest lie she had ever told? Could they really become a happy family?

'I'd love to jump in feet first, Peter, but . . .' How could she put it into words?

'I've just got out of a relationship with your best friend, and there's a lot at stake? I know. Truly, I understand, Jess. I don't want this to go south any more than you do. Let's take it one day at a time. I know you have Ollie to think about. But you know I love that little guy as if he were my own.'

His words pleased her and scared her in equal measure – and made her deceit so much worse. 'Sounds perfect.'

Jess tried to relax, and sipped more of her chocolate.

'So, how upset was Ricki?' Peter ventured.

Jess sighed. 'I think she was shocked mostly, which is fair enough. I was pretty good at hiding my feelings for you from her; from everyone,' she finished with a wry smile. 'She knows you two have broken up, but I understand how seeing that would have hurt.' *Just like you'd be hurt if you knew she'd done the same thing*, thought Jess, but she forged on. 'I reckon she'll be fine now she's said her bit. She might not even worry about grumbling to you.'

'She's entitled to,' he said sadly.

'So, what are we doing tonight on the boat?' said Jess. A change in topic was due, and might be the only thing that stopped her from spilling Ricki's secret.

'I don't know. To be honest, something quiet would be nice. No drama and no dancing,' he said wincing. 'You know how sore my legs are?'

Jess laughed. 'It's all good exercise. It's your surfing replacement,' she added.

He groaned. 'Don't mention surfing. Talk about withdrawal. Do you know how hard it is for me to be on the water without my board?'

'I can imagine,' she said teasingly.

'Hey, I'm serious. I even go out on deck to smell the salt. If I close my eyes and feel the swell I can almost trick myself.'

'We have to be back on the boat this afternoon,' she sighed.

'I know,' he said sadly. 'Spoilsport.' He nudged her shoulder and gazed at her like kissing her again was his only thought. And for now, she allowed it to be hers too.

⚓

Though the beach was a perfect spot for kissing, they didn't do much of it. Instead it was nice to walk and talk, holding hands as their feet squelched on the wet sand and the cool sea water lapped at their ankles. The sun was warm but the breeze coming off the ocean was fresh.

Peter lifted her hand and frowned at her bare arm. 'Do you still wear the bracelet I bought you?'

Jess cleared her throat and glanced out at the ocean, watching a seagull flying low over the waves. How did she explain to Peter that the one object she treasured from him was now lost? Well, not lost but stolen. She was sure of it.

For her sixteenth birthday Peter had given her a silver bracelet and her first charm to add to it: a silver circle with the number sixteen in the centre. The following year he added to it with a silver heart, then an apple to represent her studies as a teacher. Every year the collection grew and she wore it always, until the clasp broke.

She sighed. 'The clasp broke. I was going to get it fixed, and then it disappeared,' she said with a sigh.

'Disappeared?'

'Stolen is my guess.' He frowned as she continued. 'It was on my dresser at Mum's place, and then after one of Chris's visits it was gone. I think he took it, along with a few other things we've had go missing.' Jess looked down at the sand, her heart heavy. 'I don't know what to do about Chris. He's like Dad, but instead of alcohol it's drugs.' She stopped walking and faced Peter. 'I'm worried about him, about Mum. I don't feel safe around my own brother,' she said truthfully. 'What kind of a sister am I?'

'You're a good one. Chris is a grown man. It's his life, not yours, and I know you want to save him but some people have to hit rock bottom before they can find their way back up.'

'I've tried to talk to him, to get through to him, but he keeps putting up walls. He feels like the world owes him something, that *we* owe him something. He just keeps taking.'

'I guess all you can do is be there when he needs it. Don't worry about the bracelet. I still have you, that's more important.'

He let go of her hand and moved a strand of hair from her face, then caressed her cheek. His thumb brushed across her lips and suddenly there was fire burning low in her belly. The way he stared at her was so passionate. As if to prove it, he dropped his head and kissed her.

It was when they came up for air and continued along the beach that the guilt ate at her. She should tell Peter about Ollie. Now. Before it was too late, before she was too far gone. But the words wouldn't come.

Her throat constricted, as if refusing to let her share her secret. A battle of wills raged and before she knew it the time for speaking up had passed as Peter began to talk about a big job he'd landed for a new office building.

'I'll need to find two extra guys to help, I think, but it will be worth it.'

Eventually he stopped talking and was watching her. 'You okay? You still worrying about your brother? Or Ricki?'

It was neither, but she ran with it. 'Bit of both. Do you think Ricki will get past this?'

'I think she's in the process of trying to work out what she wants too. She might be angry now, but you mean the world to her, so I don't think she'll break up a friendship over this.'

And if anyone knew Ricki better than Jess, it was Peter. 'Yeah, you're right, I suppose.' Ricki looked back the way they had come. 'We should probably go wait for the bus. It's nearly time to head back.'

'Yep. Go and face the music.' He scanned the beach then stopped when he got to Jess. 'I don't want to go. This has been awesome. Just you and me. Like old times.'

'I know. It feels so right.' So much so it scared her. Ollie. Pete. The two deeply invested loves seemed to come with the risk of a bigger shattering heartbreak.

They kissed, one last time, then wrapped their arms around each other and held on tight. Jess breathed him in, felt his heartbeat against her chest and the pressure of his strong arms. 'Can we stay like this forever?'

'I'd be happy with that.'

As they made their way towards the road, she knew she'd remember their beach walk forever.

26

Abbie

ABBIE HAD HALF-EXPECTED RICKI OR JESS TO JOIN HER IN the ANZAC Centre, but in the end she was happy they didn't. She enjoyed the solo meander among the photos, memorabilia and information walls about the soldiers. The last time the girls had come to the heritage-listed Princess Royal Fortress all those years ago they were more interested in talking to each other and exploring the fort; this time Abbie let the history engulf her, the fact that more than a hundred years ago this was the departure point for the first convoy of ANZACs on the way to the battlefield. Their last sight of home was King George Sound; its calm waters with rocky islands dotted around, one with a lighthouse. It gave her something else to think about as she explored the amazing telescopic-looking building and then weaved her way down the decked runway to a beautiful sitting area.

'You know,' she said to the only other person at the decked Convoy Lookout, a man admiring the view, 'you are probably sitting right where a big gun had been placed back in 1914, ready for any oceanic attacks. Nice quiet spot, isn't it?'

'It was quiet,' Alex teased, and then gestured for her to join him. His dark eyes drank in her expression. 'Bit sad in there?'

'Yes and no. I loved reading about the lighthouse girl. Can you believe some of those soldiers sent her postcards from Egypt? What an effect one girl could have. I think she must have been something they could hold onto, the last connection to home. Reading all the stories makes my problems seem small and insignificant.'

'Do tell?' he asked softly.

Abbie let out a sigh that sounded as exhausted as she felt. 'Problems going on with my friends. Secrets and indiscretions, surprises.' She shrugged. 'We came here to celebrate, but today all we've done is yell at each other.'

'Friends fight; it doesn't mean the end.'

Abbie smiled weakly. 'I know. It just sucks. The whole point of the trip was to be together, have fun, reminisce . . . but it's been one disaster after another.' The wind blew, ruffling her dress against her legs.

His eyes dropped to the scar on her neck. 'So, tell me what it's like being the ship's doctor,' she said quickly.

Alex smiled. 'Well, it's okay when I get to meet people like you,' he said with a wink. 'Otherwise it's mainly seasickness issues. But my cabin is cool, bigger than most and my colleagues are great and easygoing.' His fingers tapped on his thigh, rhythmically. 'So, are you with that guy that I've seen you with?'

'Peter? No. He's a good mate. He was dating Ricki, but as of last night he's now with Jess.'

Alex's eyebrows shot up. 'Ohhhkaaay. Kind of sorry I asked,' he said with a chuckle. 'I take it that's causing some of the problems with your friends?'

'Yeah, one of many. I don't think we have enough time for me to explain it all. I'd rather spend our time on happier topics.'

Alex nodded. After a moment he leaned towards her, his brow creased. 'What's this from?'

And before Abbie could answer, Alex had reached over and touched her surgery scar, with professional scrutiny.

It took all her effort not to quickly put her hand over it.

'It actually looks good. It's healing well.'

A small line of puckered pink skin sat like a big elephant between them. It was more than just a scar, and Alex knew it.

'Yeah, good. Thanks for your professional opinion.'

He ignored her jibe; his serious eyes held her locked, unable to escape his next question.

'Lymph node clearance, or melanoma?'

Abbie pressed her lips together. But she didn't have to say anything.

'What stage?' he murmured, not even waiting for her to confirm.

Her breath hissed through her teeth. Just hearing it said out loud made it feel real again. 'Hodgkin's Lymphoma.'

'Which has a good survival rate.'

Abbie had heard the same optimism from her doctor. 'I don't know what stage I am yet. I have those tests when I get back. I was only diagnosed just before this trip.'

The great thing about saying this to a doctor was that she didn't get the pity party, instead she got a face that nodded with understanding. A face that had seen this many times before and didn't hold the emotion she knew would come from her friends.

'So, you've had the dodgy ex, no job, friendship fractures and this to deal with?' He nodded as if things made more sense now. 'Do your friends know?' he asked.

'No. I don't want to worry them. And I don't want all the messy emotions.'

His voice cracked with concern. 'Does anyone know? Family?'

'Ah, nope. My parents are away, travelling around Australia. If I told them they'd come rushing back, and I don't want that. They've been saving for this trip all their lives. They deserve it.' *Another subject would be great*, she said silently. Thinking about her parents was not something she could do right now.

'You're going to handle it all on your own?'

'If I can, yes.'

'You don't have to, you know. It won't kill you to let them in.'

Abbie gave him a pointed look.

'Or you could tell no one. Sure. But if you want someone who's in the know,' he said tapping his nose, 'I'd be happy to go with you for your staging or talk you through anything you don't understand.'

She smiled, and for the first time in a while she meant it. 'Thanks, Alex. I'd appreciate that. Even a catch-up drink after this cruise?' she said. 'It would be nice to have someone to talk to about it without worrying my friends and family.'

His lips were smooth and curled up as he smiled. 'Good. I'd like that too.'

Alex was like a breath of fresh air.

'Gosh, how did we get to the point where you know my

big secret and yet I know nothing about you except you're the ship's doctor?'

'You know I'm divorced.' He smiled but it was strained.

'Not over it?'

'I am now, but it was hard at the start.' He looked out to sea and pointed out the big grain ship coming in.

Abbie stayed silent. She felt he had something weighing him down too.

'I've known Sarah most of my life,' he said, then smiled wryly. 'In country towns everyone has known everyone most of their lives. After we got married everything seemed like it was going great. I could see our future laid out before us. And then . . .'

Abbie nodded; she knew only too well how quickly things could change.

'We fell pregnant.' His lips twitched, his hands tightened into fists. 'She made it to full term but . . . our daughter was stillborn.' His voice cracked slightly.

Abbie clenched her fist against her chest, her heart going out to him. 'I'm so sorry, Alex. That must have been . . . I can't imagine.' Instinctively she reached across and took his hand, hoping his fingers would relax.

'The worst part is, I'm a doctor, I should have known something was wrong. Even Sarah mentioned she hadn't felt the baby move in that last week. I feel like I failed her and myself and our child.'

Abbie started to reassure him but he spoke over her.

'I know there's nothing we could have done, and I shouldn't blame myself, but I can't help it.' He paused, his eyes shifted, cold. 'She once screamed at me that it was my fault, that I should have checked when she was concerned.'

He let out a long, slow breath, his fingers relaxing. 'It's like she read my mind. She apologised later, but I still felt like I could have saved our baby if I'd just checked. Anyway, we couldn't get over the loss. Somewhere in all that we stopped communicating, and we fell apart. Sarah found someone else, maybe because I was too busy punishing myself, or maybe she needed someone different to take her mind off it. Either way, our marriage ended.'

'Oh, Alex.'

He unclenched his other hand and moved it across to place on top of hers. 'I've never really spoken about it to anyone. It's always been too hard.'

They sat in silence for a while, listening to the birds in the native bushland around them.

'What was her name?' Abbie eventually asked softly.

'Evie.' He smiled. 'She was perfect. I can't help but feel the burden.'

There was so much she wanted to say, but nothing seemed right. Nothing would take the pain from Alex or bring Evie back to him. So, she just squeezed his hand tighter and they sat like that for ages until his phone went off.

'Damn, sorry. It seems one of the cooking staff has cut their hand pretty badly. I'd better go,' he said standing up. 'Thanks, Abbie. Today meant a lot.'

She smiled and nodded, a little sad as he walked away, out of sight.

'It meant a lot to me too,' she said quietly.

⚓

The friends sat in the Italian restaurant on the boat together, yet miles of unspoken distance separated them. Jess was avoiding looking at Ricki, Peter was avoiding looking at Jess so they didn't flaunt their feelings in front of the others, Ricki was avoiding looking at Peter, and Abbie was off in her own world trying to ignore the high level of awkwardness.

Before dinner she had gone to the top deck with Peter and Jess, and together they had watched Albany disappear while Ricki watched from another deck. The *Eden* had moved like a swan through the islands and cliff edges as it left the harbour and amazing beaches, the sun sinking below the hills, gold tipping the trees and bushes and lighting up the few clouds in front of them. It seemed even more enchanting watching it all from the top of the *Eden*, the salty breeze in their faces, the crispness of the air and the birds they could hear from the nearby islands. It was a weird feeling, from being on Mount Clarence looking out to sea to now being on a boat looking back at the land. Abbie had sought out the small lighthouse on Breaksea Island and tried to imagine being a soldier off to war. Like a ticking time bomb, fate unknown. Kind of like how she felt with this cancer. There was no surety, no clear path.

'Well, this is horrible, and I don't mean the meal,' she said eventually, pushing her empty plate away. She wanted to fade away into the darkness.

'Mmm, I'm going to get a drink. I'll see you guys later,' was all Ricki said before she stood and left the restaurant.

'Well, I guess we should let her go if she needs space,' said Peter as he watched her leave, his face tight. He shifted in his chair, trying to get comfortable. 'What shall we do?'

'Actually, I think I might turn in,' Jess said, watching Ricki walk out of the restaurant. 'It's been a big day.'

'Okay, I'll walk you back,' said Peter, but Jess put her hand on his. 'No, I'll be fine, really.' She smiled. 'One step at a time, yeah?'

Abbie saw the look between them and suddenly needed to be outdoors. 'Well, sleep tight, Jess. I'm going to head up on deck for some air and a glass of red. How about it, Peter?' she said as she headed out towards the lifts. Towards fresh air and less emotional baggage.

Peter caught up with her near the pool, where Abbie was standing at the railing gazing over the edge to the churning water below while sipping her wine. The rail was cold but she gripped it tightly as the vertigo dragged her closer to the water.

'It's such a weird sensation,' Peter said, looking over the railing beside her. Abbie looked around to see that they had the deck to themselves, not counting the person over the far side asleep under a blue-and-white striped towel.

'Do you ever wish upon a star, Abbie?' Peter asked, his eyes pointed towards the heavens.

The dark sky, no clouds in sight, was filled with stars, the Milky Way bright and easy to see. The summer night was crisp on her skin. There were many stars, but none she wanted to wish on. 'When I was a kid, sure. But as an adult I think I've forgotten to look up and even see them. We're so hopeful as kids – it's easy to believe in magic – but now I feel jaded, like life is passing me by.'

'Kids are yet to be burned by life,' said Peter.

'Yeah, but what about the sick ones? Even the dying ones still seem to smile and want to live.' Abbie had done some volunteer work for Telethon and visited kids at Princess Margaret

Hospital when she was twenty. They were ten times braver than she was, she'd bet her right leg. Actually she would bet her whole cancer-infected body. *Please somebody take it away*, she almost prayed to the night sky.

She sighed as she looked up again. Was she praying to God? To the universe? Would anyone listen or care? The prayers of the millions of people who had died from cancer before her were never answered, so why did she think she would be special? Good people died, bad people lived. It was life, and in her case it kept getting worse, as if crumbling around her.

'That's true. What is it about a night sky that makes you feel philosophical?' Peter pointed up. 'Maybe it's knowing there are so many galaxies out there. We're just specks. A moment in time.'

'I think you need another drink,' said Abbie with a laugh.

'Now, there is some wise wisdom right there. Do you want another one while I'm going?'

She managed a smile as she looked at her half-empty glass. 'Yes, why not. Thanks Peter.'

⚓

Looking over the rail, sipping the last of her wine, something about the white caps mesmerised her. Was it the unknown lurking below, or the idea that it could hold a quick death? All she would have to do would be to climb the rail and fall over the edge. A small splash. Would she have to expel her breath on the way down so she didn't pop back up?

Was it crazy that this seemed preferable to the way Gramps went?

Peter would come back, and there would be no sign of her. Would anyone see her go over? Would they care? Would they search the boat and wonder where she was hiding?

It was a strange calm that had overcome her. She tried to lift herself up further but slipped, her glass smashing against the rail. Glass splintered into her hand and wrist as her wine splashed across the deck.

There may have been a hint of pain but she didn't feel it now. *Hope they don't charge for the glass*, she thought calmly. Forgetting the water below, Abbie stepped back down and sat on the nearest chair. Her drink had gone everywhere, she could feel the damp on her skin and through her soft blue dress. The light wasn't great, but she couldn't miss the dark splash of red on her dress and wine spots along her skin. Lifting her arm into the light she saw deeper red tendrils trailing down her arm. So much blood. Time slowed, seconds became minutes and each blink, each breath was carried out in slow motion.

Abbie picked out some glass embedded in her hand and placed it in a small pile by the chair. Blood seemed to ooze out faster as the shards piled up.

Below her hand the deck was a dark circle, as if wet with water, and it was growing larger by the second. She watched the lines, like fat texta marks drawn over her skin, flow from her. She felt no pain.

The salty air scent intensified and became metallic.

Abbie lay back, with her arm hanging by her side and stared at the stars. If only the cancer was leaking out of her body with it – drip, drip, drip – until the last cancerous cell departed.

It didn't work like that, if only.

Abbie closed her eyes and wondered how long it would take. She clenched her cut hand, and felt the blood throb out faster.

When Peter came back she didn't see him approach. She didn't hear him. She was lost in a quiet peace.

'This wine had a funny name but it sounded—'

His feet stopped at the base of her chair.

'What's . . . Abbie, is that *blood*? Abbie!' His voice rose with each word.

Abbie opened her eyes and saw him reaching for her arm, their drinks discarded on the deck beside her chair.

'Bloody hell, Abbie!'

She watched calmly as he ripped off his shirt and wrapped it around her hand and wrist.

'What *happened*, Abbie?'

Abbie could sense his anger and worry, but she felt nothing. Maybe a little disappointment that he'd returned so soon.

'Jesus. It's everywhere,' he said, looking at the mass of blood by her chair and the footprints he was leaving in it. 'I could bloody use Ricki right now.'

He shook his head and checked his shirt was firmly in place. 'Hold this. I'm going to get help.'

He ran for the door and Abbie looked down at her wrapped hand. *A shame*, she thought slowly. She could unwrap it, let the flow continue – but Peter was back in seconds.

'They're getting help,' he said as he rushed to her side, shirtless. 'It'll be okay soon. What happened?'

He went to touch her face but pulled away when he realised his hands were covered with her blood. There was even a smear of red across his abdomen.

'Sorry. My glass broke,' she managed to say. She felt tired. Happy, groggy, sleepy.

'Can you stand? Let's get you into the light so the doctor can see how bad it is.' Peter held out his hands, waiting.

Abbie didn't move. Instead she closed her eyes.

'Abbie, talk to me.'

He could beg all he liked, but she didn't want to ruin the silence. She heard two voices.

'She's here, quickly. See, it's everywhere.' Peter swore.

'Righto. She's lost a lot of blood,' came a calmer voice. 'I think it's best if we get her straight down to the medical centre.'

Abbie liked the sound of his words, smooth and in control. Not like Peter, who was now in a right panic. It felt familiar and gentle, probably like all the doctors she'd met recently. *Do they teach you how to talk at university?* she thought lazily. She opened her eyes to see who had such a voice, to find Alex beside her. The face of a god, tanned and with dark eyes like endless souls. His lips smooth but pulled into a hard line. Ah, yes, he was the doctor.

'I'll carry her,' Peter said.

Before Abbie had time to protest, Peter had picked her up as if she were a doll.

Abbie blinked when they got inside into the lights. Peter was following Alex, who was wearing his uniform white pants and shirt. She'd never seen him in his work wear before. He looked so important, like the captain of a navy ship.

'This way.' He directed Peter into an elevator.

Someone went to join them in the elevator but Alex stood in their way and pressed the button to shut the door. 'Sorry, please take the next one.'

The woman's eyes bulged when she looked behind him and saw a shirtless Peter holding a blood-stained Abbie. Abbie almost smiled.

They stopped at deck five, and by the time Peter had carried her all the way to the front of the ship he was starting to grunt.

'Do you want me to take over?' said Alex beside them.

'No, I got it,' he puffed.

'Am I heavy, Peter Pan?' she murmured. 'You should have flown us here.'

'How can you joke at a time like this?' he said gruffly, but he held her delicately, as if she might break.

Alex opened a door and indicated. 'In here, pop her down on the table. Thanks.' Again Alex's calm, familiar voice made her feel at ease. 'I've got it from here,' he said after Peter sat her on the edge of the examination table.

Peter stepped away, back towards the door. 'You'll be okay, Abbie. You're in good hands. I'll be right outside.'

Abbie gave him a reassuring smile – he needed it, his face was so tight and serious – and then turned to Alex, who stood beside her, to give him the same reassuring smile, to let him know that she was fine.

'Hi Abbie. We really must stop meeting like this,' he said with a small grin as the door closed behind Peter. 'So, how did you manage to do this?'

She heard drawers opening and then Alex was back adding gauze, tweezers and other supplies to the trolley beside the table. He put on gloves then reached for the makeshift bandage around her hand.

'It's nice to see you again,' she said ignoring his question.

His dark eyes watched her carefully, as if assessing, but still lined with amusement.

'Are you going to tell me what happened?'

Abbie sighed. 'I broke my glass,' she said glancing down at her hand. Under the lights it all seemed so much more violent. The bright red, the deep gashes, puckered white and pink skin and glass she'd missed.

'Oh, yuck.'

'Yes, you did a stellar job. I'll just get the rest of the glass out before I stitch up a few of these cuts.'

Abbie's focus was suddenly clearing up far too quickly.

'Would you like to lie down while I do this?'

She nodded and he helped her lie back onto the small pillow and then lifted her legs up on another.

'Just rest your arm out here and I'll work my magic,' he said.

She watched his face, trying to read his thoughts as he fussed over her cuts, his brow creased. It was too quiet in this cold, square room.

'How are you feeling?' he eventually said.

'Okay. A bit dizzy.'

'I'm not surprised. You lost a lot of blood.' He cleared his throat. 'Not many patients of mine have cut themselves and let the blood flow. Most stem it with something.'

Her heart raced with his observation. It was as if he could see through her shields. 'What are you implying, doc?' she said, wondering where his frankness had gone.

He paused mid-stitch to stare at her. 'Did you do this on purpose?'

Ah, there it was. She preferred his straight question. Abbie tried to take no notice of the needle in his hand, and instead focused on his intense gaze. 'No, I didn't do it on purpose. I actually was thinking of jumping overboard,' she said honestly. His face didn't alter, but she did notice a small twitch in the corner of his eye. 'Then I broke the glass by accident and, well . . .' Her words died away. She didn't know how to express exactly what she'd been thinking.

'Does this have anything to do with your scar?' he asked, nodding towards it. 'Abbie, your cancer has a high recovery rate. Hodgkin's Lymphoma isn't always a death sentence. You can't give up yet, you don't even know what stage you're at.'

'I know. I got scared.' Then she found herself blubbering out her experience with her granddad. 'Every time I visited Gramps he asked to be put to sleep. He wanted out. He'd had enough of fighting. He lost so much time in that hospital. He told me he wished he'd never found out he had cancer, so he could have lived right up until his death. And I get that, Alex, I wish I could have given that to him and to all of us. To have memories of him at his best living life and not suffering. When I think of him all I see now is the skeleton man with pale skin and bloodshot eyes who was pleading for release. I struggle to remember him happy and healthy.'

Alex covered up the stitches with gauze and bandaged her hand. 'I understand that too, Abbie. I really do. But all I'm saying is don't give up yet, not when you don't have all the facts. You're still so young.' Alex had paused and was watching her. 'Please?'

'Life can be pretty messed up,' she said.

After a moment he stood up. 'Well, I think you're good to go. I suggest lots of water and sleep. Do you need anything for the pain?'

She shook her head. This was just a scratch compared to what may come. Time she started toughening up.

'I'll help you back to your room.'

Abbie was about to protest and say she could manage – until she tried to stand and nearly toppled over. Alex grabbed her quickly, holding her against him.

'I'll take a hug as thanks any day,' he joked.

'Ha ha.' But she did enjoy his warmth and the comfort of his arms. He held her probably longer than was professional, but she wasn't going to lodge a formal complaint anytime soon. It felt like something they both desperately needed.

He leaned back, dark eyes drinking her in for a moment before he helped her out of the examination room, into the front office. Peter stood up suddenly when he saw them. He was still shirtless, stains on his pants, but the blood had gone from his abdomen and hands.

'All good?' His worried expression was enough to crumble anyone's high.

'I'm fine, Peter.'

He glanced at Alex as if he didn't believe her.

'She's all stitched up and ready for sleep.' Then he turned to Abbie. 'You might be dizzy for a while, so be careful when you get up in the morning or during the night.' He gave her some iron tablets to take.

'Yes, doc.'

'I can take her,' said Peter moving to her side.

'Okay. I should stay here and clean up. Still on duty. Come and see me down here in the morning.'

Abbie nodded. 'Thanks, Alex. I will.'

Anything to see him again.

Without a word Peter put his arm around her waist and took her weight. She put her good arm around him and hung on as he walked her slowly back to her cabin. It wasn't until they stopped outside her door that she finally broke the silence. 'Thanks, Peter.'

She hugged him, keeping her hand out awkwardly. It was starting to throb.

'You had me worried, Abbie. I've never seen so much blood before. Don't freak me out again,' he laughed, but it was strained.

She hated knowing she'd caused that.

27

Jess

JESS WOKE UP AS THE CABIN DOOR OPENED.

'Sorry, didn't want to wake you,' said Peter as she rolled over to switch on a light.

'That's okay,' she said and blinked a few times at the sight of Peter half-naked and helping Abbie to her bed. 'Where's your shirt?'

That's when she noticed the bandage on Abbie's hand. 'Oh God, what happened?'

'Abbie had a fight with a glass. She's okay, just needs sleep.'

Jess threw her covers back and sat up.

Abbie held up her good hand. 'I'm fine, Jess. Go back to sleep. I'll tell you about it in the morning.'

'Your dress is covered in blood. Let me help you take it off.'

It was hard to get the dress off without smearing blood over everything it touched. Peter went into the bathroom and came back out with a couple of wet flannels. Jess took one and Abbie the other as they cleaned the blood off her skin. Abbie stood

232

in her underwear and rubbed at the blood on her belly. Peter picked the dress up from the floor.

'Peter, don't bother. Just chuck it out. I'll never wear it again.'

Jess saw something flicker in Abbie's eyes but it was gone before she could figure out what it meant.

'Okay.'

When Abbie was clean enough she put on her nightshirt and crawled into bed.

'I really want a shower but I don't think I could stand for that long.' Abbie's voice trailed off. She groaned as she snuggled her head against the pillow.

'The doctor said she'd lost quite a bit of blood, so she'll be dizzy. I practically carried her here.' Peter sat on the seat and leaned forward, shoulders hunched. 'If she wakes up we might need to help her to the bathroom.'

'You want me to make up the floor for you again?' asked Jess.

'Yeah, I think so. I'd like to be here, just in case you need me.'

'Thanks,' Jess said with a tired smile.

'I'll go next door and grab some stuff, have a shower. I need to talk to Ricki too.'

He left but Jess stayed sitting at the table, awaiting his return, watching Abbie snore softly. Jess was too wired to sleep, too curious to know exactly what had happened.

She heard a gentle knock on the door fifteen minutes later and opened it to see Peter and Ricki standing in front of her, holding bedding supplies.

She bit her tongue as they dumped the pillows on the floor. Ricki kept a blanket wrapped around her as she sat beside Jess. Peter sat the other side of her; he smelled fresh from the shower and her body gravitated towards him until she gained control.

'What's going on, Peter?' she asked him, surprised he had Ricki with him.

'That's what I'd like to know too,' Ricki whispered. 'He pulled me from the bed and said I had to come here.'

'It's important,' Peter whispered. 'I'd do this in our cabin but I don't want to leave Abbie alone.'

Jess glanced at Ricki and they both frowned, their interest spiked.

'What happened with the glass?' asked Jess.

Peter went on to explain what he had seen. 'She was sitting back while the blood ran out. What would you have done in that situation?' he asked them both in hushed tones.

'I would have stopped the flow,' said Ricki.

'Me too. Put something on it at least until I got help.'

'Well, that's just it,' said Peter. 'Abbie did none of those things. It was as if she wanted to die. But that's not all. It's worse.'

He glanced over to Abbie: no movement, just the soft snoring.

'The doctor was someone she knew, she'd met him before. Alex, I think she called him,' said Peter.

'Oh, yes, he's nice.' Ricki smiled.

'Well, they didn't know I could hear them when Alex asked about her scar.' He tapped near his neck and leaned in closer. 'She had something cut out . . .'

'Yeah, it was a mole or something,' inserted Jess.

Peter sucked in a breath as he shook his head seriously. 'No. They were talking about Abbie having Hodgkin's Lymphoma.'

Jess's chest started to ache like she was out of breath. 'That's cancer, isn't it?' she said turning to Ricki. Ricki's eyes were glistening as she nodded and reached for Jess's hand. 'No way.'

But Peter continued to nod, the repetition like a frightened child rocking back and forth. It was all sinking in. Cancer. Cancer was everywhere, but surely it couldn't have invaded her friend's body.

'I can't believe it. Why didn't she tell us?' whispered Ricki. Peter shrugged, his face gaunt in the half-light.

'Oh, no, Abbie.' Jess looked at her hand gripped in Ricki's and knew this was real. 'Why wouldn't she tell us, or let us be there with her for the operation?' Her other hand went to her mouth in disbelief. 'What does this mean?'

Ricki shrugged. 'I don't know.'

Jess was after statistics. What were the survival rates? What treatment options were available? How long would this last? So many questions. 'Will she be all right?' It was a question for both of her friends but neither responded. Instead they sat in silence. The ship rocked; midnight passed, but no answers came.

'She can't die,' said Jess softly.

'We can't think the worst,' said Peter. 'We have to be supportive. Abbie wouldn't want us to fall apart. It's why she hasn't told anyone. No one knows except for her doctors and now Alex.'

'Really? She's done this all by herself?' Ricki cursed. 'I mean, Jim left her and her job's gone. Shit, she's had it rough and here we are fighting over nothing.'

Jess saw the guilt, anguish and regret in Ricki's brown eyes and all over her pale face twisted with worry.

'It puts our lives into perspective, doesn't it,' mumbled Jess.

Peter cleared his throat and they turned their attention to him. It was clear that he knew more and it wasn't good.

'Spill, Peter, what else did they say?' Ricki leaned forward.

'Alex asked her if she'd done this on purpose. I think Abbie has been thinking about ending her life—'

Jess gasped then covered her mouth quickly.

'Oh, no,' said Ricki. 'It's what her granddad had wanted.'

Jess's stomach churned as she remembered the night Abbie had broken down, telling them about his slow, painful death. It was the only time throughout their friendship that she'd ever seen Abbie truly distraught. She was angry too, but they'd seen that on plenty of occasions. Abbie was the strong one. If a pet died she buried it and moved on. *That's life*, she'd say. She had her own way of dealing with emotions and pain, whereas Jess would have cried for weeks and not wanted to face the world.

'It's okay. I think Alex convinced her otherwise. He mentioned "staging",' Peter said.

'Yes, to see what stage her cancer is at,' said Ricki. 'I just wish she'd shared this with us, let us in. We're her best friends.' Ricki looked at Jess. 'Regardless of what's happened, *you* are my best friends. We might be angry at each other but I hope the friendship will always stay strong. We all make mistakes . . . yes, some more than others.' Ricki's smile was pained. 'But that doesn't mean I want us to fall out over it.'

Jess nodded. 'I know, Ricki. I feel the same. We need to be united for Abbie,' said Jess.

Ricki straightened up and smiled tiredly. 'And she'd want to see you happy. So please, if you two want to be together, then don't stop because of me. I think we all need to be happy.'

'And understand each other's feelings. Let's focus on Abbie.'

Peter was hunched over, tired looking, shivering slightly but he nodded to show he agreed. Ricki moved so she could share her rug with him.

'So, there's a chance she'll be fine after treatment?' Jess asked Ricki.

'Yes, but it all depends on how far the cancer has developed.'

Jess yawned, and seconds later her friends caught it too. 'We should catch some sleep so we can talk to Abbie in the morning.'

'How should we bring it up? You know, without her being angry enough to attack us with a fork,' said Peter.

Ricki and Jess smiled at the shared memory of Abbie literally chasing Peter with a plastic fork during lunch one day in school. He'd made some sexist comment about an area that was off-limits to the girls, which had been imposed by the year twelve boys. Abbie didn't take well to segregation and discrimination. Peter had been scared for his life, and he'd worked hard to have that rule changed.

'Over breakfast?' Jess offered. 'Pile her plate with food, hide the cutlery and hope she understands where we're coming from. Tell her we care and we want to be there for her.' Jess glanced at the shape in the bed. Abbie hadn't moved.

'Sounds like the best plan we have.' Peter stood and stretched. 'Well, I'm going to sleep on the floor, in case she wakes up and needs someone to carry her.'

Ricki shimmied out of the blanket they shared. 'Take this. I'll go back to bed, but let me know if you need me, please?'

'We will,' said Jess.

She walked Ricki to the door but before she could open it Ricki turned and hugged her.

'No matter what happens, I love you guys.'

'I love you too, Ricki. We'll talk more in the morning. Night.'

Ricki laughed as she went out the door. 'It's already morning,' she said before disappearing.

Jess closed the door, turned around and ended up in Peter's arms. He'd been there, waiting, understanding. He hugged her fiercely. It was exactly what she needed. Right now, the realisation that Abbie could be dying, that this very minute her body was being attacked by an army of silent killers – it was too horrible to be true.

Tears fell, wetting Peter's clean white T-shirt. He smelled like soap, but that soon faded as her nose clogged up from her crying.

'I know, Jess. Come on. We all need some sleep so we can put our best foot forward tomorrow.'

Jess reached for his hand and tugged him towards her bed. Suddenly she was beyond exhausted. Somehow they managed to fit on the tiny single bed; Peter's back was against the wall and she was cocooned in his arms. It might have been a different story trying to get to sleep on her own, but this time, with the warmth and safety of Peter, they were both sleeping before she could mumble, 'Thanks.'

28

Ricki

RICKI DIDN'T SLEEP AT ALL. HER BRAIN WOULDN'T STOP. IT tried to imagine Abbie sick. Abbie's funeral. A world without Abbie. It was a dark, terrible place and she pictured it all as she tossed and turned, her bed resembling a teenager's room by morning. And the bed felt empty without Peter, like missing a blanket or favourite teddy.

She untangled the sheet from around her waist and legs. 'Well, that was a waste of bloody time.'

As she showered and dressed, it dawned on Ricki that if they brought up Abbie's cancer at breakfast it could cause a scene. Abbie didn't care what people thought, so an outburst was possible. But then again, right now Ricki didn't care either.

Abbie was sick.

Her lips started to quiver first, then tears pooled faster than she could blink them away.

'Get a grip, Ricki,' she ordered herself.

· She'd done enough crying last night and had the puffy eyelids to prove it; now wasn't the time to make it worse. After spending longer than usual on her make-up, Ricki left the cabin to stand outside the one next door, her hand poised ready to knock.

Who knew this was how their trip was going to turn out? Somehow, the journey just didn't seem over. No, it had only just begun.

Peter answered when she finally knocked. 'Hey, Ricki. Ready?'

'Yep,' she said. 'All okay?' she whispered, finding it easier to talk to Peter than she had expected. Things were different between them, she could feel that already, but it wasn't difficult to be in each other's presence. Not when Abbie was their main focus.

He nodded. 'The girls are getting up. I'll go next door to dress. I'll be back.'

He scooted past her to their cabin. Ricki put on a smile and continued inside. 'Morning, I hope you all slept better than me,' she said.

Jess was pulling up her jeans. 'Morning,' she said before throwing on a grey T-shirt.

Abbie looked at her strangely, so she walked over to where she sat on her bed and gestured to her hand.

'How's it feel?' Go into nurse mode; that was a safe place. 'Peter said you'd done a doozy job,' she added calmly. 'I do worry about your ability to stand, Abbie.' Ricki smiled and saw Abbie relax.

'I know. And I wasn't even wearing heels.' Abbie held it out for Ricki to inspect. 'It's aching a little now, but Alex can fix that, I'm sure,' she said with a smile.

'Alex?' she said, playing dumb as she unwrapped the bandage.

'He wants me to go see him today. I'll head down after breakfast.'

She stood up gingerly, Ricki was at the ready.

'I'm okay. I think I can manage a shower on my own. If you hear a noise like a wet seal landing on the floor, then come find me.'

Ricki helped her put her things together for the shower and then turned the taps on.

'Can totally tell you enjoy giving your patients sponge baths. Did you want to give me one?' Abbie teased.

Ricki shook her head. 'Oh, no, I prefer grumpy old men. Cleaning you would ruin my run of wrinkly bodies.'

Abbie chuckled as Ricki stepped out of the bathroom and joined Jess.

'How does she seem?' Jess whispered.

'Okay for now. At least until we tell her we know. But knowing Abbie, she'll pick up on us acting weird first.'

'Well, your *good morning* was right out of *Mary Poppins*.'

Ricki sat on the edge of the bed while Jess brushed her hair. 'I know. Overcompensating.'

Jess sat quietly on the bed, looking deflated. 'So, who's going to be the one to say something?'

Ricki sat beside her. 'I don't know. Maybe see who finds the best moment?' She reached for Jess's hand. 'How did you sleep?'

Jess went to speak, but nothing came out.

Ricki almost smiled when she realised why: Peter had spent the night in this cabin. But Ricki wasn't upset. They had more important things to worry about.

'Okay, actually, but I woke up early and my brain hasn't stopped since. I can't believe it's real.'

'Me too. I still hope we're all wrong.'

Ricki walked to the bathroom and opened the door a fraction. 'All okay in there?' she called. 'No sea-life rescue needed?'

'Ha ha. I'm fine. I even managed to get over this bath without tripping.'

'Goodo.' Ricki shut the door.

'She sounds okay,' said Jess from her bed.

Ricki rolled her eyes and nodded. 'She's fine.'

Abbie needed help getting her bra on and buttoning up her jeans, but the rest she managed on her own.

When Peter returned, dressed in stonewash jeans and one of his surfing shirts, they headed to The Pantry for breakfast.

⚓

'So, what's everyone up to after we get off the ship?' said Ricki, doing her best to sound casual as they made their way through plates piled high.

'Well, Mum's coming to pick me up. I can't wait to see Ollie. I've missed him so much,' said Jess. 'And then I'm hanging around for a bit before I head back to Wandering. No rush home with term break on.'

'So, we can all catch up some more before you go?' asked Ricki, then regretted it when Abbie suddenly stopped eating and looked between Ricki and Jess, now seemingly on glowing terms again. 'Be nice to spend some more time with Ollie,' Ricki added quickly.

'I have plenty of work waiting for me,' said Peter.

'I'll be packing to move,' said Ricki. 'Any chance I can rent one of your rooms Abbie?' The table had gone quiet, except for Peter, who seemed to be choking on his eggs. Maybe she should have mentioned this to him first.

Abbie went a shade of pink, her mouth moving but no words coming out, as if she was backpedalling but going nowhere. 'Oh, um . . .'

Ricki realised that if she moved in with Abbie then it would be hard for Abbie to keep her cancer secret.

'I don't know.'

'Why, what are you hiding Abbie?' Ricki asked and felt bad when her friend went white as a sheet. She was already pale from blood loss!

Well, I've got to do it now, she thought. Ricki scrunched her hands into tight balls and swallowed hard. 'Abbie, we know about your disease.'

Abbie's jaw dropped. 'Say what?' Abbie looked as if she'd just been blindsided, twice in a matter of seconds. Confused and ruffled.

'The cancer, we know about it,' said Jess, putting down her cutlery. Her words were rushed and nervous. 'Why didn't you tell us? We're your best friends. We want to help.'

'How do you know?' Abbie's words were soft but shaky like a volcano about to erupt. She pushed her plate away as her dark eyes darted between Jess and Ricki before turning to Peter beside her. They zeroed in. 'You.'

Peter sighed. 'I had to tell them what I overheard, Abbie. We all care for you.'

Abbie's face grew redder and Ricki resisted the urge to run away from the table.

'It was nobody's business, Peter! Not yours, not theirs, nobody's but *mine*,' she said pointing into her chest hard. 'It was *my* choice to keep it quiet and now you've screwed it all up.'

People eating beside them paused, heads snapping in their direction. Silent expressions and awkward glances passed around.

'Let us be there for you,' said Ricki. She didn't know how to calm Abbie, nor the right words to use, but as explosive as Abbie could be, they had never run from her yet. It was all bluff; deep down they knew she was hurting and struggling to cope. She'd drown before she'd ever ask for help, even now she was fighting, but so would Ricki. She would not give up on her friend, ever.

'I can't cope if everyone knows about it. Already I can see the pity in your eyes and it's making me so wild. I kept it to myself for a reason, Peter. I can't believe you'd do this, it wasn't your secret to tell.' Abbie's fists clenched and shook with emotions threatening to burst free.

'I'm sorry, Abbie, but I believe it was the right thing to do.' Peter held firm, as if he were face to face with a charging bull.

'Well, you know what?'

Oh no, thought Ricki. She'd heard this tone before. It was usually followed by, 'Payback's a bitch, baby.'

'I believe telling you that you're Ollie's father is the right thing to do, and that Ricki cheated on you. But is it my place to say something? No, it's not. But seeing as you feel people have a right to know everything, then have some your own way.'

Abbie grabbed her bag and stormed out of the restaurant, leaving a hush in her wake. It wasn't until the other patrons went back to their meals that Ricki repeated Abbie's harsh words in her mind. Over and over until they made sense. With wide eyes she glanced at Jess. She felt like a balloon about to pop. 'You two, behind my back?'

Jess looked like she'd jammed her hand in a mincer at a sausage factory. 'No, Ricki, this was before you guys got together.'

Ricki felt herself deflate, but then she realised. 'So, that was true? Ollie is Peter's?'

But Jess wasn't listening, she was staring at Peter, tears falling down her cheeks.

Peter was frozen in his seat, watching Jess in disbelief.

'Ollie is mine?' His voice was uncertain.

'I'm so sorry, Peter. I've been meaning to tell you. Honest.' She paused, then took a shaky breath. 'That night we spent together that you don't quite remember, I ended up pregnant with Ollie, but I didn't know until I was nearly six months. The reaction you had after that night left me with no doubt you didn't want me and by then you and Ricki were happy together and I didn't want to come between that,' said Jess, before a sob broke free. His face was unreadable. 'Please forgive me. I did what I thought was right.'

He stood up, looking at Jess as if she were a stranger. Ricki had so many emotions, but none could be close to what Peter was feeling. He looked utterly betrayed by the one person he'd loved most of his life. *Jesus*, she thought. *How many more secrets are there? Surely that's it?*

'Ollie's mine.' He shook his head again. 'You kept that from me? How could you?' His face scrunched in pain and anger. 'I can't believe you'd do such a thing, Jess. I . . .' His words faded away.

Peter closed his eyes and shook his head before turning and walking out. His exit was silent compared to Abbie's, yet it resonated just as much.

'Peter!' Jess cried as she fell into sobs, clearly not caring where she was or who was watching.

Ricki reached over and hugged her.

'Oh, Peter, I'm sorry,' mumbled Jess.

Ricki rocked her like a baby while trying to get her head around Peter being a father, and that while Jess went through the whole pregnancy on her own, Peter knew nothing. Did Jess really keep it quiet to protect Peter and Ricki's relationship? Straightaway she knew the answer: of course Jess would put her friends' happiness before hers. Maybe she thought the night was a mistake and didn't want to ruin Peter's life too. Ricki wanted to know more details, but Jess was in no fit state to talk. Her devastation was enough to halt a raging army.

All the people Ricki loved most were hurting. Where did they all go from here? Could they weather this storm?

One thing was certain: no one would ever forget this trip.

29

Abbie

ABBIE COULDN'T BREATHE SHE WAS SO ANGRY. SHE STOPPED halfway down the stairs on the way to the medical level and cursed, then stamped her foot because there was nothing to throw or hit. Between her anger, blood loss and stomping away from her friends so fast, she felt dizzy.

With a deep breath she sat for a minute on the step and waited for the spell to pass.

'Bloody hell,' she grumbled between her teeth.

She hadn't given it a thought that Peter had heard the conversation with Alex about her cancer. If he'd heard that, then he would have heard about her suicidal thoughts. *Damn*, she thought, slamming her hand down loudly on the step, *did he tell them that too?*

An old couple walked past her.

'Are you all right, love?' asked the old man with his socks halfway up his legs and his shorts to his knees.

'I'll be okay, thank you.' But was she?

They continued on their way, the old man holding his wife's hand. Abbie watched, knowing she might never experience old age. The wrinkles, the aches, the memory loss and having friends die around you. Would it be a bad thing to miss all that?

With a grunt she lifted herself up using the handrail. If the oldies could traverse these stairs, then so could she. Abbie took her time, walking slowly to the medical centre.

Alex was there with another woman, also in medical uniform. He looked up when Abbie entered and smiled. 'Hello, I'm glad to see you're still with us,' he teased.

'I didn't want to waste your perfect stitches, did I?' she replied, harshly, not jokingly as she had planned. His eyebrow shot up but he said nothing.

The woman moved towards her, her eyes on Abbie's bandaged hand.

'It's all right, Neve, I'll look this over. Your shift's done.' Alex stood and walked around the desk.

'No worries. Thanks, Alex.'

'Come in,' he said, gesturing Abbie to the examination room and offering her a chair. 'So, how do you know my stitches are perfect?' he said.

'Ricki. Being a nurse, she couldn't *not* look at them this morning.' Abbie frowned, her anger rising as their sad faces flashed in her mind. So much for trying to save them from the worry and pain. Bloody Peter.

He pulled up another chair and sat beside her. 'Ah, I see. You're in good hands, then. How are you feeling?'

'Like absolute shit.'

His eyes seemed to darken, but he didn't say anything.

'Peter overheard us talking and told my friends about my . . . this . . .' She couldn't say the words and instead waved towards her scar. 'I didn't want them to know and now he's gone and ruined everything.'

Alex caressed her hand. 'Is it really that bad to let your friends in? Will it kill you?'

They both smirked.

'Quite possibly,' she added.

'It can't kill you any quicker, at least.'

She grinned again as his big dark eyes watched her carefully.

'And what else is bothering you?' he ventured.

'How do you know something is?'

He shrugged. 'You seem worried. I get you're upset about your friends knowing and angry at Peter for telling, but is there something else?'

Abbie sighed and sat back in the chair. 'I was a complete bitch.'

He didn't move, just sat and watched and waited.

'I was angry at Peter, so I told him some secrets that weren't mine to tell. It was a spur-of-the-moment thing, and I think I'll regret it forever.'

'Sounds serious.'

'I'm sure you don't have the time to hear about it.'

'I do.'

'And you're a doctor, not a counsellor,' she added.

'I'd like to be your friend, though, and friends hear each other out. You know a fair bit more about me than most people I know.' His smile was full.

It started to warm her heart.

'If you tell me while I check your dressing, we can kill two birds with one stone.'

Abbie nodded, and he began to unwrap the bandage.

She kept her voice low, conscious of the room's echo. She wouldn't make that mistake twice.

'I told Peter that Jess's baby is his.'

Alex's eye twitched a bit and he exhaled. After a moment he asked, 'And Peter was dating Ricki?'

'Yes, until recently. But they weren't together when Jess got pregnant. Jess has always loved him, so they should be together. They've been best friends since forever, and I ruined that. Peter will be devastated she's lied to him.'

'That's not your fault, Abbie. You weren't the one who kept that from Peter. It was Jess's decision.'

'I know. I do. But I still feel shit about it. I hope he can forgive her. Those two have never kept secrets from each other.' She tried to laugh but it came out as more of a snigger. 'We all promised never to keep secrets from each other. I don't know where it went wrong. Did we grow apart?'

Alex was nodding with every word. Their eyes met, and it was as if she had finally found someone who understood everything. Understood her.

'If Jess is a decent friend she won't hold it against you, and Peter will come around. But if your friends want to be there for you, then you should let them. You'd miss them if they were gone. Besides, think of the fun you'll have. Make them wait on you hand and foot. You're going to need some help in the future, no matter which direction you choose to take.'

His words were serious but gentle. And he was right.

'And think about this: would you want to know if it was Jess or Ricki who was sick?'

Abbie, in that moment, tried to imagine it and straightaway knew the answer. 'I'd want to know and I'd want to be there for them every step of the way. I love them.'

'Exactly. So, why can't you let them love you?'

His words packed a punch, as if he'd hit her with a boxing glove. 'They probably want nothing to do with me.'

'Have a bit more faith in your friends. Time helps.'

He was right. She liked how he wasn't afraid of her or the drama she seemed to attract. 'Thanks, Alex. Are you working all day? Any chance we could catch up? Last day on the boat and all.'

He smiled. 'I'll have an hour for lunch. Do you want to meet at twelve by the pool?'

'I'd love to. So, it's all good?' she said, gesturing to her hand.

Alex was wrapping it back up. 'Yeah, it'll pass. No infection. Now, go and rest up.'

He walked her to the door and she paused, not wanting to sever the connection yet. As she watched him, uncertain, Alex reached out and touched her arm. He didn't say anything, but the corner of his lips rose. Her heart raced in reply.

He nodded to the corridor and she smiled and walked away, looking over her shoulder once to find him still watching her.

⚓

After enjoying an hour relaxing on the top deck, Abbie looked up to see Ricki and Jess walking towards her. Jess was a step behind Ricki, her face cautious.

'Yes, you were a right bitch, but you're our bitch and we still love you,' said Ricki as she sat down beside Abbie. Jess sat beside Ricki sideways on the layabout chair.

Abbie's insides were in chaos. She turned to the two girls she'd shared so much with. Jess's face was red and blotchy, and it made Abbie feel even worse. 'I'm sorry, Jess. I wasn't thinking.'

Abbie was hoping for abuse, or something that would make her feel better, but Jess merely sighed.

'It was bound to come out one day, Abbie. I can't be with him and pretend he's not Ollie's father. Not that we'll probably be together anymore, but, you know,' she said with a flick of her hand. 'I created the mess.'

'I guess all our secrets are out on the table now,' said Ricki.

Ricki's cheating hadn't even been a stone thrown in a smooth lake, not one ripple it made on Peter. He was too focused on the tsunami. Abbie sat cross-legged in front of them. 'Unless anyone has any others they haven't shared? Maybe now's the time to spill?'

They all looked at each other.

Jess spoke first. 'I love Peter, and he's Ollie's dad. And I'm scared I've lost my brother to drugs,' said Jess.

'Oh?' said Ricki.

Jess nodded. 'There's nothing I can do about it. He won't listen to Mum or me. I'm scared. He's not the brother I remember and I don't want Ollie around him. And that saddens me no end.'

Ricki put her hand on Jess's lap. 'And I cheated on a perfectly good man. And I still want to go overseas, and I'm unhappy.'

'I didn't know that,' said Abbie.

'How could you? Aren't we good at hiding how we really feel? Even to ourselves? I've lied to myself the most. Nothing is stopping me from my dream except myself. I needed a wake-up call,' said Ricki.

'My God, you are so right. I've fought my feelings for Peter for so long that I even believed it wasn't real. Until he wanted to marry you, then it hit me with such force. You can only push something away for so long.' Jess frowned. 'Now any chance with him is gone.'

'Don't say that,' said Abbie. 'He's hurting, he needs time. We all need time. Pete loves you and he loves Ollie. He'll realise he has everything he's ever wanted right at his fingertips. He'll forgive you, I believe that. Will you guys forgive me for not telling you? I guess I was lying to myself too. Maybe I thought it wasn't real, that the doctor got it wrong. Even though the other half of me is preparing for my death.'

Ricki scoffed. 'Don't say that. We're not ready to think like that, Abbie. Please, let's take one step at a time. We want to be there with you when you go for your staging. Will you let us?'

Ricki and Jess reached out and touched a knee each.

Abbie felt the emotion she'd been trying to push deep down and keep locked away. She was strong and didn't want to show defeat, but these two beautiful girls had a way of breaking down her walls. Her nose prickled with the onset of tears.

'I would love to have you both with me. On one condition?'

'Anything,' they said together.

'No one else knows. None of my family, old workmates, no one. I don't want my parents to know, or find out accidentally from someone else. Not yet.'

Jess and Ricki glanced at each other and nodded.

'I promise. Just us,' said Jess.

'Me too. I'll talk to Peter, make sure he's on board.'

Abbie nodded. 'Thanks. I appreciate it. Love you guys like crazy.'

'That's 'cause we *are* crazy,' said Jess.

Jess smiled even though Abbie had just crumbled her world, and because of that smile Abbie was going to do everything in her power to make things right between Peter and Jess. *I won't die till it's done.* Inside she laughed; as if she had any say over her death.

Best she start as soon as possible.

30

Jess

'COME ON, JESS, I KNOW YOU'RE HURTING, BUT OUR FRIEND has cancer – what's more important right at this moment?'

Ricki was right. Peter was alive. He might hate her right now, but he was here, and there was always a chance he could forgive her. Abbie, on the other hand . . . time was precious.

With Ricki's help Jess had cleaned herself up and they'd gone to find Abbie. And the first thing Abbie had done was apologise. Really, how could Jess hold it against her? Abbie had been trying to deal with cancer by herself and she'd lashed out. Hadn't they all done that to some degree when backed into a corner?

As they sat, chatting quietly, Jess had a feeling of calm. 'You know, it feels like when we were kids. We were so close then, nothing would stand in the way of our friendship. Lately we've drifted apart. Was it our secrets, our unhappiness that built these walls between us?'

Abbie plucked at the bandage on her hand before pressing her lips together. 'I feel as close to you both as ever, and I don't want that to change. Maybe we needed this trip more than we realised. Sure, it was majorly screwed up at times, but look where we are now.'

Jess smiled at Abbie's raw words but knew she was right.

'What will you do about Peter?' asked Ricki softly.

Jess glanced up, and with both Abbie and Ricki watching her intently, she couldn't deny it. 'I can't see how the future is going to go, if Peter doesn't want to be with me. What will happen to Ollie? Will we have to share him?' Jess clutched her chest at the horrible thought.

'Not if you and Peter can work it out,' said Abbie. 'He loves you, no matter what he's feeling now.'

'Yeah, but you can love someone and still not be able to live with them. I've broken his trust, and I don't know if I can ever get it back.'

'How about we get off this boat and sort the rest out as we go?' said Abbie. 'Hey,' she added, turning to Ricky suddenly. 'Yes, you can live with me. I have a whole house to myself.'

'Really?' said Ricki, looking brighter, and relieved. 'That would be great. I'll go back to grab the necessities and move the rest later.'

'When's your appointment?' Jess asked Abbie.

'The day after tomorrow, at four.'

Abbie was matter-of-fact, but before Jess could ask for more information, Alex found them; Jess couldn't help but notice that he looked rather sexy in that white uniform.

'Hello, lovely ladies. I like seeing all these gorgeous faces.'

He zeroed in on Abbie and held her smile, and as Jess saw the spark in Abbie's eyes she realised she wasn't the only one admiring Alex's well-fitting uniform.

'Hey, Alex, is it lunchtime already?' she said checking her watch. 'Wow, we've been talking away the time.'

Alex sat beside Abbie, as if he had nowhere else more important to be. 'Will I be cramping your style if I join you for lunch?'

'No, you two go ahead,' said Jess and watched Abbie nod. 'Ricki and I can occupy ourselves.' She turned to Ricki. 'Maybe a swim?'

Ricki nodded, and as they both watched Abbie and Alex walk away, Jess looked across the deck and froze.

'Umm,' she mumbled quietly when she saw Peter watching her. Normally she could read his expression, but not this time. It was so cold and shut off. It took all her effort not to run over to him and beg for his forgiveness, but she knew it would be no use; he would only escape. The intensity of his eyes and the set of his jaw told her he was nowhere near ready to speak to her.

She touched her chest, the ache so painful it hurt to breathe. Even if she lost Peter, she still had Ollie. It was that thought alone that kept her going. She mouthed the words, *I'm sorry.* He turned away, and her knees started to give out just as Ricki grabbed her arm. She didn't hear the words her friend offered, just let their warmth give her strength to move forward.

⚓

'We're home,' said Ricki, sitting up from the makeshift bed they had made up by pushing the two singles together. It reminded them of their teenage years.

Jess sat up, blinking the sleep from her eyes, and pulled the curtain back to see the Fremantle terminal just metres away. 'Yep, we're home,' she repeated excitedly as she jumped out of bed.

Before long they left the cabin for the last time and made their way down to the exit point, signing off the boat at their allotted time, and heading to the gangway, then onto land. Fremantle looked extra bright this morning, the buildings glowing with the sunlight, cars busy along the roads, everything was back to normal as if the clock had begun to tick again now they were back on land.

'Do you think we should've found Peter?' Jess asked, looking back.

'He wasn't in the cabin. Not much else we can do. He's a big boy,' said Ricki softly. 'We need to give him some space, even if it's hard.'

Jess nodded sadly as they headed into the terminal, pausing only once to take their last look at the *Pacific Eden*.

'Well, that was quite a trip,' said Ricki.

'I don't think I'll be forgetting that cruise any time soon,' agreed Jess.

'I can't believe it's only been a few days. Feels like weeks.' Abbie shook her head.

As they collected their bags inside the terminal, Jess couldn't help but search for Ollie at every moment, wondering if her mum was there yet.

'Peter hasn't left yet,' said Ricki, pointing to his bag.

'He'll be okay,' Abbie said, not unkindly, and wheeled her bag outside. 'And Jess,' she called back with a smile, 'there's someone else here waiting to see you.'

As Jess moved quickly to join her, Abbie pointed down the steps of the terminal. 'Ah, I bet he's missed his mummy.'

Jess turned to where she was pointing and almost squealed at the sight of her mum with Ollie in her arms, coming up the stairs.

'Ollie!' she cried. As Ollie realised who it was, his face lit up and his chubby arms reached out for her. April nearly lost her grip of him as he tried to squirm from her arms with no regard for his safety.

With Ollie firmly in her arms, Jess hugged him and kissed him all over, feeling whole again.

'You two are so cute together,' said Ricki as she and Abbie approached. 'His eyes. Oh my God, I can't believe I never noticed how much they're like—' She suddenly stopped herself, and forced a cough.

Jess froze. But the secret was out of the bag now, and it was only going to keep spreading.

'What?' said April, smiling hesitantly. Then her grin widened as she waved past Jess. 'Peter!' she called out.

Now Jess's heart started to race as Peter paused beside them. She'd never seen his gorgeous face in so much turmoil, in all the years they'd known each other. His gaze burned through her as if searching to find the girl he used to know.

She could tell by the strain of his body that he was about to turn away and leave; she had to stop him, just for a moment.

'Do you want to say hi to your son?'

Ricki and Abbie sucked in breaths beside her but stood firm, giving her courage.

Meanwhile, her heart continued to pound.

Peter's body was tense, his hand white where it clutched his bag. But his eyes flickered and left her face to drop to Ollie's. His face softened and his shoulders relaxed.

'Jess, what's going on?' said April, with uncertainty.

Peter sighed. 'Sorry, April. It seems Jess has fooled us all. She didn't tell anyone, and probably wouldn't have. Apparently, I'm Ollie's father.'

She could almost feel his hurt. Suddenly, he turned and walked away, and he didn't stop until he was on the other side of the train overpass. Not once did he look back.

'Give it time, Jess.' Ricki touched her arm, but Ollie tried to pick her fingers off. 'Little guy wants you all to himself,' she added with a chuckle.

'Jess, can you explain what just happened?' said April. She was looking from Jess to Ollie as her coloured scarf fluttered around her neck. Yet her face wasn't upset or angry, only confused.

'We'll go get a taxi,' said Abbie, ready to escape. 'Call us later and we'll sort out tomorrow.'

'Okay, I will. Bye, love you guys.' Jess hugged them both then watched as they walked to the taxi stand.

'Honey?'

'Can we get home, Mum, have a cuppa first and then I'll tell you all about it?' Jess finally turned to her mum. 'I need a coffee.'

April reached for her bag and nodded. 'I would really like some answers. Is Ollie Peter's son?'

'Yes, Mum. He is.' Jess reached out and held her mum's arm. 'I'm sorry I lied to you. I'll explain when we get home.'

'All right. Let's go,' she said as they headed to the car. 'I'm not sure if he'll go back in his seat. Doesn't look like he'll leave your arms.' She smiled softly at Jess. 'We've both missed you.'

'Thanks, Mum.'

⚓

Jess smiled as April put a packet of choc-mint biscuits on the table; they had always been their special-time biscuits. Funny how an item of food could hold so many memories. Just like Peter with the hot chocolate. A rush of sadness hit her. Would this be the end of that?

April waited until they had settled Ollie with a cup of milk and a biscuit, then taken their first sips of coffee before asking her initial question. 'So . . . Peter?'

Jess looked her straight in the eye so there would be no doubt. 'Yes.'

A single word that made so much difference. While Ollie sat on her lap, covered in chocolate but deliriously happy and unaware that this conversation was based on him, Jess poured out her story – everything, from the night with Peter through to the way it had all come out on the boat, except for Abbie's health condition.

'I knew you loved Peter, I just wasn't sure if he felt the same,' said April.

'You knew?'

'I'm your mum. Of course I knew.'

Jess smiled. 'Well, I thought I knew how Peter felt, Mum. His reaction made me lose any hope of being with him so I made a choice and in the end it was the wrong decision, but at the time I thought it was the right one.'

April smiled. 'We're all guilty of that, sweetheart. We can only try to do what we think is best.' Her smile broadened. 'I am glad, though. I'm glad Ollie now has a real father – and a sweet, caring father at that.'

'I ruined any chance with Peter by keeping Ollie from him. But I'm okay with still being a single mum. At least Ollie will know his dad and have Peter's family. I'm just not sure I want to share him.'

Her mum smiled sympathetically, and Jess felt some more weight fall from her shoulders. At least her mum wasn't angry; she was pleased and prepared to listen. Jess wasn't sure that Peter's parents would be so forgiving.

'You'll be fine, don't worry. Ollie is happy, and that's the main thing.'

April was right.

Ollie *was* happy, and he'd grow up with a dad who wasn't anything like her own.

31

Ricki

RICKI WAS FIRST IN THE TAXI DROP-OFF.

'I'll keep your bags, and see you soon. Good luck,' said Abbie.

'Ta.' Ricki shut the taxi door and waved before facing the house that had been her home for the past year. It was a great house in a good area, four by two, with large cream bricks and a gunmetal-grey roof. The gardens were easy to manage, and Peter was diligent in spraying weeds in the paved driveway and paths. He'd bought it four years ago. Peter was the most organised, stable guy she knew. He was always working for his future: buy a house and pay it off, work hard. He was a good man, and she didn't want to blame him for her unhappiness. Life was about living, experiencing and emotions. The good and the bad. You had to laugh to cry. You had to love to hurt. You had to jump to fall or fly. And Ricki had decided it was time to fly.

With a deep breath she headed up the front path and tapped hesitantly on the large oak front door.

'Why are you knocking?' Peter asked when he opened the door. 'This is still your home.' He stood back as she walked in.

'I know. Sorry. It felt weird to waltz inside. I'm going to move in with Abbie for a while. Is that okay?' she asked warily.

'Yeah, of course, but don't feel like you're not welcome here. I don't want it to be bad between us.' Peter touched her arm.

It was a simple gesture that meant a lot and she felt a strange release.

'Wow. Thanks. And I'm sorry. I haven't been myself for a while.'

'Stop apologising, will you?' He smiled. 'Come on. Do you want a cuppa?'

He was quiet as he pottered around the kitchen getting cups and putting the pods in the coffee machine.

'Are you angry with Abbie?' she asked eventually.

Peter turned as she sat on a stool by the kitchen bench.

'No. I'd rather know than never find out.'

'He does have your eyes, you know. So easy to see now I know.' A long pause. 'So, how are you feeling about all that?'

Peter finished their coffees before answering. 'I don't know,' he said as he sat next to her, sliding her cup over.

'Thanks. I think we both need this.'

'I think I need scotch in mine.' He sipped his and then put his head in his hands. 'I don't know what to think, Ricki. I have a son.'

Ricki rubbed his back. 'It's a good thing, Pete. He's a gorgeous little boy, so like you. How can he not be a good thing?'

'But I don't even remember the night I slept with Jess. I just don't understand why she didn't tell me about it.'

'Only Jess can explain that,' replied Ricki. 'But I do know that you're so important to her, she couldn't risk not having you around as a friend. I get that.'

'If I was so important you'd think she'd at least tell me about Ollie,' he grumbled.

'True. But we're all human.' She sipped her coffee. 'And I truly believe Jess was doing what she thought best at the time. She didn't want to ruin our relationship because she knew you'd go to her the moment she mentioned Ollie. You really should talk to her about it. At least hear her out.'

'I don't know if I can just yet. I still can't believe she did this to me. I've missed out on so much already.'

'Have you?' Ricki asked gently. 'You were there through her pregnancy, you were there at Ollie's birth and his first birthday. Don't you think maybe she's made sure you didn't miss anything?'

Peter grunted, which gave Ricki a small hope that she might be getting somewhere. The more they talked the more confident she felt in her decision to end things with Peter; he really was meant to be with Jess. For a moment she thought about apologising for cheating on him but realised now wasn't the time and, quite frankly, he had bigger fish to fry. It had probably been over for them for a while with Peter having feelings for Jess. Even though he didn't realise.

She wanted her two friends to be happy. She wanted Ollie to grow up in a loving family environment.

'You do know she was going to walk away from us all if we got married?' he said. 'She would have taken Ollie and I wouldn't have seen either of them. She was prepared to do that knowing I was his father.' His fists clenched, turning white. 'I'm not ready to face her.'

Ricki put her hands up, surrendering before Peter popped a blood vessel.

'Don't give yourself an ulcer, Pete. How about you help me pack up instead,' she said gently; any distraction would be good. 'Please?'

He sighed. 'Yeah, sure. Why not. We can fit more in the back of the work ute. I'll empty the tray.'

'We won't need lots of room,' said Ricki. 'It's not like I have much.'

It was true. When she had moved in, Peter's house was fully furnished, so she only needed her clothes and a few personal items. Had she lived like this because she knew one day she would fly away overseas?

'You won't need much at Abbie's either,' said Peter as he finished his coffee.

'Depends what Jim took with him.'

'I doubt Abbie let him take anything,' Peter said with a grunt that bordered on a chuckle. Then he sighed, the brief light fading from his eyes. 'I'll just go do a few jobs, then unpack the ute. Yell out if you need anything,' he said rising from his stool.

Ricki grabbed his hand before he could leave. The touch didn't bring any sensation but warmth; a different sort of love. It hadn't for a while now, she realised. 'Thanks. It means a lot that we can stay friends. It's going to be a shit time with Abbie coming up and I think we'll all need each other, no matter what's happened.'

'Yeah, I know. But I'm still struggling with Jess.'

'Give it time. Don't shut any of us out. We're all still *your* friends too.' Ricki's curiosity bit. 'Are you going to tell your parents?'

Peter groaned and shrugged. 'No. Not at the moment. I need to get my head around it first. I can't handle their onslaught of questions when I have a million of my own.'

'You know who has the answers.'

'You're a dog with a bone, Ricki,' he growled.

'Yeah, but I'm right. And I don't want to see Ollie miss out. Jess had a shit father and—'

'I'd never be anything like him,' interrupted Peter, his face suddenly fierce.

Ricki knew that if anyone hated Jess's father more than Jess did, it was Peter. Seeing what Jess suffered had helped shape Peter into the man he was today, what made him so protective and sensitive. He'd seen the bad side of man and it couldn't help but affect him.

'I never said that, Peter. You'll make a wonderful dad. Just don't let your issues with Jess get in the way of being there for Ollie.'

Ricki realised she'd hurt him greatly the moment she'd finished. Peter would never let anything get in the way of Ollie. After watching Ollie come into the world he'd vowed to Jess he would be there for both of them forever.

'I already love him to bits,' he whispered.

'I know you do. I'm sorry.' She gave him a soft smile. 'I'll go and start packing.' She tugged on his ear playfully. 'I'll miss you though.'

'No you won't. You'll only miss my cooking and cleaning

up after you. I hope Abbie knows what she's in for,' he teased, a cocky grin appearing on his face.

'You might miss my mess,' she shot back, relieved to glimpse the old, happy Peter.

'You know what, I think I probably will to a degree. It'll feel lonely in this big house by myself.'

'Then invite people around. Have Ollie over for a play date?' He looked shocked, but she continued before he could voice his objections. 'He's your son, so you're entitled to see him. You might have to buy some toys, though.'

She could see that his brain was ticking over. 'Just don't go overboard and spoil him rotten.'

Peter nodded as if that's exactly what he'd been thinking. No doubt planning a cubby for the backyard. Maybe doing up one of the spare rooms for him, with a cool bed and toys.

He shook his head, as if trying to clear his thoughts. 'Okay, let's get this stuff moved. It's time.'

When all the boxes and bags had been squished into both vehicles, Ricki returned to see what she'd missed.

'You forgot this one,' said Peter handing her a photo frame.

It had been hanging in the lounge room. A collage of photos that Jess had made her for her twenty-fifth birthday. Photos of Ricki, Jess and Abbie when they were young having tea parties, then more at school in their hated green uniforms, and others at various dress-up parties. A journey of their friendship over many years.

Now she had everything.

32

Abbie

'HONEY, I'M HOME!' ABBIE WALKED INTO HER HOUSE AND dropped her bag with a chuckle. Soon she could say that because Ricki would be here. The thought actually made her feel good. No more empty house. Feeling alone. Adrift. Her friends were here to guide her and be an anchor point. Feeling puffed, she made her way to the kitchen, turning on lights as she went, and sat on a stool. The house was quiet, still. The sooner Ricki got here the better.

After lunch – noodles while watching *Orange is the New Black* on Netflix – Abbie went to sort out a room for Ricki. Previously a makeshift gym that doubled as a guest room, it had been completely cleaned out besides the bed. Ricki probably wouldn't mind going back to a single bed for now – after all, she wouldn't be hanging around for long. There were dreams to chase.

All right for some, she thought and then cursed herself; she was stronger than that. But how amazing would it be to walk away from this current life and go overseas, maybe start ticking off a bucket list?

The thought grew to a point where she sat in the office, dug out a notepad and pen and started to list all the things she would love to see and do.

1. Machu Picchu. For obvious reasons.
2. The Northern Lights. Again, obvious.
3. To bungee jump. Purely for the adrenaline kick. And anything else that's risky and fun.
4. Ireland.

It had been a dream to visit Ireland since she'd met a boy at school who'd moved from Cork. Abbie had totally fallen for his accent, and being around his family had always resulted in many laughs. She needed laughs. Life should be full of laughter, and if she had to go to Ireland to laugh, then she would! Even if it meant having a drink at every pub, it was a burden she would take on.

Abbie paused and smiled at the growing list.

She turned when she heard a bang at the front door. Flipping over her notepad, she left.

'Bloody hell, about time,' said Ricki as Abbie opened the door. Her arms were full with boxes, and bags hung off them too. 'Do you know how hard it is to knock with your foot and keep your balance?'

Ricki staggered past as Abbie held open the door. 'Straight into the old gym room, Ricki,' she said, then got a shock when Peter walked past, his arms also loaded.

'Hey, Abbie.' He gave her a simple smile, nothing that said he was ready to be chummy mates again but enough that Abbie knew she was forgiven.

'I really am sorry,' she muttered as she followed behind.

'Don't. I'd rather know. Secrets are burdens best let out.'

Abbie touched his arm. 'I'm glad, Peter. I do love you,' she said.

He stopped by the door, turned to her and smiled. 'Yeah, me too, ratbag!'

Abbie burst out laughing; things couldn't be too dire if Peter felt able to tease her. But as she watched him move, every step heavy, his head down, she suddenly felt heartsore at the thought of him putting on the same kind of mask she had resorted to.

'Do you want to stay for dinner?' she asked him. 'Not sure what we're having yet, but something I can order in.'

Peter stepped into Ricki's room and put the boxes he carried on the bed. His eyes took in the small room and single bed but he didn't say anything.

'No, thanks anyway, Abbie. I've got a load of work to get sorted for this week.'

Then he shocked her by striding over and pulling her into a hug. 'But I wish you all the best for tomorrow and I hope you get good results.' He pulled back and his eyes washed over her face. 'Don't be a stranger, yeah? Keep me informed.'

Abbie could only nod as her throat constricted, her tongue dry and stuck to the roof of her mouth.

'Right, I'll go and offload the rest of Ricki's things and I'll be out of your hair.'

In less than half an hour they were done. Peter had let Ricki take the desk they'd shared and so her laptop was now set up on it not far from the bed, and her clothes were in the small built-in wardrobe.

'What about the other stuff?' said Abbie pointing to the boxes.

'That can stay in there,' Ricki said with a shrug.

Abbie opened the nearest one and found it full of DVDs. 'Oh my God.' Abbie pulled out the one that had caught her attention. 'Remember this?'

'Ha! Of course. Best movie ever.'

They smiled at each other, remembering their teenage years snuggled together watching *The Goonies*. Jess had introduced them to it. It had really been her favourite movie; she had wanted to be a Goonie, find a pirate ship full of treasure and save her family. Except it wasn't from a property developer – no, Jess wanted to save her family from her dad.

'Let's watch it while we have our dinner,' she said, feeling nostalgic.

And so they did. With delivered Chinese food and the red wine Ricki had brought, they ate, drank and laughed out loud as they repeated parts of the movie word for word.

'It's a giant piggy bank,' said Abbie with an expression that set Ricki spluttering into her wine.

'I wish Jess was here. She did Chunk's Truffle Shuffle to a T.'

'Yes, she did,' agreed Ricki.

Abbie glanced at Ricki over her wine glass. 'Do you think she's all right?'

Ricki thought for a moment, then smiled. 'Yeah, I think so, Abs. Time heals all.'

Just not in my case, thought Abbie.

⚓

Abbie woke feeling like a woman on death row. All she needed was an orange jumpsuit and chains and she could shuffle to her judge and jury at the hospital.

She was lying in bed staring at the ceiling when she heard Ricki. 'Hey. You want a coffee?'

'I'd love one, thanks.' She smiled. 'I guess there are perks to having a flatmate.'

'Totally,' said Ricki. 'And you don't have to sleep with me either.'

Abbie laughed and when Ricki returned with two cups she joined her in bed.

'Today . . .' Ricki started but her words died. Her head fell back against the bed head and she sighed.

'Today is screwed. I know,' said Abbie for her.

'Yeah, let's go with that.'

'What does one wear to the hospital?' Abbie asked her friend as they started to get organised.

'Something you feel comfortable in.'

Abbie ended up going with leggings and a long white top. Who knew it would be so hard to dress for an occasion like this?

Jess arrived and they piled into her car. 'Hello ladies. How was last night? Thanks for all the photos, I wish I'd been there.'

'Don't worry, you'll have to come over and we'll watch it all again. *The Goonies* never gets old,' said Ricki.

By the time they'd reached the hospital they were all in better spirits. Even Abbie was going in with a bit more hope.

At the entry waited a man with the sexiest eyes she'd ever seen. It had only been a day, but she'd missed them.

'Good morning, lovely ladies. Great to see you all again,'

said Alex as they reached his side. His words were for all of them but he only had eyes for Abbie.

Her cheeks felt flushed under his gaze. It intensified when he reached out to kiss her cheek.

'Hi, Alex. Thanks for this.'

'Thanks for texting me so I could come. I couldn't imagine being anywhere else. Shall we go?'

Alex and Ricki looked at ease as they guided Abbie and Jess into the hospital and in the direction of the scanning department.

When Alex's hand slipped around hers she didn't pull away. Instead she gripped him firmly, her heart racing for the wrong reasons.

Their steps seemed heavy against the boxed corridor. Abbie felt glances directed at them, people looking them up and down as if trying to figure out if they were visiting someone – or worse. In the waiting area they sat on cold white chairs, as if squished together on the last available iceberg while sharks circled.

When she was called up, they all stood.

'Please, wait here. I can be stronger without you by my side,' she said truthfully. Seeing their worry only made her more anxious. Without them she could put on her brave face, and hopefully fool herself and the doctors.

'Are you sure?' said Ricki, gripping her hand.

She nodded.

'It's just the scans, so sit back and relax,' said Alex.

And he was right. There would be no answers today. Just tests.

Once inside she got the final rundown of the PET-CT scan. She'd heard it before, and this time all she could think was: *Will the machine pick up how terrified I am?*

Abbie opened her sweaty clenched hands and tried to air them out. She had to put a hospital gown on and take off all her jewellery.

A radioactive drug, or tracer they'd called it, was injected into a vein. She had to wait nearly an hour for the drug to spread through her body and tissues. Then she was taken to the scanning room where the radiographer helped her onto the narrow bed and made sure she was comfortable. She was informed to stay as still as possible as the bed moved into the scanner and it began rotating around her body.

'Now try to relax, this can take up to an hour,' the radiographer said.

She tried to remain calm in the cold, alien room, but so much was riding on these results. Cancer everywhere, or just a tiny chunk? A lot of chemo or a little? Breathe in, breathe out. *Stop thinking about it all, Abbie,* she scolded herself.

Think of something else. Something good.

Alex.

Something fun.

The list.

Add things to the list.

5. Kiss Alex on top of the Eiffel Tower.
6. Ride a motorbike along Route 66.
7. Have sex with Alex in some remote secluded beach bungalow.

She started to see a theme here. In the midst of her test she smiled. *Hmm, lucky this isn't a brain scan where they could see my thoughts.*

33

Jess

'WAITING IS SO HARD,' SAID JESS. THEN SHE FELT TERRIBLE for saying that when Abbie was stuck in there being staged for cancer. She shouldn't be bloody complaining. For the tenth time she stopped her hand from automatically going to her mouth, ready to chew the first nail it reached.

'What are your thoughts, Alex?' asked Ricki. 'Have you had much to do with this type of cancer?'

He shook his head. 'No, not a lot, but I did call a mate who is a great oncologist. I want Abbie to see the best doctors and have all her options available.'

Ricki sighed, and Jess knew exactly what she was thinking.

'Abbie isn't one for hospitals and suffering,' Jess explained. 'She doesn't like stretching things out.'

'Yeah, but Abbie's still young. She can battle through this and have plenty of life left,' he added.

They talked around in circles while they waited, bouncing back and forth between hope and despair, Alex trying to answer any medical questions they threw at him.

'Hey.'

Jess looked up from the nail she'd been picking to bits to see Peter standing in front of them. 'Hi, Peter,' she said softly but he ignored her, his focus on Ricki.

'I was in the area and thought I'd stop in. How does she seem today? She been gone long?' he asked. 'Hi, Alex,' he said at the very end, shaking his hand.

'She's coping the best she can. She could be in there for another hour yet. Are you going to stay and say hi?' asked Ricki.

Jess was watching Peter, hoping for any sort of response. A glance in her direction, even if it was a glare.

'No, I've got to get to my next job. I was so close I couldn't help but stop in. Just let her know I came by – or not if you think it will annoy her,' he said with a small smile. 'Give her a hug for me.'

Ricki put her hand on his chest, a familiar gesture that she did naturally, and Jess found herself jealous that she couldn't be the one to do it. She ached to touch him.

'Will do, bye.' Ricki waved as he walked away.

He didn't look at her, not once. Not even a glance. She was not invisible. She was still the mother of his child. She had to say something. Jess chased after him, calling his name, her voice echoing down the cold, hard corridor.

'Please, Peter.' She reached out to him, touching his arm. He stopped but spun around as if burned by her touch. It made her gut twist in sadness. 'Will you give me time to talk this over with you? Don't you have anything you want to say or ask me?' Anything. Jess would take anything from him right now. Just a word. Even if it was angry and hurtful.

His blue eyes, wild and bright, seemed to sting as he looked at her.

'No.' He breathed in deeply and let it out slowly. He went to leave but stopped. 'Actually. I wouldn't mind seeing Ollie at some point. Work out some times for visits. I think it's only fair that I get to spend time with him and get to know him properly.'

'Yes, of course.' This was a start. 'Shall we work out a date or—'

'I'll text you when I'm free with a date and time,' he cut in, his jaw clenched.

'Thank you,' she began to say but he'd turned and was walking away, the moment well and truly over. But it was a small breakthrough, she was sure.

'How did that go?' asked Ricki when she slumped back in the chair beside her.

'It's a start. He wants to see Ollie.'

'Of course he does.' Ricki smiled. 'No one could resist Ollie's charms. Give it time, Jess. Peter will come around.'

Ricki sounded so sure, but Jess didn't feel the same. Peter had never looked at her with such distrust before.

The clock clicked over another hour before Ricki sat up. 'Hey, look.'

Jess turned to see Abbie gingerly approaching them. Alex went straight over to help her. Her face was pale, her eyes tired.

'Well that was fuc— Hmm, fun,' said Abbie, eyeing the kids sitting in the far corner with their mum. 'Felt like I was being probed by aliens.'

'Shall we go get a coffee?' asked Jess, unsure of what else to say. Of course she had questions about the procedure, but now wasn't the time to pepper Abbie with them. All Jess could do was hope that Abbie would tell them once she could relax away from the hospital.

'Bloody fabulous idea. Alex?' said Abbie.

She looked worn out, leaning on Alex for support. If there was a strong wind they'd have to hold her down. Jess forced herself to not stare at her friend's frail body, fighting the guilt that came with not realising sooner that something was seriously wrong. How long had Abbie brushed away the symptoms, ignored the signs and pushed on in her determined, tough-woman way? Abbie was the girl who as a kid continued to play netball with a fractured foot.

'I'd love to, if that's okay.'

'Of course. I have to get back to work tomorrow, so let's make the most of today,' said Ricki.

They drove to their favourite cafe down the road from Abbie's house. Alex followed behind in his black European car.

'I like him much better than Jim,' said Jess, as she watched Alex find a parking spot nearby. 'Something so gentle that comes in such a manly package, if you know what I mean.' Ricki smiled at her description but was nodding her head in total agreement.

'So do I,' said Abbie as she watched Alex get out of his car. 'So do I.' She turned in her seat towards Ricki. 'Hey, do you mind if I invite him over for dinner?'

'Of course not.' Ricki's hand paused on the door as she was about to climb out. 'Do you want me to disappear?'

'No, stay. I just want his company, not his body, if that's what you're thinking,' she said.

'Never,' said Ricki who chuckled as she climbed out.

Jess tried hard over the coffee and cake to focus on Abbie as she spoke about the scans, and on Alex who added the technical jargon, but her mind kept wandering to Peter. In her head she played out fantasies of Peter coming to Wandering, falling in love with the little town and Jess, and them becoming the family she'd so longed for.

Only, life never did go to plan. Would reality be Peter finding another girl and Ollie spending the rest of his life going back and forth between two families? Maybe Jess would find another man, although right now it wasn't something she could fathom. Yet, anything was possible over time.

Time.

Time was something Abbie probably hated. Waiting for her results. Waiting to see how bad it was. Waiting to know if she had time. Time to live. Time to love. Time to experience.

Anytime Jess felt bad about her situation with Peter, she only had to think about Abbie. Things could always be worse.

34

Ricki

RICKI HAD SNUCK OFF TO BED AT AROUND TEN, LEAVING Abbie and Alex deep in conversation.

She hadn't heard Alex leave, but his car was gone when she left for work in the morning. As she arrived at the hospital she quickly tied her hair up in a ponytail and checked her watch. On time, just. It felt funny going back to work, especially knowing that Miguel wouldn't be there. The place wouldn't seem the same. Plus, life had changed so dramatically in such a short time. She felt free in a way she hadn't been for a long time as she walked down the familiar corridors, and not even the prospect of a grumpy Heather deterred her.

'Ah, good to see you could make it, Ricki,' said Heather the moment she spotted her.

'With minutes to spare,' Ricki returned with a smile.

Heather frowned. 'Um, hurry up, then, get on with shift change.'

Ricki remained standing by the nurses' desk and smiled more broadly. 'Just to let you know, Heather, I'll be putting in my resignation today,' she added, her voice chipper.

Heather stared at her. 'Seriously? I've had to move Marni on after some missing medication and now you're upping and quitting!'

Teresa had brought some paperwork to the desk and almost skidded to a halt. 'Say what? Are you for real?'

'Totally,' Ricki replied as she sorted out her handover paperwork and went to find the roster. 'Who am I handing over to?'

'That would be me.'

That voice. It set her body on instant alert, like tiny bubbles of champagne popping beneath her skin causing her body to zing.

'You're still here,' she said spinning around to face Miguel. Oh, and what a face it was. It had never been far from her mind, and now he was smiling at her as if she were standing on a beach in a bikini not in a hospital in her plain uniform and ponytail.

'My final shift. I fly out this afternoon.'

'Now I wish I didn't have to work. I could have come and seen you off. Although,' she smiled as they fell into step beside each other, easily, naturally, 'I *did* just quit. If only it was effective immediately,' she added with a chuckle.

Miguel froze and reached for her arm. 'Seriously?' He glanced back to Heather, who'd been watching them with a stony face full of disapproval.

'Seriously. I'm going to write up my letter today. I'm getting out of here, Miguel. I also heard Marni's gone?'

'Yes, lots of changes happening in a short time. Heather's

head will be in a spin. Me, Marni and you all gone. So spill. What happened on that cruise to make you come back and quit?'

His warm hand remained on her arm as he stood close, making her instantly aware of his scent, his body.

'The short version is I broke up with Peter, found out he is the father of my best friend's child, and that my other best friend has cancer.' It seemed so absurd to say it like that, so flippant when in reality it was anything but.

'Oh, Jesus, Ricki. I'm so sorry.'

He pulled her in for a hug, warm and tight, and as he held her the tears flooded her eyes so suddenly it shocked her. It was as if she'd finally let go of everything that was simmering under the surface.

'Do you want to talk about it?'

'I do, but we better get this handover done first.' But Ricki found herself telling Miguel all about their cruise as they moved between patients. Talking to him was easy and she did feel better for it.

'So, now it's just waiting for the results,' he said as they left the last patient on his list.

'Yep.'

'Tell me, why have you quit? Has it got something to do with Abbie?'

'No. Maybe. I don't know. I just know that I haven't been happy. Things between Peter and me weren't great, and it was an amicable split, which is good, he's a great guy and friend. But it's been listening to you that's made me realise why I'm not happy. I need to make a change.'

Miguel was smiling. 'And?'

'I'm going to go overseas and make my dream a reality.'

Miguel scooped her up and jumped, letting out a whoop of joy. 'Yes! You won't regret it, Ricki. I *know* this is your calling.'

He put her down but kept hold of her hand.

'I probably have you to thank. Only thing now is, I'm hoping someone can help me,' she said smiling.

'Oh, Ricki, of course I'll help you. Come to Cambodia with me. I know you can't right now, but when you're ready, would you be willing to come and help us? We could use more great nurses.' He squeezed her hand. 'And I'd love to have you by my side.'

His eyes sparkled and her heart raced in response.

'I didn't want to break up your relationship,' he continued, 'but I'd be lying if a huge part of me hadn't hoped you'd want to come and be with me. I've never met anyone like you, Ricki. You have so much to give, and the way you are with your patients is one of the things I adore about you.'

He pulled her closer, dropping his voice to a whisper. 'Is this real? Will you really come with me?'

She brushed her thumb against his hand. 'I'd love to.'

He sighed. 'I don't want to let you go,' he said.

The warmth of their joined hands was a furnace in the cold hospital. And they were drawing looks from the other nurses. *Let them talk*, Ricki thought.

They looked at each other for a moment.

'Okay. Bye,' said Miguel eventually. He leaned over and kissed her lips quickly before walking off.

Ricki watched him leave, and every time he looked back her heart raced.

'Just because you've told me you're quitting doesn't give you the right to neglect your patients and slack off, Ricki. I'll put in a complaint if this keeps up.' Heather had snuck up behind her, making her jump.

'Yes, Heather. I'm right on it now.' And Ricki gave her a big smile, because nothing could change how happy she felt.

35

Jess

JESS WAS OUT IN THE SUNSHINE PULLING WEEDS FROM HER mother's garden while Ollie played nearby with a plastic shovel, burying some of his toys in the dirt she'd cleared of weeds. April sat under the shade of a scraggly tree in a foldout chair and knitted two bright colours together. Apparently it was a sweater for Ollie. *I suppose orange and blue is better than pink and green*, Jess thought. April wasn't much of a green thumb, but growing up Jess had often helped Peter's mum in the garden with planting pretty flowers and pulling weeds. Over the years Lucy had taught her so much, about when to feed, when to prune. Whenever Jess came home she'd do bits in the garden, not that her mum really cared for it but she did appreciate what Jess could accomplish in a small time.

'Chris came around while you were gone,' said April, her needles clicking.

Jess stopped and glanced at Ollie, her first concern. She hated the feeling that came with the mention of her brother, which was then followed by guilt. She wanted to be a better sister, but he was making it hard. 'When was that? What did he want?'

April stopped, watching her daughter. 'Ollie was asleep in your room when he came.'

Jess relaxed a bit.

'He wanted some money.'

'Mum, please tell me you didn't give him any? You know what he's going to do with it.' Jess felt her muscles clench. She'd once loved her brother so much it hurt. But now, that love was slowly growing into fear. Fear that she no longer knew him. Fear that he was more like their father than anyone wanted to admit.

'He was in trouble and had to pay someone back, so I gave him what cash I had to help him. How could I not? He's my son. I tried to tell him to come to me for help, that I want to see him happy and clean.'

Jess gave a small, cynical laugh. 'I bet that went down well.'

April frowned. 'He's still your brother. He's made bad choices, but I can't give up on him and neither should you.'

'Maybe not, Mum, but he's old enough to help himself. He can change his life if he wants to.' Jess had never said it, but she sometimes wished her mum had given up on their father sooner. Maybe then Chris wouldn't be like this. Maybe then she wouldn't have her own fears and insecurities. Maybe then her mum would be a happier, stronger woman. But it wasn't to be; life was what it was and nothing Jess could do would ever change it.

'He didn't have the bond you shared with Peter's family,'

April said pointedly. 'Maybe if we worked together to get him into a rehab program, we could make him see a better way?'

April's knitting was sitting forgotten on her lap as she gazed out across the backyard, but it was a blank stare. She was probably imagining a world where Chris was better. The young boy who once loved to hug his mother and show her his Lego creations.

Except the real world was what they lived in, where her best friend had cancer, her dad was an abusive alcoholic and her brother's drug habit was way out of hand.

'I don't like Chris coming around here, Mum. Not when you're alone and especially not while Ollie's here.'

April scoffed. 'What do you think he's going to do? I'm his mother,' she said, matter-of-factly. The clicking of knitting needles started up again.

Yes, and you were my father's wife and look how that turned out, Jess thought as her phone chimed. Brushing the dirt off her hands onto her jeans, she pulled it from her back pocket. Peter's name filled the screen and her finger shook as she swiped her screen open.

Shielding her phone from the sun, she read his message. *Are you free to bring Ollie over this afternoon, please? I've knocked off early from a job.*

And that was it. No smiley faces or kisses, no greeting or sign-off.

Immediately her thoughts raced, tumbling into each other. Would it just be Peter, or would Lucy and Eddie be there to see their grandson? What would they think of her? If their reaction was anything like Peter's, she was almost too scared to find out.

We'll be over in an hour, she replied and then deleted the three kisses she'd automatically added.

Jess got up and brushed down Ollie. 'Mum, I'm going to take Ollie over to Peter's for a bit.'

April nodded, her eyebrows raised. 'That's a step forward, honey.'

'I hope so,' she said with a heavy sigh. She touched her mum's shoulder on the way past, a thank you of sorts. 'See you when we get back.'

Jess had a shower with Ollie, put on fresh jeans and a shirt, and one of her favourite denim outfits for her son. She hadn't been this nervous in years. She fussed so much, Ollie started to grizzle at her.

'Sorry, Ollie. Mummy is out of sorts. Shall we go visit your daddy?' she said, picking him up. His eyes watched her. Yes, it was a strange new word. *Daddy.* 'You have your dad's eyes, did you know that?' she said softly to him.

He was still and quiet, as if he knew this conversation was important and new. Maybe he felt it, a change in his mum. She had never spoken about Peter that way before. Never mentioned him as *Daddy* to Ollie or even to herself. The words felt strange on her lips but she liked saying them. The truth of the word was freeing.

On the drive to Peter's house, Jess kept glancing back in the mirror to check on Ollie and chatted to him nervously.

'Peter is your daddy and you're going to spend some time with him. You already love hanging out with him, and did you know he was there when you were born? He was the first person to hold you after me.'

Ollie sat quietly, soothed by the sound of her voice, which helped Jess survive the trip. Pulling up into Peter's driveway almost made her feel ill. She'd helped him find this house, and she'd even helped him furnish it. So entwined in each other's lives they were, until now.

Jess let Ollie walk as she threw her large nappy bag over her shoulder. It was full of the essentials plus his favourite toys and some food. She didn't know what Peter had, or what he planned to do, but she figured he mostly simply wanted time to look at Ollie, to talk, connect and feel his own flesh and blood. To bond.

'Come on, up the little step, that's right, good boy. Now knock on the door,' she instructed Ollie.

He smiled as he banged open-handed on the door. Everything was a fun game. If only Jess felt that instead of the acid swell inside her gut.

The door fell away quickly as it opened and Ollie almost stumbled forward. Peter was there and kneeled down to his height.

'Hey, Ollie.' Peter reached out a hand to help guide the little man inside.

Ollie reached for him without hesitation, with a trust he didn't show many people.

'Thanks for bringing him over,' said Peter, but his gaze never left Ollie's face.

It cut to her core that he wouldn't look at her, but she pushed it aside. She had caused this, after all, and she would endure her punishment.

Jess put down the nappy bag against the wall and wondered if she'd be offered a coffee, or would that be pushing it?

'Can I have him for an hour?' Peter asked as he produced a small pink doll's pram from the opposite wall.

Ollie went straight for it and began to push it along the carpet.

'My neighbour had a few things. She only has girls, though.'

'Oh, Ollie won't mind. I think boys love the prams as much as the girls,' she said with a smile. To think Peter had gathered some things for Ollie; it was sweet. Then she realised what he'd asked. 'An hour?' she repeated, confused.

Finally he looked at her. Jess had missed him so much it hurt. Tears prickled her eyes as she devoured his familiar face.

'Yes. Is it okay to leave him here with me for an hour, or longer if there's something you want to go do?' he said.

'Oh, right.' Jess felt suddenly silly. Peter didn't want her here, only Ollie. Her face grew hot as she looked down feeling suddenly lost.

'Do you not trust me with him?' he said, his voice slightly deeper.

'No, of course I do. It's just, I don't leave him with many people. Only Mum and Marian. Of course I trust you.' She couldn't stop the flutter in her chest. The stupid hope that he might have wanted her here as well. 'Um, if he gets upset I packed his favourite toys.' She watched Ollie push the pram into her leg, a big smile on his face. 'But I'm sure he'll be fine,' she added. 'I guess, I'll go then,' she said shakily but forced herself to give Ollie a big smile.

Jess headed to the door. Why did she feel like she was being torn in two? Of course she trusted Peter, he'd protect Ollie with his life. It wasn't that. But was it the thought that she had to share Ollie now? He wasn't just hers. Peter had a right and say in how Ollie was raised; he had a right to be Ollie's father.

Peter didn't see her to the door, instead he sat on the floor and watched Ollie push the pram around him, his eyes drinking in Ollie like never before.

'Bye,' Jess said softly, and slipped from the house quietly, like she used to when Marian first started watching Ollie. She knew that if she didn't make a big fuss, then Ollie wouldn't even notice she'd gone.

The moment Jess shut the front door she felt the sob building in her throat, painfully pushing its way up. She made it to her car and slammed the door shut just as the tears fell. Quickly she drove around the block and parked by a house with a big tree on the road verge before her strangled cry erupted.

Where was she to go? What was she to do? Besides, she couldn't drive and cry at the same time without causing an accident. So, she cried a block from his house until she managed to get a grip. She didn't want to go back in to pick up Ollie looking red and blotchy.

She reminded herself that she wasn't losing her son; that Ollie was gaining a wonderful dad – the best person she knew. Peter would forever be in their lives and Jess truly was happy about that. She just hated the way he looked at her now.

After composing herself, Jess checked out Facebook, and then called Abbie to see how she was going and to tell her about Ollie and Peter.

Abbie listened as Jess poured out her feelings. She felt bad and selfish, but Abbie reassured her she wanted to hear it all.

'The distractions are always good,' she'd said.

'What are you up to today?' Jess had asked.

'You know, moping around feeling sorry for myself. It's as if now I know I'm sick I'm feeling all the effects, whereas before,

I'd pushed them aside. I'm pretty tired, but I'm keeping busy helping Ricki look at the work she'll be doing in Cambodia. And I've started a list of things I want to do, a bucket list of sorts. I even have some I wrote down about Alex,' she admitted.

'Oh, that's great Abbie. I like Alex a lot. He's very calm and grounded.' And she was rapt that Abbie had shared this with her.

'Yeah, he is. Hey, come over for dinner tonight so we can show you where Ricki's going. It's amazing, Jess. I envy her so much for chasing her dream.'

'Ricki gallivanting around the countryside like Mother Teresa,' mused Jess. Abbie's words had hung heavy, but Jess knew that Abbie didn't want sympathy; she wanted normality. 'I'm glad she's finally doing it. I'm proud.'

'So am I,' Abbie had said.

Jess smiled. She started her car and drove back to Peter's place. Hearing the strength in Abbie's voice gave Jess renewed power as she walked towards the front door to collect Ollie.

'Hey,' she said with a smile when Peter opened the door.

His eyes flicked across her blotchy face, his lips pressing into a thin line briefly.

'Was he good?' she asked, moving inside.

Peter shut the door behind her and nodded. 'Yes, he's awesome.'

And she could tell he meant every word. Finding out that Ollie was his son would only strengthen the bond that was already there, she was sure.

Jess found Ollie on the kitchen floor with some pots and pans, banging lids onto them like a drummer.

'I remember Mum letting Scott do this when we were little.'

Peter smiled and Jess's insides melted like butter. Then she had an idea.

'Hey, would you like to have him tonight? Abbie wants me to come over for dinner and I thought, I could bring him back later. Well . . . only if you want to?'

Peter stood still, his mouth slightly open. 'Really? For the night?'

Jess shrugged. 'If you want. He usually sleeps through, but I can't guarantee it.' She didn't have to worry about Peter changing nappies or bathing and feeding Ollie – he'd done it all before, though never on his own. 'You'll be fine with the rest, I'm sure.'

'Yeah, totally.' He was grinning like a kid, and she couldn't help but smile. She'd made him happy. It felt like a small win, but a win nonetheless.

'When is Abbie going back for her results?'

It was the first question Peter had asked her in a while; it felt like an opening.

'In two days. We'll all go in with her.'

He nodded slowly, the weight of her results heavy for them both.

Jess cleared her throat. 'I can come and get him at any time, just call me. I'll come and pick him up in the morning so you can get to work.'

'Yeah, that would be great. I can hang around for a bit anyway. The perks of being the boss,' he said.

'I'll drop him off on my way to Abbie's. I'll bath him and bring his portable cot. For breakfast he loves eggs.'

Finally Ollie stopped banging and looked up at Jess. He lifted his arms, smiling.

'Hello, my little drummer.' She hugged him and kissed his forehead. 'Did you have fun with Pet— Daddy?' She glanced up at Peter, studying his face. Did he like hearing those words? Her tongue flicked around her mouth as if getting used to the words herself.

'It feels good to finally say it,' she admitted. 'I really am sorry, Peter. I never meant to hurt you. I was being selfish, protecting my own heart and I tried to pretend I was doing you a favour by not ruining your life.'

Peter squeezed his eyes closed, and Jess wished she could take back her words. He still wasn't ready to understand.

'I'll see you in an hour or so,' she said quickly and headed for the door.

'Yep,' he replied.

'Mummy just has to take baby steps, Ollie,' she muttered under her breath as she got to the car. 'Baby steps.'

36

Abbie

WITH HER FRIENDS RALLYING AROUND HER, ABBIE WONDERED why she hadn't told them sooner, why she hadn't trusted they would understand what she needed. There had been moments when she could read the sadness in their eyes, but mostly they put on a brave face and gave her the light, flippant humour that kept her going. There had to be laughter, if not they might all cry forever.

Alex had been amazing. A stranger who was fast becoming a close friend, maybe more. Abbie didn't want to start anything, just in case. It would be cruel. But she'd still take his sincere hugs and random touches. He brought warmth when she was frozen.

'There's no place I'd rather be,' he'd said when she'd opened her door to find him standing there.

There was something soothing about his presence. She could never feel alone, and he *was* easy on the eyes. His dark eyes captivated her, and his smile was infectious. And then there was his laugh.

'Are the girls coming too?' asked Alex as he stepped into the house.

He wore jeans with a grey polo shirt. It wasn't a fancy shirt but a well-fitting one that she guessed was a favourite for the way it fitted his upper body so well. He made himself at home on the couch and waited for her to join him.

'Yes, they were adamant that they come for the results. Nothing I could say would change it.'

'They love you very much.'

Abbie felt the heat rise in her cheeks hearing Alex speak of love. *God, what is wrong with me? I'm not a teenager!* she silently but happily scolded herself. She thought she'd never have such feelings again, those giddying nerves at being so close to a man and yet she was comfortable beside Alex.

'Yeah, they're keepers,' she said with a smile, sinking into the couch beside him with her leg folded beneath her.

Alex reached for her hand and threaded his fingers through hers. She let him. It was easy, and nice.

'So, when are they arriving?'

'Soon, I guess. Jess has to drop Ollie off at Peter's place and Ricki will finish her shift soon. She's loving work now she knows she only has a week left.'

'Yes, it's great when you know it's coming to an end.' He paused, licked his lips and then breathed in before adding, 'I'm floating around with no permanent job at the moment too. I just refused the hospital position I was offered.'

Abbie shook her head, suddenly worried. 'You did what? Why?'

'Yes, it was all for you, Abbie,' he teased as if having read her thoughts. 'No. Actually it was because I didn't like the job and it would mean I'd have to keep working with Brian who's an old dinosaur and treats the hospital like an army base. I was thinking of doing more boat cruises. You know, things that are more fun. I'm sick of mundane. I don't want to be stuck working all day every day in a job I don't like, burned out when I'm forty. Which isn't that far away.'

Abbie could see the uncertainty in his eyes. The loss of his child and his marriage had changed all his plans, all his ideas for his future. He was a little lost, without a purpose. She knew that feeling.

'You became a doctor because you are smart and amazing. But don't let it control your life because you feel that's what you have to do now. If I've learned anything, it's that being happy is important. I don't want to get married, have kids and work right now. I want to see, taste, explore. I want to travel,' she said, then added with a smile. 'Wait here, I've got something to show you.'

Alex's eyes were sparkling when she returned with her bucket list; she knew he'd understood her perfectly.

'I've started this. No matter what happens next, no matter what my results are, I'm going to work my way through this list. Even if I have to sell my house to fund the travel. Life's short, Alex. I want to really live it.'

As he read down her list, his smile grew – and that's when she remembered exactly what she had written on the list after she got back from her scans. *Sex with Alex. Kissing Alex.*

'Oh, I like this list very much,' he said. 'I hope you accomplish all of them.'

His cheeky smile made heat flush her body, not just her cheeks.

'I forgot I had those on there,' she said, then looked him square in the eye. 'But it's the truth.' Abbie wasn't about to run and hide from embarrassment. The truth was not shameful. 'Do you want to come with me?'

'Well, I definitely have to be there for a couple of them,' he said with a wink.

Abbie laughed and squeezed his arm playfully.

Alex suddenly sobered, putting his hand over hers. 'Abbie, I want you to know that whatever the results are today, I'll be here for you. I know we haven't known each other long, but this feels right. I like you so much. When I'm with you I feel alive, the happiest I've been in a long time. So, what I'm trying to say is, that no matter what your results are, I'm here to stay. As a friend, as a doctor, as more, however you want me.'

Abbie studied him closely and thought of her reply carefully. 'I won't have you wasting your life to nurse me, Alex. I don't want to hurt you. In saying that, I love your company too.'

'Good. I'm glad that's said. We're a good pair, you and I. Don't you think?'

'A couple of crackpots.'

Jess arrived and let herself in as Abbie was still laughing, and Alex quickly folded the bucket list and slipped it into his back pocket.

'Hi, don't mind me,' she said. 'I have the giggles, and no I haven't been drinking.'

Jess frowned and glanced at Alex for confirmation.

He put his hands up. 'I swear. I didn't steal laughing gas from work either.'

'Oh, that would be cool if you could,' said Abbie. 'I like that form of treatment.'

With the sound of that word, *treatment*, Abbie felt the shift in the air. As if she'd whipped away the fun and shined a spotlight on the real reason they were gathering together today. For a moment she seethed at herself.

'Ah, let's move on,' she said after a moment. 'How was Peter when you dropped Ollie off? He's loving having him still?'

Jess plonked herself down on the chair beside the couch. 'Yeah, it seems to be going well. Ollie's happy. Is it bad that I was hoping he'd make a fuss when I leave?'

'Not at all,' said Abbie. 'You're his mum, you're *supposed* to be his favourite.'

That drew a smile from Jess, so Abbie continued. 'Any progress between you and Peter?' Abbie still felt like she had caused this mess, even though Jess had forgiven her, and she desperately wanted to see all her friends happy.

'I don't know. He's talking to me at least, well in passing but not about anything serious, nothing about us or our relationship. But I think his time with Ollie is helping. I'm just worried about what will happen when the school holidays are over and I head home.'

'Has he told his parents yet?'

Jess shook her head. 'I don't think he's ready yet. Too angry still—'

'Sorry, I got held up in traffic. I can't wait until I'm out of the city and in some remote village where people walk everywhere,' said Ricki as she barrelled into the house like she'd been blown in from a hurricane. 'Oh, hi, Alex. I'm going to have a quick shower. We've got time, yes?'

'We've got time,' said Abbie as Ricki went to her bedroom.

'I don't think I've seen her so carefree. That old Ricki sparkle is back,' said Jess. 'I'm so happy for her. And jealous.'

Abbie chuckled. 'Yeah, me too. I'm actually thinking of flying over and visiting her. How great would it be to see Ricki in the environment she was meant for?'

Jess smiled; if she thought Abbie might be too sick to do that, she didn't say. 'Maybe we should both visit. I can always leave Ollie with his dad now.'

'Look at you go. Free babysitter.' Abbie glanced at Alex. 'See, there's always a silver lining,' said Abbie.

⚓

'Do you want us to stay here or come in?' asked Jess as they stood in the waiting room.

Abbie smiled, but it was hollow. 'Stay. I'll be okay.' She took a few steps towards the doctor who'd called her name and paused. 'Actually, Alex, would you mind coming? I'm worried I won't remember a word of what he says, plus you'll understand it better. If you don't mind,' she added.

'I don't mind at all.'

Alex stepped towards her and Abbie saw her friends relax knowing that she wouldn't be alone. Alex stopped her just outside the doctor's door, his warm hand on her arm. 'Breathe,' he told her. 'You can't control what comes next.'

And that was hard for her. Abbie couldn't figure out her future. Some moments she pictured herself in a hospital undergoing treatment, sometimes it was travelling with Alex by her side. Sometimes it was her funeral. She'd had some grim thoughts with knowing what her gramps had been through, but suddenly now, standing here with Alex she felt strangely optimistic. Many had survived this cancer, statistics were good, there was no reason she couldn't undergo treatment and live a happy life with Alex. A ball of hope started to unravel and thread its way through her body. Hope was something she didn't normally believe in. Too much hope made for a bigger crash, but a little bit was okay, surely?

Abbie held out her hand, Alex took it and together they went into the doctor's office.

He was waiting for them and gestured for them to sit. Abbie tried to read his expression, to second guess what he was about to say. But as she was quickly learning, all doctors had a game face.

Doctor Mathias shuffled the file on his desk. Her file.

'The results came back not as we hoped,' he said finally looking across to Abbie.

She felt Alex stiffen beside her. No small talk, straight to the point. As Abbie preferred. But there was that stupid word. Hope.

'Spit it out, doc, what stage am I?'

His sideburns suddenly looked quite grey and his eyes tired. He didn't need to look back down at her results, instead his gaze remained on her.

'I'm sorry, Abbie. The results came back stage four.'

Alex cleared his throat while she frantically tried to remember what stage four meant. It wasn't good, she knew that much.

'In stage four the cancer is found outside the lymph nodes throughout one or more organs. In your case it's in your lymph nodes and quite a few organs: your lung, liver and bone marrow.'

Abbie glanced to Alex, and his pale face told her all she needed to know.

'We call it "advanced unfavourable" due to you having the following risk factors.' Doctor Mathias glanced down briefly to consult his notes. 'Your blood albumin level is low, along with your haemoglobin levels, and . . .' He paused.

Maybe he could tell it all meant nothing to her.

'Well, it's not good, is what all that means. Not in your favour.'

Finally she found words. 'So, what happens from here?'

'A combination of chemotherapy and maybe some clinical trials of new combinations of chemotherapy. Hopefully we can see some changes.'

In other words, her cancer was so advanced they'd use her for trials to see if any of the treatments would work. Or was she being optimistic? Maybe none of them worked.

'Sounds bleak,' she said. Glancing at Alex, she could tell he was thinking the same thing.

Yet Abbie didn't feel anything. She felt numb.

Alex asked some clever doctor questions that Abbie never would have thought to ask and doctor to doctor they talked in that other language. She sat there and picked at a fingernail as she thought about her future. Did she even have one? The bits she did understand of the doctor-speak focused on how gruelling her treatment would be. It might give her five years. A lot of pain and suffering for a few extra years. And what would her quality of life be like then? Her chance of survival was beyond slim, it was near impossible.

Abbie was in a bubble; everything beyond it was blurred. They left Doctor Mathias's office with information and another appointment to start formulating immediate treatment. As they walked towards her friends, Abbie held her hand out to stop Alex. 'I'm going to go for a walk down to the park we passed coming in. Can you tell them for me? I don't want to be here for it.'

Alex watched her with heavy eyes but he didn't offer her sympathy. He knew her well enough already that it was not what she wanted right now. Instead he caressed her face briefly, that touch offering more comfort than any words could.

'I will. We'll go to the coffee shop next door and wait for you.'

'Thank you, Alex. I just need a moment.'

Then she walked off towards the doors. Jess and Ricki stood up, their gazes flicking from Alex to her and back to Alex as he walked towards them while Abbie did not.

Abbie wanted her friends to have time to put on a brave face. And right now she couldn't take any form of pity, sadness or tears. But she needed time alone. Time to figure out what all those doctor words had meant and what she wanted them to mean.

Only then could she face her friends.

37

Ricki

RICKI WANTED TO CRY. SHE COULDN'T LOOK AT JESS, WHOSE eyes were rimmed red and watery. Instead she focused on Alex as he talked them through Abbie's diagnosis. Words she'd heard before rattled around the air between them.

Chemotherapy. Clinical trials. White-blood-cell count. Low lymphocyte count. Liver. Lungs. Lymph nodes.

But connecting them to Abbie made the words carry a weight they'd never had before. One glance at Jess's face showed that none of it was making sense to her, even though Alex was trying his best to explain it in simple terms.

Jess sucked in a shaky breath and asked the one question Ricki was too afraid to ask. 'Will she survive it?'

Alex sighed. 'There are no guarantees with this stuff, Jess,' said Alex. 'Her chance of survival is only guesswork at best, and the statistics for stage four with her low counts aren't good. It all depends how the cancer reacts to the treatments and if her body can handle it.' His words were heavy and didn't make it any clearer. 'But it's so aggressive, unless there's a miracle clinical trial, I can't see her surviving it.'

Jess's lips pressed together so hard they went white.

'Okay. How much time?' she stammered.

'I'm sorry, Jess. I honestly don't know. It could be a few months, it could be a year, it could be five years.'

He sounded how they all felt.

'What can we do for her?' said Ricki. 'I've dealt with this before but never with someone I love. I suddenly feel so useless.' Some nurse she was. And what made it worse was knowing she had everything ready to book her flight to join Miguel in Cambodia. How could she get excited about seeing him again, about flying overseas and being in an amazing place while Abbie had so much pain ahead of her?

Jess asked, 'If she does all this stuff, the chemo, the new trials, will it all work?'

'I doubt any of it will work, but the specialists will try it and hope for some positive outcomes,' said Ricki. 'Like shrinking of tumours, or slowing the growth rate.'

'In the meantime Abbie is sick and needs help.' Jess shook her head, her eyes pressed closed.

Ricki glanced towards the coffee-shop door. They had decided that if Abbie hadn't returned by the time they'd had their coffee they would go to find her.

'Bloody hell,' Ricki said, her bottom lip quivering with anger. She wanted to rage at the unfairness of it all. But who would listen and what would it solve? Nobody and nothing. Abbie would still be sick.

Jess held her hand and squeezed it so hard the pain felt good, it gave her a moment to get a grip on her emotions.

'I hear you. I'm trying hard to keep a lid on this too. Abbie's going to walk through that door soon and we need to be strong.'

Jess was right. They'd end up bawling and Abbie would be the calm face to comfort them, because that's just who she was.

'I should cancel my trip,' said Ricki.

'No!' said Alex and Jess together.

'You know she'd hate that,' said Jess.

'Yes, I *would* hate that,' said Abbie.

Their coffees were just a brown stain inside the cups.

'Can we go home?' asked Abbie before any of them could think of something to say.

⚓

'Jess, I'm okay. Go and pick up your gorgeous boy and hug him for me.' Abbie didn't want her to fuss anymore.

'I know there isn't anything I can say or do. But I love you like crazy and you know how to find me if you need me,' said Jess.

They'd sat on Abbie's couch talking quietly for the past two hours. They had huddled around Abbie's laptop and googled everything they could find on stage-four cancer, discussing the various cases they came across. Alex helped to make sense of the technical parts. Now Jess had to leave to collect Ollie.

'I know, Jess. Thanks. Thanks for being here.'

The girls hugged and Ricki had to look away and swallow the lump in her throat. She'd bet a hundred bucks that Jess would probably cry all the way home.

'Can you tell Peter for me? I know he's been waiting for news, but I can't do it. It feels so weird to go around telling people I have stage-four cancer and I have no clue if I'll survive. Quite frankly, it's screwed.'

Jess nodded. Her hands were balled at her sides, nails digging into her hands to stop her from falling to pieces. 'I will. No one else will know, Abbie.'

'Thanks.'

Jess left and Alex stood. 'I should probably go too.'

Abbie looked suddenly afraid, the most she had been all day. 'Do you have to?'

Alex smiled and reached for her hand. 'No, I don't have to. I thought you might want some time to yourself.'

'No. I'd really like you to stay. Stay and hold me,' she added at a whisper before falling into his arms.

'I can do that with my eyes closed,' he said, wrapping her close to him.

Ricki didn't bother giving an excuse to leave, she just got up and went to her room. She smiled and sighed heavily, thankful that Alex was around.

Ricki lay on her bed, thinking. It was torture, trying to find an answer but knowing there wasn't one.

Her phone rang, jolting her out of her thoughts. For a moment she felt a wave of relief when she heard Miguel's voice. Before she could even ask about his flight to Phnom Penh he got straight to the point. 'How did it go?'

Ricki sighed and then told Miguel about Abbie's bleak future.

'Oh, Ricki. I'm so sorry. Do you want to postpone the trip?'

'I do, she doesn't. Abbie doesn't want me to put my life on hold. She knows how important this is to me, and I can't make her see that she's much more important. I can do Cambodia any time. I want to be with Abbie. For now Cambodia is the last thing I want to think about.'

The phone line wasn't great, but she still heard Miguel's deep sigh. 'I wish I could be there for you too. I want to hug you so tightly it hurts,' he said.

Tears prickled her eyes and she felt a swell of longing for his arms. A shoulder to cry on. Someone to hold her and tell her it would all be all right. 'I wish you could too,' she managed to squeak out before the first tear fell.

'If you get time, I'd love you to email me with more stories,' she said.

'Sure, I can do that. Bye, Ricki. I'll call again next week. I miss you. Thinking of you. Call me if you need to. Okay?'

'I will. And Miguel?' She paused. 'Thank you.'

They hung up and her smile faded as real life with all its ugliness came back.

Ricki held it together right through making dinner, not her best attribute but she managed with a simple apricot chicken, didn't even burn the rice, and they got through the meal with light-hearted banter. What else could they do?

'This is good, thanks, Ricki. You're improving,' said Abbie.

'Ha. Wonders never cease, hey?' she said with a chuckle.

Out of nowhere Abbie ended up being the one to mention what they were all thinking. She'd eaten half her meal and then pushed the rest away.

'This is so screwed up. I can't stop thinking about it. Distractions are good, but the moment they're done I'm back thinking about this stupid cancer. And what pisses me off the most is that I know that thinking about it isn't going to make it go away. So, why do I waste my energy on it? I want to forget it. I'm tired and I don't want to be sick. I don't want to think about chemo and what my options are. I don't like any of it.'

Ricki pushed her food around on her plate while Alex didn't even bother to try and eat his dinner.

'And I hate it more when I feel the "poor me" crap. I don't want to crumble, because none of it changes a thing.'

'Being angry is good. I can handle angry,' said Ricki.

'I own angry.' Abbie huffed and then her shoulders drooped. 'But it's tiring. I have to think this through. It has to be my choice. No doctor is going to make me do something I don't want to. I won't be their crash-test dummy either.'

Abbie glanced at Alex and smiled, and he rolled his eyes, grinning as he traced his finger along her arm.

'Abbie,' he said, 'there's no right or wrong way to cope with this. There are no right or wrong feelings. If you want to throw something, go for it. Scream, I'll warn the neighbours. You want to cry, we'll hold you. Just know that no matter what, we'll still be here.'

Alex's words were so beautiful that Ricki had to mop her face with her shirt sleeve. Abbie wasn't immune either, she let her tears roll down her face as if they weren't even there.

Eventually Ricki started to clean up while Abbie said goodnight to Alex. When she came back from waving him off she looked paler than normal.

'You okay?'

She shook her head. 'I was hoping he wouldn't leave. I don't want to sleep by myself tonight.'

Ricki went over and hugged her. 'You won't have to. I'll come sleep with you.'

'Thanks. I'd like that.'

So, they went and had showers, put on their pyjamas and crawled into Abbie's bed and decided to watch a few episodes of *The Vicar of Dibley*. Both wanted something funny, but Ricki found her tears of laughter were borderline floodgates about to open and never close.

It wasn't until they turned the TV off and Ricki lay on her side hugging Abbie that she felt the full force of the quiet night ahead.

'This is nice,' said Abbie, hanging onto Ricki's arm that wrapped around her.

And it was. Ricki couldn't imagine any place she would rather be than here, listening to the rhythmic sound of Abbie's breathing, the warmth of her body and the feel of her heartbeat.

Ricki lay awake, listening to Abbie until a gentle snore indicated deep sleep. Then, and only then, did Ricki's fears finally overtake her as she silently cried beside her friend. Only the scent of Abbie's fresh apple washed hair eventually calmed her into sleep.

38

Jess

JESS FLOPPED ONTO THE OLD COUCH AND SANK INTO ITS saggy folds. She couldn't move even if she wanted to, because once this couch sucked you in it would take another person pulling to get you out. But when Jess needed comfort and none was available, this old couch was the next best thing. Jess tried not to think about the years of dirt, food and bugs it housed. Right now she was too exhausted. Too mentally drained. Too annoyed and angry and sad.

Her mum was in her room asleep. Ollie had long ago been put to bed.

She'd kept her tears in check during the whole drive to Peter's. Even after he'd opened the door and saw Ollie she managed restraint.

'How did it go?' Peter asked before she'd even stepped inside.

She'd felt his eyes all over her, reading her face; he'd probably known the moment he opened the door.

'That bad?' he'd said while Jess had gone straight for Ollie and picked him up.

She'd needed her baby's closeness, to feel his little heart beating and all the comfort that gave, because she wouldn't get it from Peter. He stood an uncomfortable distance away from her at all times now, to the point where she almost had to raise her voice to cover the space.

'No, it's not good news. She's got the worst stage possible and her treatment looks bleak. I don't even think it's really sunk in yet.'

'Shit.'

He'd said it with such emotion that Ollie had jerked in her arms, his head thrown in Peter's direction as his eyes watched his dad cautiously.

That's when Jess had bit her lip so hard a burst of blood had coated her taste buds. The pain, the metallic salt taste had all been a distraction from Peter's feelings. Jess couldn't fall to pieces. The one thing she wanted most was Peter to hold her so together they could let their fears overcome them for a moment. Only, Peter was still angry and hurt. She saw it outlined in his eyes, like permanent marker it wasn't going anytime soon.

'How did Abbie take the news?' he'd said, screwing up his face as if he'd just been punched in the gut.

'She's shell-shocked, we all are. Alex tried to help us all understand what this could entail. Lots of treatment, new clinical trials but even after all that she might only have a few months or years.' Jess had paused to breathe, to try to swallow the lump that ached in her throat, but it didn't help. Neither did Peter's intense gaze. 'She doesn't want anyone to know, at all, and she doesn't want us upset around her.' Even as Jess had said the words, tears had won, rolling down her cheeks and Peter's face had gone blurry.

He didn't move. Didn't offer a hug or gentle reassuring words. No, he'd stood awkwardly with one hand tucked into the pocket of his jeans and the other arm draped across his body like a shield, clinging onto his elbow. It was when he looked away from her that she knew all was lost.

It was as if a bullet had shattered her heart into tiny fragments. Abbie, now Peter. It was too much to handle and she still had to get Ollie home safely.

With a steely resolve she didn't know she possessed, Jess had picked up Ollie's nappy bag and headed for the door. She didn't bother to wipe the tears from her face. 'Thanks for having Ollie. I better get him home.'

It had been hard to walk away from Peter, that familiar scent and those warm arms she craved, but she did it. Kissing Peter on the beach had been amazing, that small moment when the future seemed so wonderful. Now it hung over her head, the torture of something snatched away. What was worse was that it was her own doing. It would have been so much easier to endure this if she didn't have those memories, the softness of his lips and the electric feel of his tongue.

When she got back to her mum's house she remained in this automatic mode, going through the motions of organising Ollie's dinner and bath and then her own dinner. She put on a few loads of washing and cleaned up. Meanwhile her mum watched her with wary eyes.

Yet here she was now, in this suction couch, holding back the churning waves that crashed against the wall she'd put up. Once she started crying she might never stop.

The tears came anyway, as if she had any say in the matter. Followed by sobs, which she stifled with her rug. Tissue after tissue, a mountain of them piling up beside her as she sat there not really watching TV until she fell asleep from sheer exhaustion. April woke her at two o'clock.

'Go to bed, honey, you'll be stiff and sore otherwise.'

The TV was off and the house was eerily dark. April helped her to her room, where she crawled into bed fully clothed and went back to sleep before her mind could engage.

⚓

Jess woke late the next morning to find April playing with Ollie. He was dressed and had eaten. She caught her face in the mirror and it shocked her. Her eyes were still puffy from the tears she'd shed. 'Damn it.'

'Go and have a shower. I've got this,' said April with an understanding smile.

'Thanks, Mum. I'll miss this when I go back to Wandering.'

'I'll just have to visit more.'

Jess paused in surprise.

'Really? I'd love that, Mum. You're always welcome.'

April smiled and Jess felt tears threatening again and made a hasty exit.

But the shower felt good, and she even put on make-up afterwards, mainly to hide her eyes. If she looked better, then maybe she'd feel better.

The sound of an angry voice made her falter, the soft pink gloss paused by her lips.

She recognised the voice. After a few more seconds she registered the sound of her brother and grew angry herself.

He shouldn't be here. And where was Ollie, she worried as she headed straight to the kitchen where April was speaking calmly.

'I don't have any money here, Chris. But if you calm down I can help. Please, you're scaring Ollie.'

The closer Jess got the louder she heard Ollie's cries and Chris's booming voice. Jess stepped around the corner and gasped as she saw Chris standing in the kitchen tapping a large carving knife to his forehead. His movements were erratic, his hair greasy and at odd angles. April stood a few metres away with Ollie in her arms. Toys were at their feet and a carrot was on the kitchen bench half chopped.

Ollie was pushing his head into April's neck and his arms and legs crawled to get further away from Chris. April was having a hard time keeping hold of him he was moving so much.

Jess had her heart in her throat and quickly spoke as she moved to Ollie.

'It's okay, Ollie, Mummy's here,' she said trying to get his attention.

'What are *you* doing?' said Chris waving the knife in her direction. His other hand jiggled beside him before he pressed it hard against his head.

'Mum, take Ollie away, please.'

'Chris, put the knife down, love,' said April, not moving. 'It's your mum. You know me. Let me help you,' she pleaded.

Chris pressed his free hand to his face and rubbed his eye, and Jess took this moment to step closer. He jerked his hand away when he caught her movement and jabbed the knife in her direction. His eyes may have been familiar, so was his face, but it wasn't her brother standing there, she didn't recognise this person at all. A quick glance at her mum showed her that

April felt the same. Even though April's voice was calm, there was fear edged around her eyes, cautious and prepared.

'I don't want your help!' he yelled, his body doing a dance as if covered in crawling bugs.

The knife in his hand seemed like a loaded gun ready to go off. Jess felt panic rising.

April stepped away but Chris moved in closer.

'Where is it?' he asked gruffly.

April shot Jess a pleading look as if to say she had no idea what he wanted. Did Chris even know?

'Just give me Ollie,' said Jess as she moved towards them. Nothing was more important than getting him safe and away from this situation.

April quickly turned to hand him over, but he was so agitated he cried harder and fought to hold onto her.

In all the reaching, pushing and pulling as Jess tried to untangle his grip on April's shirt, she didn't notice the little sting much. She noticed it the second time, though, and if anything it made her more focused on getting Ollie.

'Ollie, it's Mummy. Shush, darling,' she said close to his ear so he could hear her. Finally he opened his eyes and saw her, and suddenly his grip on April eased and he went to Jess willingly. 'I've got you now,' she said as she started to move away. But something wasn't right. As she went to move nothing happened and she felt the floor coming towards her. She rolled at the last second so Ollie was on top of her, protected from the fall.

April screamed. There was a clatter of metal hitting the floor and the sliding door was wrenched open. Jess opened her eyes; her first thought was for Ollie's safety. Why had she fallen? What had she tripped on? Had she hurt Ollie?

She felt him wriggle on top of her. He wasn't crying.

'Mummy, Mummy,' he said raising his hands, wanting her to stand back up.

His hands were red. It was like paint. But the smell was all blood.

'Ollie?' she almost shrieked.

April was beside Jess reaching for him, touching him, pulling him off her. 'It's not Ollie. Jess, it's you. Oh my God. So much blood. Oh my God. Where's my phone?' she cried.

Jess tried to lift her arm to stop her mum leaving. She wanted her baby. Wanted to see for herself if he was all right. She tried to get up but felt faint. What was going on?

That's when she saw the knife on the kitchen floor, its blade tainted with colour. The floor had splashes of red but next to her was a pool of it and it was spreading. *Where's it coming from*, she wondered hazily.

April came back without Ollie but she moved straight to Jess's side and lifted her slightly to press tea towels against her back and side.

'Hold these, honey. Please.' April had reached for Jess's hands and pressed them against the towels. 'Press firmly until I can call for help.'

Jess didn't reply or nod. She felt strange. Suddenly it dawned on her, the stinging sensation and all the blood. Chris had done this? Why? Nothing was making sense.

Was she going to die? Her hands were stained with her own blood. It was everywhere.

Before the black started to edge her vision, before she finally slipped into the darkness, she thought of Abbie and how strange if would be if she died and Abbie survived. Who would have guessed that?

39

Abbie

'I'M SORRY.'

'Thanks, Peter.' Abbie hugged him and let him into the house. 'Did Jess fill you in?'

'Sort of,' he said with a shrug. 'We're not really communicating that well.'

'Well, you'd better get your shit sorted, Peter. She loves you. That's what really counts,' she said and watched him grimace. 'Take it from someone who may die soon. Life is short. Love while you can.'

'Abbie!' Peter shook his head. 'It wasn't that bad, was it?'

She shrugged and smiled. 'Nah, I've probably got a few years. They can't tell me. Maybe the treatment will give me extra time or maybe it will kill me quicker. I can't seem to get an exact expiry date from them,' she said with a shrug. 'I just know that it's imminent and unavoidable.'

Peter gave her a grin but she knew it was just a brave face.

'Where's Ricki? Driving you nuts already so you kicked her out?' Peter asked, making himself at home on her couch.

'She's in her room searching for her passport. She's not the most organised girl.' Abbie joined Peter on the couch. She'd been reading some of the travel books Ricki had collected over the years, dreaming and making notes of the places she'd love to see. Places to give her hope and a reason to fight. She had a feeling she was going to need a big load of things to keep her fighting. The thought of the treatment and trials was frightening her more than the thought of death. Death would be peaceful and easy compared to the hard slog ahead. She wasn't even sure she wanted to do any of it. But would her friends understand if she chose otherwise? Maybe they'd get angry, tell her family and then it would be a mess. Abbie didn't want a mess, she wanted tranquillity and happiness, laughter and exhilaration.

She'd said as much to Alex. Bless him he'd agreed and said he just wanted her to be happy.

'If there's ever anything I can do, Abs, you know, anything at all, please let me know. Even if it's cleaning out your gutters.' Peter shrugged. 'I want to be useful.'

Abbie didn't reply, just reached out and patted his leg. She could understand how they were feeling. It wasn't something they could fix or help, so feeling useless and powerless would eat at them.

She picked up the book she had left face-up on the table. 'I hope I get to travel to Cambodia and see Ricki in action. It's one of my dying wishes,' she said.

Peter cringed, but he made an effort to recover quickly. 'I didn't realise how much she wanted to do it. But I'm glad she is.'

'Aw, thanks, Peter. You don't know how happy that makes me,' said Ricki who was standing by the passageway. She continued towards them and sat on the other side of Abbie.

The couch was squishy and they were pressed closely together but it felt good. The touch, the closeness was what Abbie was craving right now. As if it could all be the last touch and she needed to make the most of it. To show them her love.

'Did you find your passport?' she asked.

'Yep. It was in a shoe.'

They all laughed just as a phone rang.

'It's mine.' Peter fished his phone from his pocket. 'It's Mum.' A few seconds later Peter's body suddenly shot forward, his focus totally on the phone call.

'What? Say that again? What's that noise, I can hardly hear you. Is that Ollie?'

Abbie and Ricki shared concerned glances.

'Oh my God. Which hospital? We'll be right there.'

'What's going on?' said Abbie. She couldn't wait any longer. 'Is Ollie okay?'

'It's not Ollie, it's Jess,' said Peter before talking to his mum. 'Stay calm. Find Ollie's giraffe and he should calm down. I'll be there soon. Bye.'

He ended the call and stared at his phone, meanwhile Abbie was ready to shake him.

'What's going *on*?'

Her words were enough to shake him from his trance. His eyes were big with worry and he was pale like he was going to be sick.

'It's Jess,' he almost squeaked. 'She's been stabbed. Mum said there were cops and an ambulance at April's house. She found April and Ollie covered in blood. Mum's freaking out and Ollie won't settle.'

'Shit,' said Abbie, heading straight for her car keys, then realised Peter was parked behind her. 'We'll take yours. Can you drive?'

'Yeah, I'll be fine.'

They practically ran from the house, locked up and piled into his work ute.

'How the hell was she *stabbed*? Where was she?' asked Abbie trying to imagine the scenario.

'She was at home. It was Chris off his trolley.' It came out as a growl. Peter was angry, he was trembling so much he couldn't lock his seatbelt in.

Ricki spoke first. 'Oh my God. Chris.'

'Arsehole,' Abbie said loudly. 'We're all dying while dicks like him are walking around. It's insane. I don't care if he wasn't in his right mind. If anything ... if ... I'll kill him myself.' Abbie was so angry she couldn't formulate her words properly. She just wanted to scream every swear word under the sun.

'Did she give you any other information?' asked Ricki as she did up her seatbelt. 'How bad is Jess? Any specifics on her wounds?'

'Mum's only just arrived at the hospital, she drove April and Ollie there in Jess's car. She said they were taking her straight in to operate.'

Ricki swore. That wasn't a good sign. Abbie clenched her hands as Peter reversed out of the driveway and headed to the hospital.

'She wouldn't die, would she? Ricki? Could it be that bad?'

Peter was at a red light, his words were shaky, his knuckles white where he gripped the steering wheel.

'I honestly don't know, it depends what the blade has cut, how much blood she's lost. There are too many factors I don't know. We'll find out more when we get there,' she said.

'Have the cops got Chris locked up?' Abbie almost growled.

'Not yet. He took off afterwards.'

Peter was so pale that Abbie was worried he might be sick. But they managed to make it to the hospital in record time. He'd hardly turned off his ute before his seatbelt was off and he was out the door.

In the emergency waiting room they found April, Ollie and Lucy.

Peter stopped so suddenly that Abbie ran into his back, but when she recovered she realised why. The scene before them was awful. April and Ollie were coated with blood, Jess's blood.

'I'm sick of the sight of blood,' he whispered.

Abbie only just heard him and felt bad for her part in that. She nudged him forward. 'Any news?' she asked.

'We rushed right here, we didn't even think about a change of clothes or Ollie's bag or . . .' April's voice faded away as she dropped to a chair and looked at her hands. She'd obviously washed them, but maybe it was harder to cleanse the vision from her mind.

'Darling, here,' said Lucy, bringing Ollie to him. He had blood on his pants and shirt and was distressed and wouldn't stop moving or crying. 'Please help me get him out of these clothes.'

Together they undressed Ollie down to his nappy. Ricki gathered wet paper towel from the bathroom to clean any spots on his skin, and she reminded them to put Ollie's clothes into a bag in case the police needed them.

'It's okay, Ollie, Daddy's here.' At his words, Lucy frowned as if she'd heard wrong or couldn't make sense of anything in this moment. Peter tucked Ollie into his arms and started humming to him. Slowly Ollie settled, his hand gripping the front of Peter's shirt and his eyes never leaving his face.

'He looks exhausted.' Abbie wanted to hold his little hand but didn't want to set him off again. 'What happened?' she asked softly, turning to April.

April sighed, tears rolling down her cheeks. Abbie encased her hands in her own and massaged them slowly. 'It was Chris?'

April nodded and sniffed. 'He wasn't himself. Jess wanted Ollie safe and away from the knife. Her only focus was Ollie. She didn't even react when he . . . She went down with Ollie in her arms. Protected him, of course. But the blood, it pooled out everywhere. I tried to stop it. Ollie was crying. Jess. I can't lose my girl.' April began to sob loudly.

Abbie did her best to comfort her while Ricki ducked off to find out what she could.

'Poor Ollie,' said Lucy to Peter. 'What happens if—'

'He won't be alone, Mum. He's my son, your grandson.'

Abbie turned to see Lucy's reaction. Even April took a deep breath to calm herself.

Lucy was looking at Ollie, nestled in Peter's arms. 'He's your son? Why didn't you tell me?'

'I only just found out myself,' he said. He bent down to kiss Ollie's forehead.

'Oh.' Lucy didn't say anything else, just watched the interaction between her son and his child. 'Oh my.'

'It's okay, Mum. I'll tell you all about it one day. Right now I need to know if Jess is okay. I need her to be. We both do, hey kiddo,' he said while watching Ollie.

Ricki came back and they all looked up, eager for any news. Abbie had never felt so on edge, not even when waiting for her own results. It seemed so much worse when it was someone you loved.

'Well?' she asked, hurrying Ricki up.

'I tried hard but they couldn't tell me much. We won't really know until she's out of surgery. I can go with you April, they might tell you more.'

April nodded and pulled at her sweater where some of the blood had stained. 'I need to get this off.'

Abbie helped her pull it off without smearing blood over her face.

'I'll go back and get you some fresh clothes,' said Lucy.

'And Ollie's nappy bag, please, Mum, and some clothes and—'

Lucy put her hand on Peter's shoulder, cutting him off. 'It's okay, darling, I know what a baby needs. I have been there before,' she said with a warm smile. 'I'll sort it out. You just try not to worry too much. Both of you,' she said aiming her last words at April. 'Jess is a fighter. Always has been.'

'I'll stay here until you get back,' said Abbie.

Time seemed very slow when you checked your watch every two seconds but there wasn't much else to do in the waiting room. Abbie paced for a bit, flicked through some magazines but couldn't read a single word. She watched Ollie sleep in Peter's arms. 'Would you like me to hold him for a bit?' she offered.

'I'm fine. I don't really want to let him go,' he said as he pressed his lips together, his Adam's apple bouncing up and down. 'I can't lose Jess, Abbie. I just can't.'

His voice cracked and Abbie's heart lurched. ''Cause you love her to bits, am I right?'

Peter was watching Ollie, eyes swimming with tears, as he nodded and let out a breath. 'More than I ever thought possible.' He lifted his eyes to Abbie, just for a second, just to add weight to his words before they dropped back to his son. 'She hurt me, but I never stopped loving her, not for a minute. I just wanted her to hurt like I was hurting. But I still love her.'

'I hope you tell her that.'

He nodded, sighing like a massive weight was draped across his shoulders. 'I hope it's not too late.'

'It won't be,' said Abbie reassuringly. But she didn't know for sure. She had no clue about anything these days. So much was happening it was hard to know if she was swimming to the surface or deeper to the sandy floor at the bottom.

'Hey, guys,' said Ricki, returning with April. 'We have a bit of news.'

Lucy walked into the waiting room at that moment, Ollie's nappy bag hanging from her shoulder and two more bags in her hands. 'Hi, sorry I took so long but I got Jess some things as well as you, April, and then some food for Ollie and a few sets of clothes for him. Has there been any news?'

'There has been, Lucy, thank you,' said April as she took the bag from Lucy and touched her arm in thanks.

'The knife cut her spleen and there was massive bleeding. They're trying to stitch her back together,' said Ricki.

Abbie could tell she was choosing her words, keeping it simple and understandable.

'But the good news is they think she'll be okay,' said April. 'She has a great chance of recovery.'

'Thanks to April's quick thinking. It could have easily gone the other way.'

Relief seemed to pour from their bodies as tension eased from tight muscles and breaths were expelled.

'How long until we can see her?' asked Peter.

Ricki sat down beside him. 'It will be a while yet. They haven't finished surgery and then she'll be out of it for a while.'

'That's okay, I'm not going anywhere.'

'I might duck out and buy some supplies,' said Abbie. All this time waiting had given her time to think, time to figure out what really mattered to her. She wanted to act on it now.

They all nodded like they'd heard her but no one took much notice as she slipped out the door with Peter's keys. She didn't start the ute straightaway, instead she pulled out her phone. After a quick call to an old workmate to set a plan in motion, she made the call that mattered the most.

'Hey you, are you busy right now?'

'No,' replied Alex. 'Why?'

'Jess is in hospital; she was attacked by her brother. And, I have a proposition for you.'

'Oh, bloody hell. There's never a dull moment with you guys, is there? Righto, I'll head straight to your place. Then you can tell me everything.'

She could picture him shaking his head as he hung up and headed for his car.

Abbie started the ute. She had enough time to shop before getting home to meet Alex. She knew after their chat he would come back to the hospital with her; he was that kind of person. It seemed like a kick in the guts that she finally found the right guy for her and she wouldn't get to grow old with him. But on the other hand at least she was with him now. Life wouldn't be the same without an Alex. Or a Jess, Ricki and Peter. And little Ollie.

Really, she'd been lucky in the life department.

40

Jess

JESS HEARD MUMBLING VOICES BESIDE HER. SOFT WORDS SHE listened to before she tried to open her eyes.

'Should we bring Ollie in?'

It sounded like her mum's voice. Just the mention of her son seemed to snap her out of her drowsy state. She opened her eyes and tried to focus on the ceiling.

'No. He'll cry when he sees her. I don't want him to get upset.'

Peter's voice. Her Peter.

I want to see Ollie, she tried to say, but the words didn't come. Instead she turned her head to the side and forced her eyes open.

'Oh, honey, how do you feel?' said April, rushing to her side and taking her hand. 'You do know how to worry us all.'

Jess looked to Peter, who was smiling and agreeing with April. Had he really been worried?

'Ollie?' she managed to get out. She needed to see her son. Was he okay? Nothing else mattered to her at this point.

'Don't worry about him. He's playing outside with Lucy. They're having some grandmother–grandson time,' said Peter.

Her eyes widened.

'Yes, Mum knows. Um, April, do you mind if I have some time with Jess?'

'Not at all.' April bent over and kissed Jess's cheek. She smelled like her favourite lemon-myrtle soap and old clothes.

'I love you,' April whispered before moving away from the bed. 'I'll be back shortly with Ollie.'

Peter nodded and moved to the side of her bed. He pulled the chair closer and sat down so his head was almost level with hers. He reached for her hand.

His warm fingers made her forget the funny feeling around her waist. 'Am I okay?' she asked.

'You'll be fine after a bit of rest here in the hospital. Don't worry, we'll look after Ollie. But you should be back on your feet and as good as new before you know it.'

Jess took a moment to formulate her next word. 'Chris?'

She felt his hand shake as he replied. 'They found him wandering the streets. He's sleeping it off behind bars until the police can talk to you.'

Jess closed her eyes for a moment. She still couldn't believe that any of this had happened. Her own brother. All those years growing up together and it had turned out like this?

'Don't think about him now. Ollie will be here in a minute and he's been dying to see you. But first I need to talk to you.'

He cleared his throat and Jess turned her head to watch him, study him as he stroked her hand.

'Having you end up in here wasn't fun at all, Jess. We all thought we might lose you and it . . . it was too hard to even contemplate.' He dipped his head and kissed the top of her hand. When he lifted his head his eyes were glassy. 'You'll always be my best friend. I can't imagine life without you. You hurt me a lot, keeping Ollie from me, but that's the past. I want to move forward with you. If you'd died,' he stumbled over the word, 'I would have never forgiven myself.' He paused.

Jess realised she was holding her breath.

'I love you, Jess. I need you and Ollie in my life. It's just not worth living without you both in it.'

She was flooded with euphoria but still a part of her hesitated. Did he mean it? 'Really? You can forgive me?' she whispered through cracked lips and a dry throat.

'Yes, I forgive you. I don't want to waste any more time. I want to be with you and Ollie. That's what matters to me. Can we make this work?' He fumbled for a minute and then had something in his hand. It was the little metal ring with a red heart from the machine in the shopping centre. 'It's funny, I couldn't remember why I kept this but I did. Makes sense now. I know it's not much but it's the only way I could think to show you just how much you mean to me.' He put it onto her finger. 'I'm not proposing marriage, just yet,' he said with a cheeky grin, 'but I am proposing we be together and see where this takes us. There's so much to work out, it won't be easy – but please know that I love you.'

'I can guarantee it won't be easy,' she smiled and nodded. She gripped his hand. 'I love you, Peter. Always have.'

He smiled and leaned forward so he could drop a soft kiss on her lips.

'Now, hurry up and get better so I can do that properly,' he said.

Jess wanted to ask if she was really awake or imagining this. Yet the pressure of his hand and his lips were real and so was the masculine scent that tickled her nose.

A rustle of clothes and movement by the door broke the magic bubble.

'Here's your mumma,' said April as Peter moved to the side to let them in. 'Abbie and Ricki are dying to come in too, but we've been given orders to take it easy on you. So, only a few at a time and rests in between. But this guy couldn't wait any longer.'

'Mummy, Mummy, Mummy,' said Ollie with his arms outstretched. It looked like he was trying to use April as a springboard to launch himself to her but April held on fast and brought him to the bed.

'Be careful with Mummy,' she said, trying to stop him from crawling all over her.

Peter ended up helping to hold Ollie away from her abdomen; a wayward foot wasn't what she needed.

'Just lie beside Mummy.' April tried to keep Ollie calm while Peter kept his legs still.

Jess kissed him and he tried to kiss her all over her face. His little wriggly body was warm and familiar. He was happy and well. What more could she wish for?

'Thank you.'

Peter leaned over her bed and kissed her forehead and then brushed her cheek softly with his knuckles, tucking her hair back behind her ear. 'See you soon.'

What she saw in Peter's eyes in that moment was exactly what she'd dreamed of all these years. And more.

⚓

The next time she woke Abbie and Ricki were in her room and she felt a little better. She had a drink and let Ricki fuss over her.

'You look much better,' said Abbie.

'Yes, I agree,' said Ricki. 'Your surgeon is very happy with his handiwork. Expects a full recovery.'

Jess smiled. 'So he tells me.'

'Man, you know how to give us all a heart attack,' Abbie tutted.

'I'm impressed you didn't swear,' said Jess.

'Oh, I want to, but it's a hospital,' she said with a wink. 'So . . . Peter. Well, he was very worried.'

Jess closed her eyes for a moment, remembering. Soft lips. 'Did I dream it?'

'No, honey, he's not about to let you go any time soon. But seriously, next time I'm sure you can find a safer way to make him come to his senses,' teased Abbie.

'Yeah, bit extreme, Jess.' Ricki smiled as she took her pulse.

'Will you sit down, woman. You're making me nervous. Where's Ollie? What time is it?'

Ricki stopped fussing and stood by her bed. 'Ollie's at home with Peter and your mum. Don't worry, he's being totally spoilt.'

Jess went to sit up suddenly as fear gripped her but the pain sent her crashing back to bed.

'Hey, hey, none of that!' ordered Ricki. 'Don't stress. They're at Peter's place. And Chris is under watch. It's all okay. Peter's parents are going to clean up the house so you don't have to be reminded of . . . you know?'

'Just rest. Everyone is safe.' Abbie shot her a warning look as if she would duct tape her to the bed if needed.

The rush of pain and fear had worn Jess out and she sank back into her pillows and felt suddenly very tired.

⚓

'Good to see you're getting some colour back.'

Peter was sitting in the chair with Ollie on his lap. Abbie and Ricki also lounged in chairs, reading books and magazines.

'Don't you lot have anything better to do?' she asked.

They dropped their reading material and smiled.

'Nope. Watching you sleep is as good as it gets,' said Abbie. 'But you'd better be on your feet by next week so you can see us off at the airport.'

Jess frowned. 'What? *We*?'

Ricki and Peter shared a glance that she couldn't interpret.

'I'm flying off as well,' Abbie announced. 'And I thought I'd go at the same time as Ricki – only one trip to the airport that way.' Abbie was smiling, clearly pleased with herself and the happiest Jess had seen her in a while.

'Where?' Was there a treatment centre overseas that she'd found? Had they received good enough results for Abbie to try it?

'Alex and I are going to Paris to see the Eiffel Tower and then off to Italy, then Cambodia and then . . . well, we've left it open.'

Jess lifted her hand and rubbed her head. 'I don't get it. What about your chemo and treatment?'

Ricki looked down at her lap and Peter reached out for her hand. And that's when she knew. It was Abbie through and through.

'You're not having any treatment, are you?' Jess asked.

Abbie shook her head slowly.

'Oh.'

'I'm sorry, Jess. I know it's not what you want to hear, but it's my life, my choice and it's about the only thing I have control over at the moment. I've put my house on the market, put things in play. You know what it was like with Gramps.'

'Yeah, but he was older,' Jess said even though she knew it didn't matter to Abbie.

'I won't be coming back. I want you both to remember me as I am now. How I've always been.' Abbie pulled out her phone and waved it at them. 'I'll be posting everything I do on Facebook for you and the family. I want you all to see how much I'm enjoying life and living. This is how I want you to remember me, with a smile on my face. Please tell me you understand and will support me on this?'

Jess didn't know what to say, so she spoke the truth. 'Abbie, I love you.' Tears sprang forth, she had no control over them. Just like no one had any control over Abbie. When she made up her mind about something it was impossible to stop her.

'I know, Jess. I love you too, so much.'

Jess flicked a tear away and nodded. Abbie had a way of making everyone see her side of things. In the end they only wanted Abbie to be happy.

'Alex?' she asked.

'Alex is happy to help me on my mission. He's going to cart the drugs around to help me keep going. He's under strict instructions not to fall in love with me. Not sure I can say the same in return, though,' she said. 'But that's what life is about, isn't it? Love and loss. We all die at some stage. I'm just more prepared than most.'

'Wow, seems like you've done a lot while I've been out to it,' said Jess. Her chest was heavy with the reality that Abbie was not going to be around to see Ollie grow up. It seemed so unfair.

'It's been in the back of my mind since I was first diagnosed. You know that. I thought about escaping it all but at least this way I can get the most out of my life before it's over. I'm my own god.'

Ricki laughed then. 'Yeah, we always thought you had a God complex,' she sniggered.

The laughter took the edge off the pain and because Abbie was happy they put aside their fears and opinions on the matter.

'Come on, then, better show Jess your plans so far,' said Ricki. 'She's started a colour-coded file. I'm under the green one. She's letting me find my feet in Cambodia before she visits,' said Ricki while Abbie pulled up a folder from the floor.

'Yeah, well, that way you'll be able to take us to all the cool spots and be our guide,' said Abbie.

As they discussed her travels it felt like Abbie was off on an amazing adventure, not to her death. In a way it was still hard to believe she was dying.

When it was time for them all to leave, Jess was exhausted and even a little jealous of everything that Abbie would see. Not many people got that chance. If Jess was dying she'd just want to be with Peter and Ollie as much as possible.

She'd been so close to dying, so close to not seeing Ollie or anyone she loved ever again. The more she thought about it the more Abbie's trip seemed like a wonderful way to go. On her own terms.

41

Ricki

RICKI PULLED THE HUGE BACKPACK FROM HER SHOULDERS and dropped it at her feet. The airport was buzzing with people dragging luggage towards the baggage drops. Ricki's flight wasn't until later; Abbie and Alex would leave first. To Paris.

'I can't believe it's here already,' said Jess.

Ricki gave her a quick once-over, seeing if she was in any pain or discomfort. She was happy to see Jess taking it easy, Peter making sure she walked slowly and rested. He wouldn't let anything slip past his notice.

'You and me both,' said Ricki. 'I'm so excited, and Miguel has been sending me photos of everything. I can't wait.'

Alex stood beside Abbie, casting a watchful gaze over her. Ricki bet they'd be sleeping together very soon if they weren't already. It made her happy and sad for them. It was only going to end up hurting Alex, but judging by the look on his face he couldn't leave Abbie's side even if he wanted to.

Ricki sighed. Both her friends would be taken care of. 'I'm going to miss you guys so much. Text me, call me, send me photos, I want it all, okay? I don't care what it costs.'

'I agree,' said Jess. 'I want every photo of all the crazy daredevil things you do, Abbie. I don't want to miss a moment. I'll be living through you.'

'I'll take good care of her,' said Alex.

'And I want photos of Ollie and you guys too. You'll want to unfriend me once my photos start clogging up your Facebook feed,' she said with a smile. 'Do let me know how Chris is going in rehab. You're a brave and caring sister to try to stand by him after all this.'

Jess glanced down and shuffled her stance. 'It's only because Mum really wants to give Chris a second chance. She believes he can get clean. I'm trying to do what's right and to be forgiving. Had it been Ollie . . .' Jess's words faded away and they all nodded.

'Yeah, I hear you.' Abbie glanced at them both, her eyes shining. 'You girls are amazing. I want you to know that. Don't ever change. You're the best friends a girl could ask for and I will take you with me everywhere I go.' Abbie touched her chest.

Her smile faltered, sliding from her face, mirroring their sadness. Abbie had spent this last week visiting her family and friends, letting them know she was leaving on this great adventure, none of them aware of the ticking bomb inside her body. Just the way Abbie wanted it. Happy goodbyes.

'Come on, you guys, this is a happy occasion not a sad one.' Abbie almost stamped her foot.

Peter had his arm around Jess as tears rolled down her face.

'It's okay, I brought tissues,' said Jess, fishing them from her handbag.

Ricki held out her hand for one, and wiped away her tears. 'Look what you started, Jess.' She hadn't bothered with make-up; it would have dribbled off her face onto her shirt if this kept up.

'I didn't do it, it was Abbie.'

'Me? Bloody hell, now you've got me going.' Abbie swiped at her face before opening her arms. Jess shuffled into them first and then Ricki followed suit and the three of them clung to each other while airport travellers blurred past. The noise of the airport faded away and all Ricki could hear was the sniffles of her friends and their soft laughter. Their breaths caressed her face and she wanted to remember this moment forever. The sweet almost spicy scent of Abbie's hair and her familiar perfume, the way her small body tucked against hers so familiarly and the sound of her voice. Thinking about this possibly being the last time she would ever feel these things made her heart break. A life without Abbie seemed too horrible to contemplate.

'It isn't goodbye,' said Abbie through her tears. She shook Jess's shoulder as if to reinforce her words. 'Okay? You promised to come and see me in Cambodia so we can all be together again.'

For one last time, it seemed to echo unsaid.

Jess would fly across, she would drop everything to go over at the same time as Abbie. Ricki wouldn't fall to pieces now, she had to think of that future moment when they would be doing this again.

'I'm looking forward to it already,' said Ricki.

'Me too,' said Jess.

Abbie laughed through her tears. 'Me three.'

Had anyone passed them by, they would have just thought it was an emotional goodbye between friends. Three friends with no more secrets except the one they kept for Abbie. Three friends with a bond that would last lifetimes.

42

Abbie

If you girls are reading this letter, then I guess I finally found peace. Probably a good thing, as this gallivanting around the world is exhausting but also the most amazing thing I've ever done. I can truly say I have no regrets. None.

I can't really tell you anything that you don't already know. I love you both more than you could imagine. And I know I will miss you wherever I've gone. Hopefully I get to watch over you both. Actually, I know I'll be there. Every time you swear, that will be my influence. Every time you stand up to someone, that will be me holding you strong. Every time you cry, it will be me catching your tears.

It's taken a few attempts to write this letter. I don't really know what to say but then I didn't want to go without a last word. You know me! Besides, I wanted to make sure you knew how much this crazy woman loved her best friends. And if it's written down on paper, then you can keep it forever and never doubt it.

Always remember me happy. Because I was. Right until the very end. Seriously, I thought I was a goner after that bungee jump in Germany and that slip down the steps in Machu Picchu. I could have so easily gone as randomly as any other stranger on travels. But lying on the Waikiki beach, with Alex by my side, soaking up the sun and listening to the waves crash against the sand beats croaking it in a sterile hospital any day.

Thank you for supporting me. Thank you for trying to understand. Thank you for loving me enough to let me go. You guys are awesome. Never forget that.

But now I ask of you one thing. Please take care of Alex for me. He may need some strong shoulders to support him for a while. Please remind him how much I loved him and encourage him to live life fully and to be open to love again. He deserves it. He has so much to offer someone special.

Thanks. I owe you both one. If you want to name your kids after me, that's okay too.

Alex just asked me what I was laughing at. He thinks I ask too much!

Right, I must go. The waiter is here with my drink and I'd like to finish this book too.

Take care, my friends. Love you forever.
Abbie xxxxxx

Epilogue

THERE WERE WHALES IN THE OCEAN, SHE COULD SEE THEM breaching, then diving under the blue water, creating white splashes. 'Oh, wow!' Jess couldn't help the tears that suddenly appeared at such a sight. But up on top of Mount Clarence she enjoyed it with mixed emotions. The cliffs and islands that sat in the dark blue ocean around Albany brought a smile to her face. It was still a magic place, regardless of the sadness that swept around her heart like the warm breeze catching her skirt.

'Are you okay?' Peter's warm hand slid into hers.

'Yeah, just remembering the last time we were here with Abbie, we were fighting, of course,' she said with a chuckle. 'I miss her so much,' she said as fresh tears appeared.

His voice was raw. 'I know, babe.'

He drew her back against his chest and nuzzled against her neck while his hands wrapped around her large belly.

'Ollie, stay on the lawn where we can see you, please,' she called out as he started to chase a bird into the bush. He was easy to spot in his Thomas the Tank Engine shirt and red shorts.

'Come and join us up here, buddy,' added Peter.

Ollie ran towards them, the blond waves moving on his head as his little arms pumped, up the decked ramp and straight into both their legs. He buried his head between them before smiling up at them. Then he moved to climb up on the bench chair beside them.

'Careful,' Peter warned. He held out his hand for him. 'Can you see the whales, Ollie, look down there,' he said pointing.

'Where, Daddy?'

Within seconds Ollie grew tired of trying to see something and ran back down the ramp.

'He has your energy,' said Jess.

'Maybe this next one will have your smile,' he whispered into her neck right before he kissed it.

Jess felt the baby kick and smiled. She missed both her friends, but at least Ricki came back to visit, next time would be for the baby's birth. She hoped Abbie would be there in spirit.

'I'm so glad we came back here. Abbie wanted us to experience the ANZAC stories and to remember this place, remember what we went through while we were here. The good with the bad, she'd said.'

'Sometimes I think she knew more than most of us,' said Peter.

And he was right. The fact that Abbie had included a bucket list for her and Ricki with her goodbye letter made her live on in their quests to fulfil them. Visiting Albany again had been at the top of the list. How she was going to get to the little village in Italy with soon-to-be two kids, she had no idea but the thought of visiting places Abbie had been was something she was going to do. Even if it took her a lifetime. For Abbie.

Jess smiled and turned to kiss her soul mate.

'Don't think I'll ever get sick of that.' He chuckled and hugged her tighter.

Jess stepped back and Peter paused. 'Is it time to go?' he asked.

She checked her watch and looked across to see Ollie running in circles on the lawn. She turned in Peter's arms so she was back looking out to sea and towards the old lighthouse on the island.

'No, not yet. Let's stay a little longer.'

Acknowledgements

FIRSTLY, THIS BOOK WOULDN'T EVEN BE HERE IF IT WASN'T for Rachael Johns. One day she called me and asked if I wanted to go on a cruise with her for three days. Of course I said yes and we had a great time talking books, reading books, brainstorming books, drinking cocktails . . . We talked about cruise books and ideas flowed and book titles were flung around the room. Rach landed *Secrets Between Friends* like a seasoned pro – my go-to girl for titles. When we get together, magic happens and I'm sure we could create and write a heap of books with our two creative minds. Our history has been intertwined from the very early days of our writing, and helping each other is just what we do. I look forward to our next adventure where we can plan some more books. Thank you Rach. Thanks for giving me the support to attempt this new direction.

Another special lady who needs plenty of thanks is my publisher, Rebecca Saunders, for seeing something in my words and my story. Thank you for being so excited, taking me on and sweeping me up into new unexplored territory. It's been a great journey and I look forward to the next one. Also the rest of the team at Hachette, thanks Karen Ward, Jordan Weaver-Keeney, Fiona Hazard, Chris Sims, Essie Orchard, Christine Fairbrother, Kelly Jenkins, Dianne Murdoch and the amazing editor Claire de Medici. I'm in such good hands with you guys. I'm feeling the love.

I've had outside help; thanks Nadine Owen for answering all my weird questions and finding solutions for my problems. And to all my friends who help, as always, be it books, coffee, chocolates and fudge (Jeni), chats, laughter – thank you for keeping me sane. Even though we don't catch up as often as I would like, when we do it's as if time's stood still.

Thanks to 'the boys' for giving me a job on your farm, fitting in around my writing and many other 'things' that take up the days. I have the best of both worlds.

To my parents, especially Mum who comes to events with me, and my family for understanding and being so supportive, thanks. Jacinta, thanks for trekking to Henty with me, it was awesome. (Let's do many more!) And Julene, cheers for helping at Wagin. I have amazing friends and family. Without them it would be so much harder to keep juggling all the things I do. Big hugs.

To the readers, thank you! I hope you enjoy this new step in a slightly different genre. But I'm still a country girl at heart.

SEPTEMBER 2018

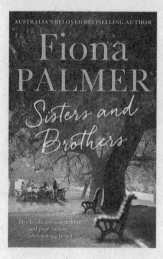

Emma, a nurse and busy mother of three, has always
dreamed of having a sister.

Michelle, at 46, wonders if it's too late to
fall in love and find her birth parents.

Sarah, career woman and perfectionist homemaker,
struggles to keep up with the Joneses.

Bill, 72, feels left behind after the death of his adored wife.

Adam can't stop thinking about the father he never had.

A poignant novel of family, secrets, connections and moments
that may just be life-changing, *Sisters and Brothers* will both
break and warm your heart in a way that only bestselling
Australian storyteller Fiona Palmer can.

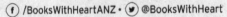

hachette
AUSTRALIA

If you would like to find out more about Hachette Australia, our authors, upcoming events and new releases you can visit our website or our social media channels:

hachette.com.au

f HachetteAustralia

🐦 HachetteAus

📷 HachetteAus

👻 HachetteAus

Before becoming an author, Fiona Palmer was a speedway driver for seven years and now spends her days writing both women's and young adult fiction, working as a farmhand and caring for her two children in the tiny rural community of Pingaring, 350 km from Perth. The books Fiona's passionate readers know and love contain engaging storylines, emotions and hearty characters. She has written nine bestselling novels and *Secrets Between Friends* is a Top Ten national bestseller.